A CLOUD OF SUSPECTS

ALSO BY LAURENCE GOUGH

The Goldfish Bowl
Death on a No. 8 Hook
Hot Shots
Sandstorm
Serious Crimes
Accidental Deaths
Fall Down Easy
Killers
Heartbreaker
Memory Lane
Karaoke Rap
Shutterbug
Funny Money

A CLOUD OF SUSPECTS

LAURENCE GOUGH

National Library of Canada Cataloguing in Publication

Gough, Laurence
Cloud of suspects / Laurence Gough.

(A Willows and Parker mystery)
ISBN 0-7710-3512-8

I. Title. II. Series: Gough, Laurence. Willows and Parker mystery.

PS8563.O8393C46 2003   C813'.54   C2003-901131-3
PR9199.3.G652C46 2003

We acknowledge the financial support of the Government of Canada
through the Book Publishing Industry Development Program and that
of the Government of Ontario through the Ontario Media
Development Corporation's Ontario Book Initiative. We further
acknowledge the support of the Canada Council for the Arts
and the Ontario Arts Council for our publishing program.

Published simultaneously in the United States of America by
McClelland & Stewart Ltd., P.O. Box 1030, Plattsburgh, New York 12901

Library of Congress Control Number: 2002116589

Typeset in Minion by M&S, Toronto
Printed and bound in Canada

McClelland & Stewart Ltd.
The Canadian Publishers
481 University Avenue
Toronto, Ontario
M5G 2E9
www.mcclelland.com

1 2 3 4 5   07 06 05 04 03

This book is dedicated to the ones I love.
My family, my friends. You know who you are.
I hope you know how much you mean to me.

Death is . . . the sure extinction that we travel to and shall be lost in always.

– Philip Larkin

Seize the moment. Just remember all those women on the *Titanic* who waved off the pudding trolley.

– Erma Bombeck

1

nothing but blue skies

The alarm was set for 6:00 a.m. Colin awoke from a dreamless sleep at 5:55. He rolled over on his back and stared up at the ceiling, focusing his energy and collecting his thoughts. He'd had a woman friend over. It had been a long and exhausting night. He smiled, remembering just how exhausting it had been.

At 5:59, he reached out and blindly turned off the alarm. It was a ritual he had followed, day in and day out, seven days a week, for more years than he could remember. He rolled out of his king-size bed and padded, naked except for his black silk boxer shorts, across the carpet to the massive wall of green-tinted glass that overlooked False Creek. He pressed a button in the wall. An electric motor hummed quietly. The drapes twitched and then split in two and retreated towards the end walls, flooding the room with dappled light. Colin unlocked the pair of triple-glazed, ten-foot-wide glass doors and pressed a silver button. Another motor hummed. Despite their mammoth size and weight, the twin panels of glass slid easily aside on their metal tracks and nylon rollers.

Colin stepped outside, onto the fifty-foot-long balcony that ran the entire length of his apartment. The sun was just coming up, and the ornate Italian-marble tiles were pleasantly cool to the touch. He wriggled his toes and spread his arms wide, and took a deep breath. From the balcony he had a view of the width and breadth of False Creek, the broad pedestrian walkway almost directly below him, and the long, graceful sweep of his classic wooden schooner, *Gull*. He'd bought *Gull* at the beginning of the summer. The thrill of ownership hadn't yet begun to fade, and he still felt a soaring in his heart when he gazed down at her flowing lines, varnished wood, and glinting brass work. The boat was moored at a prime slip in the condominium complex's private marina. She wasn't the biggest boat in the marina, but Colin was damn sure she was the prettiest.

The sky was blue everywhere he looked, and the temperature was already twenty-five degrees Celsius. The city had been sweating through a week-long heat wave. Today looked like more of the same. Colin wasn't complaining. He reached down inside the silk boxers and gave himself a scratch, and then turned and went back inside the apartment. He had a 7:30 breakfast meeting set up with a couple of guys who'd flown in from Calgary looking for an investment opportunity. The way Colin saw it, he was their man.

He was in the shower in the ensuite bathroom, shampooing his hair, when the Barenaked Ladies' latest hit suddenly blasted at him over the wall-mounted speakers. The stereo wasn't on a timer. An electrical surge wouldn't make it come on . . . would it?

He was rinsing the shampoo out of his hair when the bathroom door swung open and someone walked into the room. The shower had clear glass walls, but they were steamed up, and the streams of soapy water running into his eyes didn't help. Colin said, "Who's there?"

There was no answer. The roar of the pressurized water from the shower's several nozzles was suddenly deafeningly loud.

He wasn't worried. He'd given his new endless love a key to the apartment. Sometimes he lost track of what day and time his housekeeper, Mrs. Rubie, was due to come by to do the housework.

He peered into the steamy, swirling mist. "Mrs. Rubie? Is that you?"

Maybe he'd imagined it. He must have imagined it. Had he left the sliding glass door leading to the balcony open? He didn't think so but wasn't sure. He rinsed the last of the shampoo out of his hair. His eyes stung. As he reached to turn off the water, something very, very fast moved in his peripheral vision. He spun around. He must have hit the cold water tap, because the blast of water from the half-dozen wall-mounted nozzles was suddenly scalding hot. He cried out. The water beat at him, turning his skin bright red. He fell backwards, against the glass wall.

From the other side of the glass came a low, guttural moan. Colin yelled, "Who is that? Gimme a break, I'm freaking out in here!" The water was unendurably hot; so hot he couldn't get at the taps to turn them off. The shower and bathroom rapidly filled with steam, dense and impenetrable as heavy fog.

He shouted, "Who's there! Get out! Take what you want and get out! Just take everything and get out!" The music pounded at him. The water beat down. He screamed, "Get out! The police are coming!"

Christ, if he didn't get out of the shower he was going to be boiled alive, like a fucking lobster. He pushed open the glass door, stepped out of the shower, and was immediately knocked down from behind, hitting his head. A darkly malevolent eye stared down at him. An arc of white-hot pain screamed across the back of his neck at the base of his skull. Hurrying steps padded into silence.

He simply could not believe this was happening to him. It was so exactly like every ridiculous, B-movie horror flick he'd ever seen that it didn't seem real. He sat up and stared blankly at the thin trickle of blood that flowed down his shoulder and heaving chest. He reached behind him. His probing fingers explored the slippery wound. He was shocked and frightened by the depth of the puncture, the ragged edges of his violently torn flesh. He glanced around the overblown bathroom and took heart in the false belief that, because he saw everything in so much detail, with such enormous clarity, he must surely be caught up in a nightmare.

Then the blood welled up, and poured over him in a hot red flood.

He looked around as whoever had attacked him moaned again, a gut-shuddering animal sound that made his heart lurch. Something moved in the fog. A dark shape. He shouted, "Don't hurt me!" His assailant smashed him against the wall. He felt a sharply burning pain in his side. A piece of skin as large as the palm of his hand flapped against his hip. A rack of thin white bones gleamed in a bubbling sea of red. He scrambled backwards against the glass wall of the shower, and was attacked again. He put up his arm to defend himself. A fan of blood vanished into the fog. The tiles were slippery with blood. His arms flailed wildly. Distorted Hula Hoops of blood splattered on the walls.

He lay in a fetal position on the tiles, alternately squealing with horror and blubbering with fear. When he finally stopped screaming, it was only because he was too exhausted to continue. The steady roar of the shower reasserted itself. The music had stopped. He cocked his head, listening. The seconds crawled by, and then sped up, tearing past him at breakneck speed, in a blur of fear and tick of blood, before once again slowing down to a crawl. After a few moments he managed to stand up. His naked body shook as if he dangled from a thousand wires. He snatched a towel from the rack and pressed it against his side. The floor was pink with diluted blood.

The bathroom had two doors. One led to the master bedroom; the other opened into the apartment's central hallway. The door to the hallway was ajar. Colin hobbled stealthily over to it, opened it a crack and cautiously looked out. Behind him, clouds of steam billowed silently out of the shower. The hallway was empty. The thick off-white carpet was marked by blobs of pink that faded as they moved away from the bedroom door and towards the kitchen and entry hall.

Colin stood there for a moment, leaning against the door frame, lightheaded from shock and loss of blood, weirdly proud of himself for knowing that it was important for him to think straight, horribly conscious of his blood weighing down the towel pressed against his ribs. He told himself he was going to be okay. The cut in his side looked like hell but it was nothing serious, only a flesh wound. Spill a cup of coffee, and what a mess; it looked like the cup had held a couple of gallons. A paper cut on the ball of his thumb could make his desk look like a slaughterhouse.

There was a phone in the bathroom. He turned and looked behind him. He couldn't see anything because of the steam. There was a phone in the living room, and another in the kitchen, but no way would he follow in the path of those gruesome stains on the carpet.

He'd use the phone in the bedroom. If the line had been cut he could use his cellphone, which should be in the charger on his night table, beside the bed. If he couldn't find the cellphone, it was just a hop, skip, and a jump to the balcony. If he went out there and screamed bloody murder, somebody was bound to hear him. The way he looked, nobody in his right mind would think he was kidding. The cops would be pounding on his door before he had time to draw his next breath.

Colin shut the door to the hallway by leaning against it. This door, like every other interior door in his apartment, was oversized, intricately carved, and crafted of sold oak. The doors had been salvaged from a doomed Shaughnessy mansion. Colin had paid a thousand dollars each for eight of them. The hardware he'd had fitted was solid brass and of the finest quality. Unfortunately, the doors leading to the bathroom had simple passage locks that were easily bypassed by anyone armed with a flathead screwdriver or a credit card. He locked the hallway door anyway, knowing that every pinch of time he could buy himself might save his life.

The music started up again. Jann Arden's "Sleepless."

Colin cracked open the door to the bedroom and looked out. The bedroom door to the hall was wide open. The walk-in closet's mirrored doors were shut. He opened the door a little wider, until he could see his unmade bed. His cordless telephone stood upright on the night table beside it. The cellular was in its docking station.

He gripped the doorknob tightly and pushed open the door a few more inches, muscles tensed.

The bedroom was empty.

He hurried to the bed, snatched up the cordless phone, and dialled 911. A huge silence yawned into his ear. He dialled the number again. Something was wrong, but he couldn't think what it was. Then it hit him: the phone's dial pad hadn't lit up. He turned the phone over. The battery compartment's plastic cover was missing and the battery had been removed. He stood there by the side of the bed, staring blankly down at the useless phone as if hypnotized. He dropped the cordless. The towel slipped as he snatched up the cellphone. A fresh wash of blood poured down his belly and curled into his genitals. Groaning, he pressed the bunched-up towel against his wound. Blood from the saturated cotton splattered on his leg, and on the bed, and carpet.

The cellphone felt wrong. He turned it over. The battery was gone.

Colin shrieked in rage and fear as a heavy weight smashed into him. He spun around so fast he overbalanced and toppled sideways. The muscles and tendons of his wrist were laid bare. Blood spurted from the gaping wounds. His fingers were limp and useless. The phone thudded on the carpet. His assailant was somewhere behind him. Something tore fiercely into the small of his back. He shrieked for mercy. His knees buckled. The pain was unbearable, as if a burning hot wire embedded deep in his spine had been forcibly uprooted, torn from his flesh. A waterfall of blood filled his eyes, blinding him. He tried to wipe the blood away, but there was too much of it. He rolled across the bed and fell clumsily to the carpet. Whimpering in fear and pain, he crawled through a sea of red towards the balcony.

It took him almost a full minute to cross the twenty feet of carpet to the huge wall of glass overlooking the south shore of False Creek. He sensed, rather than saw, the summer light streaming in through the window. His heart pounded in his chest. He was terrified, and was having difficulty getting enough air into his lungs because his nostrils were clogged with blood. Blood from a gash in his forehead ran down into his mouth, making it difficult to breath. Blood filled his throat, choking him. He spat clots of blood, and coughed a fine red mist.

He sobbed with relief when his splayed outstretched hand touched the cool panel of glass. The pair of sliding doors leading to the balcony was to his left, only a few feet away. He crawled along the base of the wall, his fingers groping at the metal track. It wasn't until his blindly questing hand bumped up against an unyielding wall of polished concrete that he realized the doors were closed.

He struggled to sit up. He got to his knees and slapped at the door, leaving a random pattern of bloody handprints on the glass. After a few moments he fell back, exhausted. He was very sleepy. The pain was fading, and he had almost stopped bleeding. He shut his eyes. His breathing had been fast and shallow. Now it slowed.

The glass door slid open, gliding silently on its nylon runners, until there was an opening barely wide enough for Colin to pass through.

Colin imagined he heard the thin keening of a strong wind flailing a barbed-wire fence.

Something that felt like a pad of wet sandpaper slithered across his face. He made a clotted gurgling sound that might have been a plea for mercy. He felt a sharp pain in the back of his neck, and then his heart stopped beating, and he died.

He was rolled over onto his back.

A blade ripped into him, savaging him.

When it was over, the sliding glass door was shut and locked, and the curtains were drawn.

Colin McDonald was going to miss his appointment with the wealthy oilmen from Calgary. He would also miss a date with his dentist, and another date with several minor business associates. The oilmen shrugged off their disappointment and hit the hotel bar. Colin's business associates were accustomed to being treated with disdain, and thought nothing of his absence. The dentist managed to fit someone into the half-hour he'd scheduled with Colin, but instructed his receptionist to bill him for the missed appointment all the same.

More than twenty-four crucial hours would pass before Colin's housekeeper, Mrs. Rubie, entered his apartment and found his body.

In the meantime, *Gull* lay quietly at her slip, and Jann Arden's "Sleepless" played over and over and over again.

2

the needle and the damage done

Jan had outlined the fist, changed colours, and started filling in the knife that the fist was tightly grasping when the bead curtain rattled and Harvey pushed his way into her tattoo studio and back into her life. There was just enough room for him to pull up a chair and thump his skinny ass down on it. Jan's customer crossed and uncrossed his legs, and was still. Harvey rolled and lit a cigarette, glanced around for something he could use for an ashtray. Jan gave him a warning look. Her customer cleared his throat. Harvey was five-six and weighed a hundred and thirty pounds fully dressed in a thunderstorm. He shoved the smoking match into his ponytailed hair, and grinned up at her. He'd always had a great smile, despite a brutal overbite. During the time he'd been gone, the prison dentist had worked wonders on his alignment. Jan almost smiled back.

She said, "Learn anything?"

"About what?"

"Like, how to stay out of jail?"

"Let's hope so." He tilted his head and exhaled a chain of smoke rings straight at her.

Jan said, "You just get out?"

"Couple weeks ago."

She smiled. "Got something you want me to get rid of?"

Harvey said, "Aren't you smart."

"Smart enough."

The guy in the chair was listening with both ears and everything in between, trying his best to make sense of the conversation, break the code. Harvey tagged him at about three hundred pounds. Bordering on enormous, and clearly blissfully unaware that he was a decade past his prime. Harvey sure did admire the guy's Harley, though. He looked the guy square in the eye, and reached out his hand. "I'm Harvey. Jan's old man. I used to be a criminal, but now I'm reformed, on parole, and totally harmless."

"Toby," the biker said. He let Harvey take his paw.

Harvey said, "That your panhead?"

Toby nodded. He pointed at the lurid jailhouse tattoo on the back of Harvey's hand, then jerked his head towards Jan. "She do that?"

Harvey laughed. He said, "You better hope not."

Jan said, "Stay still, please."

Toby wore oil-stained Dayton black leather motorcycle boots that weighed about five pounds apiece, a pair of black Levi's riddled with battery-acid holes, and a sleeveless Ozzy Osbourne T-shirt, Ozzy's smirk lost behind a mouthful of live bat. Toby had hair all over every visible inch of him except for the palms of his hands and his shaved skull and the rectangle Jan had clear-cut on his biceps, for the tattoo.

Harvey sized him up. Somebody's sweet baby turned to somebody's bone-cruncher, now run to fat. The T-shirt didn't have any food stains on it. Toby probably thought he was all dressed up, totally irresistible. Sweat poured off him, but the look on his face told Harvey he was enjoying the pain.

Jan paused to wipe blood from the guy's arm with sterile pads. She tossed three bloody pads in the garbage one after another.

"How long has it been, Harve?"

"Fifty-eight months, fourteen days." Harvey flicked ash at the worn linoleum floor. Bull's eye. He said, "I lost track of the hours and minutes and seconds about the third week in, and I'm not going to bullshit you about it."

"Well, that's a big relief." Jan went back to work on the knife, filling it in. Toby had wanted a silver blade smeared with red. She'd suggested stylized blood, bright red flames. Like on a car? Yeah, like on a car. She liked the way the knife was turning out, violent but undeniably artistic. Too bad her walking billboard was three hundred pounds of moron, barely smart enough to sit tight for three or four minutes at a stretch while absorbing a minimal amount of hurt.

She paused to wipe the arm clean again. Toby was breathing hard, through his nose. She said, "Want me to take a break?"

Harvey said, "What for, you tired?"

She went back to work. Harvey wordlessly offered her a hit on his cigarette. She ignored him. He said, "Want a drag?"

"I quit."

"Before or after lunch?"

"Five years ago, Harvey."

"How come?"

"For Tyler."

Harvey shook his head. Not getting it, as usual.

Toby said, "What'd you do, you pulled all that time?"

"Poured a beer on somebody's head."

"You got five years for a little thing like that?"

"Hell, no." Harvey laughed, started coughing, thumped himself on the chest. "In remand, there was a guy bothered me in the showers. Ever had one bad thing lead to something even worse?"

Toby nodded.

Harvey said, "Well, that's what happened."

It did, too. Just like that. Harvey had dropped his soap, and the guy had turned and looked at him, waiting to see what he'd do. Harvey had picked up the soap, but had been careful to bend his knees and keep his back to the wall. The guy thought that was pretty funny. Harvey had told him where he could shove his sense of humour. The guy had unwisely tried to kick him in the balls. Harvey had grabbed his foot and twisted hard. The back of the guy's skull had bounced off the tiled floor. Harvey had stuffed his bar of gritty prison soap a long way down the guy's throat, shoved chunks of another bar of soap deep into the guy's nostrils. He'd foamed up like a rabid dog. The wardens crashed the party in time to save the guy's life, but not his brain. Harvey pleaded self-defence. The jury found him guilty of aggravated assault but recommended leniency. The judge wasn't buying it. He gave Harvey twelve years, less time served waiting for trial.

Harvey was a model prisoner, kept his nose clean except for a couple of times when circumstances forced him to defend himself. He'd whittled his sentence in half, got out eight days before his thirty-fifth birthday, wearing six-year-old socks, shoes, shirt and pants, boxer shorts, the gold-colour Timex with the dead battery. He had almost five hundred dollars in his pocket, money he'd earned and saved during his time in the joint. He spent a hundred on a used black leather jacket he'd bought at a pawn shop, another ten on beer in a skid-road hotel, three hundred on a .38-calibre snub-nose Colt and a plastic bag full of bullets.

He'd used the Colt to bust up a card game and scored eighteen grand plus change. He'd spent twelve of that on a five-year-old meltdown-red Pontiac Firebird that had been owned since new by a mechanic who'd died in a big hurry when a hydraulic lift failed and a Jeep TJ fell on him. Harvey had made himself look sad and opined that these things happen. He stopped himself from adding, usually only once. The dead wrench's wife had given him a good price on the car. She'd even let him bunk with her over the weekend, while he made sure it was the right vehicle for him. He'd forgotten the Colt when he left. For all he knew, it was still tucked under her pillow.

He'd driven the Firebird right across the country, east to west, sunrise to sunset, three thousand miles and more, in three long nights and four endless days, across the boundless, rolling, golden, glorious dustbin of the prairies and over the Rocky Mountains, down into the wet, green depths of the rain forest. In Vancouver, he'd found a cheap but clean hotel on Kingsway, a ten-mile-long strip of asphalt that was home to endless used-car lots and Vietnamese restaurants and drab three-storey condos whose windows were permanently shut against the roar of traffic and endless blizzard of toxic wind-blown grit.

Jan said, "How did you find me?"

Harvey gave her a playful grin. "I got your letter. You mentioned a *job*, remember?" The way Harvey said the word *job* made Toby look up.

She nodded, hard at work, not giving him much of her attention, just enough to let him know she was aware of him. Concentrating, she bit gently down on her lower lip. Harvey loved it when she did that. So sexy. He wondered who her current sweetie was, and how long she'd been with him. Not long, probably. Whoever the guy was, he was about to learn the hard way that it was time to find someplace else to sleep.

Harvey got up, went outside, and flicked his butt into the gutter. A matched pair of motorcycle cops cruised by on their Harleys. The cops wore white half-helmets, but everything else about them was black as sin. Black uniforms, sunglasses, nightsticks, guns, leather stomp-'em boots, and tight black leather gloves. They looked exactly like L.A. cops, and from the dribs and dabs of info Harvey had picked up during his period of incarceration, they pretty much misbehaved like L.A. cops, too. He waved as they went by. Neither cop paid any attention to him, but they made a pretty, synchronized right turn at the end of the block. When he heard the rolling thunder of their V-twin engines going down the lane behind Jan's shop, he knew they were coming back for another pass at him, would want to have a word. He didn't have a problem with that. He'd dumped the Colt, and the card game he'd busted had yielded up eleven separate sets of I.D. Three of the driver's licences had such bad pictures that he could pass, in a pinch. Add it all up, he had more lives than your average cat.

rabbit ears

Peter Markson stared out his living-room window at the stricken condominium complex across the street. For the past few months, the eight-year-old complex had looked as if it had been swallowed by a gigantic bile-green tent caterpillar. Workmen had torn off the stucco cladding and fibreboard, revealing fields of perky mushrooms, rain-soaked insulation, and mouldy black swaths big as a kingsize bed.

The whole city was riddled with waterlogged buildings. There was such a strong demand for repairs that in some cases the same heartless scumbags who'd hidden behind the numbered construction companies that were responsible for the original mess were now behind the numbered companies that repaired them. Naturally, these businesses hired the same consultants and workmen who had earned them huge profits the first time around.

Peter tired of looking at the condo. His fingers slipped from between the thin metal blinds. He stood there by the window for a moment with his hands dangling at his sides, and then he walked slowly into the kitchenette and drank some lukewarm water from the tap. When he had quenched his thirst he went back into the living room and flopped down on the sofa and turned on the TV. He enjoyed TV. He could count on TV to always be a wonderful, wonderful experience. TV never let you down, twenty-four hours a day, 365 days a year. If you were bored you could flip channels. He had only twelve, but it was more than enough.

He went over to the TV and turned it on. The TV was a Magnavox. It was old but reliable. There was a box on top that the cable went into and then out of again. The box allowed him to change channels with a remote, just like on a newer model. But first he had to turn the TV on manually. He didn't mind that at all. His secret unclean truth was that he really liked touching the TV. Some people might think there was nothing wrong with that. He wondered if they would feel the same way if they knew he enjoyed touching and looking at the TV a lot more than he enjoyed touching and looking at his wife, Janey.

Peter sat down on the sofa. He took the remote out of his pocket and pointed it at the TV and ran through all twelve channels, up and down and up and down again, as if he were a pianist warming up.

If he was sober and his timing was right, he could sometimes make people living on different channels mouth each other's lines. Or he could flip rapidly back and forth between channels and get nothing but a silent black screen. He had been doing a lot of that, lately. It took a certain amount of skill. This morning he had spent half an hour of his valuable time watching an infomercial on achieving unbelievably enormous wealth by simultaneously manipulating the real-estate market and one's fellow human beings. The infomercial's gorgeous host assured her viewing audience that very little financial and absolutely no moral capital was required. That was a good thing for Peter, because he hadn't held a job for more than a year. Janey didn't know it, but they would have been in one big financial mess if it weren't for the inadvertent generosity of people so unbearably and irrevocably stupid they made after-dark withdrawals from isolated ATM machines.

Easy money, once you'd learned the trick of convincing your victim that you would shoot him dead if he didn't cooperate.

Easy money, until last night, when a stupid woman had ignored all his carefully worded instructions. She had screamed when he had told her to be quiet, and kicked him when he warned her not to resist, ripped his black ski mask off his face when he snatched at her purse. The ATM's security camera caught him in sharp focus. This morning, he'd recognized himself the instant the "Crime Stoppers" picture hit the screen. The pictures showed him dancing around like an idiot, snatching at his mask and her purse in turn, firing the gun and blowing quite a surprisingly tidy hole through the bank's glass door. There had been more stilted pictures of him fleeing into the darkness, tangled up in such a blind panic that he'd forgotten all about his getaway bicycle. The cops would have found the bike by now, dusted it for fingerprints or DNA, or whatever. He knew nothing about forensics, but he knew for a dead-as-a-run-over-dog certainty that his carefree life as an armed robber had pretty much hit the wall.

When Janey found out, she'd leave him again. Pack her bags and put on those boots that were made for walkin'. She'd left him many times before, for a bewilderingly wide variety of reasons. One time he'd forgotten to reassemble the newspaper so all the sections were in order when he'd finished reading it, and she'd stormed out the door and hadn't come back for a week. No, eight days. He didn't know beans about the law but he knew that attempted armed robbery was an offence a lot more serious than failing to reassemble a daily newspaper, or forgetting to clear out the dishwasher or wax the kitchen floor. This time she'd leave him for good. No, for bad. He couldn't picture life without Janey.

He went into the bedroom and threw himself facedown on the unmade bed. The alarm clock told him it was five minutes past three, but the alarm clock was a damned liar, because Janey set it ten minutes early, to give herself a little more time in the morning, so she could make herself pretty before she went to work.

Janey got off work at four-thirty. Unless she missed her bus, she'd be home in less than two hours. She was going to have a foamy screaming fit when she walked in the door and saw he hadn't done any housework or even begun to think about supper.

Maybe someone would turn him in by then and save them both. Peter rolled over onto his back. He clutched her pillow to his face, and smelled her perfume. His life as he knew it was almost over. Maybe if he pressed down on the pillow extra hard, he could smother himself to death . . .

Nope.

The lawyers would portray him as a violent armed robber who'd recklessly fired his deadly weapon during the commission of his crime. The jury would hate him with a passion. He'd plead for mercy, but they wouldn't care. He'd get ten years, maybe even twenty. Because of the nature of his crimes, they'd dump him in a maximum-security institution, a great, ugly lump of concrete and barbed wire, where his fellow convicts pumped iron and watched daytime soaps and slaughtered each other just to relieve the boredom. Like Alcatraz in that Clint Eastwood movie. He wouldn't last a week in a place like that. Somebody would shove a sharpened spoon into his chest because he wanted his toothpaste, or didn't like the way he combed his hair. His lungs would fill with sticky-hot blood. He'd fall down and die. The end.

Peter tossed the pillow up in the air, so high it almost hit the ceiling. He caught it and threw it again. Wouldn't Janey be surprised if she came home and found him lying in the bathtub with a bullet in his brain! But he wouldn't be around to see the stunned expression on her face, so how much fun would that be?

Better to wait until she got home, explain the situation, and see how she reacted. See if she was going to straighten herself out and try to be helpful, or stuff her suitcase and run for her life. Give the woman a chance to do the right thing. If she failed the test, it would be all her fault and he could do whatever he pleased, in terms of taking her with him, and stuff like that.

good vibrations

Toby swung a leg over his motorcycle as if it were a very small but seriously overweight pony. He took his own sweet time putting on his beanie-style micro helmet, wraparound oil-slick shades, and cool, fingerless, black leather gloves. Then, just as he grabbed the handlebars, he remembered that he had to take the gloves off so he could get out his Zippo lighter with the Harley logo, and his smokes. He lit a cigarette and jumped on the bike's kick-starter. The Harley coughed twice, and died. Toby cocked an ear and tilted his bike from side to side, listening for gas sloshing around in the tank. He tried the kick-starter again. The bike made a mechanical gargling sound, as if it were being strangled to death. He sat there for a moment, looking cool, and then pulled meditatively on his smoke and unscrewed the gas cap and peered inside. Couldn't see much with his shades on. He took them off and tried again. Sure was dark in there. Ash fell from his cigarette into the tank. He flinched, screwed the cap back on, looked around, and saw Harvey watching him from across the street. Toby was in the middle of giving Harvey a hard look when his boot slipped in the puddle of 50-weight oil that had leaked out of the bike in the past half hour. Harvey blew him a kiss. Toby reared up and took another futile shot at starting the bike. His beanie-style helmet slid forward over his naked, sweaty skull.

Harvey finished his own cigarette and flicked it arcing across the street.

Toby kicked the Harley again. The bike roared to life, the engine shuddering painfully. Sunlight skittered off the polished chrome and cool, tinted mirrors. Toby stomped the Harley into gear. The heavy clunk of misaligned steel was drowned by the roar of his shotgun exhausts. He cranked the throttle and tore off down the street, trailing a roiling blue cloud of oil.

Harvey went back inside, shut the door behind him, shot the deadbolt, and turned the SORRY WE'RE OPEN sign around so it read COME BACK WHEN WE'RE OPEN, STUPID.

Jan was still in her little room, cleaning her instruments. He waited patiently until she was finished, and then took her in his arms and held her as tight as was reasonable. She smelled of expensive perfume and wide-open spaces. He wanted to kiss her but knew he better not try. Later, maybe, but not now. When the time was just past just right, he let her go, and stepped back. She saw the carnal glow lurking in his eyes and said, "I've got a boyfriend."

"I'm happy for you."

"It's a serious relationship, Harvey. I don't fool around, and neither does he."

"You hope."

Jan didn't say anything.

He said, "You living together?"

"Off and on."

He rolled and lit a cigarette.

Jan said, "Everybody I know smokes. Why is that? If I ask for one of those, tell me no."

He smiled. "I'll never say no to you. Haven't you figured that out by now?"

"Gimme a fucking cigarette."

"No way."

She patted his cheek. "You're a good boy, Harve." Her knuckles were red and her skin smelled of bleach. She said, "Want a Coke?"

"Sure."

She opened the bar fridge and took out two cans and opened them both. Harvey took his and sat down in the antique dentist's chair he'd given Jan when she'd signed the lease on her first tattoo parlour, eight years ago. In all that time, it didn't look as if she'd made a whole lot of progress. He stretched out his stubby legs and drank some Coke. He was aware that Jan was watching him as closely as if he were a train. He knew what she was thinking. She wanted to know if he still had what she needed. He didn't blame her. If she'd asked him point-blank, he wasn't sure he'd know what to say. Prison did strange things to a person. If you wanted to survive, you had to change in ways you'd never have thought possible. Harvey had decided long before his trial was over that he wasn't going to be anybody's sweetheart. Inside, a black lifer named Marvel Durwood had taken a shine to him. When the time came to bend over or stand up, Harvey snapped the right-side nylon arm off his glasses and shoved it deep into Marvel's gaping nostril, slammed it home with the palm of his hand. Marvel's eyes rolled up in his bowling-ball head. His knees buckled, and he dropped. Hit the concrete so hard the impact had been heard from one end of the cell block to the other. There had been a lot of blood, but no witnesses. Marvel was past talking. The three-inch long spear of nylon had showed up in the X-rays. Harvey didn't wait for the guards to notice his glasses were broken. He requested an interview with the warden, sat down in a plain wooden chair in front of a rolling camcorder and told the world how it had gone down. The warden filed a report, but it hadn't gone anywhere. Marvel had six inches and more than a hundred pounds on him, was in for life on a multiple-murder rap, and had already killed two of his fellow convicts. Truth was, the only person on this planet or any other who had ever cared about Marvel Durwood was Marvel Durwood, and he couldn't even count on himself any more, because he'd been messily but effectively lobotomized.

But after that, with two brain-dead inmates on his sheet, Harvey had been the very model of a modern model prisoner.

Jan shook Harvey's shoulder. He looked up at her, seemed mildly surprised to see her standing there. She said, "What in hell were you just thinking?"

"About Marvel Durwood."

"Who's that?"

"A guy I knew in the joint." Harvey smiled. "Me and Marvel were the best of platonic friends. We watched out for each other."

Jan said, "I guess it must be good to have a friend in prison."

"It's a priceless thing, lemme tell you."

Jan nodded. She said, "I told you before you went in that I wasn't going to dry up like a prune waiting for you. It was your own fault and nobody else's that you went in. Beating that man up just because he was attracted to you. That was stupid, Harve. All you had to do was say 'no thanks,' and you would've been just fine."

"Maybe."

"Why should I have spent five years being lonely? Tell me what good that would have done."

"Made you gladder to see me now."

"I'm glad to see you."

"But not for the right reasons. I want us to be man and wife again and all you want is somebody to help you pull off a score. I'm love, and you're all business." He put his hand over his heart. "How do you think that feels?"

"I don't want anyone else in on this," said Jan. She wore a pair of lace-up knee-high black leather boots it must have taken her at least an hour to put on, and tight blue jeans and a pink T-shirt decorated with sequins. The T was snug. Anybody could see she wasn't wearing a bra. Harvey's palms felt sweaty. He tightened his grip on the Coke can, and tried not to stare. Jan was watching him.

He said, "Did you say something?"

"I said that I don't want you inviting any Marvel Durwoods or any of your other loser convict buddies in on this."

"Fine with me."

"Everybody's got a mouth, but hardly anybody can keep a secret. You trust me and I trust you, and Matt Singh's in because it was his idea. But that's as big as the party gets."

"Okey-dokey."

"Just the three of us," said Jan. "Nobody else."

Harvey drank some more Coke. It barely qualified as lukewarm. Was the bar fridge working, or just for show? He swirled the Coke around in his mouth, and let it slide down his throat. He had at least a thousand questions that needed answering. Quite a few of them revolved around their son, Harvey Jr. Called now by his middle name, Jan's father's name, Tyler.

Harvey the absentee ex-con father said, "Want to go somewhere, grab a bite?"

"Love to, but I've got a date."

"Break it." Harvey smiled. He put his fists together, thumb to thumb, and then twisted his wrists as if he were snapping a bone.

Jan said, "Thanks anyway."

Harvey bit down hard on the anger boiling up inside him. He said, "I'd like to see my son, if that's okay with you."

"Tyler's on a camping trip."

"Don't call him that."

"It's his name. He's been Tyler for the past five years, and he isn't going back. Get used to it, or take a walk."

"Where is the cute little tyke?"

"Golden Ears Park."

"Oh yeah?" He didn't watch out, she'd be sending the kid off to Europe.

Jan said, "He's coming home in a day or so. He'll be tired, not at his best."

"You tell him I was getting out?"

Jan nodded.

"Tell him I wanted to see him?"

"I said it might be a possibility."

"What'd he think about that?"

"He knows you love him. I tell him that on a regular basis. But he's only eight years old, Harve. He can't remember the last time he saw you, and he doesn't really know anything about you."

Harve said, "I always remembered his birthday."

"You should've sent him a card, so he'd know."

"Easy for you to say, but how in hell . . ." He realized he sounded like a whiner, and shut up.

Jan saw the hurt in his eyes. He had six years on her, but she'd grown up faster than he had. She was smarter, too. Whose fault was that? Nobody's. She said, "You can see him Sunday after dinner. Bring some chocolate ice cream. Chocolate's his favourite. You can visit a while, eat some ice cream, get to know each other."

"Sounds good."

"You can afford it, buy him some Lego. A spaceship."

"Lego spaceship," said Harve. He finger-wrote the words in the air.

Jan smiled. She said, "Don't steal anything. You get tossed back in jail, you're useless to me."

"What sweet sentiment."

She leaned over him and kissed him chastely on the cheek. She smelled like a flower garden in the sun. Harvey hoped and prayed it didn't take her long to mend her broken heart when her new boyfriend suddenly disappeared, never to be found again.

so far away

Janey Markson sat on the edge of her queen-size bed, surrounded
by a blizzard of tear-drenched tissues, book-ended by a mis-
matched pair of City of Vancouver homicide detectives. Janey
repressed an inappropriate smile at the thought that the tissues
looked like a flock of miniature doves that had died en masse in
mid-flight.

Jack Willows had no faith in Janey Markson's grief. He'd have
bet next week's paycheque that her river of tears would dwindle
and die as soon as the Kleenex ran out. He tried but failed to make
eye contact with Claire Parker. Janey was a receptionist at a hair
salon. The salon was downtown but upscale. Janey had spent a lot
of money on her clothes. She dressed well and provocatively.

Parker seemed lost in thought. Willows was pretty sure he knew
what she was thinking about. Hadrian, Hadrian, Hadrian.

Willows said, "I know you've already been over most of this
with the attending officer, but would you mind going over it again,
for me?"

Janey nodded. She made a visible effort to collect herself, grabbed
a handful of tissues and wiped her eyes, and suddenly burst into
another rainstorm of tears. She blew her nose, destroying another
handful of tissue. It had been a long day. Willows had a hunch it
was going to keep on getting longer.

Popeye Doyle stepped into the room, an unlit cigar propping
up his mouth. The weight of the cameras and related equipment
made his shoulders sag. He said, "We're done with him, he's
all yours."

Parker had Janey Markson stretch out on the bed, and suggested
that she try to relax. Janey nodded again, snuffling. Parker
squeezed her hand and assured her that she and Willows would
be back shortly.

Peter Markson lay facedown on the living-room floor. His right
hand clutched the TV's remote control. A cylindrical shaft of

bright chrome-plated metal protruded from the left side of his back, just below his wishbone. Willows crouched down beside the body. His arthritic knee cracked painfully. Now that he was closer, he could clearly see that the spear of metal was made up of the two sections of a "rabbit ears" television antenna that had been tightly bound together with black electrician's tape. The bulbous safety tips on the antenna had been removed with a pair of needle-nose pliers, and the hollow rods had been filed to sharp points. The roll of tape, pliers, file, and a brief handwritten suicide note lay on the blood-specked carpet a few inches from Markson's outstretched left hand.

Parker circled around so she could read the note. She had perfect vision, but Markson's writing was so small and cramped that it was all she could do to make out the words. It was hardly worth the effort. Markson's last thoughts were generic and pedestrian, unenlightened. About the only thing you could say in the author's favour was that he'd been brief.

Parker said, "This is so depressing."

"You're right," said Willows. "Why is that, anyway? Usually, there's nothing like a suicide to brighten up my day." His bad knee popped again as he stood up. He'd lost the cartilage as a result of a rugby injury back in his high-school days. Now, all these years later, he was paying the price. He patted himself down, found his Advil, and popped a couple of the small brown pills into his mouth.

Parker said, "How long has it been since you last rode the bike?"

Willows swallowed the pills. In fifteen or twenty minutes the pain in his knee would vanish like fog. Parker was always criticizing him for his lack of commitment to his exercise regime. He was supposed to ride the damn bike for fifteen minutes every day, and then lie down on an exercise mat and stretch the tendons behind his knee for another quarter of an hour. The bike was a stationary, recumbent model. It had cost him almost a thousand bucks. He had quickly learned that few things in life were less rewarding than riding a deconstructed bicycle to nowhere. He was certain that, in the dreary aftermath of all that work, his knee always hurt more than it would have if he'd only left well enough alone. Human beings were designed to wear out. Unnatural exercise was just asking for trouble. He smiled. It had taken a while, but he'd finally figured out what was bothering him.

"Claire?"

Parker turned towards him. The breeze coming in from the sea lifted the blinds. The slats were open. Parallel bars of light and shadow raced across her face, and then the breeze died and the blinds fell rattling into place. Parker couldn't see the ocean, but she could smell it. Her eyes darkened. She hugged herself and said, "Did you say something, Jack?"

Willows was paralyzed by deep-seated fear and an aching, wholly irrational, anger. He felt as if he were spiralling helplessly into unlit depths. His heart pounded and his lungs burned. His wife had never looked so beautiful, or lost.

3

love and trucks

Jan loved Tyler with all her heart. She missed him every single minute he was gone. But at the same time, being a working single parent was a bitch, and she refused to feel guilty for taking pleasure in the rare luxury of having no one to think of but her own sweet self. She'd come home from work to her stifling sublet two-bedroom apartment, stripped naked, cranked up the stereo, cracked open a bottle of cheap but ice-cold Sauvignon blanc, and run a tub. She'd been soaking for half an hour and two glasses of wine, and felt blissfully calm for the first time in months.

It had been a shock seeing Harve, after all those years. Harve was Tyler's father, and a secret, buried part of her no bigger than the faded picture inside a heart-shaped gold locket would always love him, and wish him the best. But that was about it. Five years was a long time. She hadn't consciously thought about it, but when he walked unannounced into her studio, she realized that she had irrationally hoped his long years in jail would have smoothed the sharp edges off him. She spent five long minutes listening to him tell her how much he missed her, blah blah blah, and knew for a rock-hard certainty that her husband was meaner and more self-centred and ruthless and cold than he had ever been. He was a danger to her, and to all the people around her, including and maybe even especially their darling son. She drained her wine-glass and reached for the bottle. If Harve ever laid a finger on Tyler, she'd kill him.

In the meantime, sad to say, she was in desperate need of the sonofabitch, and there wasn't a damn thing she could do about it.

She was surprised and vaguely alarmed to see that the bottle was two-thirds gone. Her boyfriend, Sandy, wasn't much of a drinker. He wouldn't think it was all that great if he showed up and she was drunk. But a little bit tipsy was okay. Tipsy was relaxing. Tipsy was fun.

Jan sat up, and poured herself a half glass of wine, and settled back down into the warm, soapy water.

Sandy buzzed her an hour later, on time to the minute. Jan was still in the bathroom, her hair done, makeup applied, dressed now in tan shorts and a pink tank top she'd picked up at Milano's half-price sale. She gave herself a last quick once-over in the mirror, ran her fingers through her hair, and turned and headed for the door, excited, wanting to hurry but holding herself back. She was almost at the door when she remembered she'd forgotten the goddamn deodorant, and had to go back to the bathroom and rummage through the medicine cabinet for the Ban. In her hurry, she knocked over a bottle of Aspirin. The cap hadn't been screwed on. The little white pills, dozens of them, had an awful lot of bounce. She scooped up as many as she could find. Sandy was a very tidy person. She had never met anyone half as organized. He never said a word, but she could tell he hated it when he came over and the place was a mess.

The buzzer rang again. She'd offered Sandy a key the second time he'd stayed over. He'd been nice about it, but had turned her down. She'd been so shocked that she'd babbled on for ten minutes about how she didn't offer a key to every self-centred sonofabitch she met and that if he thought . . . Etcetera, *ad nauseam*, for sure.

Jan was still thinking about how badly she handled rejection when she opened the door. Sandy wore freshly ironed jeans, a dark blue shirt hanging unbuttoned and loose over a pale blue T. He had brought her a bouquet of long-stemmed roses and baby's breath. She could tell by the way they were wrapped that they'd come from a florist, not a corner store. Sandy almost always brought her flowers, and they were almost always roses, eleven red and one white. When she'd asked him about that, he'd told her red was for passion and white was for purity. Eleven red, one white. Jan thought that more or less defined their relationship. Sandy's driver's licence said he was twenty-one years old, and she was pushing the dreaded big three-zero.

Sandy said, "You look great." He smiled his killer smile. "Gorgeous, actually. Did you do something with your hair?"

"Washed it." Jan accepted the roses. He gave her a quick kiss on the mouth as he slipped past her into the apartment. She loved kissing him, could have kissed him all day long, if there weren't even better things to do.

He shut the door and locked it, casual but quick.

"We alone?"

"Were you expecting somebody?"

"Shouldn't there be a cute little kid around here somewhere?"

"I told you last night that Tyler was going camping for a few days."

Sandy nodded, remembering. "With the neighbour and his kids, right? You trust the guy?"

"He's a fireman," said Jan.

Sandy nodded agreeably. But what did Jan think, that all firemen were saints? Or that the mere fact of their exalted profession absolved them of all sins? Sandy had met more than his fair share of smoke-eaters. Most of them were nice enough guys, but about 90 per cent of them had been divorced at least twice, and most of them had kids they didn't see all that often, and lots of them drank too much, and smoked a little dope, when nobody was looking.

He followed her into the kitchen. Got a vase down from a high cabinet for her and then opened a cold bottle of Chardonnay while she took care of the flowers, filled the vase with lukewarm water, cut away the excess leaves and trimmed an inch off the stems, emptied the plastic pouch of preservative into the vase and carefully arranged the roses and baby's breath, placing the white rose where it would have the most visual impact. Jan was an artist. You could see her talent in just about everything she did, no matter how inconsequential. It was one of too many wonderful things about her that made it hard for him to keep his balance, stay cool and detached.

She put the flowers on the table in the flow-through dining area, and then the two of them sat down on the living-room sofa. Sandy poured two glasses of wine. They clinked glasses.

He said, "To you and me, babe."

Jan sipped her wine. The Chardonnay had cost twice as much as the bottle she'd been drinking from earlier. That one, what was left of it, was in the back of the fridge, hiding behind the lettuce and carrots, waiting for her to be alone again. She hoped the bottle was in for a long wait but wasn't holding her breath.

Jan said, "How was your day?"

"Okay. Guy came around, installed the dish, and set everything up for me. I spent most of the morning flipping channels. You?"

"Not too bad. Kind of slow in the morning, but it picked up after lunch." Jan told him about the piercings she'd done, not going into detail because he had a weak stomach. The first time they'd gone out, she'd described with some degree of pride a complicated multiple tongue-piercing she'd done that morning, and he'd lost his colour and had to step outside to gulp some fresh air and settle himself down. She told him about Toby and his desire to have a blood-stained Bowie knife tattooed on his arm. He'd brought along pictures of the knife ripped out of a book, and had paid in cash from a wad of scuffed hundreds big enough to choke a dinosaur. Jan said she was pretty sure that if you put a straw to the bills, you could probably suck another fifty dollars' worth of coke off them.

Sandy said, "You think the guy was a dealer?"

"He sure as hell looked the part."

Sandy laughed and asked her another question that showed he was interested in her story. He was a good listener. Kept his eyes on her, and nodded his head every so often, made small sounds of amazement or consternation, asked exactly the right number of intelligent questions. Jan finished telling him about the knife tattoo, and then she put her wineglass down on the coffee table and snuggled up to him, thigh against thigh, letting the weight of her breast fall on his muscular arm. They kissed for a while, nice and slow, warming up, and then Sandy tilted her head up so he could look her in the eye.

"What is it? Something wrong? Do I need to brush my teeth?"

Sandy shook his head. He said, "Something's bothering you. What is it?"

"Nothing."

He sat up a little straighter. "Bullshit. Is it Tyler?"

"Tyler's fine." Jan scratched her arm. She leaned forward to retrieve her wineglass, stretching out more than she had to and holding the moment, conscious of her breasts pushing at the thin material of the pink tank top, giving him an eyeful but at the same time feeling emotionally distanced because he was right, something was wrong, and it had everything to do with that sonofabitch Harve. She drank some wine, and felt a little better, and drank a little more wine. Not much, just a sip.

Sandy hadn't moved an inch since he'd asked her what was bothering her. She had never in all her life met anyone who was half as patient. The first time he'd come over, the babysitter was late and Tyler was still up, running around the apartment in his pyjamas, venting the last of his steam. Eight years old, but he'd instinctively known Sandy for the rival he was. He'd blind-sided Sandy as he sat on the sofa, hit him with a metal dump truck that weighed a couple of pounds, easy. Smacked him on the kneecap and then swung viciously at his head and missed by inches, but only because Sandy saw the blow coming, and ducked. Some dark part of Harve in there, inside the child. Jan didn't want to think about that. She had offered

Sandy ice for his knee, but he'd said he was just fine, no damage done. The sitter had finally showed up, and Sandy had taken her out for dinner. No dancing, though. He'd taken her home early, still limping as he walked her to her door. He had graciously declined her offer of a nightcap. She didn't waste any of her precious time wondering whether he'd spurned her because Tyler had assaulted him or because he didn't like her perfume, or had done the math and figured out that she had almost a decade on him, or whatever. You couldn't please everybody. There was no point in giving yourself a migraine worrying about it.

When he phoned a couple of days later and asked her if she wanted to take in a movie, she couldn't have been more surprised.

Sandy sat up a little straighter, startling her. God, she'd been aching to see him all day long, and here they were, alone on the sofa, and she'd forgotten all about him, her mind wandering. She smiled. Here she was having an out-of-body experience when it was an *in-body* experience that she so desperately craved.

Sandy said, "Where were you?"

"Thinking about when Tyler hit you with the truck."

"Wishing he was here so he could whack me again?"

"Of course not."

She drank the last of her wine and snuggled up against him, casually rested her hand on his thigh.

She said, "You can kiss me if you want to."

Sandy said, "I'll try to remember that." He looked serious but the light in his eyes told her he was kidding, teasing her. She'd never met anyone as passionate as Sandy, but he took a little more winding up than most of the guys she'd known. She'd thought at first that he was repressed, but it was a lot more complicated than that. There was a shyness to him. As if he didn't know himself, wasn't sure who he was. That was okay with her. She kind of liked it, to be honest. When they were together it was always a learning experience for both of them. What made it really exciting was that they were both learning something entirely different. It had to be the age thing. That, and a boy's own innocence, slowly and deliciously eroded.

It drove her crazy, just thinking about it.

straight up no chaser

The waiter brought Willows' Cutty Sark, Parker's bowling-pin-shaped green glass bottle of Perrier, and a tall glass and a lowball glass full of ice cubes to the table. He poured half the Perrier into the tall glass and set it down in front of Parker's empty chair. Willows shifted slightly as the waiter placed the Cutty and ice cubes in front of him. The ice shifted, rattling in a subdued way. The waiter said, "Was there anything else? Did you want to see the menu?"

Willows shook his head, no.

The waiter went away. Willows reached down and around with his right hand, and adjusted the angle of his holster so the butt of his Glock wasn't digging into his ribs quite so irritatingly. He should have left the gun in the trunk of the car. It made him a little nervous, packing iron in a bar.

He thought about Janey Markson, how surprised she had been by her husband's sudden, violent death. She'd had no idea he was an armed robber. Peter had told her all sorts of lies when he'd gone out at night. He was going for a walk, to Starbucks, to the library to do some research ...

The true story, Peter Markson had kept a set of burglar's clothes and a ten-speed bicycle in his ratty, ten-year-old Econoline van, had driven around the city until he saw an ATM he liked, parked a few blocks away, changed into his black jeans and black, long-sleeved T-shirt and black sneakers, stuffed his black balaclava into his pocket, and rode the bike over to the ATM, hid in the shadows until somebody who looked like a victim used the machine. It was lucrative work. Most people had an arrangement with their bank or credit union that allowed them to withdraw four or five hundred dollars a pop. If Peter hit two ATMs a night, he was often grossing eight hundred to one thousand dollars. His operating costs were almost nil – coffee and doughnuts and a few dollars' worth of gasoline. Of course, the wear and tear on his psyche had been considerable . . .

Janey Markson had said, "What van? Peter owned a car?"

She'd switched to the past tense in the blink of an eye. Willows hadn't been surprised.

Parker came back from the washroom. She touched Willows' shoulder as she sat down. The overhead pot lights glinted on her diamond engagement ring and gold wedding band.

She said, "What a day."

Willows nodded. "Yeah, it was, wasn't it." Now that she was sitting at the table, he could take a drink. He took a very small sip of Scotch. Parker twirled the straw in her glass. She looked out the window at English Bay. It was a little past eight, but the city's informal "sunset club" was already starting to gather, dozens of people sitting on the grass banks and on the many logs arranged neatly on the beach, parallel to the shore, like giant pick-up sticks. By sunset there would be several hundred people on the beach, all of them facing the setting sun, and the sea. It was as if they expected, or at least hoped, that some kind of all-knowing god would rise up out of the depths and clue them in to whatever it was that woke them in the middle of the night, gave them the three-in-the-morning sweats. One time only, pre-Jack, Parker had joined the sunset crowd. It was a spooky experience. Everybody was very quiet, as if conversation were forbidden. When the last pink traces of the sun had faded from the sky, people had started leaving. They'd stood up and walked away in total silence, like zombies. Weird.

Parker drank some Perrier. She watched a trio of bikini-clad in-line skaters propel themselves powerfully down the sidewalk. During the past few years Vancouver had developed a well-deserved reputation as a "no-fun" city. It had started when the police had arbitrarily and illegally forbidden citizens from frequenting the Robson Street area to celebrate a Stanley Cup series win, and had snowballed as the city's tight-ass bureaucrats repressed or out-right banned more and more civic events. Greek Day, one of her personal favourites, was apparently gone forever. The Parks Board morons had even stripped the hoops from the Kits Beach open-air basketball court, because the sound of kids having fun had irritated a few taxpayers across the street from the court.

Parker drained her glass and poured herself a refill. Fortified, she turned to the matter at hand. It wasn't going to be easy to broach the subject, but if she raised it quickly she knew it would go easier on both of them – especially her.

She said, "Jack, I can't do this any more."

"Drink Perrier?"

She leaned back in her chair, collected herself, let him see in her eyes that this was not the time for bullshit, and tried again.

"Jack, I can't do this any more."

"You just got back."

"That's true."

It was, too, almost. But that was beside the point. Being separated from her beloved son was driving her crazy. She was a crazy woman, armed with a 10-millimetre Glock.

Willows said, "Give yourself some more time to adjust."

"I don't want to adjust. I want to be a mother."

"You are a mother." Willows almost added, "and a damn fine mother, too." But wisely decided against pushing his luck. During her term, Parker had gained twenty pounds. No problem, because his love for her was more than just skin deep. Then, during the last few weeks of her pregnancy, she'd lost her sense of humour. She'd worked hard to shed the extra pounds, but he couldn't remember the last time she'd laughed out loud. Except, rarely, at something brilliant Hadrian had done or babbled.

"I want to be a full-time mother," said Parker. "Not someone who says goodbye to her son at seven o'clock in the morning and comes home too tired to see straight, just in time to tuck her baby into bed."

Willows stared down at his Scotch. He felt the anger rising up in him again, and struggled to push it back. He and Claire had talked about the problems of parenthood for hours on end. They'd reluctantly decided they were in no position to have a child. Not yet, anyway. Maybe in a few years, but not now. When Parker told him she was pregnant, he was concerned, even frightened. But he was also deliriously happy. He knew there wasn't a chance in the world that Claire would abort the fetus. If she'd suggested abortion as a way out, he would have argued vehemently against it, done everything he could to stop her, short of locking her in the basement.

"Something else has been bothering me," said Parker. "How much of the crap I put up with during a shift do I bring home with me? Nobody understands what babies sense or absorb. Will Hadrian look into my eyes and see Peter Markson's body lying on the floor?"

"I seriously doubt it," said Willows. He added, "No, he won't," and knocked back half his Scotch.

Parker made a show of checking the time. It had taken a real effort to convince her to stop on the way home for a drink. He'd hoped they could relax for half an hour, take a rare break between the exhausting tedium of work and the eternal sameness of their domestic life together.

Parker said, "We should go."

Willows drained his glass, and signalled for the check. The waiter had been watching them. He said something to the bartender, who rang up the tab. Willows suspected the waiter had been keeping an eye on him because he believed he and Parker were going to start shouting at each other. Fair enough. The waiter put the check down in front of him. Willows calculated the tip as he got out his wallet. He'd never waited tables, but he knew it must be hard work. He considered himself a generous tipper. Tipping was an integral part of the dining experience, not an optional expense. If you couldn't afford to tip properly, stay home and stare at the TV. He tossed twelve dollars on the table, and pocketed the receipt.

Parker had done the math. Her face was tight. She pushed back her chair and stood up. Willows stepped aside to let her past. He followed her as she wended her way past the noisy, crowded tables and out of the bar. As they exited the building the dam burst.

"You overtipped. Again."

"I might want to go back there some day."

"I don't doubt it."

"Claire, it was only a couple of dollars."

"It's your attitude, Jack. That's what bothers me, your need to impress people you don't even know. Your wasteful attitude."

This was so unfair, Willows wasn't bothered by it. Parker hadn't finished her Perrier. Was that such a terrible waste? Willows didn't ask. He had two children from his previous marriage. Sean had left home and Willows didn't expect him to ever come back. In September, he hoped, his daughter, Annie, would be going into third-year Arts at the University of British Columbia. Annie had just broken up with her boyfriend. During term she had a rented room near the campus and she rarely came home, except to do her laundry.

Willows considered that he'd been an average parent at best, though he gave himself credit for recapturing lost ground after his first wife left him. When Parker told him she was pregnant, he'd relished his second shot at fatherhood. He was older, and wiser. Not nearly as prone to explode in fits of anger.

He had told Parker he had no preference as to the sex of their child, but secretly hoped it would be a boy. He loved Annie's older brother, Sean. He was proud of him, and what he had done with his young life, but there was a distance between them that Willows believed was entirely his fault, and it nagged at him.

Parker was silent during the ride home. Five days a week, Hadrian put in a ten-hour shift at a nearby daycare facility. Willows and Parker quickly learned that the daycare staff cut no slack where late arrivals were concerned. Their overtime rates were usurious, but the worst part of it was the visible anger they radiated when a parent didn't pick up his child on time. Willows and Parker had sought extra help. Their next-door neighbour had recommended a retired nurse named Miriam Witherspoon. Miriam was in her late sixties but had excellent references, a kindly disposition, and boundless energy. In the span of a few short months, she had almost become a member of the family. Willows supposed that to Hadrian, she *was* a member of the family.

Maybe that's what Parker was so upset about . . .

For Detective Jack Willows, this was a major insight.

4

days off

Claire called in sick the next morning. As Jack dressed, she told him she had an upset stomach and a headache. He wasn't quite as sympathetic as she thought he should have been. Maybe he didn't believe her. Small wonder, since she was lying through her teeth.

Jack said, "Want me to leave the car?"

"No, take it." He'd already kissed her goodbye and was lingering by the door. Claire waved him out of the bedroom. As soon as she heard him shut and lock the front door, she sat up and reached over and picked up the cordless and phoned the daycare.

"Hi Wendy, this is Claire Parker. Hadrian won't be coming in this morning. No, he's fine. We both needed a day off, that's all. Thank you, we will. 'Bye now."

Claire hung up, and swung out of bed. It was just past seven. Hadrian was usually awake by six, but this morning he hadn't made a peep, probably because she'd kept him up late the previous evening. She'd heard about babies who woke at their regular hour no matter how little sleep they'd had. Hadrian wasn't one of them, thank goodness.

Jack had cut a doorway in the wall between the two bedrooms. Claire moved soundlessly across the wall-to-wall, and peeked into the curtained bedroom. It took her eyes a moment to adjust to the dim light. Hadrian stood bolt upright in his crib, holding tight to the closely spaced bars with his tiny little fists, staring fixedly at a moth batting against his nightlight.

Claire held out her arms as she walked towards him. She smiled and said, "Hello, my darling!"

Hadrian's face crumpled. He burst into tears.

a girl's best friend

There was nothing to eat in the house, so they went out. Sandy drove a late-model Toyota pickup with a bench seat. Jan liked to sit close, snuggle up against him with her hand resting on his thigh. He was a careful driver, not reckless and wild like a lot of men she knew. If somebody cut him off, it didn't seem to bother him in the least. When she asked him about it, he said he'd witnessed a terrible accident shortly after he'd started driving and it had made him a more thoughtful and better driver.

Jan was in the mood for seafood. Nothing fancy. A bowl of clam chowder or a crab salad, something along those lines. Definitely not fish and chips. Nothing deep-fried. Given the geography, there weren't a whole lot of seafood restaurants in town. Even more surprising, there were only a handful on the water. Vancouver had miles of wonderful beaches, but there was nothing much to do but swim or lie around on the sand, or play volleyball, if you were feeling athletic. Why was it impossible to find a restaurant on the beach, somewhere nice where you could sit outside and enjoy the sunshine and the view, and a decent meal and a glass of wine? She told Sandy what she'd been thinking, and added, "It's as if scenery and a fine dining experience are mutually incompatible around here."

Sandy smiled and said, "'Mutually incompatible'?"

Jan said, "I learned that phrase from the marriage counsellor, when he was telling me why I should split up with Harvey."

Sandy nodded. Jan had told him about Harvey.

She said, "Anyway, am I right, or am I right?"

"You're right," said Sandy. "There's that place across the street from English Bay. With the upstairs, downstairs, and the big outside deck."

"Is it expensive?"

"That's up to you. But I'm buying, so don't worry about it."

"You're buying me lunch?"

"It's a limited-time offer that may never be repeated," said Sandy. "You can choose to use it, or sit back and lose it."

"I want a crab salad and a bowl of clam chowder and some fresh sourdough bread and at least two glasses of dry white wine."

"Sounds good to me."

Jan snuggled a little closer, and casually rested her hand again on his thigh. He was such a sweet guy, but jam-packed with contradictions. Careful with his money one day, generous the next. When she'd first met him a couple of months ago, at a Starbucks, she'd asked him what he did for a living, how he earned his daily bread. He'd said he was between projects. She had no idea what that meant but hadn't pushed it. He wasn't a friend of a friend of Harvey's, and that was really all that mattered.

After lunch they went for a walk on the beach. There were plenty of gorgeous women around, some of them in bikinis so outrageously skimpy Jan wasn't sure she'd feel comfortable in them, even though they were legal. Sandy was an extremely observant person, but he was also sensitive, and smart. If he ogled other women, he took care that she didn't know about it. What she did know, with a comforting certainty, was that when she was with him, he treated her as if she were the only woman in the whole damn world. Harvey had been just the opposite. When he spotted a good-looking woman, he'd made a point of staring at her, acting as if Jan didn't even exist.

Jan was still feeling the effects of the lunchtime wine when they got back to her apartment. The alcohol and long walk in the sun had given her a slight headache. A couple of Aspirin took care of the headache. A cool shower perked her up. She dried herself off and strolled into the living room and sat down naked on Sandy's lap as he read the morning paper. Pretty soon, she'd sweet-talked him into taking her to bed . . .

feeding time

The answering machine's flashing red light caught Parker's eye as she entered the house. She shifted Hadrian to her left hip and hit the machine's playback button. Jack told her he was in a situation, would be home late.

Hadrian wriggled in her arms, and then, without warning, burst into tears and started screaming deafeningly. Parker went over to the sofa and sat down and gave Hadrian her nipple. He bit her, and then screamed again and slapped at her with his little hands. God, but her breast hurt. Parker controlled her anger with an effort.

Hadrian's eyes were squeezed shut.

Tears flowed down his pudgy cheeks.

He blindly groped for her breast.

Parker shifted him in her arms to make things easier for him. She flinched as his questing mouth found her nipple.

This time, he suckled contentedly. If Parker had her way, Hadrian would stay on the breast for the next year or so, or at least as long as she could manage it. On work days, she had to express her milk into bottles that Miriam or the daycare staff warmed up. Thinking about it made her jealous. In the evening and on her days off she could hold Hadrian in her arms and watch him suckle. Staying off the bottle wasn't easy, but she firmly believed it was worth it, for health reasons and because of the bonding that went on between them, the heat of his small body, the touch of fingers, the eye contact.

When Hadrian had been fed and burped, Parker took him into the shower with her. More often than not he peed in the shower, but she didn't mind. He obviously loved the sensation of the water beating softly down on him, because he wriggled excitedly in her arms and made the most amazing cooing sounds, and sometimes shrieked with glee, so loudly it hurt her ears.

When they'd bathed, Parker dressed Hadrian in a long-sleeved Gap T-shirt and blue-and-white gingham shorts. No socks or shoes, because of the heat. She wore a black one-piece bathing suit under shorts and a sleeveless T. She carried Hadrian on her hip as she made herself a tomato and cucumber sandwich, and put together a small picnic basket. Hadrian was a big fan of apples. Apple juice, apple sauce. She put an extra jar in the hamper, and wrapped a spare diaper around the jar to help keep it cool. Hadrian watched her closely. He pointed at the jar of apple sauce and excitedly said something neither of them understood.

Parker said, "We're going to have a day at the beach. Do you remember the beach, Hadrian?"

Hadrian wasn't giving anything away.

Parker said, "We're going to go for a swim and then we're going to flop down on a blanket on the sand, in the shade of that big umbrella you love so much, and then we're going to have something to eat, and watch the world go by. We have to wear a hat and sunglasses, but it'll be worth it, because it'll be so much fun."

Hadrian frowned. He had a faraway look in his eye. He was having a bowel movement. It was the strangest feeling. What was going on down there? His eyes widened. His head jerked from side to side.

Where in the world was that wonderful smell coming from?

5

nuance is everything

Harvey wanted to move in with Jan so he could sleep with her and watch her cook his meals, and also so he could play with Tyler if he felt like it, teach his kid the kind of valuable stuff fathers taught their sons. He had no idea what kind of stuff that might be, but reasoned that he would be able to figure it out instinctively.

Harvey wasn't a patient man but he wasn't stupid, either. He knew he wouldn't be doing himself any favours by trying to rush Jan. That was fine with him. If he had to wait a day or two before getting into her pants, he could do that. Probably.

He rented a room in a cheap hotel on the sunny side of Main Street, a few blocks from the train and bus terminals and the elevated rapid-transit line that could speedily take him to or far away from the city. The room was small and dirty, and smelled like a large rat had crawled under the bed and died. The roar of traffic was a brain-numbing constant, but Harvey didn't mind, because it was a temporary situation. All he needed was some place to hang his hat for a little while, so Jan wouldn't rip into him about wrongly making assumptions. But that didn't mean he had to stay there night after night, suffering in manly silence.

He'd never admit it to her, but he'd hung on tight to Jan's sweet memory every single day and night of his stretch in the joint. If the image that had festered in his brain wasn't a dead-perfect match for the woman she'd become, well, that wasn't his fault. It was just something that happened, was all.

He sat down on the sagging, sorry-ass excuse for a bed, and lit a cigarette. Five years was just short of forever. He hadn't expected Jan to lock herself in a closet, all that time. But he hadn't expected her to slip a new hombre into her life, either. Or if she did try to replace him with someone else, he expected her to drop kick the guy out of her life the moment she laid eyes on him. What else could she do? They were man and wife. A team. Plus, Tyler was his son. His own flesh and blood. If that didn't count for anything, what did?

A cockroach scuttled across the scabrous carpet. The damn thing was so big it should've had a licence plate. The roach bumped up against his boot. Its antennae or whatever the hell they were called tickled the black leather. Was it sizing him up? He took a long pull on his cigarette and flicked ash at it. The length of ash hit the roach and exploded like a tiny bomb. Stunned and disoriented, the roach whirled around and around in a frenzy until Harvey rained on its parade with the heel of his boot. He bore down hard, grinding the roach to muck. But when he finally lifted his boot, the thing was still alive, wriggling erratically, as if its battery needed replacing. He stomped the roach again and again, until it wasn't an insect any more, just flattened pieces of an insect.

Harvey took a long pull on his cigarette and said, "That's what I'm going to do to your boyfriend, Jan. Squash him like a bug."

A passing truck drowned his words. He waited until the truck was gone and then he said, "That's what I'm going to do to your boyfriend, Jan. Squash him like a bug."

Was roach better?

Harvey said, "That's what I'm gonna to do to your candy-ass boyfriend, Jan. Squash him like a roach."

Nope, too specific. Confusing.

Harvey practised saying *I'm gonna squash you like a bug* until he was certain he had it down pat. It took him a long time to get it right, crammed full of evil menace and impending doom. By the time he was finally satisfied with his delivery, he'd smoked half a pack of cigarettes and had a fresh appreciation for Arnold Schwarzenegger, and the acting profession in general.

Squash you like a bug!

Get it wrong, it sounded ridiculous, like some kind of dumb kid's joke. "Squash you like a *bug* squash you like a bug *squash* you like a . . ."

Somebody pounded on his door. A wheezy voice shouted, "You okay in there, fella?"

Harvey yanked open the door. A heavyset guy wearing jeans and a red-and-black-plaid flannel shirt stared down at him. The fingers on the guy's left hand had all been cut off just below the first knuckle. Harvey figured the guy for a disabled logger. He grabbed two handfuls of flannel and said, "*I'm gonna squash you like a bug!*"

Harvey's room was on the third floor. He could hear the ex-logger thundering down the stairs all the way to the lobby. He went over to his window and looked down. The hotel door banged open. The logger turned right when he hit the sidewalk. He'd stopped running, but he sure was walking at a brisk pace.

Harvey lit another cigarette. The thing about Jan was, she wouldn't hang out with a punk. Which meant vile threats might not do the trick.

What if Jan's boyfriend decided to squash *him* like a bug? What would he do then?

Harvey thought it over. He decided he needed to buy himself a large-calibre mothafucka handgun. Something big enough to blow a hole in a battleship.

best laid plans

Jan and Sandy made love twice and then she drifted off. When she woke up it was past seven. Sandy had left a note on the pillow. He told her he'd had a great time, it had been a perfect day and he was crazy about her, but there were some things he had to do and he'd probably be working late, would call her in the morning, around eleven.

Jan balled up the note and threw it at the wall. She was furious, but mostly at herself. She'd worked hard to arrange Tyler's camping weekend, and it wasn't just for his benefit. It was for her, too. She should have told Sandy she wanted him to spend the night with her, instead of hoping he would choose to stay simply because he could. He was a guy. She should have spelled it out for him. Told him outright that she'd sent Tyler away and that it was the first time in her son's life that he'd been away from home and she worried about him even though she thought the trip would do him a lot of good. But all of that was totally beside the point, because the real reason she'd let Tyler go camping was because she wanted to be with Sandy all night long, make love and fall asleep in his arms and wake up and make love again, and have a leisurely breakfast in bed with him. What was wrong with her, that he couldn't find it in himself to stick around for one single night?

Jan got dressed and walked eight blocks to the nearest liquor store and bought a bottle of rye. On the way back she stopped in at Blockbuster and rented a couple of movies she'd been meaning to see. Back home, she made some toast, scrambled some eggs, poured herself a rye and 7-Up and settled down in front of the TV. The rented movie ended at a few minutes past nine. By then she considered herself reasonably but not by any means excessively drunk. She decided to treat herself to a double feature, and slipped the second movie into the VCR. That film ended at quarter past eleven. The bottle of rye had a pretty serious dent in it by then, but she was still fairly steady on her feet. She rummaged through the cupboards. There was nothing to eat but Arrowroot biscuits and Cap'n Crunch cereal. She poured herself one last drink, rye on the rocks, because she was out of 7-Up, and sat back down in front of the TV just as they switched from the national to the local news.

The lead item was about a late-night shooting in Metrotown, in the suburb of Burnaby, half an hour's fast drive from her apartment. There had been an ambush and gunfight in the mall's underground parking lot. Hundreds of terrified shoppers had run for their lives. Two men had died: the intended victim and a mall cop who had been caught in the cross-fire. The victim was known to the police, who believed he was a highly ranked member of a local gang.

There was amateur camcorder footage, jerky and blurred, of a burly female RCMP officer pushing back the crowd, then a slow pan past a yellow Porsche Boxster to a bullet-riddled body. The camera zoomed in, and steadied. The image of the dead man's face cleared, like something rising up out of turbulent water.

Jan's glass hit the carpet, and rolled. Her hands flew to her mouth. She said, "Oh my God." Her words sounded small and lonely.

The dead man was a friend of Harvey's named Matt Singh. Jan had met him just after Harvey took his fall, when she'd taken Harvey's Cadillac in to have it detailed. She'd wanted the Caddy to look as sharp as possible, so she'd be able to get top dollar for it. She and Tyler had needed every cent she could lay her hands on. Harvey didn't need the car because he wouldn't be doing any more driving, not for quite a stretch, anyway . . . Matt had taken an interest in Jan. He'd told her he knew somebody who might be interested in the car. They'd gone clubbing a few times but one thing hadn't led to another, and they had eventually gone their separate ways. At the time, Jan wasn't quite sure why. She'd told herself the chemistry wasn't there for her, though that wasn't exactly true.

When Matt called her out of the blue a couple of years later, and asked her if she was interested in making a thousand dollars in five simple minutes, she told him to go to straight to hell. He came around that same evening, knocked on her door, and before she could say anything, told her all she had to do was walk across a parking lot.

Jan said, "That's it? Walk across a parking lot?"

"Yeah. And when I say five minutes, that's five minutes max. You're probably looking at something like thirty seconds of actual work."

"What's the catch?"

Matt laughed. He had the whitest teeth she'd ever seen on somebody who wasn't a movie star. He said, "You have to look really sexy, show a lot of cleavage, a lot of leg, lots of real juicy attitude . . ."

"I can do that."

Matt said, "I know, I seen you do it."

Jan smiled. "And that wasn't even on purpose," she said, "because I didn't like you all that much, and I still don't."

"Don't matter. All this is, is business."

Jan sat him down on the sofa and got him a beer. She said, "Okay, I put some nice clothes on, and take a stroll across the parking lot. Then what?"

"Nothing. That's it. See, what you are is a distraction. You do your distracting and then you beat it. The only way you could have a problem is if you walked in a big circle instead of a straight line."

"In the meantime, you're going to be doing what?"

Matt smiled. "Not just me. You remember Billy Zeman?"

"The bartender, skinny black guy with the crooked teeth, at that new place on Granville, with the fake palm trees? How could I forget him?"

Matt nodded. "Me and Billy are doing an ATM. There's two guards, both armed. One shoves fresh money into the machine while his partner keeps an eye open for trouble."

"And that would be me."

"Nothing to it," said Matt.

"When do I get paid?"

"Right this minute, that's what you want."

Jan held out her hand, palm up. He handed her a fat envelope sealed with a length of clear tape. The envelope had her name on it, written large. She said, "You're a dime short, it's like I got nothing."

"In that case, count it."

Jan ripped open the envelope. It was stuffed with twenty-dollar bills. The bills had been in circulation for a while. She counted them out on the coffee table. Fifty, in ten piles of five. She shoved the money back in the envelope and tossed the envelope on the table. She said, "I got a kid I got to take care of. For him, there's nobody else but me."

"Lucky bastard."

"I want another four thousand, when you're done."

Matt laughed. "Forget it."

"Okay, three."

"There's plenty of good-looking women around, Jan. You sure you don't want the job?"

"Sure there are, but how many of those women can you trust?"

"Fifteen hundred."

"We're back to four," said Jan. "Ten, if anybody gets shot."

"Nobody's gonna get shot."

Jan said, "Okay, then it's four, for a total of five thousand dollars. If there's a fuck-up, you don't know me."

"Fine."

"I mean it, Matt."

He laughed again, throwing back his head. His gums were black. He said, "A blind man could see that you're serious. Don't you worry your pretty little head, Jan. We got everything all figured out. It's the perfect score, and it's gonna go smooth as yogurt."

Jan had almost backed out at the last moment. Her fear of what Matt might do to her had kept her in the game. In the end, Matt had been right about the score. He'd worked everything out perfectly, and it had gone exactly as he'd said it would.

Except one of the armoured-car guys had been shot in the head at point-blank range, when he'd pulled his gun. He'd been in a coma for more than four long years, died just over two months ago. Funny how things turned out . . .

The morning after the robbery, Jan read about the shooting in the paper. She learned that the guard was expected to survive, and that the thieves had gotten away with four hundred and sixty-eight thousand dollars. She'd called Matt on his cellphone to complain about her small piece of the action. Before she could say a word, he told her to watch her mail, and slammed down the phone.

Two days later she found a small package with no return address in her mail box. She went back into her apartment and locked the door and ripped the package open. It contained ten thousand dollars in a wide variety of denominations, the promise of another five grand every second month for the next year, and a terse type-written note warning her to keep her mouth shut and not to make any unusually large purchases.

Jan rented a safety-deposit box from her credit union. She let the money add up for six long worrying months, and then she paid cash for a low-mileage three-year-old Pontiac Sunfire, and treated Tyler and herself to a pressure-relieving trip down the coast, all the way to L.A. They'd spent two full days at Disneyland, toured Universal Studios and a bunch of other zany tourist hang-outs, ate at decent restaurants, stayed up late, and slept in even later. It was heaven, while it lasted.

Matt still owed her ten grand when the payments stopped. She asked around. He'd tried to rob a nightclub. The bouncer had beaten him half to death with his own gun. He'd pled, and taken a five-year hit. Jan visited him a couple times. He'd lost a tooth in a fight and felt sick about it. She voluntarily contributed a few hundred dollars to his prison account, giving him some much-needed juice.

He'd got out a couple of years later but hadn't been in touch until a month ago, when he'd dropped by unannounced to tell her about a score he'd been working on. He'd somehow found out that a wholesale diamond merchant was expecting a shipment of uncut African diamonds. They were blood diamonds stolen from a mine. He told her there had been a firefight at the mine, and more than twenty men, security personnel and miners and thieves, had been shot dead.

Jan said, "Are you trying to tell me the diamonds don't belong to the person you're going to steal them from?"

"That's right."

Matt smiled. His smile was perfect again, the missing tooth replaced. He leaned a little closer, and lightly touched Jan's arm. "What they do, they cut the diamonds and then they use a laser to carve a tiny little polar bear into the stone. It's so small you can't even see it with the naked eye."

"How sweet."

"What the bear does, it's a guarantee the diamond came from a Canadian mine, dug out of the ground by well-paid Canadian miners. What *that* means is some cute babe can slip a couple carats on her finger and not have to worry about whether some poor African bastard was exploited to death. Like she'd give a rat's ass anyhow."

"You're a cynical person, Matt."

"If you got a couple of hours, you can ask me why." He gave her arm a squeeze, and let go. "Point is, we pull the robbery, the jeweller can't whine to the cops. He's in a box, totally fucked. All he can do is go home to his wife and bitch about how rotten life can be."

"How much money are we talking about?"

"Don't even ask."

Jan said, "Do you have any idea what it feels like to be paid thirty thousand dollars for a crucial part in a robbery that netted your partner almost half a million?"

"Didn't I do the right thing?"

"Not really."

Matt gave her a very direct look that was a challenge and a warning. He said, "Some guys would have handled the situation in a completely different way."

"Think I wasn't ready for that?"

"Don't kid yourself. Please don't take this as a threat, but if you're going to mix with people like me – not me personally, you understand, but people like me – then you got to always, every last minute, be thinking about the well-being of Tyler. Because in the end that's how they'll get at you, through him."

Jan stiffened and drew back.

Matt said, "That security guy at the club, beat the crap outta me? I could've shot him, but I chose not to. I chose to take the rap, instead of killing a man. You know me, Jan. I'm not, at heart, a violent person. Even if I was looking at life, I am sure as hell not the kind of person who would ever harm a child. But the thing is, you and I can't do this job alone, it's gonna take at least three of us."

"Why me, this time?"

"'Cause you took care of me while I was in the slammer. Visited me, put that money in my account. You were my friend. Now it's my turn, if you're interested."

Jan looked into his eyes, shrugged. The simple truth was that the money from the ATM robbery was long gone. Worse, her tattoo business wasn't all that profitable. If business didn't pick up in a hurry, she was going to lose everything, and she'd have to go on welfare. There was no way she and Tyler could have a decent life on the miserly pittance the government doled out.

Matt told her about the jeweller, Andrew Cooper. Cooper was a boozer. Matt had met him in a downtown bar, told the guy he was an ex-cop with his own security business, handed him his gold-embossed business card with the four-colour picture, but backed off in a hurry when the jeweller told him he was already covered. Cooper was a lonely guy. Unfortunately for him, he and Matt had found other things to talk about that night.

"Like what?" said Jan.

Matt said, "All kinds of stuff. The best brand of vodka. How the real estate and diamond markets have both been depressed by the trend towards late marriages, or no marriage at all. The high cost of insurance . . . Fascinating stuff like that."

Night after night, Matt smiled through hours of boozy conversation so tedious a normal human being would have been driven to smash his lowball glass on the bar and slit his own throat. As the days and weeks slipped by, the two men became close friends. Or so Cooper thought.

The most interesting thing Matt learned, after a long night of heavy drinking, was that, two or three times a year, Cooper bought large quantities of African black-market diamonds.

"Isn't that illegal?" said Jan.

Matt said, "Bet your ass."

home sweet home

Claire heard Jack unlock the front door at three minutes past midnight, by the bedside clock. She listened as Willows kicked off his shoes and padded down the hall and into the kitchen, where he rattled around for a few minutes before he made his way upstairs. She was mildly surprised when he walked quietly past the open bedroom door and into Hadrian's room. She tensed when she heard his voice, low and soothing, but a little garbled. Jack had been drinking.

Claire listened carefully as he walked out of the nursery and down the hall the few short steps to the bathroom. The light snapped on and then he eased shut the door. A few moments later she heard the low thunder of the shower.

The drumming of the shower suddenly stopped. Claire heard the glass door slide sideways in its tracks. She decided that she would pretend to be asleep when Jack came to bed. It was late. She'd had a long day. She'd spent too much time in the sun. She was tired. They both needed a good night's sleep. In the morning she'd call in and take another sick day, and try to get Jack to take a day off. She'd drop Hadrian off at the daycare and drive straight home and make a big breakfast. When they'd finished eating, they would talk.

Claire rolled over on her side so when Jack came to bed she would have her back to him. Her heart was pounding away, beating fast as a hummingbird's. She tried to get her breathing under control, but it was hard, because for some reason it felt as if she were suffocating, couldn't get enough air in her lungs.

Jack's side of the bed sagged under his weight. She smelled his soap and shampoo.

Claire realized she was terrified. She knew Jack had spent the day at 312 Main, watching grainy ATM tapes so he could tie Peter Markson to as many robberies as possible. He'd told her he'd be at it for days, but that hadn't stopped her from constantly worrying about the possibility that he might, at any time, be killed in the line of duty. She was terrified for Hadrian, because if Jack was killed he would never know what a fine man his father was, would only know Jack as a series of disjointed second-hand memories, vague images shallow and haphazard as snapshots.

Jack laid his hand gently on her shoulder, as if he somehow knew what she was thinking.

"Claire . . ."

She turned towards him. She struggled to control herself, but it was no use. She shuddered from head to toe, and burst into a flood of tears.

Jack held her tightly. He told her he loved her.

Claire knew it was true, because it had to be true. She clung to her husband, and knew the weight of his sorrow, and the weight of his tears.

6

rise 'n' shine

Hadrian woke Claire at 6:15. She rushed into his room to find his mattress and bedding and Hadrian himself smeared with vomit. He stood at the bottom end of his crib, fully erect, his little fists gripping the railing. As soon as he saw his mother, the volume of his screaming tripled. Claire scooped him up in her arms. Her first thought was that he could have choked, and her second thought was that he smelled disgusting, and her third thought was that she was getting vomit all over her pyjamas, and after that it was nothing but guilt, for thinking of herself when her child was in crisis.

Hadrian was flushed, his plump cheeks a fiery red and his eyes too bright. She didn't need a thermometer to tell her he had a fever. She shot a resentful glance at Jack as she cut through the bedroom to the bathroom, and was surprised to see that he wasn't in bed. Where the hell was he? She expected to find him in the bathroom, but he wasn't there, either.

She called out his name, tentatively at first and then loudly, with unrestrained anger, as she hurried into the bathroom.

She heard hurrying footsteps on the stairs, but it was her twenty-year-old stepdaughter, Annie.

Annie took a half-step into the bathroom. She gave Claire a look that Claire irrationally judged accusing, and said, "What happened to Hadrian?"

"What does it look like? He threw up. He's got a fever."

"Sorry," said Annie. Her tone making it clear she meant she was sorry she'd bothered to ask.

Claire ran the tap and soaked a hand towel with cold water. She squeezed out the excess water and wiped Hadrian's face and hands clean, tossed the towel in the sink and soaked a washcloth and draped it over his forehead.

Hadrian stopped screaming. His tiny fingers plucked at the towel.

Annie said, "Is there anything I can do?"

"Get my bathrobe from the bedroom closet. The old one. It's pale green, with white stripes."

"Be right back." Annie hurried off. Claire fumbled with the vomit-slippery buttons of Hadrian's pyjama top. As she undressed him, he windmilled his arms. His small fist caught her flush in the eye. It was as if a bolt of lightning had exploded into her brain. For a split second, she was blinded by the intensity of the pain. She hurt so much she couldn't think, and tightened her grip on Hadrian for fear of dropping him. Her eye throbbed. Tears streamed down her cheek.

Annie came back with the robe. She said, "What happened to your eye?"

"I got punched."

"Hadrian punched you?" Annie was simultaneously shocked and amused. She said, "You're going to have a black eye. A real shiner. You should put a cold compress on it before it swells up."

Parker held her temper. The pain was ebbing, and her vision was restored. She said, "It was an accident. I'll be okay. Is your father downstairs?"

"I doubt it. The car's gone." Annie hesitated, and then said, "Did you guys have a fight last night?"

"Of course not."

Annie allowed herself to look puzzled. Claire felt herself blushing. She laid Hadrian on his back on the counter. She managed to get him out of his pyjama bottoms and diaper.

Annie said, "Yuk, what a mess. Can I go to bed now?"

"At this time of the morning? Shouldn't you be getting up? Where were you, last night?"

"Out."

Claire nodded, too busy to argue. She said, "Thanks for your help."

Annie bridled. "You don't have to be sarcastic."

"Really? I thought it was my turn."

Annie stomped off down the hall as loudly as she could in her stockinged feet. Claire folded up the dirty diaper and put it aside. She kept Hadrian pinned in place with her left hand while stripping off her pyjamas. There was vomit in her hair, on her breasts. She desperately wanted a shower but that would have to wait. She rested Hadrian on her knee as she bent and filled the tub. The day had hardly started and she was already wondering how she could possibly get through it. She tested the water, and adjusted the flow. She wanted it cool, but not cold. Hadrian suddenly lost his temper and pummelled her face with his fists. She yelled, "Stop that, it *hurts!*"

He took a deep breath and opened his mouth to scream.

Parker eased into the tub. Hadrian's tiny feet turned the water to froth. She gave him her breast. That shut him up.

Men. If they weren't all alike, it was a very close thing.

firepower

A fight down on the sidewalk below his open window woke Harvey at a few minutes past eight. His room had a toilet and a shower, so he didn't have to join the line of grumbling bastards that snaked down the hallway past his door. He showered and shaved, got dressed, lit a cigarette, and strolled up the shady side of Main Street to a McDonald's, where he read the sports section of a complimentary newspaper while eating three Egg McMuffins washed all the way down with four cups of strong black coffee. After breakfast, he walked back down Main Street, north towards the harbour and mountains. Behind him was an elevated Sky Train station and track that he didn't believe had existed when he was back-handed his sentence.

To his left, three identical high-rise apartments blocked the view, or would have blocked the view if there'd been a view. The high-rises had been half-built when he'd gone inside. He smiled, thinking that in some ways he was kind of under construction himself. Always changing, hoping to better himself in some small way.

He'd met a lot of guys in the slammer. Most of them were still there. The vast majority of those that had got out would soon be back. A life of crime wasn't all that bad, really. The cops might nail you, but probably wouldn't. If they did, chances were pretty good a butter-brain judge would let you off easy in the mistaken belief that you were truly repentant and would never do another crime, now that you'd been caught. But if you were a reasonable person, why wouldn't you continue your career as a crook? Nothing engaged the mind like plotting a caper. Putting a crew together was a lot more fun than a backyard barbecue. Actually pulling off the crime was almost as good as sex, and sometimes maybe even better. Not working a regular job was the cherry on the cake. There was a reason nine-to-fivers were called *stiffs*.

True, crime was a risky business. It was generally true that, the more often you got caught, the heavier your sentence would be. But getting caught was a learning experience. It tended to sharpen your concentration. Every time you got caught, it made it that much less likely it would ever happen again. Harvey had pulled twelve hard years in a maximum-security institution for his first known offence. His lawyer had advised him to plead guilty, and that's what he had done. The judge liked that. How could you be truly repentant if you wouldn't admit you'd done wrong? Harvey had sheepishly ducked his head and sworn on his mother's grave that he was sorry for what he'd done and would never do it again. The judge hadn't climbed down from his pulpit to give him a great big hug, but Harvey could see it was a near thing.

Twelve years was a long time to spend in one place, but it wasn't like the days and weeks and months were wasted. They just became kind of predictable, that's all. Not that twelve years added up, the way the system worked, to a grand total of twelve full years. It was a lot more complicated than that. First you had to subtract whatever time you'd served waiting for your hour in court, and then you could get your original sentence chopped by one-half for being a model prisoner. On both sides of the wall, there were thousands of rules and unseen legions of bureaucrats busy making up dozens of new rules every single day, but there was only one rule that was worth worrying about – *don't get caught.*

It seemed to Harvey that he'd hardly had time to get comfortable before the screws were insisting that his time was up and showing him the door.

One of Harvey's fellow cons had tipped him to a dump on Main called The Western Hotel, and he found the hotel without much trouble. A blond stripper was hard at work on a stage not much bigger than a postage stamp, working a brass pole in the soft-core glare of pink and blue spotlights. She was kind of lumpy, like her implants might have shifted, but pretty tasty-looking all the same. Harvey stood just inside the door, letting his eyes adjust to the dim light, watching the stripper bump and grind, chew gum, swing around a shiny brass pole, clumsily lip-synch the lyrics to "Stairway to Heaven."

There were half a dozen customers in the bar. None of them were well-dressed or looked in the tiniest bit affluent. Harvey sat down at a front-row table. A thin waiter with hairy arms asked him what he'd like to drink. Harvey ordered a pint of draft and a packet of beer nuts. The waiter was quick. Harvey dropped his roll on the table. He peeled off a five and told the waiter to keep the change, kept his eyes on the stage as he ripped open the package of beer nuts with his teeth. The blond stripper fluttered her eyelashes at him. He tossed one, two, three beer nuts into his mouth and wondered what else she'd flutter at him, if he asked her nice.

He'd knocked back about a half-inch of beer when a kid in a black leather coat shuffled up to his table. The kid had the body of an overweight fireplug. A white scar under his eye looked like a tiny half moon. He had pudgy hands, fingernails that were bitten bloody, identical cheap silver skull rings on all his fingers and both his thumbs. The skulls had eyes made of beads of translucent red plastic that caught the light and glowed brightly.

Before the kid could pitch him, Harvey told him to take a seat. The kid sat down. He looked a little worried. No wonder. Harvey's roll sat there on the table, almost a thousand dollars in well-used fives to fifties. The cash took up a lot of space. It looked like it weighed a ton and would last forever. The kid wanted every last penny. Harvey could see his hunger in his beady little eyes.

Harvey said, "What's your scam, kid?"

"You a cop?"

"No, I'm a criminal. The name Bill Shale mean anything to you?"

The kid shook his head. "No, why?"

Harvey said, "He's my parole officer. Thought you might know him."

"No, I don't think so."

Harvey said, "Not yet, anyway." The kid was dying to ask him what kind of work he did, but knew enough, barely, not to ask. Harvey said, "Armed robbery. Tried to knock off a nightclub, the Roxy."

"I been there."

"This was about three years ago. The bouncer jumped me. Black guy, size of a refrigerator. I had a choice of shooting a bunch of holes in him, or going quietly."

"You blast him?"

"Lay down on the floor with my paws in the air."

"How come you didn't shoot?"

"He was a nice guy. Married, or at least wearing a ring. Soon as I gave up, he stopped punching. I had to ask myself if a few years of my time was worth his whole life. The answer was no."

It was Matt Singh's story as told to Harvey by Jan, but Harvey told it well. The kid was genuinely interested, as if he expected to run into the identical scenario himself some day and wanted to know how to behave when the time came. He said, "I still don't get it."

"Why I didn't shoot?"

The kid's eyes went slightly out of focus as they drifted across the unfurled roll of money. The pupils swelled as the eyes snapped back to Harvey. He said, "Yeah."

"There was seven or eight of them, the bouncer and manager and a couple bartenders and waitresses or whatever and their boyfriends. I shot one of them, I knew I'd have to shoot them all."

"So?"

"I was armed with a revolver. Six bullets. The bouncer's coming at me at about fifty miles an hour, arms spread wide, smiling like he just won the lottery. I had about a millionth of a second to do the math on six counts of murder at twenty-five years each."

"If you were caught."

Harvey sipped his beer. He said, "I'd never murdered anybody before. I had no chance whatsoever of killing all the witnesses, unless they were unusually cooperative, and lined up in a row so I could knock off more than one of them with a single bullet. I knew that if I'd fucked up in the smallest way the detectives would track me down and either arrest me or shoot me to pieces, depending on their mood.

"Either way, I'd never get to belly up to the counter and order another Big Mac and chocolate shake, unless I lived to be about a hundred and eighty. That seemed doubtful. Still does." Harvey smiled. "What've you got for me, kid?"

"Wanna score some drugs?"

"Do I *look* like a dumb-ass scumbag addict?"

The kid shook his head, no. He said, "Anything else you maybe think I might be able to do for you?"

"Like what, helping me across the street?"

Harvey drank a little more beer, ate a few more nuts, drank a little more beer. He hunched forward in his chair. "I'm looking to purchase a large-calibre handgun." He leaned back. "You can help me with that, start talking. Otherwise, fuck off."

"I know a guy."

Harvey leaned forward again. "The cops come knocking on my door, I'll hunt you down and kill you."

"I wouldn't rat you out."

"Can you get me a piece," said Harvey, "or not?"

The kid sat there, nodding but not saying anything, until Harvey was about ready to punt him through the ceiling. When "Stairway to Heaven" finally ended, and the last cloying notes had faded away into the general hum and rattle and hiss of the bar, the kid turned towards the stage and snapped his fingers. To Harvey's surprise, the blond stripper jumped lightly down off the stage and came rolling over, her hips churning. She was a big hunk of woman, moving in five or six directions at once, and she looked like she was all business.

The stripper rested a hip on the table. She said, "What's up, Richie?" Harvey decided there was a lot more he could learn about breast augmentation. Hers looked real, but he knew they couldn't be. He wondered if she wore a bra when she wasn't working, and if Frederick's of Hollywood had her size, or if she had to get them tailor-made.

The kid said, "He needs to talk to Anders."

"Buying or selling?"

Harvey said, "Buying." He didn't like them talking about him as if he wasn't even there, and he let it show.

The woman said, "Hi, I'm Charlene." She lifted her hand to her mouth, did that thing with the thumb and pinkie that irritated him so much. "Got a phone?"

Harvey shook his head, no. She gave him a disbelieving look. He didn't blame her. It seemed as if everybody had a cellphone growing out of his ear.

Charlene said, "You can stare at them if you want to."

Harvey jerked his eyes away. He said, "I'll try to remember that, in case I ever get the urge."

She laughed. "Don't kid yourself. I get off in half an hour. Stick around, you might learn something worth knowing, and wouldn't that be a change." She jerked her head at Richie. "Give him twenty and tell him to fuck off."

Harvey peeled a ten and two fives off his wad and shoved them across the beer-stained and cigarette-burnt table with the tips of his fingers. Richie grabbed the money and pushed back his chair and headed for the door. He was even slower and more awkward on his feet than Harvey had imagined. From the back, he looked like something that was born to be brought down by wolves.

The music started up again. The stripper held out her hand. She said, "Help me up on the stage." Harvey sat there as if glued in place. She said, "Don't worry, nobody's gonna try to steal your fucking tiny little insignificant bankroll."

He said, "Maybe that's not my only problem."

She gave him a knowing look, and turned away laughing. Her laughter was surprisingly light, good-natured, and feminine, and seemingly genuine. Harvey watched her climb effortlessly up onto the white shag stage, the muscles in the backs of her legs bunching up, rippling, gliding smoothly under the pastel lights. In prison he'd spent anywhere from four to six hours a day in the gym, pumping iron with the other white guys, bulking up, making himself strong. By the time he was released, he could bench press twice his own weight fifty-two times in a row, fourteen sets of three reps, in twenty minutes flat.

He figured Charlene could take him easy, in more ways than one.

another home sweet home

Sandy lived on Napier Street, in a genteel part of the city's East Side. His open-plan apartment was an illegally converted one-car garage. The garage was old and small, but its green-painted cedar-shake siding and white trim lent it a certain charm. The apartment's single small window faced the untended backyard, tall grass and a garden run wild, the rusty, falling-apart swing set left behind when his landlord's wife ran off with their three small children and the door-to-door milkman. But there was a big skylight, and you could prop it open with a pole, if you felt like some fresh air.

He parked his pickup in the lane close against the cinder-block wall that butted up against the garage, so there was room for local traffic to get past him. He set the dual alarm systems and the tempered-steel bar that hooked onto the steering wheel, then got out, and locked the door with his remote. A lot of cars got broken into in his neighbourhood, but that didn't mean much, because it seemed like the entire city was riddled with thieves; shattered safety glass glittering like diamonds along the side of the road everywhere you looked.

He glanced casually around as he walked down the narrow brick-lined sidewalk that led to the converted garage's only entrance. The back door of his landlord's house swung open, and the man's middle-aged girlfriend stepped out onto the back porch with a wicker basket overflowing with laundry. She gave him a meaningless smile, the kind of smile that told him that he'd better keep his distance, if he knew what was good for him. He unlocked his door and pushed it open. Behind and above him, the clothes-line squeaked.

The answering machine's message light blinked red. Number of messages – 3. He hit the play button. Jan told him she needed to talk to him. She told him not to call her back, just come right over as soon as he could. She'd be waiting for him, any time of the day or night. *Click.* She'd called back a minute later to add that it was urgent, but not what he thought it was, if he knew what she meant, but they could do that anyway, if he was in the mood. Giggling, she hung up.

The third call was from his sister. She rambled on about what great weather they were having, ran out of steam, told him she loved him and missed him, and abruptly hung up without saying goodbye.

Sandy went into the kitchenette and got himself a Coke out of the fridge. He ran cold tap water over the top of the can, wiped it dry on his T-shirt, popped the can open and drank thirstily. Jan's message hadn't given anything away, but he was pretty sure he knew what she wanted. She wanted nobody but him. Endlessly, if not forever. On the other hand, what if he was wrong? What if she wanted to talk to him about Matt Singh, or that moron Harvey?

He cleared the machine, and finished his Coke. The sugar gave him a lift, but he knew it wouldn't last. He'd been busting his sorry ass twenty-four hours a day seven days a week for so long it made him cramp up just thinking about it. So far, he had nothing concrete to show for all his hard work except a nagging, low-level fear that he might have a sexually transmitted disease.

He twisted the empty Coke can into a compressed hourglass shape and tossed it at the garbage can, and missed by a mile.

7

risky business

Charlene finished her set to muted applause. A tall redhead with a prominent Adam's apple and a five o'clock shadow took her place on stage. Charlene threw on a robe and sat down at Harvey's table. She'd been working hard. Her body gleamed with sweat, but he noticed that her breathing was relaxed. She was in terrific shape, not an ounce of fat anywhere that he could see – and there weren't many places he hadn't got a look at. He figured she had to be in her early forties. Well preserved, but fading. It must be a hard thing for a professional woman, looking in the mirror and knowing you were getting a little bit older with every tick of the clock.

He said, "Thirsty?"

"I'll have a Sprite."

Harvey signalled the skinny waiter. He pointed at his half-empty beer glass and then at Charlene. The waiter headed for the bar.

Harvey said, "What happens now?"

"What would you like to happen?"

"Uh . . ."

"That's what I thought," said Charlene.

"No, I mean . . ."

"Just hang on a sec." Charlene smiled. She said, "First things first, okay. Just let me catch my breath and enjoy my Sprite, and then I'll phone Anders and we'll get just as busy as you want to be."

She helped herself to Harvey's pack of cigarettes and his lighter, lit up. "Know something?"

"Probably."

"The very first thing I ever noticed about men is how fucking impatient they are, just like a bunch of little kids. I'm not just talking about sex, either. And I'm not saying it's the only thing wrong with them, but . . ."

The waiter brought Charlene's Sprite and a tall glass full of ice, and her purse, a large black shapeless thing outlined in sequins. Harvey slipped the waiter another five bucks. Charlene poured some Sprite into the glass. She opened her purse and fished around in there for quite some time, then pulled out the smallest cellphone Harvey had ever seen. Not that he was an expert. She flipped open the phone, daintily tapped buttons, guzzled half her Sprite. "Mmm, that's so *good*."

"My pleasure," said Harvey. She gave him a toothy smile and reached over and patted his knee. Her expression suddenly hardened. She sat up straight and said, "Hi, baby, it's me." She listened intently for a long moment, and then said, "I know, and I'm so sorry to bother you, but I got a fella here needs to see a fella like you."

Harvey could hear the guy on the other end of the line. He sounded like he'd been hibernating. Charlene said, "Richie." She jerked the phone away from her ear and thrust it at Harvey. "He wants to ask you a question."

Harvey took the phone. He said, "Hello, Anders."

"How the fuck you know my name?" The voice was deep, powerful, bad-ass authoritative.

"Charlene mentioned it to me."

"Stupid bitch." A high-pitched giggle. "Don't you quote me, now."

Harvey said, "We'll see."

That gave Anders pause. He made a sound like he was sucking at something that was caught between his teeth and was still alive and struggling. Finally he said, "Who the fuck I talking to?"

"Harvey Goodman," said Harvey. He had no idea why he'd said his last name. It just happened, that's all. Like he was back in the slammer, crouched down on all fours, looking up at the rest of the totem pole.

"You a cop, Harve?"

"Crook."

"How long you known Richie?"

"Maybe forty-five minutes. He eyeballed my bankroll. It was love at first sight."

"Gimme Charlene."

Harvey handed back the phone. Charlene listened a moment. She said, "Yeah, okay," and slapped the phone shut. She dropped the phone in her purse, and poured the rest of her Sprite into the glass of ice.

Harvey said, "You and Anders pretty tight?"

"What's it to you?"

"Just asking."

Charlene said, "We have a relationship. I'm not saying it's exclusive, or that I'm totally opposed to meeting and becoming intimate with new friends."

Harvey nodded thoughtfully.

She said, "Shall we do some business?"

"You mean, with Anders?"

"What else would I be referring to?" Charlene gave him a goofily saucy wink. She said, "Follow me, handsome. But not too close, or people will talk."

Harvey followed her out of the bar and onto the street. There was an unmarked door twenty feet to the left of the bar's entrance. The door opened on a narrow flight of stairs. Harvey followed Charlene up three flights of stairs and down one of the hallways to an unmarked door.

Charlene knocked three times, loudly. She waited a few seconds and knocked again, twice.

Harvey said, "How old is Anders, about six?"

Charlene unlocked the door with a key. She pushed the door open and stepped aside. "After you, Harve."

Harvey grabbed Charlene's arm just above the elbow. He stayed close behind her as he propelled her into the apartment, kicked the door shut behind him. They were in a short, narrow, unlit hallway, the cramped equivalent of an entrance hall. She unlocked another door. Open doorways fed into two other rooms. One dark, the other filled with a soft, golden light.

In a musical voice Charlene said, "Where are you, sweetie?"

She led Harvey into the golden light. Anders lay on his side on a green and fluorescent-orange striped corduroy sofa. Because Anders' bathrobe was a perfect match for the sofa, Harvey almost didn't see him. He'd expected somebody kind of Nordic-looking, pale and blond and athletically thin, with ice-blue eyes and a somewhat reserved personality. Anders was black, darker skinned than any black man Harvey had ever seen. Mirror-lens sunglasses covered his eyes, so it was impossible to tell if he was awake or dozing. He lay on his back, listening to music that leaked faintly from his headphones. Some kind of jazz. The lonely wail of a tenor sax lifted up, and fell back, and was lost. Anders was bald. His head looked heavy, and dense. Harvey had seen bigger men in prison, but not many of them. He pegged his host at about six-four, a solid three hundred pounds.

Anders spread his arms wide. Really wide. He hooked four inches of index finger under the headphones and pulled them off his head. The sunglasses stayed put. He sat up, and up, and up.

"John Coltrane, ever heard of him?"

Harvey shrugged.

Anders slid the sunglasses up on his forehead. He said, "What you think?"

"About what?"

Anders' wide gesture somehow encompassed his world and everything that was in it. The dazzling punch in the eyes that was the sofa, the pink sea of wall-to-wall shag carpet, a La-Z-Boy recliner with a leopardskin cover, the gaudy paintings of hour-glass nudes that covered the walls, his collection of doorknocker woodpeckers and peacock feathers, numerous lava lamps, the pulsating red and blue lights of the silver stereo in the shape of a one-eighth-scale spaceship, an elephant's foot full of Zulu-type spears, a coffee table made of a three-inch-thick slab of clear acrylic with hundreds of shiny CDs and one apparently genuine human thumb sunk in it, a massive chandelier made of interlocked deer horns from which dangled far too many shrunken-head candle-holders to count . . . There was a lot to look at, and it was all so unbelievably ugly that Harvey's eyeballs were getting whiplash. Anders himself, with his brick-flattened nose, lost teeth, burn scars, stapled-shut scalp, missing ear, and permanently stitched-shut eye, was probably the ugliest thing of all. Since Harvey was a guest in Anders' house, that didn't seem like the right thing to say. Especially since Anders outweighed him two to one.

He came up with, "Charlene sure does have a major talent."

Anders said, "You got that right." His voice was pitched so low it was almost subsonic. He reached out and yanked on a wood-pecker doorknocker's dangling cord. The woodpecker's pointed beak rattled on a split birch log. Anders pushed the mirror-lens glasses back down on his nose. He said, "Charlene is a woman of many, many talents. You can take it from me that exotic dancing is the least of them."

He yanked on the cord again, and then tilted his head towards the ceiling, as if some small but vitally important sound had caught his attention. A quintet of shrunken heads was reflected in the mirrored lenses. After a moment's silence, Anders rotated his massive head towards Harvey until he could see himself in the glasses.

Anders said, "What kind of piece you looking for?"

"Something loud. A .44 would be perfect, but I'll settle for a .357, or even a 9-mil, if I have to."

"I don't suppose you got a firearms licence?"

Harvey said, "You selling licences, or guns?"

Anders chuckled good-naturedly. The sound of his humour was like the low rumble of distant thunder.

Charlene had vanished. Harvey's turncoat imagination pictured her in the kitchen, slipping into a plastic apron and sharpening a big knife.

He said, "Where'd Charlene go?"

Anders smiled in a way that wasn't helpful. His gums were the same shade of pink as the rug. The teeth he still had left were small as baby teeth, and were crammed tightly into his mouth, top and bottom. It seemed to Harvey that there were way too many of them. Fifty or sixty, at least.

Anders plucked a spear from the elephant's foot. He tested the long steel blade with the ball of his thumb, and sucked away the blood.

A fat bead of sweat rolled down Harvey's ribs. More beads of sweat chased after the first. His throat was dry. Sweat trickled into his eyes. He wiped his face with the back of his hand.

Anders said, "What kind of budget we talking?" He snapped his fingers, rapid little pops that sounded like distant gunfire. "Show me the money, Harve."

Harvey flashed his roll, shoved the money back in his pocket. He said, "Quit fooling around. Let's see what you got, or I'm gonna have to move along."

"All business, huh?" Anders clapped his Frisbee-sized hands. "I like that. Don't worship it, but admire it. Know why? 'Cause that's the way I work, cool and efficient."

Anders stood up. It took a while.

Harvey revised his estimate of Anders' height and weight to six-foot-six and three-fifty, respectively. The man was huge. He shambled past Harvey, moving slowly and taking small, child-like steps. As he walked out of the room, ducking his head and turning his upper body sideways so he could get through the doorway, he said, "Back in a minute."

Harvey went over and stood by the window. Rusty chicken-wire stapled to the window frame made the street look like the interior of a gigantic beehive. Harvey felt claustrophobic, and trapped. He toyed with the idea of scooting, but reluctantly decided to hold his ground. He had to have a gun, and had no idea where else to get one.

Anders was gone a long time. Eleven or twelve minutes, by Harvey's cheap but deadly accurate analogue watch. Harvey had feared Anders would return armed and dangerous, intending to rob him. He was relieved to see that all Anders was carrying was a matched pair of small black lizardskin suitcases.

Anders indicated the sofa with a sweep of his massive arm. "Sit down, man, make yourself comfy. I got no alcohol, but would you care for a Sprite?"

Harvey shook his head. Anders continued to stare quizzically at him. He said, "No thanks," in case he wasn't getting through.

Anders put the two suitcases down on the coffee table. He lay down on the sofa on his side. Harvey noticed that Anders was wearing pyjamas that perfectly matched his robe and the sofa. It was weird, the way he blended in, like he was an exotic snake on the Discovery Channel. If he took off the glasses, he might disappear entirely. Anders waved nonchalantly at the suitcases. He said, "Dig in, man. Take a look, see if there's anything tickles your fancy."

Harvey hesitated, and then sat down on the edge of the sofa. He unzipped the suitcase and flipped it open. It was filled with tapered rolls of newspaper. Harvey picked one up. It weighed four or five pounds. He unwrapped the paper. The gun was a stainless Smith & Wesson .38-calibre revolver, four-inch barrel and black composite grips. A price tag was affixed to the trigger guard with a short length of string. Harvey caught the tag between his thumb and index finger. He twisted it so he could read the numbers printed on the tag in black ink.

Anders said, "That's U.S. dollars."

Harvey did the math. The gun was priced at two hundred and fifty dollars, which translated into roughly four hundred Canadian.

He rolled the revolver back up in its cocoon of newspaper, and put it aside and unrolled the paper on another gun, a black

.40-calibre Glock. He checked the tag. The price was five hundred dollars. He said, "That's nine hundred bucks. You're asking retail, almost."

"That piece is brand-new, never been fired. Plus you gotta factor in that you don't pay no taxes or licensing fees."

"What's the cheapest gun in your arsenal?"

"You already seen it – the .38."

Harvey said, "Is it clean?"

Anders chuckled. The air vibrated, and was still. He said, "It's a fucking *handgun*, Harvey. They're all dirty. That's the nature of the beast."

Harvey said, "Toss in a box of ammo and your sunglasses, you got yourself a happy customer, if you'll take three hundred."

Anders spread his arms wide. "Four hundred's cheap. Bearing in mind you also get a fifty-round box of gruesome deadly hollowpoint bullets."

"Three and a quarter," said Harvey. "That's my best offer, take it or leave it."

Anders said, "Get the fuck outta my house."

It went like that for ninety hectic seconds. Anders caved in at three ninety-five, losing a little face just to get the deal done. Downstairs in the hotel bar it had been quiet, but suddenly the compressive thump of the sound system was loud enough to make Harvey's ears hurt. Overhead, the shrunken heads danced erratically. In the kitchen, three days' worth of dirty dishes rattled in the sink. Harvey slipped a round into the Smith while Anders was counting his money.

Anders said, "'Stairway to Heaven,' my favourite."

seduction

Sandy parked his truck around the corner from Jan's apartment. He walked down the paved alley and around to the front of her building, all the way to the end of the block, and then turned

around and walked back on the opposite side of the street. In a
neighbourhood as densely populated as Jan's, it was impossible to
catalogue and keep track of the local vehicles. What he was looking
for was a couple of beefy guys slouched low in a parked car,
shining their badges. He didn't see anybody. That didn't mean they
weren't there, but it cut down on the odds. He crossed the street
and walked up to the building and rang Jan's buzzer. She answered
right away, as if she'd been waiting for him to show. She told him
to come on up, and hit the button that unlocked the glass door to
the lobby.

Sandy thumbed the elevator button and stepped back three
paces. The elevator worked its way down from the third floor.
The doors slid open. Sandy got in and hit the button for Jan's
floor. The doors slid shut. He knelt as if to tighten a shoelace,
and adjusted the suede holster strapped to the inside of his right
ankle. The holster held a .22-calibre semiauto his father had
given him. He'd practised with the weapon at a local club. It was
reasonably accurate to a range of about ten feet. Beyond that distance, the chances of hitting anything smaller than a barn were
roughly equivalent to winning the lottery. He stood up. The elevator door slid open with a faint grinding sound.

Jan was standing right there in front of him, smiling. She wore
a sleeveless summer dress in pale green with big white flowers,
some kind of orchid. She smelled great and looked even better.

He said, "You look terrific."

"Thank you." He could see she was pleased. She was a little
hard around the edges, but there was no denying she was a
beautiful woman. He guessed that Harvey hadn't been big on
compliments. They walked down the hallway hand in hand to
her open apartment door. As she led him inside she said, "Want
something to drink?"

"Ice water would be good."

"You don't want a beer, glass of wine?"

"Makes me sleepy."

She gave him a slow look. "Would that be a bad thing?"

Sandy said, "Excuse me, I gotta use the can."

In the bathroom he splashed cold water on his face and the back of his neck, and stared himself down in the mirror as he told himself he was doing the right thing, that everything was going to work out, not to worry.

He found Jan in the living room, sitting at one end of the sofa with her long legs tucked under her.

She said, "I'm having wine."

"Whatever."

She handed Sandy a wineglass full of ice cubes and water. They clinked glasses. She said, "Here's to us."

Sandy drank some water. It was so cold it hurt the back of his throat. Jan sipped at her wine. Her dress was made of one of those tricky fabrics you could almost but not quite see through. He was pretty sure she wasn't wearing a bra, and her lightly tanned legs were bare. He wondered if she was wearing panties, and felt himself stir despite all his worries. She'd told him she was on the Pill, but he always wore a rubber. He'd told her he took the extra precaution because he wasn't anywhere near mature enough to be anybody's father, but the truth was that he was terrified of AIDS.

Jan said, "Is anything wrong?"

"No, of course not."

"You seem tense."

"I'm fine, really."

Jan eased off the sofa and went into the kitchen for a second glass of wine. She came back looking flushed and a little too serious. Sandy had meant to let her lead him to wherever it was she thought she was going, but he was losing patience. Not a good thing. He made a little more room for her, but when she'd settled back down, he shifted closer, took her small foot in his hand, and gave her a gentle massage.

She stretched out her leg to make it easier for him. "That feels good."

Sandy paused in his rhythm. Her freshly painted nails were the same lurid shade of red as fresh-spilled blood.

She lifted her head and looked at him. "What?"

"Nothing, I thought I might've squeezed too hard, that's all. You've got such small bones, I don't want to hurt you."

Jan said, "Good, because I don't want to be hurt. I've already had enough of that to last me a lifetime." She was quiet for a moment. Sandy switched to her other foot. The thin gold chain around her ankle got in his way. He unclasped the chain and put it on her other ankle and resumed his massage. Jan said, "My ex-husband was released a few days ago."

"Harvey?"

"That's the one. He dropped in on me, at work. Said he looked me up in the Yellow Pages."

"I didn't know you were in the Yellow Pages."

"I'm not."

"What did he want, everything to be just like it was five years ago?"

Jan smiled. "Not even Harvey's that stupid."

"Money?"

She drank some wine and put the glass down on the windowsill, disturbing dust motes that swirled in the sunlight streaming in through the window. Sandy had noticed the first time he'd visited Jan that she wasn't much of a housekeeper. But then, he was in no position to pass judgement. Not on that particular issue, anyway. Jan said, "No, that's what I expected, that he was after my fortune, but he claimed that all he wanted was to visit me and Tyler."

"You got a restraining order, anything like that?"

Jan shook her head, no.

"How you feel about him seeing Tyler?"

"I guess it's a good idea. I mean, Harvey's his father, and Tyler knows who he is, and everything. Or, at least he knows the good bits, in a theoretical sort of way."

"You don't sound too sure of yourself."

Jan shrugged. Her breasts moved beneath the thin material of the dress. Sandy averted his eyes. He said, "You said Harvey was violent."

"Sometimes. Not always. I might have asked for it, in a way."

"How could that be?"

"I don't know."

Sandy said, "It wasn't your fault."

"Are you mad at me?"

"No, but it irritates me when you think poorly of yourself. You're working hard, being a good mother to your child. What more do you want from yourself? Creeps like Harvey make themselves strong by undermining the people around them, feeding on their uncertainty and hurt."

"Wow, you sound like a shrink."

Sandy laughed. He said, "Don't ask to see my certificate to practise, or we're both in trouble."

Jan leaned her head back against the sofa and shut her eyes. The wine and the heat streaming in through the window were making her sleepy. The conversation wasn't going anywhere near where she'd meant it to go. She needed to fortify herself with another glass of wine, but didn't want to risk getting drunk for fear she might blurt out things it would be better to let out slowly, word by measured word. Besides, she could tell that Sandy was tense, and that bothered her and put her on her guard, because as far as she could tell he didn't have any reason to be anything but relaxed.

She lifted her leg and bent her knee, giving him a look at pretty much anything he wanted to look at, if he was in the mood. She dug her toes into his thigh. "Would you mind putting my gold chain back on my other ankle, please."

"Yeah, sure." Sandy's voice was congested. Jan lifted her leg a little higher. When he'd fastened the chain around her ankle she swung her legs around and took his hands and pulled, so they stood up together, touching all along the length of their bodies.

She said, "Would you like to take me to bed?"

Sandy nodded.

Jan said, "Well then, let's go."

insomnia

Jack pulled up to the curb in front of his home. He retrieved the morning paper from the flowerbed and went inside. The house was quiet. He called out Claire's name and then hung his jacket up in the pine wardrobe in the hall, and kicked off his shoes and went upstairs. Claire was in Hadrian's room, reading as she sat in the rocking chair by his bed. She looked tired.

Jack said, "You okay?"

Claire nodded. She said, "Hadrian had a fever. He threw up, but I gave him a cold bath, and he seems to be okay."

"Do you think you should take him to the clinic?"

"He's sleeping."

Jack leaned over the crib and reached down to gauge his son's temperature for himself.

Claire said, "Don't touch him; you'll wake him up."

Jack hesitated, and then withdrew his hand. He said, "I'm going to take a shower, and get something to eat, and then go to bed."

Claire nodded, and went back to her book.

She hadn't asked him if she could make him something to eat. She hadn't asked him where he'd been. He reached down and gently laid the palm of his hand on Hadrian's smooth forehead. Hadrian's skin was cool.

Jack stayed in the shower a long time, in the vain hope that the blast of water would sluice away his tension. He towelled himself off and put on his robe and went downstairs to the kitchen, and made a cheese and mushroom omelette and toast. He read the morning paper as he ate his breakfast.

Willows went to bed but couldn't sleep. The bedroom was hot despite the open window and whir of the fan, and there was too much light, and the fitful rustling of the curtains disturbed him.

He tossed and turned for the better part of an hour and then, vexed, threw aside the sheets and rolled out of bed and pulled on a pair of jeans. As he buckled his belt, Hadrian uttered a low, indistinct moan.

Willows hurried into the nursery. He was surprised to find Claire curled up on the carpet beside the bed, sleeping soundly. Hadrian was fast asleep. He lay on his back with his chubby legs tangled in his blanket, and his small hands loosely clasping his plump cheeks, as if in comic response to something that had shocked him.

A thin band of sunlight was fragmented and deflected downwards off the many facets of a wind-up musical mobile dangling over the crib. The light turned Hadrian's face into a nest of uncertain shadows, lending him a faintly ominous air, as if he were host to a malign spirit. Willows pushed that ridiculous thought aside. Hadrian's little chest rose and fell regularly. Willows leaned over him, so close he could feel the warm puff of Hadrian's exhalations on his cheek. Hadrian's breath was normally warm and milky but this morning it was sour and noxious. This made Willows anxious. He gently laid two fingers on his son's forehead. Hadrian jerked violently at the contact, and blindly batted Willows' hand away.

Willows straightened. Hadrian was fine. A bad dream had probably disturbed his sleep. Willows contemplated what sort of bad dream a child of Hadrian's age might suffer. Unchanged dirty diapers? A milk shortage? Having to eat the same stupid Pablum day after day? Not knowing you were going to get bigger? He stepped back from the crib, and looked down at Parker. She looked so comfortable that he decided not to disturb her.

There was no point trying to get back to sleep. He'd drive down to Spanish Banks and take a walk on the beach to clear his mind, then continue downtown to 312 Main to tackle the remains of yesterday's mountain of paperwork.

seduction, part II

Annie had walked over to the Safeway for groceries. She woke
Claire when she got home. Claire reluctantly accepted Annie's
offer to drive her and Hadrian to the nearby medical drop-in
clinic. Annie – these days – was no philanthropist. Claire hoped
that all she wanted was to borrow the car, or cadge a few dollars'
spending money.

The clinic's waiting area was full, but Claire wasn't concerned
because there were two doctors and they tended to move people
along pretty quickly. Seventeen minutes per visit was the time
allotted by B.C. Medicare, but that was the maximum; there was
no established minimum time. She sat down in the last of the
vacant chairs with Hadrian on her lap. There was a play area filled
with brightly coloured plastic toys, but she didn't want Hadrian
playing with them, because it was safe to assume all the other children who had come in contact with the toys had been sick, or
exposed to people who were not well. She picked up an ancient
copy of *Oprah* magazine. Hadrian grabbed the corner of a page in
his tiny fist. He yanked hard, and ripped off a small piece of paper.
Claire took the paper away from him before he could stuff it in his
mouth, but moved the magazine closer so he could tear off another
piece of paper. The grim-looking elderly woman in the next chair
gave her an approving smile. Claire was so surprised she almost
forgot to smile back.

Patients moved in and out of the waiting room. The receptionist's phone rang constantly. Hadrian kept tearing apart the
magazine.

Claire was starting to worry about Annie when she sauntered
into the waiting room, the car keys swinging from her little finger.
Hadrian saw the keys. He held out his pudgy little hand, and yelled
ferociously. Claire didn't want Annie to let him have the keys because
she was afraid he'd jab himself in the eye, but she didn't want him
yelling, either. She let Annie give him the keys. He pulled them violently to his mouth and sucked greedily. Annie rolled her eyes.

Parker said, "The metal's cool, it feels good on his teeth."

"Whatever."

Annie was debating not going back to UBC in the fall. The official reason was that she had decided a formal education was a waste of time. In a firm voice, she'd insisted to Jack and Claire that the only thing a Bachelor of Arts degree would guarantee her was a job working the graveyard shift at Subway, slapping together low-cal sandwiches for insomniacs.

But limited career choices weren't at the heart of Annie's dissatisfaction. Her boyfriend had just dumped her, and his parting shot was that he thought she was a lesbian. Annie had been devastated. Why would he say something like that, unless it was true? Claire had taken her shopping, hoping to find some decidedly feminine clothes Annie could add to her wardrobe. The shopping trip had been a disaster. Annie felt comfortable and safe in her baggy jeans and loose-fitting T-shirts.

Claire made the crucial mistake of giving her some unsolicited advice on the basics of makeup. Annie yelled at her that she didn't appreciate being lectured and that Claire didn't know what she was talking about. Lipstick was out. Nose-rings were in! It had been quite an outburst, from a supposedly mature twenty-year-old woman. Claire had worked hard to mend the damage. She knew that Annie was going through a difficult time, and that she must have mixed feelings about her new half-brother . . .

Annie said, "Claire?"

Claire looked up. Dr. Hamilton – Randy – stood by the door to his examining room, smiling his boyish smile, and motioning her forward.

Dr. Hamilton was in his late thirties. He was tall and thin and had a shock of red hair he wore on the longish side. He was a preener, a man who had achieved his goal right on schedule, and had been basking in his glory ever since. Claire believed that younger doctors were probably more likely to be in tune with the latest in medical miracles. On the other hand, Hamilton's unlined face didn't instil confidence, and his unbridled enthusiasm, together with his apparent belief that a loud voice and active manner equated heartfelt concern, sometimes grated on her. His insistence that he call her by his first name – Randy – was another thorn in her side. She supposed her age was showing. But the clinic was a lot more convenient than phoning her family doctor and nagging the receptionist to fit her in sometime next month. Anyway, Hadrian got along with Dr. Hamilton, and that was all that really mattered.

Claire put the magazine aside and stood up. Hadrian threw the car keys to the floor and pointed at them and screamed loudly. She bent to pick up the keys and give them back to Hadrian. When she stood up, Annie was glaring furiously at Hamilton. Claire was wearing a scoop-neck blouse. Her breasts were swollen with milk, and she guessed that Hamilton must have snuck a peek at her cleavage when she'd knelt to pick up the keys. She felt herself blush as she walked towards him. He touched her arm as he followed her into the examining room.

"Hadrian feeling a little under the weather is he?" He took Hadrian from her and held him up in front of his face as if Hadrian were an inanimate object, some small thing that had attracted his attention and that he might be interested in, if the price was right. Hadrian swiped at him with the keys. His aim was true but his arms were short.

Claire said, "He had a temperature early this morning, and he was vomiting, and now he has diarrhea, and he can't seem to keep anything down."

"Getting plenty of fluids into him?" Had Hamilton just snuck another look at her breasts?

She said, "Yes, but as I said, he isn't keeping much down."

Randy Hamilton got Claire to sit Hadrian on her lap while he shone a light into his ears, nose and throat. Hadrian was fascinated by Hamilton's flashlight. Hamilton let him play with the light while he took his temperature.

He said, "He's up a couple of degrees. It's nothing to worry about. Little tyke's building up his immune system, that's all. His weight's fine and his general health is excellent." He smiled. "You're doing a wonderful job, Claire."

"Thank you."

Hamilton, standing directly in front of Claire, put his foot up on the arm of the chair she was sitting on. His posture was entirely inappropriate. She looked away. Hamilton said, "Everything else okay?"

"Just fine."

"Your husband's a cop, isn't he?"

She nodded tersely.

He said, "It must be difficult, with all the shift work."

"He's a homicide detective. He usually works a nine-to-five shift."

Hamilton nodded gravely, salting the information away. He said, "I don't suppose it's exciting as the movies, car chases and midnight surveillance and so on . . . I suppose he must have to put in a fair amount of overtime. Can't expect your average murderer to put away his knife and gun at five sharp."

Claire smiled politely. She could have bitten her tongue for discussing Jack's working hours. Hamilton was vain enough to assume she wanted him to know when she was alone at home. She said, "We work things out."

"Well, good." Hamilton stood up, and rubbed his hands briskly together. "Call me if there's a problem. As I said, the trick is to keep him well-lubricated."

Parker nodded. There was nothing in Hamilton's tone of voice that suggested any hint of sexual *double entendre*. But had she seen a teasing hint in his eyes – or was her imagination working overtime? He managed to briefly touch her again as he escorted her out of the examining room.

As Annie drove her home, Claire thought about the fact that, although the clinic had two doctors, she never saw anyone but Hamilton. She supposed that didn't mean anything, that he saw her because he was familiar with her file. Even so, she decided it was time to find another clinic.

8

on being a consumer

Harvey drove straight down Main, towards the mountains. He parked on the street, and sat quietly in the car. Half a block behind him, a City of Vancouver Meter Maid bulled her way towards him. Her face was twisted with arcane rage. Harvey reflected on the personal cost of unlimited power. Pen in hand, her knuckles white with pressure, she showered illegally parked vehicles in a blizzard of tickets. When she got to Harvey, he stepped out of the Firebird and groped his genitals as he made a show of patting himself down for change. The Meter Maid dawdled, book in hand, applying pressure as best she could. She was a blonde, kind of stocky, with bulgy calf muscles built for tackling the Alps. He thought she would've been a good match for Anders, if his name hadn't been so misleading. The Meter Maid wasn't what you'd call a stunner, but Harvey thought she looked kind of cute in her crisp white shirt and dark blue shorts, shiny black boots. She was about five-eight, a solid two inches taller than he could ever hope to be, and that helped to crank up his interest. Was it the woman he was attracted to, or the uniform? He hoped it wasn't the uni, because that would indicate he'd been institutionalized during his long period of forced incarceration, and was therefore doomed to eventually –

and probably sooner than later – recycle himself back to prison.

Harvey slid Anders' mirrored sunglasses down his nose and gave her a great big smile, crinkled up his eyes, shovelled on the charm. Lots of women, at least two of them, one unsolicited, had compared his natural good looks to the notoriously handsome film star Richard Gere. Harvey believed Gere was past his prime. He'd told both women he appreciated the compliment, but thought it failed to do him justice. He slid the sunglasses back up his nose and said, "Could I ask, you got change for a dollar?"

"You don't need change, the meter accepts dollar coins."

"I'm only gonna be here a couple minutes."

She gave him a nice smile, setting him up. "Do I look like a bank?"

In the blink of an eye, Harvey's seductive smile twisted into a black-hearted sneer. He said, "Yeah, as a matter of fact a bank is exactly what you look like." He thrust out his arm and shoved a dollar into the meter, and twisted the butterfly handle. A green light blinked. The timing needle swung around to the sixty-minute mark. Harvey said, "Quit staring at me and get back to work."

"Fuck you, Shorty."

Harvey waggled a finger. He said, "I like a woman with ambitions. Too bad for you that wishing doesn't make it so."

She turned her back on him and strode off. The ground didn't shake, but it had to be a near thing. Harvey waited impatiently for a break in traffic. He trotted across the street and down the long half block to the Army & Navy, the no-frills, Jacqui Cohen–owned department store that had been a Vancouver institution since 1919.

Harvey wandered around the store, taking his time, making a game of spotting security. The store was crammed with a wide variety of shoppers, all the way from fashionably dressed young couples to desperate welfare recipients trying to stretch their miserly pittance of a government handout as far as it would go. Harvey made his way downstairs, to the sporting goods department. When he was a kid, anybody could walk in and buy an army surplus Lee-Enfield .303 rifle and a box of hardball ammunition simply by plunking down the twenty-dollar price. No GST, either. Those days were long gone, and would not return. Now the only guns in stock were air pistols, good for irritating crows, but that was about it. Harvey went over to the fishing department and bought a double handful of one-ounce lead fishing weights and a jackknife with a fake buckhorn handle, then went back upstairs and paid cash for a pair of emerald-green canvas deck shoes, and a bright red made-in-China fedora.

The clerk punching cash-register buttons was Chinese, or maybe a Filipina, Harvey never could tell the difference. He tossed the pantyhose on the counter, but left the fedora on his head, tilted at a rakish angle like a private detective in a black-and-white movie. Affecting an exaggerated lisp, he said, "My boyfriend's six-foot-four. He's got really heavy thighs because he plays professional football. Will these fit him or are they going to be too ti-ight?"

The clerk squinted up at him. She said, "How much does he weigh?"

"Two hundred and fifty-eight and one-half pounds, somewhere in there. That was this morning. He gains as the day goes on."

"Should be okay. Are you paying for the hat?"

Harvey worked on looking surprised, then sheepish. He wasn't confident he'd pulled it off. He tilted his head and thumb-flicked the back of the brim so the fedora jumped off his head and landed upside down on the counter. The clerk rang it up, and totalled the bill.

The cash register buzzed and whirred. The clerk said, "That'll be thirty-seven dollars and fifty-four cents."

Like Harvey couldn't read the numbers for himself. He peeled a couple of twenties off his fast-dwindling roll. It was a hard world. A man had to spend money to make money, and there were no two ways about it.

grindstone

"Jack?"

Willows turned and looked behind him. Inspector Homer Bradley crooked a finger. Willows clicked his pen and put it in his shirt pocket. From his desk across the narrow aisle, Dan Oikawa gave Willows an under-the-eyebrows look. In the past few weeks, more than two dozen cheap ballpoint pens had disappeared from the desks of the six-man Serious Crimes squad. Nobody was pointing any fingers, yet. But at the same time, everyone in the squad was on his toes, eager to solve the case and bask in the resultant glory. Dan Oikawa was usually pretty good under pressure, but lately his paranoia meter had been on the rise. Willows stood. He pushed his wheeled chair up against his desk, straightened his tie, and headed for Bradley's office.

Inspector Homer Bradley was pissed. He was chronically short of detectives because of the infamous on-going "pig farm" investigation into the disappearance and possible murders of sixty-three female Vancouver prostitutes and drug addicts. The VPD had slept through years of murder, and the pendulum had finally swung the other way – a whole bunch of top-level cops were losing sleep over the Pig Farm case. Or if they weren't, they should have been. Not that it was doing anybody any good. Public confidence in the VPD was, deservedly, at an all-time low. Bradley didn't expect the situation to improve in the foreseeable future. Eventually, there was bound to be a public investigation. When the truth came out, many heads would roll.

Bradley's mood further darkened when he got the news that Parker had booked off sick, again. The world went black when he learned that Detective Eddy Orwell had bugged out for an emergency dental appointment.

He waved a pencil at Willows. "Shut the door, Jack."

Willows turned and shut the door. In all his years as a homicide detective, he'd never walked into Bradley's office without being immediately told to do *something*. It was usually the door, but sometimes Bradley wanted his window shut, or the buzzing fluorescent ceiling light turned on or off, or a chair moved an inch to the left . . . Willows supposed Bradley was demonstrating control, unsubtly reminding him that he was the biggest bear in the woods.

Willows leaned against the wall. He had to pick his spot, because most of the space was covered with photographic reminders of Bradley's decades-long service to the department. There were pictures of Bradley in chummy group poses with six chiefs of police and four ex-mayors, several aldermen, a handful of easily recognized film stars, and numerous fire chiefs and other genuine or dubious local heroes.

Bradley said, "I see Claire booked off sick again. How's she doing?"

"She's okay."

"She be back in tomorrow?"

Willows shrugged. "Beats me, Homer. Maybe yes, maybe no."

Bradley slid a slip of paper across his desk.

Willows pushed away from the wall. He spun the slip of paper around so he could read the address printed on it. He recognized the address as a luxury waterfront high-rise on the north side of False Creek. The building was ideally located between the Granville Street and Cambie Street bridges. The penthouse units had the highest per-square-foot price in the city. Willows knew all this because he and Parker, wasting time one evening a couple of years ago, had visited the presentation site. He remembered the high-pressure salesman assuring them that the amenities included but weren't limited to fantastic views, top-of-the-line appliances, genuine marble and selected hardwood floors, and European-style lighting fixtures. Neither he nor Parker had been seduced by the presentation. Maybe he'd be interested in another twenty-odd years, when he'd retired and Vancouver developers had learned how to build a watertight envelope.

Willows brought Oikawa up to speed in the elevator. They were investigating a homicide that, unless the uniformed cop who'd called it in was hallucinating, was a lead-pipe cinch for a murder investigation. Even better, the victim was Colin McDonald, the multi-millionaire developer renowned city-wide both for his appetite for beautiful young women and his ability to construct flashy-looking buildings with all the characteristics of a sieve. It was clear from the troubled look in Oikawa's eyes that he wasn't too pumped about the case, no matter how high-profile it was. Willows wasn't going to worry about it. Oikawa had always been a moody personality.

shopaholic, inc.

There was still half an hour left on the meter when Harvey made his way back to the Firebird. He was feeling cocky in his new hat, but his mood soured when he spotted the City of Vancouver parking ticket tucked under the windshield wiper. The ticket was dated and had the time written on it in a delicate, spidery hand.

Harvey slung his cool Army & Navy shopping bag into the car. He ripped the ticket in four ragged pieces and tossed it on the sidewalk, where the Bitch would be sure to see it next time she passed by.

He had the urge to track her down and give her a peek at his dark side, but told himself she wasn't worth the trouble. She had a radio and would jump at the chance to sic the cops on him. Let her own karma take care of her.

Harvey had the green shoes and red fedora and black pantyhose. All he needed now was a shirt, and a black, or green, suit. No way he was paying for a new suit, not on his budget. It seemed like everything from tobacco to bubble gum was at least twice as expensive as when he went into the slammer. A guy didn't have to be a mathematical genius to figure out that meant he was going to have to pull twice as many robberies to maintain the same shabby standard of living he'd endured before he'd been busted. If he wanted to better himself, he was going to have to stay busy.

Factor in Tyler and all the stuff he was gonna need, Harvey was going to be one seriously overworked criminal.

His first stop was a charity used-clothing store on Fourth Avenue, a few blocks west of Burrard. When Harvey had gone to jail, the building had been home to a radio station. He assumed the station had moved, or gone belly up. He followed a woman up the concrete steps and didn't complain when she held the door open for him. Inside, racks of used clothing were organized according to customer gender and type of item. There were about fifty suits to choose from. Only one was green, and it was way too big for him. No problem, except he'd have to roll up the pants to keep from tripping over them, and what if they came unrolled as he was making his getaway? He dreaded the evil crap his fellow cons would sling at him, if he got tossed back in the joint because his getaway pants didn't fit.

There were lots of black suits to choose from. Most of them looked like new – so much so that Harvey was suspicious of their origin. Had they been stripped off dead bodies by avaricious funeral-home employees? He decided he didn't care one way or the other. Not at these prices. He grabbed a charcoal Armani and a dark blue Hugo Boss and headed for the curtained changing rooms. The Hugo, with its thin-to-the-point-of-invisibility pin-stripes, suited him best. The size 48 jacket hung on him like a tent, but that was a good thing, because the extra bulk would make it harder for the victims and witnesses of his crime to give the cops an accurate physical description. The pants' thirty-inch waist was a tad loose, and the inseam was a paltry twenty-four inches, but if he wore the pants low on his hips, he'd look just fine. Not that he was trying to make a fashion statement.

But what was that weird smell? He shucked the jacket and pressed a handful of material against his nose and inhaled deeply. The suit smelled of scorched earth and mouldy cheese and rotting meat.

Harvey tried the Armani. Ditto.

He found a canary-yellow three-piece suit in a 38 Large at the far end of the rack, mixed in with the smaller sizes and a few yellow shirts. It was as if some sneaky bastard had hidden it there, intending to come back later. Harvey slung the suit over his shoulder and headed back to the changing rooms. The suit fitted easily over the drab clothes he was wearing, and had the bonus visual effect of adding a solid forty or fifty pounds to his weight. Perfect.

He found an electric-blue shirt with fake mother-of-pearl buttons that was priced at a dollar-fifty, and a yellow-and-blue-striped mile-wide tie that set him back another fifty cents, and a white patent-leather belt that was a dollar. He changed in the car, in the parking lot behind the building. There were two business establishments on his short list of places to rob. One was a drive-in hamburger joint way out on Kingsway, called Harvey's. The other place was a health-food store–restaurant combo named Caper's, that had made big black headlines a few years ago due to an employee infecting a number of innocent customers with Hep A.

Harvey liked the idea of a guy named Harvey robbing a place called Harvey's, but was leaning towards knocking over Caper's, because it was conveniently located just a few short blocks away.

But maybe it made more sense to bust Harvey's, because he was starving, and they made a great cheeseburger platter, and you couldn't find a better chocolate shake anywhere in the city . . .

But Caper's, despite a spate of negative publicity from the Hep A outbreak, did a huge business. The joint had to be rolling in dough. Plus, it was a lot closer than Harvey's.

Harvey drove three blocks west on Fourth Avenue. He parked in a Safeway lot, tilted the rearview mirror so he could admire himself. Though he didn't know it, he looked like Truman Capote's blind younger brother would have looked, if Truman Capote had had a blind younger brother. He was just about to get out of the car when he remembered that he'd forgotten to buy a pair of gloves.

No way was the Caper's caper going down bare-handed, due to the jailhouse tattoo on the back of his left hand. The tattoo was of a crudely but passionately drawn bug-eyed eagle stomping a rattlesnake to death. The artwork was in his sheet, and was bound to pop up on the screen the instant some brain-dead cop typed it into his computer.

Harvey sighed heavily. He tossed the fedora and glasses on the seat and got out of the car and trudged across the baking-hot parking lot to the Safeway. The only gloves he could find were cotton gardening gloves, white with blue flowers. He tried them on, first the left hand, and then the right. One size fit most. He glanced around, observed that he was not being observed, and deftly shoved the gloves into his pocket.

Back in the Firebird, he put the hat and sunglasses back on, shoved his new gloves into his pocket, and studied what he could see of himself in the rearview mirror. He looked weird. He wasn't sure if he looked weird *and* dangerous, but he definitely looked weird. Were the feds called feds because they wore fedoras? He shoved the keys in his pants pocket, and got out of the Firebird, and walked over to the corner and turned and looked back. The Firebird was parked facing away from him. From where he was standing, it was mostly hidden by a silver Mercedes SUV. Head for the Mercedes, he was home free.

Harvey waited for the light to change. The blindingly white pedestrian lit up and a speaker emitted a grating, bird-like cheep. He wondered how come they didn't have black pedestrian signals, as he walked across the street. He peered in through Caper's plate-glass windows as he strolled slowly past. The store was crowded. A food bar ran parallel to the sidewalk and then curved gracefully towards the back of the store. There were a few tables at the front, people of all ages eating and drinking, stuffing their healthy little veggie faces. A woman perched on a stool at a high, round table glanced at him and smiled, then ducked her head and said something to her girlfriend that made her turn and look at him. The two of them exchanged a few words and then cracked up, laughing their fool heads off. Harvey pretended not to notice. He was a consummate professional, and as such he made a point of staying calm, cool, and above all collected. He touched his new gun through the yellow suit jacket. When the time was ripe, he'd see who got the last laugh. In the meantime, he'd continue to coolly and calmly case the joint, and play the difficult against-the-grain role of a harmless geek in a loud suit.

The problem was, Caper's was a lot busier than he'd expected. There were quite a few people in the restaurant area, plus a bunch of Caper's employees in tight jeans and tie-died T-shirts, broccoli-green aprons, plus a dozen or so happy customers sprinkled throughout the store snapping up plastic basketfuls of organic this and organic that.

But really, so what? All they were was a bunch of urban house-wives and health freaks and retirees and time-lapse hippies. He used his Big Voice and waved the gun around, who was gonna argue with him?

sniffer dogs

Colin McDonald had died with his outflung right hand inches from the crumpled top of a pair of shimmering black silk pyjamas with gold piping. His initials were on the collar, monogrammed in gold-coloured thread. The pyjamas had a private label. They'd been made in Hong Kong specially for Colin.

Oikawa jealously fingered the material. He said, "How much you think they cost?"

Willows shrugged.

Oikawa said, "I'm going to look around a little, see if I can find the murder weapon, maybe talk to the girlfriend."

Willows looked up. "She isn't your type."

"I know that."

"Yeah, but can you *remember* that you know that?"

Oikawa walked out of the bedroom, silent on the thick carpet. Willows turned back to the body. Oikawa wasn't going to find the weapon. If it was in the apartment, they'd have already found it. He reached across the corpse and picked up the yellow foil wrapper from a roll of 35-millimetre film. The police photographer, Mel Dutton, had come and gone. Dutton was getting sloppy in his old age. Willows hoped it wasn't contagious. He let his eyes move across the body, hoping to find something he'd missed the first dozen times around. The killer had used a sharp-edged weapon. The cuts weren't deep, but there were a lot of them. The coroner was of the opinion that the wounds to the back of McDonald's neck had paralyzed him. Fragments of shattered spinal column glowed white against a background of blood that had dried a hard, glossy black.

Some murder victims shrieked a deafening accusation; others were mute. Colin McDonald was the quiet type. Willows hoped the Crime Scene Investigation Unit would have more luck. The wool carpet was promising, because it was a trap for all manner of evidence. If you were going to kill someone, it was much wiser to do it in a bathroom or kitchen, where there was plenty of running water, and an easily washed linoleum floor.

Willows' knees creaked as he stood up. He followed his new partner's drab monotone into the dining room.

Chelsea gave Willows a lingering glance and then turned back to Oikawa. She said, "How many times do I have to tell you that I don't have one?"

Oikawa frowned. Colin McDonald's girlfriend was a stunningly gorgeous blonde, the sort of woman you might hope to meet in a secret dream or a magazine, the kind of woman who intimidated the hell out of you just by being herself. At five-ten, Chelsea was three full inches taller than he was. Plus she was wearing spike heels that added another four inches to her already formidable height, and she had her hair tied up in a French twist that made her seem even taller. Oikawa concentrated hard on being a cop, and concentrated even harder on not being a slack-ass lecher. He said, "You're telling me you don't have a last name?"

"Yeah."

"Everybody's got a last name."

"Oh, really? What about Prince, or Madonna, or Sting?"

"That's different. They're artists, performers."

"So am I. Didn't I mention that I model, and that I'm a performance artist? Do you know what that means, performance artist?"

Oikawa shrugged.

Chelsea said, "Break it down, it isn't that hard. *Performance* and *artist*. What do you suppose those two words signify, Danny?"

"Dan," said Oikawa. He added, "I'd prefer you called me Detective Oikawa."

"Yes, and I'd *prefer* to be called Chelsea."

Oikawa didn't want to argue with her, because her boyfriend's corpse was lying on the carpet in the next room, and she was obviously distraught, if not exactly broken-hearted. But on the other hand she was potentially a vitally important witness, or even, who could say, the killer.

He said, "How are you listed in the phone book?"

"Under my name, naturally."

"What name?"

"I've only got one name. Chelsea. What's the *matter* with you? Weren't you listening, or are you fucking deaf?"

Oikawa pursed his lips. He said, "Watch your language, please." He snapped his fingers. "Let me see your driver's licence."

"I don't have one."

"You don't have a driver's licence?"

"Isn't that what I just said? What's *wrong* with you?"

"How do you get around? I don't see a woman like you riding a bicycle or taking public transport."

"You mean, like a bus?"

Oikawa nodded.

Chelsea said, "Well, you got that right. I want to go somewhere, there's always somebody wants to give me a ride. Wouldn't *you* like to give me a ride?" She waited a telling moment and then added, "If I'm alone, I take a cab." She shot a quick sideways look at Willows, who was busy rereading the notes he'd taken while he'd interviewed the housekeeper, Mrs. Julia Rubie. She said, "Can I go now?"

Oikawa said, "Not yet. We have some questions we need to ask you. Maybe you could start by telling us why you happened to drop by the apartment."

"I already told you."

"Not me, the uniformed officer. We'd like to hear it from you, to make sure we get it right."

"Okay, fine. I was at home, I got a call from Mrs. Rubie, Colin's housekeeper. She couldn't get into the apartment because her key didn't fit. She was upset, because Colin's very particular about scheduling and all that, and if he came home and found she hadn't tidied up, he'd have fired her."

Oikawa was taking notes. He nodded, and looked up. "Okay, then what?"

"I wasn't busy, so I said I'd come right over."

"To help the housekeeper with her key?"

"Mrs. Rubie is a very nice woman. She's conscientious and hard-working and has a wonderful reputation. Colin pays a little above market value for her services. That's very important to her."

Oikawa nodded.

Chelsea said, "The extra money means a lot to her because she's trying to put three children through university."

"She isn't married?"

"Her husband died ten or fifteen years ago. He was a gardener. There was an accident . . . I don't know the details."

Willows drifted over. He said, "How long did it take you to get here, from the time Mrs. Rubie called?"

"About twenty minutes."

"Was there something wrong with Mrs. Rubie's key?"

"No, my key didn't work either. There was tinfoil jammed in the keyhole."

"Who discovered that?"

"I did. We got the tinfoil out with a pair of tweezers. I unlocked the door and Mrs. Rubie and I went inside together."

"Who found the body?"

"She did."

"Mrs. Rubie."

"Yes, that's right."

Willows said, "How did she happen to have your phone number?"

"I'd given it to her a few weeks ago. I was interested in having her work for me."

"As a housekeeper."

Chelsea coloured. She said, "Yes, of course."

"Why did you go inside the apartment? Were you worried that something might be wrong?"

"No, of course not. I went inside to use Colin's phone. I knew he wouldn't mind. I had to make a call, and my cellphone battery was low."

"I imagine it must have been quite a shock, seeing him lying there . . ."

"It was terrible. It's so strange, I didn't really look at him, the first thing I saw was his hand, and all that blood . . . The way he was lying there, so still, I knew he must be dead. Then Mrs. Rubie screamed . . . Is she going to be all right?"

"She's doing fine," said Oikawa.

Chelsea took a moment to collect herself. She said, "Colin had a lot of enemies. I mean, I never met anybody who liked him. He was a very successful businessman but he had an abrasive personality, and he really enjoyed abusing his power. He was a very odd person, in the sense that he didn't seem to care what people thought of him. He once said that his own mother thought he was a jerk. He thought it was funny."

"Did he ever mention any death threats?"

"No, never."

Willows said, "Can you think why anyone might want to disable his lock?"

Chelsea gave Willows a startled look. She said, "I assumed whoever killed him did it, to give himself more time before the body was discovered."

Willows nodded. He said, "You could be right. Just between you and me, do you have any idea who the killer might be?"

"No idea whatsoever."

"Okay, you can go now. We're probably going to want to talk to you again." He gave her his card. "If you leave town, give me a call first. Would you like a ride home?"

"In a police car? No thanks." She gave Willows a quirky, under-the-eyelashes look. "Unless you're driving."

Willows said, "There's a herd of reporters down on the street. TV and radio. I don't want you to say *anything* to them until we've had time to notify Colin's family that he's been killed."

"Because I might screw up your investigation?"

"No, because you *would* screw up my investigation."

Chelsea looked deep into Willows' eyes. She said, "I'll bet you can be a real prick, when you're in the mood." She smiled and added, "Though that's not necessarily a bad thing."

Willows didn't respond. Chelsea turned and walked out of the room. Oikawa watched Willows watching Chelsea. He wondered what it was about Willows that women found attractive. He also wondered what it was about him that women found unattractive. Sometimes he blamed his height, or his Japanese ancestry. But David Suzuki wasn't exactly the tallest guy in the world, and *he* never seemed to lack for babes . . .

when the Thai salad hits the fan

Harvey hitched up his canary-yellow pants and pushed through Caper's glass door. The smell hit him like a sledgehammer. His mouth watered. He made a beeline for the deli bar. Everything was for sale by the gram, whatever that was.

A kid in a green apron leaned over the glass-topped counter and said, "Can I help you with anything?"

"What've you got with meat in it?"

"There's chicken, beef samosas . . ."

"What's a samosa?"

"A small pastry, like a miniature pie." The clerk pointed out the samosas. Harvey pointed at a bowl of noodles. "What's that stuff?"

"This?"

"No, over to the left." Beat. "Your left."

"That's the Thai salad. It's really good."

"Yeah?"

"Want to try some?" The kid grabbed a small Styrofoam bowl and shoved a few spoonfuls of noodles into it. He handed the bowl and a white plastic spoon to Harvey.

"Go ahead. Tell me what you think."

Harvey spooned noodles into his mouth. He chewed thoughtfully.

The kid said, "You're an actor, right? I seen you on . . . uh . . ."

The Thai noodles were pretty good, for noodles, but Harvey was a big meat-eater, and he was in the mood for meat. Maybe the samosas weren't as awful as they looked. What he really wanted was a burger. A big, fat, greasy cheeseburger slathered with onions, and a side of fries, and a chocolate shake so thick you could flip the glass upside down and it would take forever to pour out.

The kid snapped his fingers, smiling. "You were in that movie, the one about the armoured-car robbery. You were Walter, the guy drove the getaway car. The guy with the shotgun called you Wally, and you were so pissed you pulled your gun and blew him away. Man, you were great!"

"No, that wasn't me."

The kid laughed. "Who you think you're kidding! I'd recognize you anywhere."

"Better not," said Harvey. He put the Styrofoam bowl down on the counter. "Lemme try a beef samosa."

"I'm sorry, but I can't do that."

"What're you tryin' to pull, you miserable little punk?"

"Excuse me?"

"You give my taste buds a yank and then you fuck me around like I just walked in off the farm . . ."

The kid gave Harvey a brisk round of applause. "That's so great! How can you slip in and out of character like that? Can I have your autograph?"

"Gimme a pen."

The kid handed him a robin's-egg-blue Papermate ballpoint with a chrome button and clip. Harvey stuck the pen in the breast pocket of his suit jacket, and strolled away.

He got a bottle of organic orange juice out of a glass-front cooler, and gave the bottle a shake and unscrewed the cap and drained half the contents. Behind him, there was discontented muttering. In front of him, there was a lineup at the cash register. The two women who'd laughed at him were still at their table. Harvey guzzled some more orange juice, then slowly turned his head until he was looking directly at the two women. The one who was facing him looked quickly down at her empty plate. Harvey discreetly eyed the cash register. The clerk rang up a sale. The cash drawer popped open. It was time to do the crime.

kiss my ass

Jan lit a cigarette. She pursed her lips and blew out the match, making a big deal of it, flirting with him. She averted her head and exhaled a cloud of smoke and turned back to him and said, "What're you looking at, big boy?"

"Nothing in particular."

Sandy lay on his back on the sofa. Jan lay sprawled half on top of him. All she wore was her gold Seiko. He was naked except for one white sports sock. The sun beat down on them through the big aluminum-frame living-room window, and they were glued

together by sweat. Jan wriggled her butt. She said, "Don't lie to me
– you were looking at my ass."

Sandy said, "Yeah, I guess I was."

"You can kiss it if you want to."

"Maybe later."

Jan flicked her cigarette at an ashtray made of dark blue glass.
She said, "I'm starting to worry about you."

That got Sandy's attention. Jan gave him a meaningless smile.
He said, "How d'you mean?"

"As if you didn't know."

"No, really, I don't."

"You got your pager, your cell. Sometimes I call and don't hear
back for hours. Other times you're right there, first ring, like you
were waiting for me to call, ready to pounce."

"What are you getting at?"

Jan took another long pull on her cigarette. He felt the weight
of her body shift as she turned her head away from him, exhaled.
"There's no pattern. Most people, even if it's shift work, they aren't
available for eight or ten hours a day, because they're too busy
earning a living."

Sandy said, "Well, what can I say? I'm willing to feel sorry for
them, if you think that'll make me a better person."

"I'm just wondering what you do for a living, that's all."

Sandy reached down and patted her on the butt. His hand
rested lightly on her flesh. "Don't worry about it. All worry ever
gets you is wrinkles."

"The flashy truck," said Jan, "cute little apartment, the big TV,
stereo. We go out, it can be anywhere. You never worry about
money, always pay cash." She tilted her head for a better look at
him. Her blue eyes were serious as blue eyes can get. "When was
the last time you ate at home, Sandy?"

"You can *do* that?"

"Very funny. When we went back to your place last week, after
we had dinner at Pepita's? When you used the bathroom, I looked
in your night table for an ashtray and . . ."

She felt him stiffen beneath her, and it made her nervous, maybe even a little scared, but it was too late to stop, so she kept on. "There was a black folder in the drawer . . ."

Sandy lay quietly beneath her. His chest rose and fell. Jan took another hard pull on her cigarette.

She said, "Want to tell me about all the clippings, Sandy?"

"Not really. It's just a hobby of mine, that's all."

"Robbing and stealing?" She flicked her cigarette at the ashtray and didn't miss by much. "Stealing cars, purse-snatching, smash-and grab, burglary. You've really been working your way up the ladder, haven't you."

"That guy isn't me. Is that what you think, that he's me?"

"Why else would you keep the clippings?"

Sandy patted her bum again. He said, "Shift off me, I got to go."

Jan didn't budge an inch. She said, "The thing is, I'm *hoping* that crook is you."

He slapped her bum hard enough to sting. "C'mon, *move*."

"Don't you want to know why?"

"You're gonna phone 'Crime Stoppers,' make some easy money?"

Jan said, "How would you like to move up to the big leagues, make such a big score you'd never have to throw a brick through another display case?"

Sandy laughed. He was pretty convincing. He said, "What in hell are you talking about?"

Jan put out her cigarette. She eased off the sofa and sat down on the carpet beside him, and ran her fingers through his short, sweat-sticky hair. She said, "Diamonds. I'm talking about seven hundred and fifty thousand to one million dollars' worth of uncut blood diamonds illegally imported from Africa."

He said, "Wow!" like he didn't believe her. Pissed her off, though she didn't let it show. She said, "There's supposed to be some coloured diamonds in the shipment. Green ones, and blue, and maybe some red."

"Blue and green and red diamonds? You gotta be kidding."

"No, It's true. Red is the rarest of all." She gave Sandy the same deadly serious look she'd hit the welfare dude with, that time she'd needed a few extra bucks to make the rent. "I wouldn't be giving away any big secrets if I told you most of the wholesale diamond merchants in this city work out of the Vancouver Block."

Sandy said, "Back up a sec. What's a blood diamond?"

Jan gave him a quick primer on the world diamond market. She told him about Matt Singh, how he had become her friend, and how he'd set up the score and then been killed in a Metrotown shootout. As she talked about Matt's untimely death, she remembered that, when Harvey had dropped by the tattoo parlour, he'd told her he'd gotten out of jail a couple of weeks earlier. Fine, but then, since he was so eager to see her and Tyler, why had it taken him so long to drive to Vancouver?

A chill ran through her, as if she had been stabbed in the heart with an icicle. Had Harvey shot Matt? The timing was right. Harvey was a notoriously jealous guy, so he had a motive . . .

Sandy said, "You had some kind of relationship with Matt?"

"Yeah, a business relationship. Are you wondering if we were lovers? Not a chance. He was a really sweet guy, but there was nothing between us."

He gave her a sceptical look.

"Matt was gay," said Jan. "He didn't like women."

"Not even you?"

Jan leaned past him so she could squash her cigarette in the blue glass ashtray on the windowsill. Her nipples grazed his chest as she sat back.

Sandy had one more question. "Was Matt's shooting related to the diamonds?"

"No, not at all."

"How can you be so sure?"

"Matt was involved in all sorts of projects, and he was a gang member. The cops said the shooting was turf-related. Cocaine, smack. Don't ask me for details, because I haven't got the foggiest idea."

"No? I thought you were in business together."

"From time to time, nothing steady." Jan saw that Sandy didn't believe her. She decided to take a chance, and tell him about her role in the ATM robbery. It didn't take long. Sandy was a good listener. She was surprised how relieved she was to finally be able to tell somebody what she'd done.

Jan said, "So, you in?"

"Maybe. I don't know. That kind of money . . . Let's say, just for the sake of argument, that we steal a million dollars' worth of diamonds. What does that number mean, exactly?"

"Instant retirement, and no more sweating over the cable bill."

"No, I mean how much could you get for the stones."

"Half."

"Half?"

"Probably half. It would depend on how we marketed them, all at once or bit by bit, in dribbles."

"Got a buyer lined up?"

"Matt knew a guy. I've got his name. He doesn't know me, but . . ."

She didn't need to finish the sentence. Sandy knew from personal experience just how good Jan was at getting to know guys she wanted to meet. He said, "Anybody else involved?"

"No, it's just the two of us."

"What's my cut?"

She smiled. "Half, of course. We'd be partners. What did you think, I was going to offer you six bucks an hour to start?"

Sandy didn't say anything. That was okay, because he was as easy to read as the morning paper. Jan could see he was thinking about the money, and the risk. Half a million dollars was half a million dollars, and half of that was a quarter of a million dollars. Two hundred and fifty thousand bucks. Serious money, no matter how you added it up.

She said, "You carry a weapon?"

"Not really. A knife, sometimes, in case I want to peel an apple."

"Ever take a fall for armed robbery?"

"Nope."

"All those clippings. I didn't have time to read them. Were you ever arrested?"

"No, never." He smiled. "Just lucky, I guess."

Jan said, "The diamond wholesaler's sixty-eight years old. He's in good health, but he isn't going to put up much of a fight."

"What're you telling me?"

"Even if we got caught, if you've got a clean sheet you'd catch five tops, be out in three or less." Jan lifted her arm so he could see her watch. "What time is it?"

"Quarter past four."

"Tyler's due back sometime between five and six." She kissed him on the chest, and playfully batted her eyelashes. "Want to do something in the meantime?"

Sandy gave her a puzzled, determinedly dim-witted look. He said, "What did you have in mind?"

Jan told him exactly what she had in mind, in giddily unrepressed, obsessively graphic, three-dimensional, full-spectrum Technicolor detail.

9

lust

Chelsea hadn't seemed the least bit surprised when Willows, without preamble, suddenly offered to drive her home. She waited with uncharacteristic patience in his unmarked car's shotgun seat while he fielded questions from a mob of TV and print media. When a sharp-eyed cameraman separated himself from the mob and zeroed in on her, she responded by tucking her long legs under her and curling up in the seat with her skirt riding high up on her thighs. The cameraman's lens shade tapped against the window. Chelsea gave the camera a naughty-but-nice smile, and put away her tube of glossy lip gel and lit a menthol cigarette. If the cop car had an ashtray, she couldn't find it. She pursed her lips and blew out the match and tossed it on the uncarpeted floor. The camera kept rolling. Chelsea didn't mind. She was a seasoned performer, and had long ago mastered the fine art of looking deservedly spoiled and eternally petulant and lethally bored.

Willows pushed his way through the crowd. Chelsea saw him coming. She reached across and pushed open the door. Willows gave her a startled look but didn't say anything. He slid behind the wheel, started the engine. "Sorry to keep you waiting."

"That's okay. It was fun watching you deal with the TV crowd."
She adjusted her skirt as she straightened in her seat.

Willows rolled down his window.

Chelsea said, "The smoke bother you?"

"Yes, it does. Anyway, you can't smoke in the car. The computer . . ."

"Sorry." She leaned against Willows, resting her left hand on his shoulder and letting him take some weight as she flicked her cigarette out his open window. "Colin was always telling me I was an inconsiderate person, and it's true. But is it my fault? Jimmy told me men look at me in a way that's pathetic, and slavish, and resigned. Like they'd do anything to have me. Well, I mean, they almost train you to be a bitch, don't they?"

Willows said, "Who's Jimmy?"

"A set designer. You'd hate him. Everybody does."

Willows had no idea what she was talking about. She said, "It's all a fucking pose anyway, isn't it?"

Willows rolled up his window. He turned on the air conditioner and adjusted the vents so the blast of cold air washed across his face. The car had been surrounded on three sides by the media crowd. He put the car in gear, tapped the horn and eased slowly into traffic, then gunned it. He said, "Have you been thinking about who might have killed Colin?"

"Yes, of course." She gave him a teasing smile. "You told me to, and I'm the kind of woman who likes to do what she's told."

Willows made a right turn, drove two blocks, and parked beside a hydrant. He said, "Come up with any suspects?"

"A few."

Willows got out his notebook. He uncapped his gold-plated fountain pen.

Chelsea said, "That's a nice pen. Was it a gift?"

"A birthday present. Why do you ask?"

"My brother and I bought my dad a gold fountain pen for his birthday about five years ago. I was still in school and didn't have much money. My dad's an assistant manager at a Bank of Montreal. We thought he'd really like it, but he never used it, not once. It's still in the box, on the desk in his den. Maybe he thinks it's too flashy. Who gave you your pen?"

"My son."

"What's he do?"

Willows hesitated, and then said, "He's a student. Post-grad work. Very intense. Let's get back to your suspect list, okay?"

"Sure."

"Got some names for me?"

"Mine, for one."

"Did you kill him?"

"No, but I might've."

"But you didn't, is that what you're saying?"

Chelsea nodded. She said, "Colin was such a prick. A real animal. There were times when I . . ." She trailed off, and looked out the window.

"Why did you go out with him?"

"My shrink asked me the same question."

"What did you tell him?"

Chelsea shrugged and looked out the window.

Willows said, "Got an alibi?"

"No, I don't. I spent the night at home. I didn't have any company and I didn't make or receive any phone calls."

"A popular girl like you?"

"I watched TV and then I snorted some coke and fell asleep. Does it shock you that I take drugs?"

"To the very marrow of my bones," said Willows. "Other than yourself, who else do you know who might've killed Colin?"

"His ex-wife, Nancy. They've got three kids enrolled in St. George's and he told me she was *always* bitching about money. Colin's divorce lawyer has standing orders to make sure she never gets her support cheque on time. Colin told him to randomly vary delivery of the cheque so it's anywhere from three days to three weeks late. She fucking hates him, and who can blame her?"

Chelsea flashed her million-dollar smile. "The only problem is, Nancy's in Florida, visiting her mother."

"Who was Colin's lawyer?"

"Melvin Hartmann, Q.C. He's got offices on Georgia, in the eight hundred block."

"Have you met him?"

"A couple of times, at parties."

"What's he like?"

"A little over six feet, thirty pounds overweight. Boozer's nose, pale blue eyes, lots of wavy grey hair. Full of himself, yak yak yak, a total jerk."

Willows nodded. He said, "That it for suspects?"

"If it was up to me, I'd arrest Colin's partner, Michael Hughes. I was at Colin's a couple of nights ago. Michael dropped by unannounced. I went into the bedroom, to watch TV. I mean, you have no idea how boring those two could be when they had to talk business. About ten minutes after Michael arrived, there was a lot of shouting. Colin was really angry, very abusive."

"Do you know what they were arguing about?"

"Money, something to do with development costs. I was watching a George Clooney movie, and cranked up the sound." Chelsea looked out the car window at a man waiting to cross the street. She said, "Is that Todd Bertuzzi?"

"Who?"

"The hockey player."

Willows shrugged.

Chelsea said, "Colin doesn't like it when people drop in on him unexpectedly. Especially if I'm staying over. He was really hot. I heard glass breaking. Michael left shortly afterwards.

"I asked Colin what Michael was so upset about, but he didn't tell me, just laughed it off."

Willows said, "That's it, for suspects?"

"Not really. I don't know how many thousands of people in this city are living in leaky condos that Colin and Michael's various companies built. But there's an awful lot of them. Some of the people had to pay fifty to a hundred thousand dollars in repairs, and some of them had to walk away from their apartments because they couldn't afford that kind of money, so they were ruined. And there were lots more who sold at a huge loss, and probably won't be able to afford to buy another apartment for years, if ever."

"Colin talked to you about this?"

"He found out a few months ago that his own building, I mean the one he was living in, his 'flagship building for a new era,' he liked to call it, anyway, he found out it was leaking like a sieve. I don't know the details, but he said there was a design flaw and they were going to have to strip the cladding off the entire building. He said it was going to cost a fortune."

"Did other people in the building know there was a problem?"

"You bet they did. Everybody on the north side of the building had a problem, because the window casements were leaking. The condo's board of directors hired a Toronto company to analyze the building's 'envelope.' Colin said it was a total disaster, that it was going to cost a ton of money to fix. The board of directors offered Colin a chance to take care of it quietly, to minimize the bad publicity. But the original repair estimate was for somewhere between five and eight million dollars. Colin freaked. All his money was tied up in new projects. He was afraid if word got out that his latest so-called watertight building was leaking, the banks would pull the plug on him, and he'd be wiped out."

Willows had no idea how many people lived in Colin's building. Hundreds. At this early point in the investigation, every last one of them was a suspect. So were all the untold thousands of unhappy condo owners in all the other affected buildings in which Colin McDonald's many numbered companies had been involved.

Willows sighed heavily. Inspector Bradley had saddled him with a monster of a case. Unless the killer jumped up on his lap and confessed, he'd be interviewing suspects until the day he retired.

Chelsea rested her hand on his arm. "Are you okay?"

Willows collected himself. He said, "I'd better get you home."
Chelsea lived in the West End, in an older building across the
street from Stanley Park. It was a déjà vu drive for Willows – Peter
Markson, the ATM Bandit who'd killed himself with a TV antenna,
lived only a few blocks away. The drive across town took less than
twenty minutes, despite the heavy seasonal West End traffic.

As Willows pulled up to the curb, Chelsea unbuckled her seatbelt and turned towards him. Her skirt again rode up on her thighs
but she didn't seem to notice, or care. She gave him a very direct
look and said, "Would you like to come in for a minute?"

"Thanks anyway."

She pouted. Her lip gloss was blinding. She said, "Your mistake,
Jack. Maybe you aren't such a smart detective after all. But thanks
for the ride."

He gave her a vague, meaningless smile. He was old enough to
be her father, and he wasn't looking for any handouts, but the way
she'd said *thanks for the ride* had dripped with sexual innuendo
and careless promise. He wouldn't have thought it was possible,
but Chelsea had shocked the hell out of him. She knew it, too,
judging from the way she was staring at him. The pink tip of her
tongue darted between her lips.

Willows told himself that any man would find Chelsea attractive. He told himself that what he was feeling at that moment
didn't mean anything, that there was no need to worry about it or
beat himself up over it.

Funny how sometimes you could be simultaneously right and
wrong, for perfectly good reasons that had nothing in common.

Chelsea pushed open her door. Unburdened by false modesty
or any doubt about what she wanted, she fully exploited her short
skirt and long legs as she got out of the car.

There was no time for Willows to look away. His brain recorded
a strip of film he would play back over and over again, all day long.

lunch

Claire carried Hadrian on her hip as she made herself a cucumber and lettuce sandwich on whole-wheat bread. She'd already put the kettle on the boil. She turned her body to protect Hadrian as she poured boiling water into a pot of herbal tea. Hadrian clapped his hands in glee. He was hungry too, and he knew the routine.

Claire went to the cupboard and got down glass jars of Gerber's beef stew and Hadrian's current favourite, puréed carrots. She put him into his high chair and fastened the safety strap. He kicked his legs, and grabbed his bent-handle spoon and excitedly slammed it down on the plastic tray.

Claire said, "Are you a hungry boy, Hadrian? Would you like some beef stew, and carrots for dessert?"

Hadrian yelled, "Rats!"

"That's right, carrots."

He thumped the tray with both pudgy fists. "Rats!"

Claire took a moment to pour herself a cup of tea, and then unscrewed the metal lids of the two jars. She offered Hadrian the jar of beef stew. He pushed it away.

"Rats!"

"Stew first," said Claire. She dipped her finger in the jar and put her finger to her mouth. Her eyes widened in delight. "Mmm, yummy!"

Hadrian's spoon rattled off the teapot, skittered across the table, hit the floor, and rolled under the fridge. Tripod, their three-legged cat, bolted into the living room. Claire sipped at her tea. Hadrian watched her closely, trying to gauge her mood and determine whether he was best served by an uproarious burst of laughter or a gale of tears.

Claire pursed her lips and blew on the cup. She said, "Hot!"

Hadrian decided that was just hilarious. Claire got another bent-handle spoon from the dishwasher. She dipped the spoon into the jar of puréed carrots. Hadrian watched her closely. He opened wide. He could be such a well-mannered child, when he got his way.

After lunch, while Hadrian napped peacefully in his crib, Claire sat down and wrote a letter to the Royal College of Physicians and Surgeons, detailing Dr. Randy Hamilton's unprofessional conduct. As the letter took shape, she grew increasingly aware of the futility of her action. Hamilton wasn't as stupid as he looked. As Claire drew up a list of his offences, she quickly realized that he'd been careful not to do or say anything that was the basis for a reasonable complaint. Claire was vexed. Context was everything. The cunning way Hamilton freighted a word, the delicate outward turn of his hand, bright spark of lust in his eye. How could she possibly define and catalogue these things in such a way as to give them weight and meaning?

Fuck Hamilton. Fuck the College.

Claire had a good cry and then she made herself another pot of herbal tea and wondered for the umpteenth time what the hell was wrong with her. It seemed a little late in the game to be suffering from postpartum depression.

She went quietly into Hadrian's room and stared down at him. He lay on his back with his arms flung wide, breathing slowly and steadily. His right hand gripped one of his favourite toys, a brightly coloured plastic rattle. He was a wonderful child; everything she had wished for, and more. There was something about him that suggested a quality of restraint. She smiled, knowing she was projecting her wishes onto him. Hadrian had her grandfather's cleft chin, and she liked to think he had inherited his long pianist's fingers from her. The rest of him was all Jack.

Claire lightly pressed the palm of her hand against her son's smooth forehead. He stirred. His arms came up defensively, then settled back with a strange slowness, as if untouched by gravity. She bent and kissed him, and whispered that she loved him. He opened and shut his mouth like a fish gulping air. His breath smelled of carrots.

Claire tore up her unfinished letter to the College and went out on the back porch and angrily shoved the pieces in the yellow City of Vancouver recycling bag. Hamilton was off the hook, for now.

heist

Harvey didn't want to hurt anybody. That's why he was armed. The stainless-steel Smith & Wesson .38-calibre revolver was his insurance policy, a lethal, four-pound chunk of metal designed to minimize the risk of incoming mayhem.

Harvey circled around the lineup to the cash register. He yanked the black balaclava out of his pants pocket and pulled it over his head, instantly blinding himself. Someone very close laughed nervously. Harvey pulled off the balaclava and turned it around and put it back on again, so the eye and mouth holes were lined up in the right places. He drew his Smith & Wesson. The cash-register guy was perched on a wooden stool. Harvey gave him a long up-and-down look. He was about twenty years old, had prominent cheekbones and a thick chest and wide shoulders and long black hair tied back in a ponytail. Harvey logged him at six-two and about two hundred and twenty pounds. He believed the guy looked an awful lot like a much-younger version of that Hollywood actor who was always smashing heads and breaking arms and busting up dopers and stoned killers real good. Harvey struggled to remember the actor's name. Steven Seagal, that was it. He pointed the revolver at the cash-register guy. His name tag said *Mario*. Harvey said, "This is a stickup. Open the cash register."

Mario stared at him. His mouth fell open.

Harvey poked him in the belly with the gun. "*Now*, moron!"

Mario punched buttons. Nothing happened. He chuckled nervously. "I'm sorry, sir. But I forget how to do that."

Harvey pressed the muzzle of his gun up against the kid's head, and dramatically cocked the hammer. "If you don't open the fucking cash register right this minute, I'm gonna splatter your stupid brains all over your lap." He gestured with the gun. "I'm on a timer. Get cracking, or I'm gonna hurt a whole bunch of people."

Mario said, "I'd open it if I could but I just can't remember how to do it. My mind's a blank."

Harvey tried to screw the Smith's blunt muzzle into Mario's head. Mario said, "Please don't *do* that!" He gestured wildly and incoherently. "I can't think straight. It's like somebody chopped off my frontal lobes with a meat cleaver!"

"What in hell are you yapping about, fucking lobes. You're earning what, five or six bucks an hour, and you're ready to lay your life on the line for your company? This might be news to you, kid, but Caper's isn't some puny little mom-and-pop operation, it's part of a huge multinational outfit, they own hundreds of businesses right across the whole fucking continent!"

"How would you know?"

"I read it on a poster on a telephone pole across the street. Something to do with a Hep A outbreak, whatever that means."

"It's a contagious disease you can get from someone who handles food but doesn't practise appropriate sanitation procedures," said a middle-aged woman in the lineup. She added, "It's not like anybody died."

Harvey glanced around. All the Caper's staff had scrammed. The two women who'd been laughing at him had never looked more serious in all their lives. He waved the Smith at the crowd. "Does anybody know how to open the fucking cash register?"

"You'd better watch your language," said a child of about ten. "Or your mother will wash your mouth out with soap."

Harvey glared at him.

Somebody yelled, "Leave him alone, he's just a kid."

Harvey sensed he was losing control of the situation. He knew what to do about that, in spades. The kid was fashionably dressed in khaki shorts and an action-hero T-shirt. Harvey pressed the muzzle of the gun up against the kid's bony knee. He said, "Open the cash register, or you'll never skip rope again."

The kid laughed, as if Harvey had said something funny.

Harvey said, "I'm gonna count down from three, and then I'm gonna pull the trigger. Three. . . . two. . . . one."

Nobody moved.

Harvey wasn't sure what to do. He didn't particularly want to kneecap the kid, even though he probably deserved it. On the other hand, what choice did he have? He ripped off the kid's Nike sneaker, aimed at the little toe on his left foot, and squeezed the trigger. The cylinder revolved through sixty degrees and the hammer made a dull *click* as it struck the firing pin. Harvey pulled a few more times.

Somebody said, "It's a toy gun."

Frustrated, Harvey kept yanking on the trigger.

Click, click, click.

A fat guy in coveralls tried to jump him. Harvey slapped him across the nose with the revolver's barrel. The fat guy dropped as if he'd been shot, spurting blood and cries of anguish.

Harvey backed towards the door. He'd hit the guy a little harder than he'd meant to, but he didn't think it wise to stick around and apologize. This decision was confirmed when a bowl of pasta salad hit him square in the balaclava, half-blinding him.

The Caper's mob howled like demons as they chased him up Fourth Avenue. It was hard to run in the yellow suit's baggy pants. Harvey shied away as a standard-bred poodle tethered to a parking meter snapped viciously at him. Next time he pulled off a robbery, he'd have to try to remember to park his getaway vehicle a little closer. That or hit the gym, work himself into tip-top shape. Fat chance that was gonna happen. The balaclava made it hard to breathe. He tore it off and glanced behind him, at the howling, churning mob. Who were those guys? They weren't armed with pitchforks and burning torches but they sure had a bad attitude, for a bunch of health freaks who claimed they didn't eat meat.

10

scenery to die for

Chelsea turned to shut the car door behind her and then hesitated. She put her finger to her plump lower lip, and frowned, and said that she just remembered Colin had a Day Planner on her computer. If Willows was interested in the names and addresses he'd find on the planner, he was welcome to come in for a moment.

Chelsea's apartment was on the red-brick building's seventh floor. Mullioned windows in the original wooden frames faced to the west and to the north. The views were terrific. Stanley Park was right across the street. Beyond the dense greenery of the thousand-acre park, the Pacific Ocean heaved restlessly. There was lots of marine traffic to charm the eye. No more rowboats in Lost Lagoon, though. Years ago, a kid had tossed a rock at a duck, and the Parks Board had screamed in horror and yanked their fleet. Fun City, for sure. Beyond Lion's Gate bridge, the mountains loomed steeply. In a few months, they'd be capped with snow, and be even more determinedly scenic. On the shady side of the mountains there was a wilderness so vast and untrammelled it was too scary to think about.

Chelsea said, "Nice view, huh?"

Willows nodded. He reflexively accepted a glass of white wine.

Chelsea said, "To success." She clinked glasses and sipped delicately. "At night you can see the lights on the bridge. They're named after a local politician but I forget who he was . . ."

Willows said, "Why do you live here, instead of in Yale Town or False Creek?"

"How do you mean?"

"Well, it's very nice here. But I'd have thought someone like you would prefer to live in a more fashionable part of town."

"I got a deal on the apartment."

"From Colin?"

"Yes, from Colin." Chelsea drank a little more wine. She studied Willows for a moment, looking up at him in a way he found vaguely unsettling, and then said, "You'll probably find out sooner or later, so I might as well tell you now. The apartment's in my name, but Colin paid for it. I just moved in a couple of weeks ago, to tell the truth."

"That was nice of him."

"Not really. It was a secret loan. I had to sign a demand note for the full amount, so he could get the title back any time he wanted. The idea was to protect his money from any lawsuits or whatever that he might have to deal with."

"Have you got a copy of the note?"

Chelsea nodded. She said, "We both have copies. Well, Colin's got the original. I don't know what he did with it – probably it's in a safety-deposit box." She gulped her wine. "The note says that Colin has to give me three months' notice. You might as well know it was also a condition of the note that, in the event of Colin's death, the loan is automatically cancelled."

Willows said, "Whose idea was that?"

"Colin's. He had his lawyer draw up the note. It's very straightforward."

"Why did he do it?"

"Colin was a real fitness nut. He had a personal trainer, and a dietician. He went to the gym six days a week, was very careful about what he ate. His physician is one of the best in the city. Colin had a thorough medical exam every year. He was in excellent health."

"I don't understand . . ."

"Colin was a very careful driver. He drove a Volvo, because he believed it was the safest car on the road."

Willows still didn't get it.

Chelsea said, "Colin never went into specifics, but he told me that he sometimes had to use money that belonged to the kind of people who would be very upset if they were to suffer a financial loss."

"But he didn't mention any names."

"No, and I didn't ask him."

Willows said, "How much is the apartment worth?"

"A little over one-point-five million, in today's market. I know that sounds like a lot, for an old building like this, but the apartment is actually two apartments made into one. There's four bedrooms and a study – over three thousand square feet." Chelsea recharged her glass. "Go ahead, ask me."

"Ask you what?"

"If I murdered Colin so I could live happily ever after in my deluxe apartment."

Willows smiled. He said, "Did you murder him?"

"Nope."

"Where's the computer?"

"In the study. Follow me."

Willows followed her out of the living room and down a wide hallway. Pictures of Chelsea lined the walls. Most of them were candid shots that seemed to have been taken while she was on assignment, in various states of undress.

The computer was a Sony laptop. Chelsea had no idea how it worked. Willows sat down at a glass-topped desk. He flipped open the computer and fired it up.

Chelsea rested a hand on his shoulder. "I'm going to take a quick shower."

Willows nodded, so intent on the computer that he hardly heard her. To his surprise, the computer's files weren't password-protected. He opened the Documents folder. There were about two dozen files, alphabetically arranged. The names meant nothing to him. He opened a file, and started reading. An hour later, all he'd learned was that he'd wasted an hour of his time.

big dipper

In the afternoon Hadrian usually could be relied on to nap for anywhere up to three hours, depending on how active his morning had been. Today was different. He slept for just under an hour, and woke up screaming. Claire wondered if he'd had a nightmare. She calmed him, and then fed him slivers of cooked-to-pieces stewing beef and spoonfuls of squashed banana. Afterwards, she took him into the living room, and they played with his primary-coloured hollow plastic blocks until he tired of knocking down what she had built. By then she was feeling overheated. She ran lukewarm water into the bath, and watched Hadrian carefully as she undressed. He loved taking baths. He wasn't tall enough to climb into the tub unassisted, but that didn't stop him from trying. Claire lowered herself into the tub and then reached over and took him, chortling and squealing happily, into her arms. She lifted him up and slowly dunked him into the water. He screamed with delight and furiously waved his arms. Claire hugged him and told him she loved him. He didn't care. He wanted more water. *Wa-wa!* Claire sat him down between her legs. He slapped the water with his hands and shrieked with delight.

Claire's mind wandered. It was ridiculous, because she wasn't the least bit attracted to him, but she couldn't stop herself from wondering if she had subconsciously enticed Dr. Randy Hamilton to show interest in her.

She couldn't remember doing or saying anything that might lead him to believe she found him attractive. She supposed most women would consider Hamilton good-looking, even handsome. That didn't mean she panted after him. She was just trying to be objective, that's all. She idly scratched her thigh. She was worried about Jack, about her marriage. There was a distance between them, a lonely space that was getting wider day by day. He refused to talk about his cases. She was tired of being shut out of his life. A few days ago, she had caught herself thinking that she finally knew why his first wife, Sheila, had walked out on him. It was a terrible, terrible moment, and it had frightened her half to death.

She thought back to Jack's mixed reaction when she'd first told him she was pregnant. He had been happy, and dismayed, and not particularly communicative. At her insistence, they had talked about her pregnancy at length. Jack had said that he'd already put up with all the horrors that modern parenthood entailed, and wasn't sure he could manage it all over again, now that he was twenty-odd years older. Claire put it all down to the shock of the news. Jack had eventually come around. At least, that's what she had thought, at the time.

An unnatural silence snatched Claire from her grim reverie. Startled, she glanced down at Hadrian. He was perfectly still, staring with fascination at a water droplet taking shape on the end of his down-turned thumb.

He must have sensed that she was watching him, because he suddenly glanced up at her. His face was weirdly solemn. Claire forced a smile. He didn't smile back. Claire began to cry. She splashed water on her face. Hadrian joined in, wildly punching the water with both hands. The front door slammed shut. Claire jumped. She struggled to get herself under control. She cried out, "Who is it?"

"Me. Annie!"

A few moments later, Annie poked her head in the door. She said, "What the hell's going on in here? Are you crying?"

"No, of course not." Claire didn't consider herself an accomplished liar. But there was no denying it was a talent that came naturally.

money-back guarantee

Harvey knocked but got no answer. He pounded on the door with both fists, and kicked it for good measure, and even yelled a few vague threats, but all to no avail. He sat down with his back to the wall. Anders had deafened himself with his headphones, or he was out.

The Caper's mob had chased him down Fourth Avenue to the end of the block. Harvey had turned the corner, thinking he would lose them during the sprint through the Safeway parking lot to the car, but abandoned that idea when he saw how many people were gaining on him. These people were *fast*.

Harvey sprinted into an underground parking garage. Some kind of weird spray-on insulation made the low ceiling look like a great big fluffy white cloud. He ducked behind a van and kept low as he scuttled down the narrow space between two rows of parked cars, until he dead-ended at a glass box. There was an elevator inside the box. He jumped a low divider and trotted around to the far side of the glass box and pressed the up button. The elevator door immediately slid open. The mob screamed at him as he stepped inside. He'd expected a row of buttons, but there was only one; the elevator only had two stops, at the parking lot and at ground level. He rode the elevator up to the sidewalk. The door slid open. The mob had taken the stairs. Harvey held the door open as he waited patiently for the mob to reach ground level. He heard the thunder of feet on concrete and then the door to the stairs burst open. Harvey yelled, and they turned towards him like a flock of birds or a school of fish. He waited until they were right on top of him and then pushed the down button. The elevator door slid shut, pinching off screams of rage. He glided down to the parking lot. Nobody was waiting to ambush him. He stripped off the yellow suit and balaclava and fedora and strolled casually out of the parking lot. Nobody paid any attention to him. That was a good thing, because the silver Mercedes SUV he'd parked behind was gone, and it took him way too long a time to locate his low-slung Firebird, hidden behind the looming bulk and tinted windows of a Dodge Caravan.

Now Harvey sat down and leaned his back against Anders' apartment door. An hour crawled past on its hands and knees. Harvey almost, but not quite, dozed off. The stripper's music from the bar had given him a hellaciously painful headache. The music was so loud it made the wooden floor vibrate under his ass. He swore on his own grave that if they played "Stairway to Heaven" one more time, he'd torch the joint. All patience lost, he stood up, and pounded on the door. Still no answer. Where was that moron Anders? A thought burst suddenly into his consciousness with all the noise and force of an F-16 fighter plane on full throttle: *Maybe the door isn't locked.*

A second F-16 made a low-level pass across the shadowy landscape of his brain. *Why not give it a try?*

Ten seconds later, Harvey eased the door shut behind him, and stealthily shot the bolt. No wonder Anders hadn't been able to hear him – Bette Midler was beating up the stereo. "Some say love . . ." Harvey followed the music into the living room. Anders lay on his back on the screamingly ugly couch. A thread of drool trailed from the corner of his open mouth to the collar of his paisley shirt. Harvey went over to the stereo and yanked the plug out of the wall socket. Anders was snoring lightly. The silver thread of drool trembled with each slow exhalation. Harvey pressed the defective Smith's barrel against Anders' forehead. Anders' eyes popped open. Harvey pulled the trigger. The gun clicked. He pulled the trigger several more times, and stepped back. A cigarette butt was wedged between Anders' ear and temple. He fumbled for the cigarette, wiped drool from his face, lit up.

He said, "Talk about a wake-up call. You're the world's scariest alarm clock, Harve."

"Harvey."

Anders squinted up at him through a roiling cloud of smoke. Vertebrae crackled as he sat up. He warily eyed Harvey as he took a hard pull on his cigarette. "You look pissed, Harve. Whatsa problem?"

"The gun don't work. You might as well have sold me a cap pistol. I'm in the middle of a holdup, there's a certain amount of resistance, kid's giving me lip, I decide to blow his toe off, pull the trigger. All I get is *click click click*."

"Bummer."

Harvey said, "There was a big crowd. I got chased down the sidewalk. People were yelling, throwing food. A dog tried to bite me. It was humiliating."

"That's too bad, but there's nothing wrong with the gun." Anders held out his hand. "Lemme see it. Did you have the safety off?"

"There's no safety on a revolver."

"You sure about that?"

"Quit foolin' with me. What am I, some kinda dumb mook?"

Anders studied Harvey as carefully as a small child might study a butterfly that had alighted on the tip of its nose. After what seemed to Harvey to be a very long time, he said, "No, I guess not."

"I want my money back."

Anders snapped his fingers in a dismissive way. "We don't do cash refunds. You want an exchange, I could handle that. Got a prime .44 Magnum belonged to a little old lady, only fired it once because she missed and it got took away from her by the burglar sold it to me. It'll cost you an extra fifty, you want it. Or I could let you have a .22 Colt semiauto with a silencer, a very nice inner-city weapon." He scratched his nose. "Also, it's probably out of your league, but I got a vary rare and unusual piece that might interest you."

"Tell me about it."

"It's a 50-calibre Desert Eagle. Titanium gold finish with custom pearl grips and a six-inch barrel. Shoots 350-grain jacketed hollowpoints would drop a bull elephant. But like I said, there's nothing wrong with the piece I sold you." He snapped his fingers again. "Gimme it, lemme see."

Harvey saw no harm in giving Anders the pistol, mostly because Anders was so fried his eyeballs were steaming. Harvey knew he could take him easy as cracking an egg, if he had to. He handed the fully loaded Smith & Wesson to Anders.

Anders flipped open the cylinder. He worked the ejector rod. Six fat .38-calibre bullets fell into the palm of his hand. He put the revolver down on the sofa by his hip and rolled the bullets around in his hand, picked them up one after another until he'd examined all six. He looked up. "Nothing wrong with the bullets."

Harvey said, "That's what I'm telling you. The gun don't work. It's broke. There's something wrong with it."

"We'll see."

Anders reloaded all six chambers and snapped shut the Smith's cylinder. He cocked the hammer and tilted his massive head for a better look at the firing pin. The smoke from his cigarette made his eyes water.

He said, "Everything looks okay to me."

"What's that mean – it's fixed? You an authorized repairman, Anders? All you do is say it don't look like there's nothing wrong with it, and, just like magic, there ain't?"

"I'm not following you." Anders took a bead on his TV and pulled the trigger. The gun went *click*.

Harvey said, "What'd I tell you?"

Anders said, "Must be a dud round. That ain't my fault. If you remember, all I sold you was a gun. The bullets were like a free bonus I threw in at absolutely no cost to yourself, as a goodwill gesture. You may recall that I offered no representations as to their lethal killability."

"Stop talking like that, you're giving me a headache."

Anders said, "You think you got a headache? Watch this." Grinning, he put the gun to his head and pulled the trigger. There was a loud bang. The window behind him shattered, smashed to pieces by bullet fragments and fragments of Anders.

Harvey's mouth fell open.

Anders dropped the revolver and rolled off the sofa, knocking over the coffee table. He lay facedown on the scuzzy carpet, his hands at his sides.

Harvey said, "Anders?"

There was blood on the sofa, blood splattered on the chintz curtains and what was left of the window, blood on the carpet, blood leaking out of Anders' good and missing ear and mouth and eye. Harvey stood there, listening to the silence, waiting for screams and sirens. The silence lengthened and drew taut. He stepped over Anders and climbed up on the sofa and looked out. The view was of a dead-end alley. He picked up the Smith. The barrel was warm. There was blood on the front sight and muzzle. He was careful not to disturb the blood as he wiped the handle and cylinder of the gun clean with his shirt-sleeve, hoping to obliterate his fingerprints. When he'd finished wiping incriminating fingerprints off the gun, he jumped down off the sofa and fitted the weapon into Anders' dead-slack hand. He squeezed Anders' limp fingers around the butt, held on a moment, and then let go. The .38 thudded onto the carpet. Anders' fingers slowly spread out until his hand looked like a great big spider. Harvey studied the crime scene. The gun. Anders. The sofa, speckled with blood and fragments of glass. He took note of how the light streaming in from the bullet-punctured window was artistically stained pink by the blood smeared across what was left of the glass.

All in all, everything looked just about right. He approved of the way all the junk that had been on the overturned coffee table – magazines and butt-filed ashtray, TV remote, cribbage board and deck of cards – had spread across the carpet. But there was something wrong with the coffee table itself, something that didn't quite work . . . Harvey struggled to pin it down. Something didn't look right, but what was it? He had a sudden flash of inspiration, and kicked a leg off the table. There, that was much better. But not perfect. He scooped up a handful of cards and scattered them more widely across the floor.

Getting there . . .

Harvey continued to fiddle with the crime scene, trying his best to make it look perfect. It took a while. There were so many details to attend to that it was hard to keep track of them all. He'd shift something over an inch or two, and what he'd done would somehow, in way he didn't understand, make everything else look wrong, and then he'd have to go back and start all over again . . .

Anders' cigarette had been quenched by the flow of blood. Harvey was trying to decide if it was a good idea to light a fresh cigarette and stick it in Anders' mouth and let it burn down to his lips, when he suddenly pictured himself as a kind of morbid Martha Stewart, a kind of interior decorator to the dead. Disgusted with himself, he surveyed the scene one last time.

The titanium gold Desert Eagle was wedged between the sofa cushions, where Anders could get at it in a hurry, if he needed to. The gun was huge, but the balance was dead-perfect.

Harvey shoved the pistol in his waistband and got busy searching the apartment. He was discreetly strip-mining Anders' bedroom for cash or drugs or more guns or even a pair of clean socks, when the silence started to wrinkle his forehead.

It sure was quiet.

Why couldn't he hear the *thump-thump* of music from the bar?

Had Charlene or one of the other strippers or the bartender or a waiter or a semi-sober customer or somebody he couldn't even think of heard the shot?

Harvey decided he ought to beat it.

Just as soon as he found out where Anders had stashed his bankroll.

close but no cigar

Sandy liked his detached apartment. The little garage that could. He'd moved into the apartment six months ago, and it was a good fit. He'd spent a few bucks on a used carpet, sofa, small wooden writing desk, and a couple of lamps for area lighting. A phone line had been installed by a previous tenant, and he had the satellite dish. The TV was on now, NASCAR, a race in Charlotte, North Carolina, on Speedvision. The hushed roar of the cars and mundane chatter of the sports crew generating white noise as he worked at his desk, the laptop's screen angled to minimize the glare from the skylight.

Sandy didn't consider himself a writer, even though he never failed to laboriously type anywhere from one to five pages of notes a day; a kind of diary of certain aspects of his life. Mostly he wrote about people he met or spent time with who were of special interest to him. At the moment he was writing about Jan's plans to rob the Vancouver Block diamond merchant. As his index fingers banged away at the keyboard, he found himself thinking about the armoured-car employee who'd been shot during the ATM robbery. The man's death, together with intense pressure from his employer and his grieving, and photogenic, family, had galvanized the VPD to revisit the case. An Indo-Canadian associate of Harvey's named Matt Singh had always been a prime suspect. Harvey had the bad luck to be released from prison within days of the armoured-car employee finally succumbing to his wounds. Matt Singh had been gunned down not long after Harvey made parole.

Sandy leaned back, and flexed his fingers. Jan was an adult, a single parent with a lot of responsibilities. But at the same time, in many ways she was like a child, wasting a lot of energy on a fantasy life that would never materialize in a hundred years. He clicked the mouse to save the file, and then sat back and read over the day's notes.

Jan's plans for the robbery were haphazard and incomplete. Her story about an accomplice who'd been untimely murdered would have seemed even more ridiculously dramatic and unlikely, if it wasn't true. Sandy wondered if she intended to set him up for a fall. He dialled up his Internet server and searched the archives of his favourite Web site.

Matt Singh had been gunned down in Metrotown Mall, in the adjoining suburb of Burnaby. He'd been killed in the mall's cavernous underground parking lot, as he sat behind the wheel of his mammoth black Cadillac Escalante SUV. There was a picture of the vehicle being loaded onto a flatbed trailer. There was also a picture of an attractive female RCMP officer named Constable Ginger Greenwood, who was quoted as saying the murder was believed to be gang-related. She'd stated that there were no suspects, but the investigation was in the early stages, and they expected to make an arrest in due course. Sandy wondered what *Escalante* meant. Probably it didn't mean anything, was just another one of those made-up words Detroit was so fond of. He spread his arms wide, stretching. His wrists were bothering him. He wasn't much of a typist, though he liked to think he became a little faster and more accurate every time he sat down at the computer.

He closed the Internet connection, and returned to the start of the day's notes. There was nothing in there that hinted of the sexual aspect of his relationship with Jan. Anyone reading his notes would think that the only thing he and Jan had in common was their mutual interest in crime. He made a few minor changes, deleting or adding a word here and there for purposes of clarity, and then hit the computer's Enter and Tab keys, and devoted a six-line paragraph to Jan's request that he meet Aldo and Jackie, expatriate Iranian diamond wholesalers who had tentatively agreed to take the stolen diamonds off their hands. Sandy had told Jan he wasn't quite ready to take that step. Armed robbery was a serious business. He'd told her he wanted to think it over for a few more days. His indecision had frustrated her and made her press him even harder.

He'd almost felt sorry for her, and for Tyler. Almost, but not quite.

unbridled joy

Michael Hughes' twenty-fifth-floor downtown office had a view over the city and right across the Pacific as far as the low mountains of Vancouver Island, twenty-five miles distant. Willows idly wondered how much farther he'd be able to see if the Island weren't in the way.

Hughes' secretary had introduced herself as Mary. She was in her early fifties, very well dressed, and exuded an air of quiet competence. She motioned Willows and Oikawa towards the pair of wing chairs facing Hughes' desk.

"Please make yourselves comfortable. Mr. Hughes will be with you in just a few moments." Willows nodded amiably, and wandered over to the picture window. He looked down. The double-glazed window was about six feet wide and ten feet high. In the city, the roar of traffic was a constant, but the thick glass sealed out every decibel. All he could hear was the faint hum of the air conditioner, and the persistent ringing of a distant phone. Oikawa had been about to sit down when he saw that Willows had no intention of sitting. He stood awkwardly between the chairs and the desk.

Mary said, "Would you like coffee?"

Willows said, "No thanks." Oikawa gave him a look but didn't say anything. Mary noticed. She smiled graciously. "Would you prefer tea, or a soft drink, bottled water, Detective Oikawa?"

Oikawa grudgingly said, "I'm fine, thanks."

McDonald and Hughes' company occupied the entire top floor of the building. Willows had no idea how many thousands of square feet that added up to, but it was a lot. The overhead must be staggering. Maybe it really was true that you had to spend money to make money. But if that was the case, why wasn't he rich, since he spent every cent he earned . . . ?

Hughes' secretary fiddled with the paperwork on his desk, straightening things out, killing time, hanging around to make sure Willows didn't poke his nose where it didn't belong.

She said, "Quite a view, isn't it?"

Willows ignored her. Vancouver was hemmed in on three sides by the Pacific Ocean and the Fraser River. To the west, Boundary Road was the demarcation line between the city and the sprawling bedroom community of Burnaby.

In terms of growth, Vancouver literally had nowhere to go but up. Willows had lived almost his entire life in the city. He couldn't believe how change had accelerated in the past thirty-odd years, especially since development had begun on the north shore of False Creek, and in Coal Harbour and Yaletown. In another hundred years or so, Vancouver would be as dense as Manhattan, if it existed at all.

A mahogany door, subtly fitted into the wall behind Hughes' desk, swung open, and Michael Hughes swept into the room. Hughes was a large man, about six-foot-six, two hundred and fifty pounds. He carried his weight well, and exuded energy, and a calculated charm. He wore a banker's suit, dazzling white shirt and conservative dark blue silk tie. The tie was loosely knotted and the top button of his shirt was unfastened. He extended his arm as he circumvented the desk and strode briskly towards Willows.

"Detectives Willows and Oikawa. Michael Hughes. Pleased to meet you." The three men shook hands, Hughes retreated behind his desk.

Mary said, "Will that be all, Mr. Hughes?"

"Yes, thank you, Mary."

He waited until his secretary had left the office and shut the door behind her, and then said, "No, I didn't murder Colin. Yes, as a matter of fact I do have an airtight alibi." He used the tips of his fingers to push an unmarked plain white envelope across the vast breadth of his desk. "That contains my itinerary for the past thirty-six hours. As you'll see, I wasn't alone for so much as a single minute. I've included the names and addresses and telephone numbers of everyone I was with during that time."

Willows said, "No one's accused you of anything, Mr. Hughes."

"No, of course not. Your superiors wouldn't like it if I sued your ass for libel, would they?" Hughes smiled to take the sting out of his words. He said, "If you don't consider me a suspect now, you certainly will after you've had time to research my relationship with Colin."

Oikawa said, "How did you know he was dead?"

"It was on the radio. Mary's already fielded a dozen gloating phone calls. We're expecting quite a few more."

Willows put the envelope in his pocket. He sat down in the chair closest to the window. Oikawa hesitated, and then took the other chair. Willows said, "Why do you think we'd suspect you of Mr. McDonald's murder?"

"The terms of our contract stipulate that, should one of us die, his share of the company is automatically transferred to the surviving partner." Hughes spread his arms wide. The gesture was calculated and amateurishly theatrical. He said, "There have been times in our company's history when that wouldn't have meant much, other than the assumption of a truly horrendous debt, and a blizzard of vicious lawsuits."

"I'm not sure I understand."

"McDonald–Hughes Development is a parent company. Under the auspices of that company, Colin and I created many other, much smaller companies. Most of them were numbered companies, designed to have a lifespan limited to the amount of time it took us to finance and construct a particular building. Those numbered companies were our way of protecting ourselves from any lawsuits that might arise due to the city's faulty construction codes, in the unlikely event the buildings' envelopes didn't prove sufficiently watertight to protect them from the ravages of the elements."

Willows said, "What's your company worth now?"

"Thirty million, give or take."

"So . . ." The number had staggered Willows. He said, "Let me get this straight. When Colin McDonald was murdered, you inherited fifteen million dollars."

"*Approximately* fifteen million. Give or take. Quite a lot of money, isn't it?"

"How would you describe your relationship with Colin?"

"Strictly business."

"You weren't friends, as well as partners?"

"We were friends in the early days. Colin and I were both young, and we were both focused entirely on money, and the many truly wonderful things that money could buy. Neither of us was encumbered by what you might call a strong moral compass. We wanted fat wallets, and we didn't care what we had to do to achieve our goal. But I would say that, as we grew older and more successful, I became a philanthropist, in my own small way. Whereas Colin went in the opposite direction."

"That caused problems?"

"Not really. Not business problems, anyway. I worked hard, profits were up. That was pretty much all that mattered to him. You have to understand that Colin didn't like or dislike people. He didn't really see people as people, so much as obstacles to be surmounted. He believed emotions were a waste of time. Nobody liked him for the very good reason that he took what he could get out of you, and then he abandoned you, without apology. He was an emotional vampire. He was passionate about what he wanted, but once he'd got it, all passion fled."

"You sound bitter."

"Have you met Chelsea?"

Willows nodded.

Hughes said, "She's a beautiful woman, wouldn't you say?"

"Absolutely."

"Chelsea and I were engaged, until about six months ago. We were supposed to be married at the end of the summer. As soon as Colin saw the diamond, he went after her."

"How do you mean?"

"Tried to take her away from me. He did it, too. Took him less than a month. I wanted to kill the sonofabitch."

Willows said, "He was wearing a wedding band. Was he married?"

"Not really. That must sound odd. He and Nancy never divorced. She lives in the same building, in the apartment directly below Colin's. If you want to talk to her, you're going to have to shout. She's in Miami."

"Florida?"

Hughes nodded. He said, "Her mother's ill. Alzheimer's. Nancy's helping her move to a nursing home."

"Do you know how we can get in touch with her?"

"Her mother's maiden name was Roberts. She lives in South Grove."

Hughes' chair was on castors. He turned it so he could look directly out the window.

One of the first things Willows had learned as a cop was the value and threat of silence. He sat quietly, waiting. Several minutes crawled past, and then Hughes turned and looked directly at him. He said, "That's it. This interview is over. I'm afraid I'm going to have to ask you to leave."

Willows said, "I thought you wanted to talk about Chelsea."

"You're mistaken. I wanted to lay things out for you, so you'd know where you stood. But I'm not going to talk to you again without seeking the advice of my lawyer, and you and I both know what he's going to say. 'Zip it, Michael!'"

Hughes pointed at the envelope in Willows' lap. "As I said, everything you need to exonerate me is in that envelope. The names and addresses and direct-line phone numbers of all the people I was with during the past twenty-four hours."

Willows slid a single sheet of paper out of the envelope. The number of people Hughes had spent time with during the thirty-six hours leading up to Colin McDonald's death was impressively large. Willows recognized the mayor's name, and the names of several lesser local politicians and other luminaries.

Hughes said, "I was at a charity benefit. I always mingle. People will remember me."

The intercom chirped. He picked up his phone. "Morning, Richard. Yes, they're here now. Zip it?" Hughes chuckled, and winked at Willows. He said, "That's exactly what I told them you'd say." He listened carefully for a moment and then said, "Yes, of course. Right this minute, promise." He cradled the telephone, thought a moment, and said, "Richard wouldn't approve of me telling you this, but you should probably talk to Jennifer."

Willows thumbed the chrome button on the end of his ballpoint.

Hughes said, "Jennifer's a party girl. Gorgeous, totally uninhibited. Five stars, but very, very expensive."

Oikawa said, "How do you know her?"

Hughes laughed. "In just about every way you can think of, detective. I introduced Colin to Jennifer about six months ago. They hit it off, in a businesslike sort of way. He mentioned her name, once or twice. I don't know if they were still in touch. Chelsea's the jealous type. Very emotional. She'd have torn Jennifer's eyes out, if she'd believed that Colin was seeing her. On the other hand, Colin wasn't known for his monogamous nature."

Willows said, "What's Jennifer's full name?"

"Orchid. Jennifer Orchid. Cute, huh?" Hughes turned to the open laptop on his desk, worked the keyboard, and then turned the computer so Willows could read the address on the screen. As Willows wrote the address down in his notebook, Hughes punched buttons on his intercom. When his secretary came to the door, Hughes said, "That's it, fellas. Mary will show you out. Good luck with your investigation. If you nail whoever did it, I'd appreciate it if you offered my sincere congratulations."

Willows kept his mouth shut. Hughes' sentiments seemed entirely appropriate, for a man so out of touch with himself that he paid for sex. Or was he being a prude? If you looked at it objectively, didn't it make sense to buy what you wanted or needed, if you weren't prepared, or couldn't manage, a meaningful relationship? Hughes was honest with himself. He had faced and defined his needs, and found a way to sate his appetites in a way that didn't hurt anyone, or break any hearts. When he was single, Willows had fooled around, slept with a number of women he was physically attracted to but didn't love. In his limited experience, sex was great, but sex when you were in love was incomparably better.

In the elevator, Oikawa said, "We going to drop in on Jennifer Orchid?" Oikawa didn't rub his hands together, but his voice betrayed his enthusiasm.

The elevator reached the ground floor. They walked across the lobby towards the street. Hughes' building had a revolving door. Willows liked revolving doors. He timed his approach so he was able to step into a wedge-shaped slot without slowing his pace. Oikawa hung back, and then made his move. On the sidewalk, Willows got out his cellphone and speed-dialled his home number. Parker answered on the third ring. Willows said, "Hi. I just called to say I love you."

Willows waited out a tiny splinter of time that seemed to last forever, and then Parker said, "I love you too, Jack."

"How's your day going?"

"Okay. Hadrian seems fine. You left your lunch in the fridge."

Parker's tone was slightly recriminatory. Willows couldn't count the number of times in the last year she'd stayed up late to make him a bag lunch, and then found he'd left it in the refrigerator when he'd gone to work. He said, "I know, I'm sorry. I'll eat it tomorrow." He flinched when Hadrian shrieked into the phone.

Parker said, "Sorry. His diaper needs changing, I have to go."

Willows said, "I might be later for dinner. I'll call as soon as I know when I'll be home."

Parker said, "Goodbye, Jack."

She hung up before Willows could tell her again, a little more forcefully, that he loved her.

12

alone again, unnaturally

Sting was deep into "Every Breath You Take" when the pastel spots behind the bar flickered and dimmed. The music faltered, the beat slowing weirdly, to a lame-ass crawl. A moment later the glass-enclosed shower lost pressure. Water dribbled out of the shower head and splattered too loudly on the plastic floor, then stopped. Charlene glanced across the rows of mostly empty tables at Eddy. He was hard to see, because the stage lights were working fine, and she was half-blinded by the glare. She made a gesture, what's up? Eddy spread his hairy arms wide, gave her an exaggerated shrug, went back to polishing lowball glasses.

The music picked up. The spots behind the bar brightened. Water spurted out of the shower. Charlene swung around the pole, shook her butt with calculated enthusiasm. A drunk in gynecology row waved his arms, trying to attract her attention. The guy had been soaking it up all day long. The first time he'd waved at her, she'd sauntered over with a great big show-me-the-money smile pasted across her face, and the cheapskate bastard had lurched to his feet and tried to shove a quarter down her g-string. What did he think, just because she was a stripper, she was stupid enough to forget what he'd done?

The music faltered again, as if it had stumbled off a curb, and then faded to an irritated silence. The shower dried up. The lights over the bar died too. Eddy flicked switches, opened up the electrical panel, and poked around in there like he knew what he was doing. The lights came back on, but not the music. The other stripper, a girl from Halifax that Charlene doubted was more than sixteen years old, sat down on the edge of the stage and started popping her gum, blowing shiny pink bubbles. The guys liked that, and gave her a good round of applause, pretty noisy considering there weren't that many of them, a dozen at the most. Charlene circled the pole. Her lower back was bothering her again, and she didn't want to cool off.

The girl from Halifax slid off the stage. She ruffled a pensioner's thinning hair and walked away.

Charlene said, "Hey, where you going?"

The girl shrugged, and kept walking. Somebody outside the range of her vision booed loudly. It was hard to slur a boo, but he'd done it. Charlene told herself that if they started throwing stuff, she was out of there, and if they fired her, that was fine too, and she didn't care what Anders said. Continuing that train of thought, she promised herself that if the sonofabitch hit her, she'd walk out on him. The world was jam-packed full of assholes, and she knew from a lifetime's worth of slow learning that she could always find herself another one, when she was in the mood.

After a while, Eddy found a portable radio. He carried it over to the stage and plugged it in, fiddled with the dial until he found a local station that played hard-rock music.

Charlene walked over and tapped him on the shoulder. He looked up, startled. She said, "I'm not going into the shower with that thing plugged in. Electrocuting myself isn't part of my job description."

"Oh yeah? Maybe you should've read the fine print."

She had to laugh. Eddy joined in, so pleased with his little joke that he had to wipe the tears from his eyes. She gave him a peck on the cheek and went back to work, bumping and grinding to a tune she'd never heard before and hoped she'd never hear again.

Her shift ended twenty minutes later. By then the girl from Halifax was back at work, her eyes a little unfocused, a fan of white powder on her upper lip. Charlene went over to the bar. Eddy had her vodka tonic waiting. She knocked the drink back, and he asked her if she wanted another. She said no, just like she always did, and told him she was going upstairs. Eddy nodded. He wasn't a big fan of Anders', and wasn't shy about saying so.

Charlene knew something was wrong when she reached the top of the stairs, because the door to their apartment was wide open. Anders was a cautious man. He had explained to Charlene that, since he was a pimp and sold drugs and guns, he would be a fool not to maintain a level of paranoia that was certifiable. She hadn't argued with him, because he was right. The door had two dead-bolts, a safety chain with inch-thick links, and a steel safety-bar that fitted into a metal slot built into the floor. It would be faster and easier to chew through the wall than try to knock the door down.

Charlene walked slowly down the hall. She'd slung a *faux* leopardskin cape over her nudity and was still wearing her high heels. She deliberately made a lot of noise as she made her way towards the open door. If somebody was in there, she wanted to give them plenty of time to climb out a window.

When she was only a few feet away from the door she loudly said, "I already called the cops. You better get the hell out of there, unless you want to get arrested."

There was no response.

She said, "You hear me? I said I already called the cops. They're gonna be here any minute, I can hear the sirens."

She made her way down the short hallway and poked her head cautiously around the door. Anders lay faceup on the floor. His arms were spread wide. A gun lay on the floor by his right hand. The bullet had gone in one temple and out the other. Maybe somebody had shot him, but at first glance it looked to Charlene as if he'd shot himself. All evidence to the contrary, she found that hard to believe.

Anders wasn't the suicidal type, except for his choice of lifestyle. He liked to fool with his guns, though, and accidents did happen.

Charlene knelt down for a better look. A line of blood had flowed from the gunshot wound down Anders' forehead and through his arched eyebrow and right across the bulge of his eyeball. The man had flown away into the void, and he wasn't coming back. Ever.

She said, "You dumb fuck."

He'd fallen on the coffee table and snapped off a leg. She felt a curious twirling thrill of satisfaction. She'd always hated that goddamn table.

She walked past the body towards the bedroom. He counted his stash daily. As of yesterday's accounting, his net worth included a few thousand dollars in cash and half a dozen small gold coins he'd claimed were worth five hundred apiece, plus a thousand dollars' worth of coke, and a few other odds and ends, bits and pieces of jewellery and a couple of watches, one of them a gold-coloured Patek Phillipe he'd told her was worth at least five hundred bucks.

Any lingering doubt in Charlene's mind about whether Anders was murdered or committed suicide vanished when she poked her head in the bedroom door. Housecleaning wasn't her strong suit, but the bedroom looked as if it had been pole-axed by a tornado. Or maybe a hurricane. Truth was she never could tell the difference.

The bed had been flipped over, the bedding balled up and tossed against a wall, the mattress slashed, and the stuffing ripped out. The ceiling fixture had been smashed, and there was glass everywhere. The bedside table had been stomped to splinters, the highboy's drawers had been yanked out and overturned, all her clothes were dumped on the scruffy carpet. Charlene righted the highboy. She tried to put a drawer back, but it wouldn't fit. She scooped up an armful of expensive clothes – exotic outfits she danced in, and had spent a lot of time and thought putting together – and neatly folded everything and put it in the drawer.

She filled all five drawers and then, by a simple process of push and shove, fitted the drawers back into the highboy. One of her all-time favourite outfits was missing – a really cute black-leather cowgirl suit that she'd had custom-fitted and then spent weeks decorating with glass beads and sequins. She'd just got the suit back from the dry cleaners, and now it was gone. Obviously, whoever had shot Anders must have taken it. Charlene vaguely entertained the thought that Anders might have been killed by another stripper. It wasn't all that stupid an idea, given his wandering eye and total lack of moral fibre.

She went into the kitchen. Nothing that was capable of being shattered or broken had been overlooked. Glass crunched underfoot. Struggling not to burst into tears, she grabbed a table knife off the Formica counter and made her way back to the bedroom. The tiny closet had been ransacked. She kicked tangled clothing and coat hangers out of her way, crouched down, and used the knife to pry a foot-long piece of baseboard away from the wall. A hole had been roughly hacked in the lathe-and-plaster behind the baseboard. Anders' secret hiding place that she wasn't supposed to know about. She chipped a nail pulling out a red-painted metal box about a foot wide by eighteen inches long by six inches high.

The box wasn't locked. She flipped open the lid. The first thing that caught her eye were the neat bundles of ten- and twenty-dollar bills. Charlene estimated there was about three thousand dollars in cash. The watch was so heavy she thought it might be solid gold. The last item in the metal box was a silver semiautomatic .25-calibre pistol, small enough to fit in the palm of her hand. Charlene put the money and the watch and the pistol back in the metal box and carried the box into the living room.

What would Anders have done if he'd come home from work and found *her* body lying on the floor?

Strip off her jewellery, roll her up in a carpet, watch TV until it got dark, and then sling her over his shoulder and carry her outside, toss her in the trunk of his Olds, drive into Burnaby, find a dumpster.

She tried and miserably failed to visualize herself slinging Anders across her shoulder.

If she called the cops . . .

They'd question her, take her downtown and ask her a bunch more questions while they ripped the apartment to pieces, found all sorts of stuff they could use to bust Anders, as if he hadn't already been permanently busted.

But what could they do to her?

Nothing, she hoped. Anders was a pimp. He was a drug dealer and he sold guns. From time to time he worked as hired muscle, a bone-buster. And of course he was a thief.

She was none of those bad things. She was a stripper with a city-wide reputation, and she was, in certain circumstances, a woman who sold herself for money.

Both professions were equally legal. The only thing she had to worry about was losing her inheritance – the cash and watch, gold coins. She went back into the living room and sat down on the end of the sofa that wasn't splattered with blood, and lit a cigarette, and worked out her story until she had it straight.

The last person Anders had done business with was the ex-con with the funny name, like the invisible rabbit in that old black-and-white Jimmy Stewart movie.

Harold?

No, that wasn't it.

By the time Charlene had finished her second cigarette, she'd figured out where to hide Anders' fat bankroll, the watch and gun. She'd decided that, for the time being, all those things still belonged to him. To his estate. She would eventually inherit them, but not until things had cooled down.

It seemed likely that the killer, whoever he was, hadn't found what he was looking for. Did that mean he'd be back? Charlene had no idea. She warily eyed Anders. Was his cellphone in his pants pocket? She decided she didn't want to know. Not that bad, anyway.

She went down into the building's dimly lit basement and hid the red metal box, and then she went back to the hotel and used a payphone in the cramped lobby to dial 911.

The phone rang for a long time, and then a woman with a calm voice said, "Police or ambulance or fire."

Charlene said, "Police." Her quarter clanged into the coin-return slot. She fished it out, and gripped it tightly in her hand.

A policeman identified himself, and asked her how he could help. Charlene told him about Anders. He wanted details. She started to tell him what she'd seen, suddenly lost control and burst into tears. She was standing there in the corridor, leaning against the wall, with the telephone in one hand and the quarter in the other, crying her eyes out, when the two uniformed cops showed up. The younger one had his gun out. His buddy reached out and took the phone away from her and said something into it and then hung up. Charlene felt a stillness deep within her, as if she had sunk into the eternal darkness that lay far beneath the surface of the sea.

one big happy

Jan was in the shower when she heard the door slam shut and Tyler's tired but happy voice announce that he was home.

"Hi, Mommy! I'm baaaack from the jungle! Where are you, Mommy!"

"In here, Tyler."

His footsteps rumbled down the carpeted hall. Her son weighed sixty pounds but sounded like an NFL linebacker.

He stopped at the bathroom door.

"Are you going to the bathroom?"

"I'm in the shower, honey."

"Is anybody in there with you?"

"No, of course not."

"I have to go to the bathroom."

"Okay, Tyler. I'll be out as quick as I can."

"I have to go really, really bad."

Jan rinsed the last of the shampoo from her hair. She turned off the water and stepped out of the shower, grabbed a towel and wrapped it around her body.

"Okay, you can come in now."

Tyler pushed the door open and hurried past her to the toilet. His green corduroy shorts had an elasticized waistband. He pulled his pants down and peed noisily.

Jan said, "I'm going to go and put some clothes on."

"I forgot to lift the seat."

"That's okay, I'll clean it up in a minute."

"The toilets in the woods have seats that are nailed down. You couldn't lift them even if you remembered to. It's so the bears can't fall down the holes."

"Wow, what a good idea."

"We heard a bear last night. It crashed around and made a whole lot of noise, but I wasn't scared."

"That's my boy."

"A kid named Jerry was so scared he pooped in his sleeping bag. He had to throw it away, because it was so disgusting and stinky."

Jan said, "Sounds like you had a wonderful time."

"It does?"

Tyler had dropped his backpack in the hall. Jan stepped over it on the way to her bedroom. She dressed in white shorts and a pink tank top, and towel-dried her hair. On her way to the bathroom she yelled at Tyler to turn the TV down. He yelled back that he wasn't watching it, so why should he? Jan cleaned the toilet and followed the roar of the television into the living room.

Harvey was sprawled out on the couch, working on a beer. He was one of those guys who had minimal body hair but such a heavy beard that, if he wanted to look clean-shaven, he had to use his razor at least twice a day. Jan would have bet a six-pack that he'd shaved in the past half hour. His charcoal pants and pale blue short-sleeved shirt looked as if they'd just come off the rack. She could smell his drugstore cologne from the far side of the room. She went over to the TV and turned it off.

Harvey gave her a big smile. He spread his arms wide. Did he expect her to give him a hug? She hoped so, because rejection was good for the soul – if you had one. He said, "Do I look great, or what?"

"Didn't they teach you any manners in prison? Get your shoes off my sofa."

Harvey sat up. He swung his legs around, making a big deal of it, like he was doing her a huge favour.

Jan said, "How did you get in?"

"The door was open."

"You mean, unlocked."

"What's the difference?"

"You have no right to walk in here, make yourself at home."

Harvey raised his eyebrows and dropped his jaw, miming shock and surprise. He said, "I don't?"

"This isn't *our* apartment, Harve. It's *my* apartment. As far as I'm concerned, you're just some guy who walked in off the street. Now get out, or I'll call the police."

Harvey pulled a small black object out of his pants pocket. The Sony's remote. He turned the TV on. Jan strode across the room. Pulled the plug.

Harvey said, "Nice shorts."

"Fuck off!"

Tyler said, "You swore!" He stood in the doorway. Twigs in his hair and mud on his shoes. Her little mountain man. Jan said, "Go to your room, honey."

Tyler pointed at Harvey. He said, "Who are you?"

Harvey said, "Hi, son. Don't you recognize your old man?"

Tyler shook his head. "I don't know you."

"Yeah, you do so. I'm your dad."

Jan said, "Harvey . . ."

"Yeah, what?"

Tyler said, "My dad was killed in a train wreck."

Harvey stopped laughing when he saw the look on Jan's face. He drank some beer, picked thoughtfully at the label on the bottle.

Tyler said, "He was a hero. He was really strong and he saved a whole bunch of people's lives, and they'll never forget him."

"You must be proud of him."

"I am. Sometimes I pray for him when I go to bed at night."

Harvey nodded. He slid a quick look at Jan. What he saw in her face imbued him with strength, and purpose.

He stood up and drained his beer. "I have to go now, but I'll be back. What time do you go to bed, Tyler?"

"At eight o'clock, or else."

Harvey waggled his fingers at Jan. "See you then, sweetie."

"Don't kid yourself."

Tyler waited until Harvey had left the apartment and shut the door behind him, then said, "Who was that, Mom?"

"Nobody," said Jan, and bitterly wished it was true.

13

sail away

Jennifer Orchid lived in a beige stucco fourplex on Point Grey Road, just off Balsam. Locally, especially among realtors, Point Grey Road was known as "The Golden Mile" because it was the only residential waterfront real estate on the city's West Side. The people who lived here had clout – at their request and for no other apparent reason, the city had reduced the speed limit on the street from fifty to thirty kilometres per hour. Jennifer Orchid's fourplex was located at the eastern end of a long, curving block that butted up against Kitsilano Park. Curbside parking was reserved for residents. Willows parked in front of the building. He flipped down his sun visor so the cardboard "Police Vehicle" sign was visible to even the dimmest-sighted tow-truck driver.

Oikawa unbuckled his seatbelt. "Nice neighbourhood."

Willows nodded. Jennifer's block dipped down from the rest of the long stretch that was Point Grey Road. Consequently, it was the only piece of waterfront that didn't back onto a main thorough-fare, and was priced accordingly. To his left, across the tree-dappled street, there was a mix of unsightly modern structures and elegant shingled and turreted homes that dated from the turn of the century. Most of the older homes were large enough to qualify as mansions, and had long ago been split into strata-title condominiums. Willows had no idea what the individual apartments were worth, but he guessed they started at a couple of hundred thousand for a ground-level suite and shot rapidly upwards to half a million or more. A lot of money, for what boiled down to a small part of a large house.

It was another world on the other side of the street. Jennifer Orchid's building was the only structure that wasn't a single-family home. A small sailing club with a modest one-storey clubhouse had been built on the rapidly narrowing wedge of land that lay between the fourplex and the ocean. The ground rose up so swiftly that Jennifer and the other occupants had an unobstructed view of the water, despite the clubhouse. They had all the advantages of waterfront without the onerous taxes that went with it.

The building had four two-storey units. Each apartment had an identical varnished wooden door set in an enclosed porch beneath a gently curved archway. The effect was charming rather than regimented. A wild profusion of flowers grew in the small window-boxes beneath the mullioned windows. Jennifer's address was the second door from the right. There was just enough room on the porch for Oikawa to crowd in beside Willows.

Willows pressed the doorbell with his thumb. Deep inside the apartment, a bell chimed musically.

Oikawa said, "I know that tune." He snapped his fingers, exasperated. "It's the theme from a movie that was on TV a couple weeks ago. What the hell is it, anyway . . ."

He reached past Willows and pressed the doorbell and listened intently. Inside the apartment, the bell chimed a few notes. When Oikawa tried to press the button again, Willows slapped his hand away.

Oikawa gave him a hard look. "What the hell, Jack."

"We're not playing *Name That Tune*, Danny."

Oikawa rubbed his wrist. "Nobody's home anyway, so what difference does it make?"

Willows held his tongue. A dark shape moved behind the door's glass panels. He moved back half a pace, forcing Oikawa to step off the porch.

Oikawa said, "We leaving?"

The door swung open as far as the safety chain allowed. Metal rasped on metal. A woman wearing oversized sunglasses peered up at Willows.

Willows badged her. He said, "Jennifer Orchid?"

She nodded, and removed the glasses. Willows pegged her at somewhere between twenty-eight and thirty, maybe five-six. She wore her blond hair in a buzz cut so short it looked like fog. She had a small, delicately boned face, a sensuous mouth, and wide-set, luminous green eyes. She gave Willows a nice smile and said, "If it's about that parking ticket I got a few months back . . ."

Willows introduced himself. "Detective Jack Willows." He jerked a thumb at Oikawa. "This is Detective Dan Oikawa. We'd like to ask you a few questions about Colin McDonald."

Jennifer Orchid unhooked the safety chain and opened the door. Willows got a sniff of her perfume, and wanted more. She said, "Would you mind taking off your shoes? I just had the damn rugs cleaned, and it cost a fortune."

Willows and Oikawa stepped inside. The entrance hall was just big enough for the three of them. Willows knelt and unlaced his black brogues. Oikawa kicked out of his tan loafers. Jennifer led them into the living room. The gleaming hardwood floor was maple. The area rugs were close to an inch thick. The rugs had subdued colours, complicated geometric patterns, and hand-tied, knotted fringes. Willows didn't know much about rugs, but he suspected that the carpets were very old, likely from Persia or Afghanistan, or some obscure Middle Eastern country that no longer existed and that he'd never even heard of. All he knew for sure was that you didn't find this kind of quality in a discount store . . .

Oikawa stared out the open windows at the harbour and beyond, to the soft green bulk of the North Shore mountains. Out in the harbour, the wind was strong and the water was choppy, scooting flecks of foam across the dark blue water. He followed the course charted by a trio of wind-surfers as they raced around a massive deep-sea freighter. He watched the surfers until they had disappeared one after another behind the freighter's blunt stern, and then he became aware that Jennifer Orchid and Willows were both watching him. He said, "Nice view."

"Thank you." Jennifer indicated a cream-coloured leather sofa. "Sit down, make yourself comfortable."

Willows and Oikawa sat at opposite ends of the sofa, like two strangers that had just been introduced and instinctively knew they had nothing in common and had nothing to say to each other. Jennifer sat opposite them, on a matching leather loveseat. She was casually dressed, in faded jeans, white sneakers, and an unbuttoned white shirt that hung loose over a dark green tank top. No makeup, no jewellery. No glam at all, really. Willows didn't know what he'd expected. Something other than an *après*-gardening outfit. He supposed that if you were a high-end hooker, it probably wasn't a good idea to dress appropriately, if you didn't want to irritate the neighbours.

Oikawa sneezed.

Jennifer Orchard said, "Bless you."

"Excuse me," said Oikawa, and sneezed again. Jennifer handed him a box of Kleenex. Oikawa said, "Thank you."

Willows said, "How long have you known Colin McDonald?"

"How do you mean?"

Willows was silent for a moment, and then said, "We're aware of the nature of your relationship with Mr. McDonald, Jennifer. We don't care about that. All we care about is solving his murder."

"I wish I could help you, but . . ."

Willows smiled. He said, "You can help us, even though you might not know it. The question is, *where* do you want to help us."

"I'm not sure I understand what you mean."

Willows said, "Do you want to help us here, in the comfort and privacy of your own home, or would you prefer to go downtown?"

The coffee table had been made out of a bearpaw snowshoe covered with a half-inch-thick sheet of glass cut to fit. The coffee table held a stack of glossy fashion magazines, a pink glass heart-shaped ashtray, a sterling-silver lighter as big as Willows' fist, and a pack of filter-tipped Gitanne cigarettes. Jennifer shook a cigarette from the pack. Oikawa made a move for the lighter, but Willows was too fast for him. Jennifer inhaled deeply, held the smoke for a moment, and exhaled towards the open window. A gust of wind tore the smoke to shreds.

She said, "I've known Colin about six months." She paused to delicately remove a speck of tobacco from her tongue. "Our relationship was purely professional. Colin could be charming, when he wanted to be. There were times when I enjoyed his company. But the meter was always running." She took a long pull on her cigarette. "He liked to tell people we were friends, but he was wrong. But then, Colin was wrong about most things, when it came to relationships. He had a knack for it. A talent. Don't ask me to explain, but you'd be surprised how many guys like him, wildly successful, hard-nosed businessmen, are romantic fools." She crossed and uncrossed her long legs. "Are you a romantic fool, Jack?"

Willows smiled. "I hope so."

Oikawa sneezed three times in quick succession.

Jennifer said, "It's probably the smoke from my cigarette. I'd put it out, but I'm an addict." She turned back to Willows. "Would you care for a glass of white wine?"

"No, thanks. Water would be nice."

"Dan?"

Oikawa perked up. He said, "Water's fine with me, too, thanks." He sneezed again, and stuffed a wad of saturated Kleenex into his jacket pocket.

"Be right back."

Both detectives discreetly watched Jennifer as she walked past them to the open kitchen. She was a beautiful woman, and her every move was charged with a natural, overpowering sexuality. Willows had never seen anything like it. He glanced around. The

apartment was neat, and well-organized, and relentlessly imper-
sonal. There was no art or photographs on the walls, not a stick of
superfluous furniture, nothing at all that could be described as
revealing. The apartment had a ton of natural charm and warmth,
due to its site and architecture, but it had the aura of a dentist's
waiting room. He wondered if Jennifer owned or sublet the apartment. He supposed it could belong to a client. The nature of her
business might encourage her to lead a nomadic life. He felt a
sudden, sharp surge of alarm. Why he was thinking about her
personal life like this? He told himself it was only because of
her relationship with Colin McDonald. Willows was a pro, too.
He was trying to understand her, so he could more clearly understand the case, and that was all there was to it.

The refrigerator door sucked open. Ice cubes rattled into glasses.
The door slammed shut. Bottle caps clattered on tile. A few
moments later, Jennifer came back into the living room carrying a
tray that held glasses full of ice, two open Perrier bottles, and,
astonishingly, a plate of enormous chocolate-chip cookies. She set
the tray down on the coffee table, knelt gracefully, and poured a
measure of Perrier into Willows' and then Oikawa's glasses.

Willows said, "Thank you."

She offered him the plate. It was decorated with a circle of naked
men in a state of arousal pursuing naked women with outstretched
arms. Since all the men and all the women were identical in every
respect, and there was nothing to choose between them, it
was impossible to say if the women were running away from the
men behind them, or hurrying towards the men directly in front
of them.

Willows said, "No, thanks."

"You don't like sweets? Watching your weight?" She picked up a
cookie and held it up to him as if he were a child. Willows stood
his ground. She pressed the cookie gently against his mouth. Her
lips parted. She teasingly whispered, "Have a bite, Jack. Just one
bite won't kill you."

Willows took a small bite of cookie.

"There, that wasn't so bad, was it?" Jennifer's eyes were bright. She held his eyes as she took a sensuous, overlapping bite of the cookie. Her pink tongue flicked an invisible crumb from her upper lip. She chewed and swallowed, and then helped herself to a drink from Willows' glass. "Mmm, yummy." She turned to Oikawa with a pleasant, meaningless smile. "I forgot all about you, didn't I, Dan. Would you like a cookie?"

"Yeah, I would." Oikawa helped himself to the largest cookie on the plate. He gave Willows a twisted smile, and Willows knew that his fellow officers would be calling him "Chip," and mock-seductively asking him if he wanted a "cookie" for months or maybe even years to come.

Michael Hughes had indicated to Willows that Jennifer Orchid earned a heavy dollar. Willows believed every penny of it. He decided to slip into his all-business and nothing-but-business persona. Despite his recent problems with Claire, he considered himself a reasonably happily married man. He planned to stay happily married, no matter what. He sipped at his Perrier and said, "How did you meet Colin?"

"At a party. Michael Hughes introduced us."

"Colin's business partner?"

"That's the one." Jennifer gracefully sat on the carpet in front of Willows, her long legs tucked beneath her. She was so close that she could have rested her head on his knee. Looking up at him, she said, "Michael and I were dancing, and Colin walked by. Michael called him over and introduced him. He cut in, we danced, and he told me he'd like to take me out to dinner. I told him he wasn't my type. He laughed and said I was wrong, that I was exactly his type, and he didn't care how much it cost. I asked him if Michael had been talking out of turn. He told me he'd known what kind of woman I was the moment he saw me."

"Did you believe him?"

"No, of course not."

"Do you know why Michael would have wanted you to meet Colin?"

"I've no idea."

"But you arranged to meet him again . . ."

Jennifer thought for a moment. She said, "Colin liked to be seen in the company of beautiful women. In a relatively short time, he became very fond of me. I've found it wise not to allow relationships to deteriorate to the point where they become . . . personal. I don't mean to seem callous, or even overly protective. Things can get awfully messy awfully fast. You'd be surprised."

Willows doubted it, but didn't say anything.

Jennifer said, "To tell you the truth . . . I know he's dead and everything, but when it comes right down to it, I didn't *like* Colin."

"Why not?"

"How much time have you got? Colin's one of the few people I've met who didn't have a single redeeming characteristic. He could be absolutely vicious, the way he treated people. He was easily the most cold-hearted bastard I ever met, and I've met more than my fair share of bastards." Jennifer tilted her head and smiled up at Willows. He didn't understand the smile, or what it meant.

He said, "Can you be more specific about Colin's shortcomings?"

She shrugged, and looked away.

Willows said, "Colin give you the mouse?"

"Excuse me?"

"The black eye." Willows hadn't thought at first that Jennifer wore makeup, but as she'd talked about her ex-lover, he had noticed a faint smear of darkness beneath her left eye. He said, "Did Colin hit you?"

Oikawa sneezed forcefully into a handful of Kleenex. He blew his nose, and apologized.

Jennifer and Willows both ignored him. Jennifer said, "No, Colin never hit me, not once. I'm not into that kind of scene."

"Somebody hit you. Who was it?"

"I'd rather not say. Are you about done?"

Oikawa brushed crumbs from his lap, and made as if to stand up.

Willows said, "Hold it, Dan." To Jennifer he said, "No, we're not done. In fact, we're just getting started. We're investigating a high-profile murder. Your name came up. You've just called Colin McDonald the meanest, most cold-hearted bastard you ever met. He punched you, didn't he?"

"And then what, I lost my temper and killed him?"

"Is that what happened?"

"No, it isn't. I walked into a door."

"Have you got a pimp, Jennifer?"

"Of course not." Her mood brightened. She rested her hand on his knee. "Do I look like the sort of woman who'd spend her time lurking on a street corner, waiting for traffic?"

Willows said, "No, of course not." He lifted Jennifer's hand off his knee. "Where were you the other night?"

"I had a date, an all-nighter. I met him at his hotel. We had dinner in the hotel restaurant and then went up to his room. We had an early breakfast, and then he left for the airport. That was a few minutes past six. I caught a taxi home."

"Who were you with?"

"I can't tell you that."

"Why not?"

Jennifer said, "One of my most important qualities is discretion. I have a phone book, and calendar, but everything's written in code. No names, just numbers. My date is an MP. *A Member of Parliament*. He's married and has several lovely children. He counts on me, he *pays* me to be discreet. I am not going to let him down."

"You'd rather go to jail?"

"If I gave you his name, it would ruin my career. I've been working for eight long years, Jack, ever since I was seventeen. I think of my career as roughly equivalent to that of any other professional athlete – short but highly lucrative. When I started in the business, I hoped to be able to retire by my thirtieth birthday. I have a client list that's second to none, and I'm right on schedule. But if I rolled over on a john, everything I'd worked so hard for would be destroyed." She locked eyes with Willows. "You know as well as I do that, in my profession, there's no room for error. You're a handsome guy, Jack, and I know we could be friends. But I'm not going to risk ending up on the street, turning tricks at ten bucks a pop, just to make you happy. You want to put me at the top of your suspect list, that's fine with me."

She gave his thigh a quick squeeze and stood up. "I've had a wonderful time talking to you, but I'm going to have to ask you to leave, and I mean right this minute."

Willows reluctantly stood. Jennifer walked him and Oikawa to the door. As they stepped outside, she touched his arm and said, "Wait just a minute." She slid open a closet door. A small black patent-leather evening bag hung from a brass hook. She fished around in the purse for a moment, and then handed Willows a shiny white card with embossed lettering in elegant dark blue type. As she gave him the card, her fingers closed around his thumb. Before he could react, she tugged gently, and gave him a seductive look that told him she knew exactly what she was doing and how it had affected him. Only then did she let go.

"That's my lawyer's card, Jack. If you feel the need to talk to me again, give him a call."

Willows slipped the card into his pocket. He tried to think of something brilliant to say. Or if not brilliant, at least clever. He was still working on it when Oikawa was seized by another extended fit of sneezing. The door clicked shut behind him.

Willows stepped off the porch and moved a few paces to his right, so Oikawa was standing downwind.

all that glitters

Aldo Huff's smile lit up the booth. He swivelled his overly large head from Jan to Sandy and back to Jan. He chuckled, the sound of his good humour hard-edged as pebbles rattling in a jar. "We can't pay you anywhere near sixty per cent of the original wholesale value of the diamonds. Even thirty per cent would be a ridiculously generous offer. Twenty-five is our best offer, take it or leave it." His dark hand crawled across the table towards his drink, a highball glass full of V-8 juice garnished with a length of asparagus.

"Fifty," said Jan.

"Twenty-seven."

"Fifty-five."

"Alright then, thirty."

"Sixty."

"That's preposterous! Thirty-five."

The server had appeared at their booth while they were still seating themselves. Jan had ordered a cranberry martini, Sandy a Budweiser, Aldo the V-8 and spear of asparagus. The server had cocked her hip. "Asparagus?"

"If you have it," said Aldo, bleaching her with his huge smile. They were in the bar in the Hotel Vancouver. It was a pleasant, open, carpeted area three steps up from the marble-tiled lobby. You could sit there, have a drink, enjoy the canned music, feel expansive and vaguely exclusive as you watched people come and go. If you kept your eyes open, you might spot a passing movie star. Aldo loved the place. He knew that the hotel's restaurant was just around the corner, and that the asparagus would not be a problem.

Aldo drank some more V-8 juice. He sighed, and licked his lips. "I know you don't mean to be unreasonable," he said to Jan. "You must understand that my expenses are shockingly high. Quite staggeringly enormous, actually. And the risk . . . I shudder to think of it. If I was arrested, I would go to jail for a very long time. Who knows how short a man's life may be?"

Sandy said, "All I know is that life's too short to act like life's too short."

Jan laughed, but Aldo wasn't amused. His brow rumpled. He said, "I have no personal experience, but am told by reliable sources that prison is a terrible place. The food is poison. One's fellow prisoners are sex deviants and other undesirables, some of them quite violent."

"That's probably true," said Jan. "I mean, if I was in charge, prison's where I'd put people who belonged there."

Sandy said, "No, a first offence, white-collar crime, if you got jail time, it'd be in a minimum-security prison. Horses, golf, lattes. It wouldn't be so bad."

Aldo stroked his beard. "You speak from personal experience, Sandy?"

"Reliable sources. Cons I've known."

Aldo nodded. He said, "Think of it. Ordinary people like me, who made a terrible mistake and are suddenly no longer referred to by their God-given names, but by the simple generic 'cons.'" He took a bite of asparagus, and chewed furiously. "I don't want to be a con. What a horror that would be!"

Jan said, "Now, now. Let's not get ahead of ourselves."

Aldo nodded, and lapsed into a moody silence. Their server drifted by. Sandy ordered another Bud.

Jan said, "You hardly touched the one you got."

"Just watch me. Want another martini?"

"I prefer to stay sober, thank you very much."

"Aldo – another V-8?"

Aldo roused himself. "Why not? Live a little, isn't that the idea? Have fun, because who knows what disaster tomorrow may bring."

"It's going to be sunny all week," said their server. "Highs in the mid-eighties, if you can believe it."

Aldo smiled politely. He waited until she was out of earshot and then said, "Are you sure you can pull it off, just the two of you?"

"Don't worry about it," said Jan. "Anyway, there's three of us."

"Who is the other person?"

"The kind of guy you don't want to know."

"Three of you can do this thing?"

"Working in concert," said Sandy, "as one man." He blew Jan a kiss and added, "So to speak."

Aldo said, "The math is true, but at the same time . . ."

"No buts," said Sandy, in a voice like iron. Jan stared at him, not much short of amazed. He reached under the table and gave her knee a quick, reassuring squeeze. "The thing is," he said to Aldo, "we do all the dirty work. By the time we knock on your door, it's all over, the risky part's done."

"No violence," said Aldo.

Their drinks arrived. Aldo said, "What did you say was in your martini?"

"Cranberry juice," said Jan.

"It's a beautiful colour."

"Thank you."

"But I would like to know about this other person. The one I haven't met."

Sandy said, "Jan's ex-husband just got out of the slammer. His name's Harvey. He needs work, so we took him on. Don't worry, it isn't just a family-values thing. The guy's a driver. Lots of experience, and he's as reliable as a thief can be."

"You have a getaway car?"

"What did you think, we'd catch the number-five bus? Harvey stays down on the street, with an FRS radio."

Aldo worriedly drained his V-8. He said, "I don't know what FRS is. A gun that zaps a person with electricity, perhaps?"

Sandy said, "No, an FRS is like a walkie-talkie, except more powerful. You can get them at Radio Shack, wherever . . ."

"Yes, yes." Aldo waggled his fingers. He said, "Forty per cent of value. That's my best offer."

Sandy looked into Jan's eyes. She bit her lower lip and then nodded almost imperceptibly.

Sandy said, "Tell you what, we'll split it down the middle, fifty-fifty. How does that sound?"

"Forty," said Aldo. He tilted his glass to his lips. His tongue probed for the last few drops of V-8 juice.

Sandy said, "Yeah, okay. Fine."

They shook on it. Aldo held Sandy's hand a fraction too long. A wayward drop of V-8 juice glinted in his beard like a red diamond.

Sandy paid cash for the drinks. Aldo hadn't touched his second glass of V-8 juice. He said he'd stay and finish it, if that was all right. Sandy and Jan pushed back their chairs. As they walked away from the table, Sandy folded the bar bill in half and slipped it into his wallet.

14

hatchlings

Aldo sat quietly in his upholstered chair until Jan and Sandy had passed from view. He nibbled on his fresh drink's asparagus stalk, then tilted his body slightly for a better look out the window towards the street. After a few moments, his two would-be partners in crime walked briskly past.

Aldo pushed aside his V-8 juice. He caught his server's eye, and waved her over. She was a delicious redhead, very classy. Her name tag said *Brenda*. He ordered a double Johnny Walker Black, straight up. He was a lapsed Muslim and would freely admit, if he was pressed, that there were times when he sorely missed his religion. But never when he was drinking. He couldn't believe he had lived the first thirty-four years of his life without Rolling Rock beer, Wild Turkey on the rocks, gin fizzes, and Johnny Walker Black Label. Soon he would try a cranberry martini. He'd never had a martini, despite his fondness for James Bond films. His Scotch arrived. He told Brenda he would have another. She smiled and nodded and headed for the bar. He drank half the Scotch down, drained the rest of the glass into his mouth, and swirled the liquor around, flooded his pallet and energetically sucked the alcohol through the large gaps between his teeth.

He was halfway through his third double when Jackie, his handsome-but-foolish younger brother, joined him. Jackie wore a black double-breasted suit that was heavily padded in the shoulders. His wide black leather belt had a heavy silver-plated buckle in the shape of a pistol. Perhaps it really was a pistol. His bright red cowboy boots had spurs that jingled.

Aldo said, "What time is it?"

"I don't know. Am I late? Never mind, don't tell me. I must be late, because I always am. Always. It's an annoying habit. Why don't I do something about it? How should I know?"

"Stop talking to yourself." Brenda drifted over to their table. Aldo asked her for a glass of water for himself and a Coke for his brother.

"Rum and Coke," said Jackie.

Aldo shook his head. "No, he's only teasing. He is a devout Muslim. Alcohol is a poison to him."

"My body is a temple," said Jackie. He gave Brenda a mock-bawdy wink. "And my temple is your body." He laughed. "I don't really know what that means, actually."

Brenda moved away, towards the bar.

Jackie said, "Don't leave me, girl!" He glanced at Aldo. "Don't stare at me like that, Aldo. It's terrifying. You give me the frightened shivers."

"How did your afternoon go? Was it educational?"

"Yes, very. Jan didn't want to give me Sandy's address, but I convinced her I was just being cautious, and meant him no harm."

"What did you learn?"

"That our new friend Sandy is a security-conscious fellow. Not only does he lock all his doors and windows, he pulls his curtains so snug that it is not possible to see inside, no matter how one bends and twists."

"Well then, what did you do?"

"Nothing. You told me not to break anything or leave any marks."

"Did you hunt for a key?"

"Everywhere but up my own anus."

"On the ledge above the door, under the welcome mat, a flowerpot?"

"Everywhere, Aldo. There was a welcome mat but no key. No flowerpot at all, anywhere. I looked beneath a stone that was full of promise, but all I discovered was a seething mass of small black ants."

"You tried the back door?"

"I was everywhere you could think of." Jackie smiled slyly. He said, "I even went up on the roof."

"On the roof?"

"Yes, the roof. I climbed up on a fence and from the fence to the roof."

"You amaze me."

"I amaze myself, Aldo. Now listen to this: on the roof, there is a skylight, a hinged skylight that can be opened to let in the fresh air, or even the rain, if it was so desired."

"Did you open it?"

"It was padlocked. I could see the lock. When I pressed my face against the glass I could even see the key for the lock, dangling from a bit of string tied to the lock. It was frustrating, let me tell you. So near, and yet so far."

"But you could see into the apartment?"

"Yes, absolutely."

Brenda arrived with ice-water for Aldo and a Coke in a tall glass for Jackie, shot of Captain Morgan on the side. When she had gone, Aldo said, "Well then, tell me what you saw."

"Nothing."

"Come now, you must have seen something."

"Well, yes. A sofa and TV, an ugly thing he believes is a carpet. A small table and two wooden chairs, a computer . . ."

Jackie drank some Coke. He belched loudly, and wiped his mouth on his sleeve.

Aldo said, "You shouldn't burp. It's rude."

Jackie said, "Sandy is a very neat and tidy fellow, for his age. The fact that I saw nothing of interest could be of interest in itself, don't you agree?"

Aldo drank some more water.

Jackie had decided as he was driving to the hotel that he would not tell Aldo about the security camera that had peeked inquisitively up at him as he'd hunched over the skylight. The camera's small red light glowed brightly. Its lens was a blank eye that told him nothing. Wires led from the camera to a VCR perched on the TV. Jackie was quite sure his attempted intrusion had been recorded on videotape. He was also quite sure that, if he told Aldo about the camera, Aldo would panic, and back out of the deal.

Aldo said, "That's all you saw, there was nothing else?"

Jackie shrugged. He drank the rest of his Coke. Ice rattled against his teeth. He sighed with pleasure. The redhead, Brenda, was watching him. He was sure he could have her, if he asked nicely. His handsome features twisted as he struggled to repress a gigantic belch.

bite me

Tyler's day-camp was in the basement of an elementary school a little over a mile from Jan's apartment and about four miles from the hotel.

Jan twisted Sandy's wrist so she could read his watch. She pushed away his arm. "Hurry up, let's go." She reached for her seatbelt. "We're never going to make it."

Sandy turned the key. The truck's engine caught, and idled smoothly. He made a shoulder check and pulled away from the curb. He said, "Does it matter all that much if you're a couple minutes late?"

"Are you kidding? There's nothing more militant than a fucking daycare worker. Especially Lynda. She *hates* being kept waiting.

I'm one minute late, it's a four-hour hit, and I can't afford to throw away that kind of money."

"Not yet, anyway."

"Now is what counts, Sandy. Yesterday and tomorrow are nothing but dreams."

"Lynda's going to charge you for that much time, why don't we go somewhere, have a drink . . ."

"Are you crazy? We just had a drink. Anyway, Lynda's such a bitch, she'll wait half an hour max, and take off."

"You're kidding. She'd leave Tyler all by himself? Could he find his way home?"

"Probably. No, I guess not. I don't know. I've never been late before. When I signed Tyler up, she put the fear of God into me. Talk about rabid. She's totally into the union – should've been a longshoreman, or a fucking baseball player."

Sandy turned his head so Jan wouldn't see him smile. How threatening could a daycare worker be? But there was no denying her panic. Thinking about it sobered him. If you knew what to look for, Jan's apartment – and her life – were crammed full of signs that pointed at a tight budget. Couldn't be easy, being a single mom. He braked for a stop sign, looked left then right then left again, and drove through.

Jan said, "I never met anybody as cautious as you. Keep it up, I bet you live to be a hundred. *Then* you'll be sorry."

Sandy self-consciously rubbed the puckered scar on his forearm.

Jan knew about the arm. When he was ten, he and another kid had been out in the woods, hunting squirrels or whatever, and the other kid had tripped over a root and his gun had gone off.

"I'm just naturally careful, I guess." He smiled good-naturedly. "You really think that's something worth complaining about?"

Jan put her feet up on the dashboard. She wore her pink open-toed sandals. Her toenails were painted midnight-blue. She'd stuck tiny gold and silver stars on them while the nail polish was still wet. Sandy reached out and gave her ankle a squeeze. The stars reminded him of his childhood. All through elementary school, his teachers had stuck gold or silver stars on the pages of his notebook, as a mark of his success. A green star signified a pass, a test or homework assignment that was just barely good enough, but certainly not outstanding. You got a red star, it meant you'd really screwed up, were in danger of failing. Sandy always got silver or gold stars. No greens that he could remember, or reds. All that had changed when he hit Grade Ten. Grade Ten was his nemesis. Suddenly he just didn't care any more, and had no idea why, and didn't care about that, either. All he was interested in was music and drugs and girls . . .

Jan nudged him. "Hey, wake up. Left at the corner."

Sandy made the turn, crawled along for the better part of a block at the 30 KPH speed limit. He turned into the school's small parking lot. The door leading to the daycare was open. He could see movement inside, vague shapes hurrying around. The four-storey building was red brick. Sandy wondered if the school was on the long list of schools that were in need of earthquake-proofing. He wouldn't want his kid attending a school that was going to turn into a pile of bricks when the big one hit. The school board worked out of a brand-new glass-and-concrete tower on West Broadway. The plush, air-conditioned offices had cost millions, and had been built to withstand anything short of a nuclear bomb. He guessed that, if he had a son who worked for the school board, he'd be glad he worked in a nice, safe building. But if he was the parent of a student, he'd be pissed, for sure.

Jan pushed open her door before the truck came to a full stop. She jumped lightly down, and hurried away from him, across the asphalt and down a grassy slope, into the shadow cast by the school. He checked the time. It was one minute to six. Jan hesitated at the door, her leg cocked fetchingly, then disappeared inside. Sandy expected her to come right back out, Tyler in tow. He waited a minute, then killed the engine. The cooling aluminum block ticked erratically. A crow landed on the knee-high, white-painted fence that surrounded the parking lot. The crow worked its way down the rail towards him, then stopped and gave him a coy, over-the-shoulder look.

Sandy powered down his window. He had no idea how a crow could manage an expectant look, but this one did.

He said, "I'd give you something if I had it, but I don't."

The crow edged a little closer. Crows were supposed to be smart. Maybe this one was the exception to the rule. Jan and Tyler and a tired-looking woman in jeans and a grey T-shirt walked out of the daycare. Jan held Tyler's hand. Tyler's head was down. His kicking shoe raised a small cloud of dust. Jan said something that made him go still. Sandy guessed that the woman must be Lynda. She looked like a Lynda, though he wasn't sure why.

Tyler wore sneakers and shorts and a red-and-white striped short-sleeved shirt. He jerked free of Jan's hand and walked around her in small, rapid circles as she talked to the woman Sandy had decided was Lynda. The two adults were standing a little too close together. Lynda moved her hands expressively. Jan's posture was defensive. She looked stressed, as if she'd just been dealt some seriously bad news.

The conversation ended abruptly. Lynda reached out and squeezed Jan's arm, said something to Tyler that he didn't respond to. She stared at Tyler for a moment, and then turned and walked away. Jan and Tyler started towards the truck. Tyler tried to get Jan to carry his backpack, but she pushed it away. As they drew nearer, Sandy saw that Jan was fighting a mix of emotions. He reached across the bench seat and pushed open her door. The crow's wing feathers made a soft rasping sound as it flew away, staying low across the sun-parched grass and then rising in a graceful curving arc to settle in the topmost branches of a tall fir tree that grew close by the chain-link fence surrounding the school's crushed limestone sports field.

Tyler ignored Jan's outstretched hand. He scrambled up into the truck, and buckled himself in. The backpack lay on his bare, outstretched legs. The backpack didn't look as if it had any-thing in it.

Jan got in, and slammed the door.

Sandy started the engine. Tyler reached for the radio. Jan slapped his hand away.

Sandy expected Tyler to cry out, but he didn't, though he looked as if he wanted to. Sandy snuck a quick look at Jan. Her face was dark and full of rain. He decided not to ask any questions. For now, he was content to assume the role of a cab driver. He'd hold his silence during the drive back to her apartment, knowing that, because of the kid and her foul mood, she wouldn't invite him in. He decided that, if she surprised him, he'd turn her down.

He'd come to think the armed robbery was nothing but smoke and mirrors and idle talk. Now, post-Aldo, he believed she seri-ously intended to pull it off. He couldn't even start to imagine the tension she must be feeling, knowing that, if they screwed up and got caught, she could kiss Tyler goodbye.

A few minutes later, he pulled up to the curb directly in front of her building. He didn't turn the engine off. Jan pushed open her door and got out of the truck without a word. Tyler scuttled across the seat and jumped down to the sidewalk. He turned and squinted up at Sandy.

"Thanks for the ride, Sandy."

Sandy smiled and said, "You're welcome."

Jan slammed shut the door, then yanked it open and said, "I'll talk to you later." Sandy nodded. She said, "You going to be in tonight?"

"I don't know. Maybe. Call me on my cell."

Jan said, "Tyler bit a little girl. On the thigh." She looked as if she were about to break into tears. "Can you believe it? My kid's a fucking vampire. He didn't break the skin, thank God." She laughed bitterly. "If he does it again, they'll kick him out. In the meantime, he's on probation." She shut the truck's door with exag-gerated care, and turned and walked away without another word.

Sandy waited until she'd let herself into the building, then drove slowly away. A stew of emotions churned in his gut. The dominant emotion was guilt.

touch me

Claire was stretched out on the sofa, reading a novel recommended by Oprah, when the phone rang. Hadrian was upstairs in his crib, napping. Claire picked up the cordless and said hello.

"Hello, Claire. I hope I'm not interrupting anything. I just thought I'd give you a quick call, see how you and Hadrian are doing."

The voice was deep and authoritative. Two scoops of manly, thought Claire. She knew who it was but asked anyway.

"Who is this?"

"Doctor Hamilton – Randy."

Claire went back to her book. She had read only a few words when Hamilton said, "I hope I haven't called at an inconvenient moment. I just called to make sure that Hadrian's all right."

"He's fine," said Claire.

"It's amazing, isn't it, how resilient children can be."

Claire murmured her agreement.

Hamilton said, "I could drop by anytime, if you'd like me to examine him, make sure he's okay."

"That's very thoughtful of you," said Claire. She had intended to be sarcastic, but somehow it hadn't come across that way. She added, "But it really isn't necessary."

"Couldn't hurt though, could it?" Before Claire could answer, Hamilton said, "Tell you what, I'll call again in a day or two. In the meantime you can think it over, see how you feel." He chuckled inanely. "I don't usually make house calls. But in your case, I'm eager to make an exception."

"Really," said Claire.

"We don't have to meet at your home. Are you open to a suggestion? Why don't we have lunch together, say at the Clairmont?"

"The hotel?"

"It's only ten minutes away. Fifteen at the most. They do a lobster bisque that's really outstanding."

Claire said, "I don't think lunch at a hotel would be appropriate, Doctor."

"Too public? We could take advantage of room service, if you'd prefer. I could reschedule my appointments, take the day off. We could really make a meal of it."

Shocked speechless, Claire slammed the phone down on the coffee table, and then picked it up again, and disconnected with a harsh stab of her thumb. What kind of woman did Hamilton think she was? Had she inadvertently sent him an inappropriate signal? Claire giggled. She couldn't help herself, because when she'd turned Hamilton down, she had quoted, word for word, the heroine in the Oprah-approved novel.

She lay there on the sofa, thinking about Dr. Randy Hamilton. She wondered how many of his patients he tried to seduce. Not many, probably, if only because of the risk. It had always seemed to her, when she'd read newspaper articles about doctors who had been censured by the College of Physicians and Surgeons, that the College rarely administered more than a slap on the wrist to doctors Claire believed deserved a public flogging.

Despite the College's lackadaisical attitude, you had to be out of your mind not to realize that screwing patients was fraught with risk. She had no idea how Jack would react if she told him about Hamilton's call. He might laugh it off, but was just as likely to march into the good doctor's office and punch him in the nose.

Hamilton wasn't her type and she wasn't attracted to him, but she had to admit that he was handsome, in a compact sort of way. He certainly was jam-packed with confidence. She supposed he wouldn't be so sure of himself unless he was pretty good in bed.

In her life, she had been very cautious when it came to men. And of course there hadn't been anybody, since Jack. She thought back on that long-ago afternoon in Inspector Homer Bradley's office, when she'd first met Jack. Her new partner, Homer had said. Talk about prescient!

Hamilton wore tailored shirts that showed off his narrow waist and muscular shoulders. He must spend a lot of time in the gym, to look like that. Claire had learned not to trust men who were overly self-absorbed, narcissistic.

On the other hand, she wished Jack would spend a little more time on himself. Years of overwork, fast food, and minimal exercise had inevitably taken their toll. She'd tried to get him to go for walks with her, but he wasn't interested. Work exhausted him. He spent too much time in front of the television. Lately he had been drinking heavily. She was worried about him, worried, and afraid.

Worse, she had begun to lose her respect for him. He seemed to want so little for himself, and for her. For *them*.

If he loved her, and Hadrian, why wouldn't he try harder to take care of himself? Why did he save so little of himself for their relationship?

Claire wondered how much of herself she had revealed to Randy Hamilton. His interest in her was repugnant, but at the same time, flattering. She didn't know how she felt about it. She knew how she *should* feel, but that wasn't the same thing.

It bothered her that she had mixed feelings.

Hamilton knew damn well that she was married and off-limits. He was a snake. But then, why did she experience a little thrill of anticipation when she thought about his next phone call, the renewed invitation to spend a day with him, a day separate from everything else in her life, in a room at the Clairmont Hotel?

The phone rang, and made her jump. She picked up, and cautiously said hello.

Jack said, "Claire, I'm sorry, but something's come up. I'm going to be late. I won't be home for supper."

"When will you be in?" She knew it was an impossible question, and she despised herself for asking it.

Jack said, "I don't know. Could be an all-nighter. Don't wait up for me."

Jack's tone was deliberately bland, revealing nothing of his emotions. Claire said, "Are you okay?"

"Yeah, fine."

"How's Dan working out?"

"He's doing his best. How's Hadrian?"

"Napping," said Claire.

Willows said, "I love you. Both of you. Give him a hug and a kiss for me."

Claire said, "Wake me when you get home."

"Okay," said Willows in that same infuriatingly bland voice.

Claire told him she loved him. She didn't put much into it, and she wasn't sure why. There was a short silence, and then she hung up.

an unconscious state of mind

Harvey said, "Hi, Tyler."

Tyler stared up at him. The kid's eyes were huge. Harvey wondered about that, because his own eyes, behind his glasses, were kind of beady, and pressed in on his nose. It was bedtime. Tyler wore pyjamas with burgundy-and-pale-green stripes. His short blond hair was tousled. His small hands were wrapped tightly around the throat of a teddy bear wearing a Boy Scout hat, plastic Sam Browne belt, and a red kerchief. Harvey thought that, if it were a real bear, it would be dead by now, asphyxiated. He reached out and awkwardly patted Tyler on the head. He said, "I really am your daddy. How would I know so much stuff about you if I wasn't? Are you sure you don't recognize me?"

Jan brushed past Harvey and bent and ruffled Tyler's hair. "Bedtime, sweetie."

Harvey said, "I'm ready. I been ready for years."

She gave him a warning look, and then turned and led Tyler by the hand down the hallway to his room. Harvey shifted position so he could keep her in view. She hadn't aged a day in all the years he'd been gone. Not an ounce of fat on her. She still liked to wear tight clothes, show off her body. Well, she'd never been the shy type. Not that he remembered, anyway. He sat down on the sofa, flicked ash at the heavy blue glass ashtray. He could hear Jan's murmured voice, and wondered what she and his son were talking about. Maybe she was reading to him from a book. There was a guy named Eric Wilson who wrote mysteries that were very popular with the cons. He'd read a couple, thought they were pretty good.

He wondered if Jan was telling Tyler that his father was a loser, and not to expect to find him at the breakfast table in the morning.

Jan's voice droned on. Harvey resented whatever she was saying, even though he had no idea what it was. He got up and went into the kitchen. The fridge door had a bunch of kid's drawings plastered all over it, held on by strips of tape or giveaway fridge magnets. He yanked open the door and helped himself to a bottle of Granville Island Lager. The beer was cold, and had a nice, malty taste. Jan must be doing okay, if she could afford to buy premium beers. Or maybe her boyfriend was the big spender. He eased shut the fridge door and went back to studying the drawings. Most of the pictures were of birds or animals. A couple were of a weird-looking alien-type dude. Maybe that was the boyfriend. Sandy. What kind of name was that? It could've been a man or a woman. Or a beach.

He heard a small sound behind him, and spun around so fast he surprised himself.

Jan said, "Nervous?"

"Should I be?"

"Have a beer, why don't you."

Harvey smiled. He bumped the bottom of the beer bottle against a drawing. "That supposed to be the boyfriend?"

Jan nodded.

Harvey said, "Tyler's quite the talent. But let's hope he don't quit his day job."

Jan's face got a mean, pinched look. Harvey suddenly remembered what a ball-breaker his wife could be. He said, "Just kidding. Sure got a flair for colour, don't he? I guess he's got some of your artistic genes running around in his veins."

Jan laughed out loud.

Harvey said, "What's so funny?"

She filled a tall glass with water from the tap, and took his arm and led him back into the living room. Harvey plunked himself down on the sofa. Jan sat in a ragged, overstuffed armchair with scuffed wooden trim. The two of them were about as far apart as the room's dimensions allowed.

Jan said, "What've you been up to since you got out, Harve?"

He shrugged a little too elaborately. "Not much. Been trying to find some honest work, but I'm here to tell you, it ain't easy."

"I heard Quisno's looking for talented people."

"Maybe so, but they ain't looking for me." He took a long pull on his cigarette. Smoke leaked out his nostrils. He opened his mouth a crack and forcefully exhaled a stream of smoke until his lungs were empty, then stretched his arms wide and took a deep breath. "I dropped by the tattoo parlour a couple times. It was always closed. You playing hard to get, is that it?"

Jan said, "I've had some other projects I had to attend to."

"Like what, your new boyfriend? I thought you were a hardtop girl, was a big shock to see you running around in a pickup truck. You listen to C&W, wear a ten-gallon hat, cowboy boots, and a pleated skirt?"

Harvey's tone was teasing, but his eyes were hard. Jan said, "You been spying on me, Harve?"

"Damn right. What else have I got to do with my time? Anyway, we're still a legally entwined husband and wife, last time I looked."

"In name only, Harve." Jan drank some water. Harvey's nails scrabbled at the label on his beer bottle. She said, "You remember, I said I might have some work for you."

He didn't look up. Fragments of paper fell from the bottle to the carpet. In all the years they'd spent together, Jan couldn't remember him ever picking up after himself, or helping with the housework, or shopping . . . Or even thanking her for doing it all for him. There was no reason to think he was any less useless now. What could prison teach him, that was worth learning?

After a moment he said, "Doing what?" His voice was flat, uninterested. But his nervous fingers were busy, busy, busy. A blizzard of paper fell from the bottle.

Jan said, "If I let you in, it would only be under certain circumstances."

"Like what?"

"I'm in charge. You're the low man on the totem pole, and you do what you're told."

"You sure make it sound like a whole lot of fun, whatever the hell it is you're yapping about."

"Armed robbery," said Jan.

Harvey laughed. He said, "There been some big changes around here since the last time I looked. Armed robbery? What happened to the sweet little girl you used to be?"

"Poverty."

"The tattoo thing ain't working out too good?" Harvey drank some beer. He said, "I won't pretend I ain't interested, because I am." He gave her a disingenuous smile. "But where in hell am I going to find a gun?"

"Don't worry about it."

He pointed his trigger finger at her. "You saying you got something for me?"

"No, Harvey, I'm saying you don't need a gun."

"But . . ." Harvey got it. He said, "What's your boyfriend's name again?"

Jan didn't say anything. Gave him a hard look. He smiled and said, "Sandy's the shooter, is that it?"

"Nobody's going to do any shooting."

"Maybe not, but you damn well know what I mean."

Jan said, "Sandy has a gun. It's the only gun we're going to need, and it's just for show. We're going to rob people, not shoot them."

"You hope."

Jan leaned forward. "Shut up, Harvey." She wasn't shouting, but his ears were ringing. She said, "Just shut the fuck up, and listen. For once in your stupid life. Can you do that, Harve? Can you just shut the fuck up?"

"Yeah, sure. I guess so, if I . . ."

Harvey clamped his mouth shut. His cheeks flushed red. Thin white lines formed around the corners of his mouth.

Jan let a solid minute crawl past, by the battery-powered clock over the sink. Harvey stared at the blank TV screen as if he were watching his favourite program. He was so grim – his time in jail hadn't cheered him up one little bit.

She said, "You're the driver."

He nodded.

She said, "You can speak now, Harvey."

He ground his cigarette out in the ashtray, and lit another with Anders' Zippo. "You want me to drive the getaway car?"

"We were thinking along the lines of a van," said Jan, "but you can think of it as a getaway car if it makes you happy."

Harvey grinned broadly, but his eyes were flat as a lizard's. He said, "What're you gonna do, knock off Victoria's Secret, score a lifetime supply of clean lingerie?"

"You don't need to know."

"Just drive, that it?"

Jan nodded. She finished her glass of water and leaned forward so she could put the glass on the coffee table. Harvey eyeballed the swell of her breasts against her T-shirt. She looked up. Their eyes locked. Jan held her pose, letting him have an eyeful. Then straightened.

Harvey said, "I need to know one thing."

"What's that?"

"My share – what do I get?"

Jan had her answer ready. "Ten per cent, or a thousand dollars a kilometre."

Harvey frowned. "A thousand dollars a kilometre?"

"Or 10 per cent."

"Of what?"

"We're not sure. Probably somewhere in the neighbourhood of four hundred thousand."

"That sure is a nice neighbourhood."

Jan nodded.

Harvey said, "Could I take the thou a click against the 10 per cent, so I get whatever comes out bigger?"

"Why not?"

"Any chance of a bonus? Some kind of incentive, for a job well done?"

"Depends what you had in mind."

"You know what I got in mind," said Harvey.

Jan's white teeth pressed down on her lower lip, as if she were working out the implications of what he'd said. It had always driven him crazy when she bit down on her lip like that. She damn well knew it, too.

Jan said, "I couldn't go back to how we were, Harve. Things would have to be different. You'd have to try an awful lot harder."

"I would, I promise."

"We'd have to use the money to make a new life for ourselves. Put a down payment on a house. No flashy cars, or drugs, or . . ."

"That's exactly what I'd want for us, honey. You took the words right out of my mouth."

"You'd have to get an honest job. I don't mean right away, but soon. You owe that to your son."

"Don't I just know it."

"One more thing."

"Name it, babe."

"No more fooling around. I deserve better than that, and so does Tyler."

Harvey put his beer down on the coffee table and pressed his hand against his chest. "Swear to God, I'd be true."

"I mean it," said Jan.

"Me too," said Harvey. He eased off the sofa and moved slowly towards her, waddling on his knees. When he got close enough, he rested his head on her thighs, and slipped his arms around her waist. She smelled delicious. He wondered if she wanted him to kill Sandy. The way her woman's mind worked, one little thing at a time, he doubted she'd given it a moment's thought. Harvey snuggled a little closer. The kid had to be asleep by now. Jan had more flaws than most women, and in his opinion her worst flaw was not thinking things through. Like, how would it help if he stopped messing around with other women? He was true to her, he was going to get bored a lot sooner, and that would be a hardship on their relationship. It was the sort of thing he could never talk to her about, because she got all worked up, couldn't think straight if her life depended on it. Well, that was Jan. She'd never change. Not in this lifetime, anyway. Did he complain or whine about that? No. So why couldn't she be mature enough to accept his faults?

He lifted his head so he could look at her.

"Wanna have sex?"

Jan smiled, "You mean, make love?"

"Yeah," said Harvey.

"No," said Jan. "Not yet and maybe never."

"What's that supposed to mean?"

"Talk is cheap, Harve. You've got a lot to prove, before I'm going to let you back into my life, and my pants."

Nodding agreeably, he slipped his hand under the thin material of her T-shirt.

Jan leaned towards him. She ran her fingers through his hair, and then leaned back. Harvey cupped her breast. Yummy. Jan raised her arm. Harvey looked up. A torrent of ash and cigarette butts fell into his widening eyes. He tried to squirm away, but his hand was caught up in Jan's T-shirt.

He opened his mouth to yell something along the lines of *Don't hit me!* The ashtray thumped his skull. He fell backwards. His head bounced off the coffee table, and then the carpet.

Jan almost hit him again. She brought the heavy ashtray swinging down on his slack-jawed face and then had a change of heart and pulled back at the last moment. It was a near thing. The ashtray clipped Harvey's chin hard enough to take away a little piece of skin. His raw flesh was white, then pink, then bloody.

Jan stood up. She was a little shaky, but not bad. Harvey's eyes were closed. His breathing was deep and slow. The ashtray was flecked with blood, and cracked diagonally from corner to corner. Harvey's forehead was horribly swollen. A purpling bruise raced across his skin, from temple to eye. He'd swelled up as if something was alive in there. Jan tossed the ashtray on the coffee table. It exploded into a thousand pieces that rained down on the carpet.

She went into her bedroom and picked up the phone and speed-dialled Sandy's cellphone number.

He picked up on the first ring, as if he'd been waiting for her call. "How'd it go?"

"Not all that wonderful."

"You okay?"

"Fine."

"He still there?"

Jan said, "He got kind of frisky. I hit him with an ashtray."

"That big blue one?"

"You don't miss much, do you? He's unconscious."

"I don't doubt it. Be right up."

That startled her. She said, "Where are you?"

"Across the street."

Jan went over to the window and cracked the blinds and looked out. Sandy's pickup was parked in the loading zone in front of her building. The truck's door swung open and he got out. His phone was up against his ear.

She said, "How long have you been there?"

He looked up, waved, as he crossed the street. He was walking as fast as a man can walk and not be running. He said, "Buzz me in."

Jan said, "You better believe it." She'd been ready to do pretty much whatever was needed to get Harvey to drive the getaway car. She was glad it hadn't come to that. Say what you would about him, Harve was a bear in the sack. It had shocked her how much she had wanted him, when he'd strolled back into her life. It was crazy. Harvey was a total loser, and likely always would be.

But there had always been something between them, sexual alchemy, a white heat that burned her soul . . .

How much longer would Sandy have waited, parked in his truck outside her bedroom window, before he decided that he was the one getting screwed?

Jan didn't even want to think about that. From now on, she would have to be very, very careful. Sandy and Harvey both wanted her. Both men expected to be with her. For now, she was walking a tightrope, because she needed them both to pull off the diamond robbery. Afterwards was a different story, but she doubted she'd have to choose between them.

Harvey wouldn't let that happen.

Neither would Sandy, and Sandy already had a gun.

15

breathless

Willows parked the unmarked car in front of the Western Hotel, with the right-side wheels up on the sidewalk.

Oikawa gave him a look.

Willows said, "What?"

"It makes it a lot harder to open the door when you park like that, 'cause I got to push up, as well as out. I miscalculate, don't push hard enough, the door could swing back on me . . ."

"And break your legs?" said Willows pleasantly. He got out and slammed the door shut and strode around the car, towards the front door of the hotel.

Oikawa had to hurry to catch up with him. He was always chasing after Willows, and he hated it. Willows was a prototypical A-type personality. Why didn't he do the right thing, and have a goddamn heart attack, and die? Only then, maybe, would he slow down enough for Oikawa to keep up.

Willows pushed aside the hotel's sturdy metal-clad door and climbed a short flight of stairs to the lobby. A uniformed cop at the top of the stairs stepped aside. Willows said, "There a desk clerk?"

"In his office, over there." The cop pointed at a closed door.

"Who's keeping him company?"

"Sergeant Gramfield."

Willows nodded. Gramfield was in his late fifties, a lifer, and a force in the all-powerful police union. The desk clerk was in good hands. Three quick steps took Willows across the lobby, past the short, wide corridor that led to the restrooms and the hotel bar, and over to the stairs that led upwards to the second and third floors. Oikawa trailed along behind at a relatively sedate pace. The canned music from the bar was just short of deafening. The Western, in common with most of the hotels in the area, depended on its liquor licence to maintain any semblance of solvency.

The crime scene was on the third floor. By the time Willows reached the second floor, he was sucking wind, and sweating buckets. His heart was like a battering ram, banging away at his ribs at a frantic rate. Oikawa passed him between the second and third floors. For him, the climb up the steeply pitched stairway had seemingly been effortless. He smiled at Willows. "You okay, Jack?"

Willows nodded, too puffed to speak. He leaned against the railing. His damp shirt clung to his heaving chest.

Oikawa said, "Maybe you ought to spend a little time at the gym, work on your cardio, lose a few pounds."

Between gasps, Willows said, "Thanks for . . . the . . . advice . . . Danny." He wiped stinging sweat from his eyes.

Oikawa said, "You look like you're gonna puke. You look *like* puke. Want me to buzz the paramedics?"

"Fuck off."

Oikawa chuckled good-naturedly and continued down the hall. Willows took a deep breath, stood upright, and followed after him. Oikawa badged the cop standing by the open door to apartment 313. The cop was a rookie, straight out of the academy. He nodded to Willows. "How's it going, Detective."

"Great. Yourself?"

The cop said something Willows missed, due to the ragged catch of his own hard breathing. He entered the apartment. A short, narrow hallway led to another open door. The hallway had no architectural merit, other than to function as a simple but highly effective trap. Willows heard Oikawa say something and laugh. He followed his partner's laughter into a large room filled with a soft, golden light.

Oikawa had been talking to a uniformed corporal. He pointed at the body on the floor. "Anders Bruhn. Got a sheet on him would cover a city block. Drugs, petty theft, assault . . ."

The corporal said, "Now he's gonna have a new sheet on him – a pretty blue one, courtesy of the morgue."

Anders lay on his back, his right arm flung across an overturned coffee table. He was a big fella, about six-foot-three, maybe three hundred pounds. Despite his size, it looked as if it had taken only one shot to bring him down. Back issues of *Low Rider* and *Time* and *Oprah* lay on the floor like a spilled deck of oversize cards.

Oikawa said, "An eclectic reader, was Anders."

Willows said, "If he lived alone."

The green-and-orange-striped sofa was splashed with blood. Green bands of light flickered on the CD player. A set of Sony headphones was slung around Anders' neck. His mouth and eye were wide open. The eye that hadn't been sewn shut was chocolate brown. He had more teeth crammed into his mouth than you'd find in the average piranha. Willows had never seen a black man who didn't have brown eyes, and Anders was blacker than any black man he'd ever seen. He wore a loose-fitting, black, martial-arts-type outfit, and a black belt cut from a wide band of cloth. If he was a karate expert, it hadn't helped him much. A pair of aviator-style mirror-lens sunglasses lay low on his snub nose, tilted an angle so the lenses didn't cover his eyes. A long scar curled across his head like the memory of a model railway track.

The CD player clicked.

Music leaked from the headphones. Some kind of jazz.

Oikawa said, "Coltrane. Anders had good taste in music. Wish I could say the same about the furniture."

"You don't like the sofa?"

"Not the orange part," said Oikawa. "The rest of it isn't too bad. This . . ." He gestured widely with his arms, encompassing the width and breadth of the living room. "This seem kind of weird to you?"

"Staged."

Oikawa nodded. "That's right, staged. The headphones, magazines, the damn sunglasses. Look at the way he's lying, with his arms and leg bent like that. I've never seen anything like it." Oikawa moved gingerly around the body. He said, "You'd think the guy was posing for a goddamn Assassination Calendar."

Willows said, "We better dust every damn square inch of everything."

Oikawa went over to the stereo. He pushed buttons and twisted a dial. The green bands of light turned red. Coltrane's music rattled the windows.

Oikawa started dancing. "Know how to do the Twist, Jack?"

Willows smiled. "Not to Coltrane."

"Like this," said Oikawa.

untrue love

Annie and her best friend, Paige, had driven over to Commercial Drive to attend a poetry reading at a coffee house. They'd both dressed for the occasion. Paige wore baggy white-and-black-striped engineer's coveralls and pink sneakers with green "Go for It" laces on the left shoe and red "Get Your Filthy Hands Off Me" laces on the right shoe. Beneath the coveralls she wore a skintight flesh-coloured Lycra tank top that showed off her large breasts. You could see her nipples, if you looked hard enough. Annie couldn't help noticing that just about every guy in the place was looking. Most of the women, too.

Annie wore a plain white blouse unbuttoned halfway to her navel, a supershort pleated skirt, black knee socks, and black patent-leather slip-ons. Her bra was in the glove compartment of Paige's car. It was her new "Catholic slut" look, and it worked very well, even if she had been brought up in the United Church. Their clothes and good looks had scored them a front-row table for four. Paige had ordered and paid for a half-litre of red wine.

Annie sipped at her wine. She was still learning about wines. This particular wine was, in her opinion, barely drinkable. Not sweet enough.

She glanced around, self-consciously tugged at her skirt, and crossed and uncrossed her legs.

Paige said, "What d'you think of the wine?"

Annie shrugged.

"It's the best they've got," said Paige defensively. "I had it last time I was here. It's South African."

Annie nodded, not really listening. A couple of older guys, men in their late twenties, pushed determinedly through the crowd towards their table. The taller of the two, pale-skinned, dressed in faded jeans and a pale blue denim shirt, caught her eye. He smiled and said something to his buddy. Annie drank some wine. The guy in the blue shirt was kind of cute, but his pal was a horror show. He'd shaved himself bald, had a dyed-red soul patch that turned into a short, spiky beard, wore too much face jewellery, and had Japanese characters tattooed all over his hairless forearms. He totally creeped her out. The blue shirt put his hand on the back of the empty chair next to Annie. He said, "Mind if we join you?"

Annie glanced uncertainly at Paige.

Paige said, "Beat it."

"Excuse me?"

"This table's taken. Go irritate somebody else."

The shirt started to move away. His buddy grabbed his arm. "Hold it a sec." He turned on Paige. "Who d'you think you are, talking to me like that!"

"Fuck off."

"Fuck you!"

"Not even in your dreams," said Paige.

"Faggot bitch!"

Paige smiled sweetly. She said, "You better believe it."

The shirt said, "C'mon, let's get out of here." The guy with the face jewellery gave Paige and then Annie the finger as he retreated into the crowd.

Annie turned on Paige. "What was that all about?"

"Being a woman," said Paige.

Annie drank her glass of wine.

Paige said, "Thirsty, huh?" She gave Annie a sardonic grin, and refilled her glass. A few minutes later, two women in their mid-twenties approached the table and asked Paige if they could join her.

Paige smiled and said, "Make yourself at home."

The women sat down. The woman closest to Annie was short, heavyset, and had a sallow, puffy complexion. Her friend could have been a body double for k.d. lang. Neither woman wore makeup, or perfume. The k.d. lang look-alike wore a diamond stud in her ear.

A waiter came by with menus. Paige ordered a pasta dish. Annie said she'd have the same thing. Paige smiled, and reached across the table and gave her hand a lingering, proprietary squeeze.

The two women ordered pints of draught beer. The one with the diamond stud said, "I'm Sue. This is my friend Jess."

Paige introduced herself and Annie.

Sue said, "You guys from around here?"

"Not really," said Paige.

Jess gave her a knowing look. She turned to Annie. "West Side girls?"

Annie nodded, embarrassed, but not sure why.

Sue said, "You like poetry, Annie?"

"Depends."

"On what?"

"I don't know – what I'm hearing."

"Most poets aren't poets at all," said Sue. "They're just lazy bastards spouting total crap."

"No kidding," said Paige.

"How would you know? Are you a poet?"

Paige smiled. "Sure. Isn't everybody?"

Jess laughed. "Let's hope not."

Everybody laughed except Annie. Paige finger-poked her in the ribs. "Relax, Annie. Enjoy yourself, for once."

The beer arrived. Sue and Jess raised their glasses. Sue said, "Here's to all poets everywhere, and true love wherever you can find it."

Paige said, "That's pretty damn poetic." She and Annie and Sue and Jess clinked glasses.

Paige and Annie's pasta arrived. Paige offered to share her pasta with Sue. Annie felt she had no choice but to offer to share her meal with Jess, even though she didn't want to. She was relieved when Jess took a pass. The house lights dimmed, and somebody walked up to the podium and made a few bad jokes and introduced the first of the evening's poets. Annie didn't catch the name. Tony or maybe Toby something. He was in his early twenties, very thin, dressed in black pants and a white dress shirt unbuttoned at the throat. He had an unruly mop of curly black hair and round, black-rimmed glasses. The crowd gave him a good round of applause. He wasn't the least bit nervous. Annie admired him for that. She leaned towards Paige and said, "He's kind of cute, isn't he?"

Paige shrugged uninterestedly and looked away.

Six poets read, one after the other. Each poet was given five minutes at the podium. At the end of their allotted time, power to the microphone was cut off. One of the poets, a woman with blue hair and a sequin-speckled face, gripped the mike and shouted the rest of her poem. She ran on for several impassioned minutes, and received such a lengthy round of applause that she graduated to the next round, the following week.

When the lights came back up, Jess said, "You guys want to go somewhere?"

"Maybe," said Paige. "Depends what you've got in mind."

"We could go back to our place, drink some wine, listen to some music . . ."

Paige said, "Sounds good to me."

"I don't know," said Annie.

Jess said, "About what?"

"Everything," said Paige. That got a laugh. She put her arm around Annie and pulled her close. "C'mon, let's do it. It'll be fun."

Everybody stood up. Paige rested her forearm on Annie's shoulder. Annie felt very uncomfortable, even a little scared. Jess led them as they pushed their way through the crowd. The boy in the blue shirt caught Annie's eye. She tried to look away but couldn't. He blew her a kiss, and then turned and said something to his friend that made them both laugh. Jess grabbed Annie's hand and pulled her along. Annie tried to shake her off, but Jess's grip was strong.

thicker than water

Aldo sat carefully down on Jackie's futon. He leaned back and vigorously scratched his head with both hands. Dozens of glossy black hairs fell to his shoulders and lap. He said, "I'm going to be bald as a bald eagle's egg before my next birthday, at this rate."

"Stop feeling sorry for yourself," said Jackie. "Nobody likes a whiner."

"Nobody likes you, either, do they? Can you name one person?"

"Jennifer Orchid loves me."

"By the minute, and the hour."

Jackie smiled. He made a small gesture with his hands. "Well, yes, that's true. But I value expertise above sincerity." He flipped open a gold-plated pre-war cigarette case, took a moment to admire himself in the case's small mirror and then extracted a filtertip Marlboro and lit up with a plastic disposable lighter.

Aldo said, "I wish you'd quit smoking. It's a disgusting habit."

Jackie exhaled a monstrous cloud of smoke. "It isn't a habit, it's an addiction. I'm hooked right through the lungs." He went into the kitchen, got two bottles of beer from the fridge, went back into the living room and handed a beer to his brother.

"Thank you," said Aldo.

Jackie unscrewed the cap from his beer.

Aldo drained half his bottle. He said, "Our bodies are our temples, and we treat them like primary sewage plants."

Jackie drank some beer. Aldo had high hopes of living forever. He was forever going on and off the wagon. Unlike his foolish older brother, Jackie considered himself a realist. His idea of a long life was merely to survive the weekend's debauchery. If his sybaritic lifestyle had a flaw, it was that it was heavily dependent on cash. He said, "We are men, and therefore we must do what we must do."

"You're referring to the diamonds?"

Jackie nodded dolefully.

Aldo said, "What are you suggesting?"

"We've got to kill them," said Jackie. "Exterminate them for the worthless scum they are." He sucked fiercely on his cigarette, and threw back his head and expelled a series of five smoke rings. It was nowhere near a record, but he took consolation in the fact that all five rings were almost perfectly circular. Little doughnuts of smoke. He said, "They're thieves and scoundrels, all three of them. They've got what's coming to them, and more."

"What about Harvey? We haven't even met him."

"Birds of a feather."

"The woman, too?"

"Why not?"

"She has a child, Jackie."

"Or so she claims. Anyway, what difference does it make? She's vermin, just like the others." Jackie drained his beer and shot his cigarette stub into the bottle. The hiss of the dying cigarette excited him beyond all reason.

16

rivals

Harvey opened his eyes. The nap of the shag carpet was a ticklish blur. He rolled over on his back. Now he was staring up at the bottom of a low table. He turned his head to the right and found himself looking at the bottom half of a sofa, two jeans-clad legs from the knees down, a pair of heavy black boots. Size ten, ten and a half. Jan was a five. He rotated his head to the left and saw more furniture he recognized, and something brightly sparkling and blue, caught up in the carpet. He reached out and picked up a razor-sharp sliver of glass.

Behind him, a motor roared and something tugged at his hair. Jan was working her Panasonic vacuum cleaner, but by the time he'd worked that out, he'd already sat up in such a hurry that he'd banged his head against the underside of the table, fuelling his headache and damn near knocking himself silly, not to mention apparently knocking over a can of beer . . .

Jan said, "Goddammit!"

A man's voice said, "It's okay, I got it."

A stream of foamy liquid fell from the edge of the table onto Harvey's stomach, splattering his shirt. The liquid was cold. He sniffed the air. Beer, for sure. He rubbed his aching head. He had a lump right in the middle of his forehead. The table was moved aside. A man looked down at him. Because of the angle, he appeared to be upside down. Even so, Harvey could see he was a clean-cut, real good-looking guy, wide in the shoulder and narrow in the hip. But young. Way too young for his wife. The guy pulled up a chair and made himself comfortable. He had an open, pleasant face. He gave Harvey an upside-down smile.

Harvey said, "Who in hell are you?"

The guy offered his hand. "I'm Jan's boyfriend, Sandy."

Harvey said, "Pleased to meet you. I'm Jan's husband, Harvey. How long have I been out?"

"A long time," said Sandy.

Harvey took Sandy's hand. He squeezed down on Sandy's fingers as hard as he could, with such force that the veins and sweat stood out on his throbbing forehead. Sandy kept on smiling. He made no attempt to free his hand. But then, why would he, given that he seemed blissfully oblivious to the fact that he was in tremendous, excruciating pain. Harvey kept squeezing. Sandy reached out with his left hand and picked up his glass of beer and calmly took a small sip. He put the glass back down on the table and squeezed back, with more pressure than Harvey would have believed was humanly possible. Harvey gasped, and tried to jerk his hand free. Sandy kept up the pressure. Harvey moaned deep in his throat. Sandy let go.

Jan turned off the vacuum cleaner. In the silence, Harvey could hear himself moaning. He clamped down on his pain. Jan said, "I bet you don't try that again."

"Try what?" Harvey gingerly clenched and unclenched his aching hand. His fingers hadn't been mashed to a pulp, but his tough-guy rep had sure as hell taken a twelve-round beating. He got his legs under him and headed for the kitchen.

Jan waited until he yanked open the refrigerator door, and then reined him in. "What d'you think you're doing?"

Harvey let his shoulders slump. He said, "Okay, fine, I'll play your silly, childish game. Can I have a beer?"

"One," said Jan. "A Budweiser."

The Bud was down on the bottom glass shelf, next to a four-pack of outsized cans of a brand of beer Harvey had never heard of. It was brewed in England and was called Malpin's Best Cream Lager.

Harvey held up a can. He said, "What's this imported crap?"

"That's Sandy's."

Harvey stood there by the fridge's open door with the outsized can of English beer clutched in his aching hand, waiting for Sandy to tell him to help himself, enjoy. He waited about five extra-long seconds and then it filtered through that he could stand there forever and a day, feeling a chill from two directions at once, and never get the green light. What the hell. He popped the tab and took a long pull.

Sandy said, "Get one for me while you're at it." The way he said it made it an order rather than a simple request. Harvey drank another leisurely mouthful of beer. He swung the fridge door shut and then swung it open and then shut and opened it again, and reached down and grabbed a can of Budweiser and flipped it low and hard at Sandy's crotch. Sandy snatched the can out of the air and lobbed it back at him. He was so smooth and graceful and accurate that Harvey was a little bit impressed despite himself. He tossed the Bud in the fridge and got a can of Malpin's and walked over to Sandy and docilely handed it to him. He noticed that, as he drew near, Sandy turned his body and dropped his right shoulder and bent his left knee, so he was ready to deal with it if Harvey got stupid with the big can of Malpin's.

Harvey lifted his beer. "Here's to crime." If push came to shove, he loved Jan too much to stand in her way if she wanted to be with another man. But not this one. Sandy wasn't right for Jan. Harvey didn't think Sandy was right for anyone. There was something about the guy that wasn't quite right. Harvey didn't know what it was, but he was going to work on it until he had Sandy all figured out.

reel to unreal

Sue and Jess shared a third-floor walk-up apartment in a house on Napier, a few blocks off Commercial. In the kitchen, Sue casually put her arm around Annie's waist and asked her if she wanted a beer. Annie said no. She shot Paige a "let's get out of here" look, but Paige ignored her. Sue asked her if she was afraid she might get drunk, and laughed and gave her a quick squeeze, something that might almost have been a hug.

A burst of laughter made Annie turn and look behind her. Jess was toying with Paige's silver necklace, making a game out of nothing. Flirting. Annie had no idea if she was jealous, or not. She'd felt a pang, but it wasn't in her heart and she wasn't sure what had caused it.

Sue got a six-pack of beer from the fridge. She flicked off the kitchen light and led the group into what Annie mistakenly thought was the living room but quickly realized was a bedroom furnished with a couch and large TV. The bed was a big square of foam covered with sleeping bags. Pillows and cushions were artfully piled up at the head of the bed, against the wall. Sue handed Annie a beer and flopped down on the bed. Jess snatched the remote off the TV. She aimed the remote at Annie and then at Paige and then at Sue. "Anybody want to watch a movie?"

"No," said Annie.

"You're so predictable," said Paige caustically. She drank some beer, and smiled at Jess. "What did you have in mind?"

"Sue rented that Anne Heche movie, the one where Harrison Ford crashes his airplane into a remote island and they hate each other at first and then fall in love? We could watch that. It's supposed to be pretty good."

Annie felt the tension ease out of her. She'd seen the movie and didn't think much of it. But it certainly wasn't what you'd call threatening.

"I *love* Anne Heche," said Paige. She lay down on the bed beside Sue. Jess shoved the film cassette into the VCR, and flopped down beside Paige. The three girls stared challengingly up at Annie. Sue patted the bed and said, "Sit down, make yourself comfortable."

"I am comfortable," said Annie.

Paige said, "Fine, but why don't you sit down?"

"I don't feel like it, that's why!"

"Whoa," said Jess. "Chill out, babe."

"Don't tell me to chill out," said Annie. "In fact, don't tell me to do anything. You're not my mother."

"I'm not?" Jess laughed. Her teeth were mottled brown. She said, "Not your mother! Somebody tell me it isn't true!"

Sue and Paige both laughed a lot harder than the joke warranted. Jess popped the tab on her can of beer. Paige said, "D'you want some help with your beer, Annie?"

"No thanks."

"Annie's an alcohol virgin," said Paige.

"I am not." Annie was furious, partly at Paige but mostly at herself, for allowing herself to be baited so easily.

Jess turned on the TV. There was a long search for the VCR's remote control, until finally Sue found it hidden among the sleeping bags. She turned on the VCR, and fast-forwarded through several minutes' worth of tape. The movie started. Jess yelled at Sue to adjust the tape speed. In the blue light of the TV screen, the faces of Paige and the two other women looked drawn and solemn. All three were watching the film so intensely that Annie didn't quite believe it was real. Sue and Jess looked like people who were pretending to watch a movie, not people who were watching a movie. What were they were thinking?

Paige said, "Annie?"

Annie looked at her.

Paige said, "Come and sit down. Don't be so stuck-up."

"I think we should go," said Annie.

"Go where?"

"Home."

"I don't want to go home," said Paige. "I want to stay here and watch the movie with Sue and Jess."

"It's past ten. We won't get out of here before midnight, if then. You won't be able to drive, because you've been drinking."

"One beer isn't going to be a problem. If you had any experience at all, you'd know that a person can't get drunk on one measly can of beer."

Annie wanted to turn and walk out of the apartment without another word, but she didn't want to abandon Paige to her fate, if she had one. Paige had such a high opinion of herself, thought she was so totally hip and together. She couldn't have been more wrong, because she was even more innocent and naive about life than Annie, and that was saying a lot.

Annie said, "I've seen the movie, Paige. I know how it ends and I don't want to watch it again."

"Suit yourself."

Annie glanced around, angry, not really seeing anything in the dim light from the television. She said, "Do you have a phone?"

"In the kitchen," said Jess.

Paige said, "You gonna call your mommy to come and rescue you?"

"From what?" said Annie.

Paige clamped her mouth shut. She glared at the TV. Annie slipped out of the room and made her way cautiously around the darkened apartment. The kitchen was dimly lit by a streetlight on the far side of the alley. Something brushed against her leg, and as she drew a deep breath to scream, she recognized that it was nothing but a cat. She found the light switch and turned it on. The cat was large, and jet black, with a few flecks of white here and there. Annie knelt and scratched the cat behind its ears. It mewed gruffly, and wandered away with its tail sticking straight up.

A coral-coloured rotary telephone hung from the wall by the fridge. There was no telephone book. She decided to dial information for the number of a cab company, then remembered that BC Tel charged a dollar for directory assistance. She put three quarters and two dimes and a nickel on the kitchen counter, and dialled 411.

From close behind her, Jess said, "Oh, for Christ's sake!" She strode towards Annie and violently swept the coins off the counter with the flat of her hand. The coins rattled on the worn linoleum floor. The black cat scooted out of the room with its tail between its legs.

Annie said, "What's your problem?"

"What do you think?" Jess controlled herself with an effort. "How do you think it makes me and Sue feel when you act like you're afraid of us? We aren't going to *hurt* you." Jess's face softened as she saw that Annie was listening to her. She let out a deep breath and said, "How long have you two been friends?"

"A couple of months. We met in school. At UBC . . ."

Jess nodded. She said, "I went to Simon Fraser. I graduated with a major in Psychology. Not that it did me much good."

"How do you mean?"

"Sue and I have our own garden-maintenance business. I wouldn't say I get to use my degree in any meaningful way." Jess smiled ruefully. "Life can take all sorts of unexpected twists and turns, Annie. Sometimes it takes you by the nose and leads you where you never meant to go."

Annie didn't know what to say to that. She wasn't even sure she understood what Jess meant.

Jess said, "I'm going to tell Sue I'm tired and want to call it a night. I'll make her kick Paige out whether she wants to go or not."

"Thank you."

Jess said, "Maybe it would be fairer to Paige if you gave some thought to what kind of friend you need her to be."

Annie nodded. "I'll do that."

Jess stepped towards her. Annie thought Jess wanted to give her a hug, but all she did was take the phone out of her hand, and gently hang it up.

17

selling out

Jan saw Harvey to the door, and then came in from the kitchen with a can of Malpin's and a can of Budweiser, and a single glass, for herself. She handed Sandy the Malpin's and sat down on the far side of the sofa, about as far away from him as she could get. She clearly wasn't in the best of moods. Sandy wondered who she thought had smacked her hubby semi-senseless, him or her. She said, "I probably don't want to know, but what do you think of Harve?"

"What's *to* think? Whoever let the guy out of jail made a big mistake." Sandy raised his can of beer to his lips but didn't drink. He put the can down on the coffee table. "I guess you noticed he didn't even ask to see his son."

"Well, he had a lot on his mind."

"Yeah, himself."

"Come on, he's not that bad."

"No, he isn't. He's a lot worse."

Jan said, "Harve's parents abandoned him when he was twelve. He did six months for stealing and wrecking a car. By the time he got out, they'd moved to another town. No forwarding address. He's had a tough life."

Sandy nodded. "Just asking, but whose car did he steal?" Jan didn't say anything. Sandy said, "His father's, right?"

"How did you know that?"

"Just a lucky guess."

"Really?" Jan gave him a sceptical look that set him on edge. The diamond robbery, *heist*, Harvey had called it, then *score*, and then *boost* and then, finally, *caper*, was closing in on them. No wonder Jan was a mite touchy. Sandy told himself to concentrate on doing his job, and not rile her.

But somehow he couldn't stop himself from speaking his mind.

"Guys like Harvey are all the same. Bone-lazy. They want to take a ride, they steal whatever's closest, whatever's easiest." Sandy took a long pull on his beer. He added, "I bet it wasn't the first time he stole from his own family. I bet he stole from you, didn't he?"

Jan busied herself pouring beer into her glass. Before he'd taken the big fall, Harvey had indulged his weakness for cocaine at every opportunity, real or imagined. There was nothing worse than living with a drug addict, because an addict would do whatever it took to get his next snort. Harve had ripped her off, in large ways and small, more times than she could remember. He'd sold her TV out from under her, the stereo, microwave, a really nice area carpet she'd bought on time from The Brick. He always knew where her purse was, if she couldn't find it. He'd even pawned her Mr. Coffee machine. Every time she went into the kitchen, she was damn near astounded he hadn't made off with the fridge. It was a huge relief, like being granted an extended vacation, when Harvey was sent off to the slammer. But even then, he was a constant drain. Always sending her letters, telling her how much he loved her and how much safer he'd be if he only had a few bucks in his prison account so he could buy his fellow cons a pack of cigarettes, or a candy bar – something for them to chew on other than his own sweet self . . .

She said, "So, anyway, Harvey had quite a few things to say about how he thought the robbery was supposed to go down, didn't he? I noticed you didn't seem to have any opinions one way or the other." She managed a half-smile. "I'm not saying you were acting out of character, or anything. I just wondered what you thought about his take on the situation."

Sandy said, "Is it all that complicated? I don't think so. Basically, what we're going to do is a simple smash-and-grab. The only difference is, we're on the fourteenth floor of a downtown office building, instead of in a suburban mall, with lots of escape routes. So we have to take out the phones, handcuff the victims to a radiator or toilet, make sure they stay put until we're out of the building. But that's the only difference, the five minutes or so we need to scoot."

"What about the elevator? Harve said there'd be a surveillance camera."

"He's right, there will be a camera. That's why Harvey and I are going to wear baseball caps and sunglasses and fake beards or moustaches."

Jan said, "What worries me is that we didn't even think about cameras. What else did we miss, that could put us in jail? It's driving me crazy."

"You'll be okay."

Jan rolled the cold beer can across her forehead. She said, "I hope so." She wanted to ask Sandy how he felt about Harvey insisting that she drive, so he could be there in case Sandy needed some muscle. She had expected Sandy to veto the idea, but he'd surprised her by jumping at the idea. His enthusiasm confused her. She could understand it if he was afraid that she'd fold under pressure, but why wasn't he worried about getting stabbed in the back by his girlfriend's violent, intensely jealous jailbird husband?

Sandy had asked Harvey point-blank if he had a knife or a gun. Harvey looked him in the eye and said no, he didn't have a weapon of any kind, except his razor-sharp wit. Making a joke of something that wasn't the least bit funny.

Jan was in love with Sandy. But despite her own sense of self-preservation, and endless love and concern for Tyler, she still loved Harvey. Was it possible to love two men at once, especially when they were so different? It was sad and bewildering, but the answer was yes.

She found herself saying, "Harvey can't be trusted. You know that, don't you?"

Sandy nodded. She studied his face, but it was impossible to say what he was thinking. He drank some Malpin's, and said, "If you feel that way about your husband, maybe we should call it off."

"What? The robbery?"

He smiled. "Yeah, the robbery. What did you think I meant, you and me?"

Jan said, "I'm flat broke, Sandy. The tattoo parlour didn't work for me. I sunk every dime I owned into it, and it was the biggest mistake of my life." She thought a moment and then gave him a wan smile and said, "No, that's wrong. That honour belongs to Harvey. Call it my second-biggest mistake."

Third, thought Sandy, because by the time he'd done with her, Harvey would have been relegated to a distant second place and the failure of her tattoo business would be, comparatively speaking, a deliriously happy memory. He said, "You could sell your equipment. It must be worth a few grand."

"I owe two months' rent. Sixteen hundred and fifty dollars. Mr. Chong's a nice enough guy, but he's going to grab everything, if he hasn't already done it."

"We could drive down there, have a look. Throw everything into the back of the truck, if it's still there. You could sell it, or start over, whatever you want."

"I'd have to sell it," said Jan. "I don't know what it's worth, second-hand. Not a lot, probably."

Sandy said, "If you want, I could lend you two, or maybe even three, thousand. It'd be a loan, but you could pay me back whenever you wanted, no interest and no big rush."

"How could I pay you back, Sandy?"

"Get a job. Don't ask me where. In a gallery, someplace like that, where you could put your artistic skills to use."

"In retail sales?"

"You've got to start somewhere. That's what everybody else does, right? Tyler will be back in school in a couple more weeks. That'll make things easier. Afterwards, he could go to after-school care for a couple of hours. It wouldn't be that bad. In a couple of years, he'd be old enough to take care of himself after school, if he had to."

Jan pictured herself working eight hours a day at some rotten minimum-wage job, coming home so tired she could hardly stand up straight. Cooking dinner, helping Tyler with his homework, catching up on the housework, watching a little TV, climbing into a cold and lonely bed. Waking up too early and starting all over again. Squeezing every dollar, always worrying, never having enough. She remembered how awful it had been before Matt Singh took care of her. Buying used clothing and day-old bread, fighting with bus drivers over expired transfers . . . What kind of life was that?

Sandy touched her arm, startling her. He said, "I'm in if you are. But I've got a bad feeling about Harvey. If you want to call it off, that'll be fine with me. Will you at least think about it?"

Jan nodded, not putting much into it. Sandy drained the Malpin's and twisted the empty can into a figure-eight. Jan had a feeling that the light they shared had somehow faded, and was about to die.

the acting game

Harvey, during the lengthy period of enforced idleness bestowed upon him by this proud nation's boundlessly generous judicial system, rigorously catalogued all six of his mindsets, from suicidally depressed to catatonic-gloomy. Now he could add a seventh level to his personal hell – his *post-ashtray mood.*

He'd seen the blow coming too late to duck. Jan had popped him so hard his whole world had vibrated like a tuning fork. His first thought, when he'd finally started thinking again, was that she must have filled in her social calendar with a whole bunch of kung fu classes. He'd lain there on the rug, rendered miserable and semi-conscious by the sudden dreadful knowledge that his wife now had a right hook as lethal as her tongue. Then, as his vision cleared, he saw the shiny-sharp bits and pieces of the humble weapon that had laid him low.

He knew Jan was on a tight budget. He hoped she wasn't trying to glue the ashtray back together, because he'd walked away with a pushpin-sized chunk stuck in his scalp. His questing fingers had found the intrusive lump of embedded glass as he'd taken the elevator down to ground level. The glass was slippery with blood, but he got a good grip on it with his index finger and opposable thumb, and kind of pry-wiggled it out. The instant he plucked the piece of glass from his scalp, a waterfall of blood poured from the wound, and ran in a relatively wide stream down his relatively narrow forehead, blinding him.

He plugged the gaping wound with his little finger, and wiped most of the gore from his face with his T-shirt. He looked like hell, but every cloud has a silver lining. He'd almost made it to the Firebird when an elderly woman driving her electric scooter down the sidewalk registered his blood-spattered appearance, and fainted dead away. Her gout-swollen foot came down on the scooter's accelerator pedal. The scooter accelerated to its top speed of 10 KPH. It veered sideways, crashed into a telephone pole, rebounded onto the boulevard, and keeled over on its side, throwing the woman onto the grass.

Harvey crouched down beside her. "You okay?"

She nodded. A pair of tinted glasses lay on the grass beside her. He picked them up and put them on her. She batted her eyes at him.

Harvey looked around. No witnesses, except for a dozen starlings balanced on a wire. He said, "You should've worn a seatbelt."

The woman said, "Don't hurt me."

He smiled and said, "Why would I? Did you do something bad?" He eased her watch off her flabby wrist, wriggled her gold wedding band and diamond engagement ring off her finger, plucked a matching pair of diamond earrings off her ears, grabbed her purse, and continued on his way.

The Firebird was where he'd parked it. He drove a couple of blocks and then pulled over and emptied the purse onto the car's wide bench seat. It was a very large purse, but there wasn't much in it: a bunch of used birthday cards and a plastic bottle of evil-tasting pills, a B.C. Government health card, monthly transit pass, a badly worn pair of lightweight gardening gloves, seven five-dollar bills, a lottery ticket, roll of quarters, a small photo album stuffed full of snapshots of really ugly kids. His wound had almost stopped bleeding. It seemed he was going to live. He shoved the money and lottery ticket and health card and pills deep into his jeans pocket, and tossed everything else out the window.

He drove across the Burrard Street Bridge, into the sometimes shabby, always excessively hip neighbourhood of Kitsilano, and cruised slowly around until he finally stumbled across a spot where he could safely park the Firebird without having to worry about getting towed. He got out of the car, and started walking down the street in the direction he happened to be facing – downhill, towards the harbour. The sun had sunk hours ago, and in the spaces between the streetlights, it was as dark as dark could be.

He walked past a mix of quaint old shingled houses and ugly three-storey stucco apartment buildings completely lacking in character or charm. A pretty girl leaning against her balcony railing watched him stroll by. He tilted an imaginary hat to her, but she ignored him. He was tempted to kick down her door and teach her that it was rude to ignore people, because it made them feel small, and enraged. But he had work to do, so he kept walking. The angle of descent steepened, so his toes pushed into his boots. Sandy was another sonofabitch who had it coming. The difference between Sandy and the girl on the balcony was that Sandy was actually going to get it. Right between the eyes, when he least expected it.

Jan had told him to steal a van. The idea of boosting a Windstar or a Previa or an Econoline or a CRV or any of a thousand other boxy pieces of underpowered crap was about as appealing as yogurt. His philosophy had always been that, if you were gonna steal a car, you might as well steal one you'd enjoy driving.

Harvey thought a Corvette would be the perfect getaway car for the two of them, himself and Jan. Too bad Sandy wasn't quite dumb enough not to figure things out, if Harvey pulled up in a two-seater. Ditto for Jan. Harvey planned to make it easy on her by pumping lover boy full of bullets before she realized what he was up to. As soon as Sandy was gone, Jan would start forgetting about him. Harvey had always admired her ability to see things as they were, unadorned by regrets or might-have-beens.

The hill got a little steeper and then levelled out. He came to an intersection with a concrete "calming" circle in the middle. The circle had been filled with earth and then planted with a variety of small shrubs and colourful long-stemmed flowers. He walked over to the ersatz garden and snatched up a handful of bright orange flowers and then remembered he wouldn't be seeing Jan until the morning. By then the flowers would be dead. He tossed the flowers in the gutter and kept walking. Maybe stealing a van wasn't such a bad idea after all. Vans were anonymous and had bulk. In movies, the bad guys always had big magnetic advertising strips they could lay down on the body of the van and then rip off as soon as the robbery had been successfully accomplished. Like, "Leo's Plumbing," and things like that. Harvey had always wondered where they got the magnetic strips. Was there a special place crooks went to, when they needed that kind of thing? If not, why didn't the cops check out the local sign-making businesses, find out who had ordered the Leo's Plumbing sign, track the guy down and shoot his ass to pieces, or arrest him and make him rat out his buddies?

Harvey walked in a zigzag pattern, up one block and along the next and then up another block, and so on. Pretty soon he'd zagged himself all the way up to Broadway. He started walking back down

the hill again, towards the dark, maddeningly indistinct shape
of the mountains. It was a weeknight, and the streets were full of
parked cars. He strolled past a dark green Honda Odyssey. The
vehicle had tinted side and rear windows, but he could easily see
in through the windshield. There was plenty of room in there for a
happily reunited married couple and a ton of diamonds. Probably,
though, he should go after something a little heftier. Maybe a GMC
Savana or a Dodge Ram Wagon. Better yet, a full-size cargo van
like a Chevy Express or a Ford Econoline. Try to find one with a
big V-8 motor, something that would make Jan happy.

He turned down an alley. A dog barked at him. Its claws scrabbled on a fence. The dog was still barking when he reached the
end of the block. He looked both ways, then crossed the street and
continued walking down the alley. There were no houses here,
nothing but bland three-storey apartment blocks that dated from
the uninspired fifties and sixties. The buildings had open, ground-
level parking at the rear. If you were a thief, the world was just one
great auto mall. Harvey paused to admire a hellfire-red '62 Valiant
Signet convertible with collector plates. The Signet's top was down.
In the incidental light from the building, the white Naugahyde had
a ghostly glow. Harvey wandered into the parking lot for a better
view. A bubbly wave of excitement swept through him the way it
always did when he was about to acquire something of value and
make it, however briefly, his own.

Against all odds, the Signet's keys dangled in the ignition.
Harvey's hand closed on the driver's-side door handle. A fat man
in a white three-piece suit stepped out of the shadows. The hot
end of a cigar glowed red. He wiped his hands on a rag and said,
"Get your hand off my chrome."

Harvey said, "Sorry."

"Didn't your mother teach you that you shouldn't touch stuff
that doesn't belong to you?"

"My mother died when I was two years old," said Harvey. "She
was in a marked crosswalk when she was run over by a car just
like this one."

The guy was in his sixties, a chunky six-footer. He took off his suit jacket and slung it across the Signet's backseat. He wore a short-sleeved shirt. His arms were huge, the muscles bulging and rippling as he folded his arms across his chest. His snow-white handlebar moustache was a yard wide, the ends waxed and twisted into lethally sharp points. He had baby-blue eyes Santa would have died for. Harvey said, "It's a beautiful car."

The guy yanked the cigar out of his mouth and pointed it at Harvey as if it were a weapon. "Beat it."

Harvey said, "Excuse me?"

"You live around here?"

"Uh . . ."

"Lemme see some I.D."

Harvey backed away from the car.

"I ever see you around here again, I'll beat the crap out of you." The Signet's owner flapped the rag. He added, "Or anybody unlucky or stupid enough to look like you, asshole."

Harvey turned and beat it. He wasn't quite running, but it was a near thing. He reached the end of the block and turned left and walked to the end of that block and turned right, and decided that, when the time was right, he'd come back with a tire iron, pound the Signet into scrap.

Harvey continued to roam the neighbourhood. After a while he walked past another pretty girl on a balcony. He stared up at her and she stared back. He was about to say something clever when she picked up a cordless phone and started dialling.

He kept walking. A gleaming black Miata with leather uphol-stery caught his eye. He would have lusted after it, if they weren't so common. A pair of Oakley sunglasses lay on the passenger seat. Harvey scooped them up and stuck them in his shirt pocket without consciously thinking about it.

An overweight, affection-starved marmalade cat meowed as it eased out from under a boxwood hedge. The cat trotted towards Harvey on an interception course. Harvey got set to punt the animal over the moon. As he drew back his foot, the cat caught a whiff of his karma, and turned and ducked back beneath the hedge.

Harvey kept on walking, down one street and up the next. Hard work on a hot summer's night. Sweat ran into his eyes and made his shirt hang heavy on him. His sweat-soaked underpants clutched at his balls. Beads of sweat dribbled from his heavy black eyebrows and down into his eyes, sparkling like diamonds and blurring his vision. It had been a long day. He was tired, and he wanted a beer. But Jan was counting on him to find a getaway vehicle, and he wasn't going to let her down.

Harvey walked for what seemed like hours, until his legs turned to jelly. He stumbled across an English-style neighbourhood pub and went in. The place was about to close, but the bartender drew him a couple of pints after Harvey promised to knock them back in a hurry, and get the hell out. Harvey drank his two allotted pints and got up and walked away. He wearily turned the corner and there she was, the getaway car of his dreams.

The car, a glossy black PT Cruiser with dark-tinted windows and polished alloy wheels, was idling at the curb in front of a grocery store, the radio playing softly. Some kind of piano music, a light jazz that wormed into Harvey, made him snap his fingers and dance across the street. He was twenty or thirty feet away from the Cruiser when the driver pushed open her door and got out of the car and eased the door shut behind her. She was in her mid-thirties, but Harvey forgave her because she had a knockout figure despite her age. Her window was down. The music meant she'd left the engine running. He could hardly believe his luck.

The sidewalk in front of the store was crowded with potted and cut flowers. Harvey had expected the PT's owner to walk straight inside. When she stopped to smell the roses, he was forced to do some serious dawdling. He lit a cigarette and waited impatiently as she lingered over bunches of various kinds of flowers he couldn't name if his life depended on it. He found himself thinking about the last time he had bought Jan flowers. It was almost five years ago, the day his dumb-ass lawyer told him his appeal had been dismissed.

Jan said, "What does that mean, exactly?"

"It means I'm going straight to the slammer," said Harvey. As he'd spoken the words, his mind had spun like a whirligig in a force-ten hurricane. The happy-face truth was that he could go almost anywhere he wanted to, if he didn't need a passport to get there. He guessed that meant he was free to travel from sea to shining sea, and that was about it. Still, the freedom to take off for Halifax or whatever was marginally better than no freedom at all.

All that stopped him was Jan and Tyler. No, be honest. Just Jan. She'd put up his bail money. If he walked, she'd lose every penny, and wouldn't be waiting for him when he got out. He knew he wouldn't be able to do six months without knowing Jan was out there, waiting for him.

The PT owner plucked a bunch of white flowers out of a green plastic bucket. She held the dripping flowers well away from her body as she scrutinized them, looking for bugs, or defects, or whatever else was on her mind. The flowers must have passed inspection. Still holding them well away from her cute little body, dipping into her purse with her free hand, she turned and walked briskly into the store.

Harvey strolled over to the PT Cruiser. There were lots of people around, but nobody paid any attention to him. He opened the car door and slid behind the wheel and shut the door. The key was in the ignition. The engine was running. He pushed back the seat to give himself more leg room, adjusted the side and rearview mirrors, released the emergency brake, and put the car in gear.

The woman came out of the flower shop, moving so fast she might have robbed the joint. She checked for traffic and trotted across the street. Harvey powered down her window just as she got to the car. He grabbed the flowers out of her hand and hit the gas, made a hard right at the corner, and was gone.

18

reconciliation

Parker made Annie a breakfast of whole-wheat toast, a soft-boiled egg, and tea. She sat on the edge of the bed and had a cup of tea herself, while Annie ate her meal, and fed Hadrian bits of toast as he played with his favourite toy, a small yellow rubber duck with a bright orange bill. The duck, when squeezed, either barked or oinked or meowed or whinnied. The various sounds it made were in no particular sequence, and therefore unpredictable. Hadrian knew that ducks were supposed to quack. He found the toy end-lessly hilarious. Parker had deliberately "lost" the toy several times. Hadrian always made such a fuss about it that she'd been forced, in the interest of her own sanity, to "find" it again.

She'd brought the teapot upstairs, and poured herself and Annie another cup. In light, non-interrogative tones, she said, "When did you get in last night?"

"A little past two."

"Pretty late. Were the buses still running?"

"The driver told me I caught the last one."

"Lucky you."

Annie nodded. Parker sipped her tea. The morning had started out overcast, but a strong, gusting westerly had cleared the sky and now the sun was shining, brightening Annie's room, even though Parker hadn't drawn the curtains.

Parker said, "So, where were you?"

"Last night?"

Parker smiled.

Annie said, "Paige and I went to a poetry reading, met some people, and went back to their place and just kind of kicked around, watched a movie on TV."

"What did you watch?"

"Am I being interrogated?"

Parker laughed. "Yes, I suppose you are." When Annie didn't say anything, she added, "You haven't seemed yourself lately."

"I haven't?" Annie was flustered. She drank some tea. "You mean, because I'm thinking about not going back to school?"

"Not just that." Parker didn't know how to broach the subject. She'd spent hours thinking about it. No matter how she phrased the question, it always seemed blunt as a sledgehammer. She stood up, and went over to the window.

Annie said, "Leave the curtains, okay?"

"Your friend Paige," said Parker. "Is she gay?"

Annie jerked backwards as if Parker had taken a swing at her. Milky tea slopped over the rim of her mug and splashed onto the sheets. She blushed fiery red. Autumn in Vermont, thought Parker.

Annie said, "That's none of your business!"

Parker said, "You're right, I suppose. But why are you being so defensive? You wouldn't say that if Paige was interested in men, would you?"

Annie put the tea mug down on the tray. She lay back and shut her eyes and rolled over on her side so her back was to Parker.

Parker said, "That's mature."

Annie violently sat bolt upright. Tea slopped out of the mug onto the tray. She said, "Yes, Paige is gay. She's a flaming lesbo. So what? Who cares? Are you happy now?"

"I'm happy if you're happy," said Parker.

"Bullshit!"

"No, it's true. I've only met Paige a few times, but it seems to me that she's a young lady with a very forceful personality. It occurred to me that it was possible that Paige wanted the kind of relationship you weren't certain you were prepared to offer." When Annie didn't react, Parker decided to continue. "Sometimes, to find out who we are, we need to experiment a little. There's nothing wrong with that, but it's hard to make a rational, or true, decision when you're caught up in an emotional whirlwind."

"What's your point?"

"I guess I'm trying to say that sometimes there's a temptation, or pressure, to be far too quick to decide who we are."

"You think so, do you?"

Parker chose to ignore Annie's challenging tone. She said, "Yes I do. I really do. It starts in school, far sooner than it should, and once the pressure to decide who you are and what you're going to be has started, there's no stopping it. I realize that your sexual orientation is none of my business, Annie. All I want to do is help, if you need help. Would I be happier if you weren't gay? That's a tough question. I don't really know the answer. Speaking selfishly, I want to be a grandparent, one of these days. That's always been very important to me. I'm aware that same-sex parents do have children nowadays, but it doesn't happen all that often. To tell you the truth, I'm not even sure I approve of same-sex parenting. But even if you were heterosexual, that certainly wouldn't guarantee that you'd want to have children, would it?"

Parker moved closer, and gently took Annie's hand in hers. Annie didn't resist. Parker said, "There are very few guarantees in life, but I can tell you with absolute certainty that I love you for *who* you are, not what you are, and I will always love you with all my heart, no matter what. My love for you is boundless and unqualified, just as any parent's love for his or her child should be. You know that, don't you?"

Annie shrugged. Parker put aside her tea and lay down beside Annie. She pulled her close and hugged her tight. Annie's shoulders were thin and bony. Parker realized with a shock that Annie had been wearing loose-fitting clothing for longer than she could remember. She had lost a lot of weight. How much did she weigh?

Parker could feel Annie's ribs through the thin material of her pyjamas. She was stricken with guilt. Annie hardly ever ate at home any more. Parker knew nothing of her diet. Her mind raced. How long had it been since she'd given Annie a hug, or stayed up into the small hours of the morning so Annie could talk about the things that worried or frightened her? Months and months. She couldn't remember the last time. Hadrian had taken over her life, at Annie's expense.

Parker said, "You're very thin. Are you eating properly?"

Annie shrugged.

"How much do you weigh?" said Parker.

"I dunno."

"There's a scale in the bathroom. When you shower, I want you to take a moment to weigh yourself. Will you do that for me?"

Another shrug.

Parker said, "Your body's an engine, Annie. It needs fuel, or it can't function. Maybe school seems like too much of a challenge because your energy level is so low."

"It isn't challenging, it's *boring*."

"My mistake," said Parker carefully. "Did you want another cup of tea, before I take the pot downstairs?"

Annie shook her head.

Parker collected the breakfast dishes and put them on the tray. She had pushed Annie far enough, for now.

As she was about to leave the room, Annie said, "I'm worried about Sean."

"Me, too," said Parker.

"I wish he'd phone, once in a while. Has Daddy seen him?"

"Not that I know of," said Parker. "Sean didn't want him interfering. He told your father to stay away from him, let him find his own way."

Annie rolled over on her back. She flung her arm across her face so Parker couldn't see her eyes. She said, "They're both so stubborn."

"Yes, they are. Try not to worry about Sean. When you think about him, think positive thoughts."

"Is that what you do?"

"Always."

"Does it help?"

"It helps me," said Parker.

Annie managed a tight little smile. It wasn't much, but it was a start.

towing the line

Bob Goldman had been out of work for eight long months, and he was pissed. When he went out on his balcony to smoke his eleventh cigarette of the morning, and saw the Firebird parked in the loading zone in front of his building, he experienced a tsunami of rage. It was downright scary, how easily people got confused. They put a few hundred down on a hot car, and figured they were pretty hot themselves. There was probably a technical name for it – possession transference or something like that. Bob lit up, and carefully deposited the paper match in the tuna can that now served as an ashtray. He had learned the hard way that possession was a two-way street. You lost your job through no fault of your own but due entirely to an economic slowdown manipulated by those Heartless Big Business Bastards, and then you lost your Camry that you'd religiously made payments on for three long years, you woke up and rolled out of bed and the Camry was gone, *repossessed* in the dead of night by some prick who lacked the imagination or wits to earn an honest living.

Bob had been telling the building's brain-dead manager all summer long that branches from the Japanese plum on the boulevard hid the loading-zone sign from view. He'd bitterly complained that morons parked in the zone at all hours of the day and night. Slammed their doors, swore like troopers, laughed their stupid heads off. Woke Bob and his wife, Edith, in the dead of the night. Was that fair? Well then, why didn't he get off his fat ass and trim the goddamn tree?

Bob took another long pull on his cigarette. Behind him, Edith pulled the glass slider open, and angrily banged it shut. Fucking Edith, always on his back. If he could kick the habit, wouldn't he have done it by now? Okay, so cigarettes cost money. Was that his fault? Last week she'd threatened to cancel the cable, swore on her parakeet's grave that they couldn't afford tobacco *and* TV. Bullshit. She hated seeing him enjoy himself, was all. Every minute he spent in front of the TV watching football or hockey hurt her like a hot needle stuck up her nose. He flicked ash at the tin can. He could feel her eyes crawling all over him, knew that if he spun around real quick, he'd catch her shooting him the evil eye.

Edith worked the four-to-twelve shift at a Texaco halfway across town. She took the bus. Never left the apartment a minute sooner or later than three-fifteen. Every day, Bob found it a little harder to wait for her departure time to arrive. Her two days off a week were pure hell. She'd been angling to get him a part-time job at the station, but so far, her boss had resisted all her efforts. Thank any deity you cared to name.

Bob tried to remember if the Firebird had been parked in the loading zone when he'd stepped outside for his tenth cigarette. His mind was a blank. Ninth? Eighth? His brain trampled a field of butts. Fucking car could have been there since breakfast, for all he knew. Man, he was slipping. Losing his edge. Stuff was getting past him that he'd have fielded with his eyes shut, not so long ago. He flicked ash at the tin can, and decided he'd finish his smoke and then go inside and drop a dime on the moron. Call Buster's

Towing, brew himself a cup of instant and go back outside and plunk himself down in his front-row seat. Have a few yuks watching that smart-ass Firebird get towed straight to hell.

food for thought

Oikawa and Willows spent most of the morning chasing phantom witnesses. At eleven, they drove back to 312 Main to bring Homer Bradley up to speed.

Bradley had a piece of news of his own. He said, "The Crime Scene Unit vacuumed quite a few dog hairs out of Colin McDonald's rug. Anybody at the scene mention a dog?"

Willows and Oikawa exchanged a glance. Willows said, "Not to me."

"Me, either," said Oikawa. "Nobody in the building said anything about a dog to either one of us."

"Are dogs allowed in the building?"

"Small dogs," said Willows. "But McDonald wasn't a pet-lover."

Bradley shrugged. "Well, keep on it."

Afterwards, Oikawa fast-talked Willows into eating at Susie's Won-Ton Surprise, a hole-in-the wall joint tucked into a dent on the east side of Chinatown. Willows had followed Oikawa through a narrow doorway hung with a glass bead curtain. Susie's was a single room about twenty feet long and six feet wide. Five small tables for two were close-set against each of the long walls. The cash register was at the back. Another glass bead curtain separated the dining area from the kitchen. There were no windows and the light level was nightclub-low. Music came from speakers mounted high on the walls. A Chinese woman in a tight black dress led Oikawa and Willows to a table, and handed them menus.

Oikawa said, "Want a beer?"

Willows shrugged.

"Tsing Tao," said the woman.

Oikawa nodded. He said, "Nice and cold, eh?"

The woman nodded tersely, and turned and strode briskly towards the kitchen. Willows glanced casually around the restaurant. The only other customers were two rail-thin Chinese men in their early twenties. Both men wore loose-fitting matte-black suits, white dress shirts, no ties, and identical pairs of black dress shoes, and both had shoulder-length hair shot through with streaks of white. The man facing Willows sensed that he was being watched. He glanced up, met Willows' eye, and continued to solemnly shovel noodles into his mouth. Still staring at Willows, he chewed noisily, allowing his mouth to hang open.

Oikawa said, "Red Triangle. They own the place."

"No kidding." Willows was interested. The Red Triangle was the largest and most violent of the city's numerous Chinese mobs. Most of their money came from marijuana "grow-ops" in rented houses. The gang had suffered serious losses a few years earlier, during a deadly turf war. Since then, it had kept a low, but profitable, profile.

Oikawa said, "For a while, they used the joint to launder cash. That stopped about a year ago. I don't know why the place is still open."

"How's the food?"

Oikawa shrugged. He said, "I have no idea."

A girl of about twelve brought their beers and a bottle opener to the table. She wiped the tops of the bottles with a clean white towel, and then expertly uncapped the beers. Willows briefly considered asking her for a glass, but decided not to bother. He wasn't sure why. Maybe because she was so young she shouldn't have been working at all. Oikawa drained half his beer. He sighed happily, and leaned back in his chair.

Willows drank some of his beer. Not much, because he wanted it to last. The beer was ice-cold, and very good. The artwork on the label was a cut above average, too. He took another sip. The glass bottle was slippery with condensation. He was enjoying himself. There was no drinking on duty when he was with Parker. Maybe Oikawa wasn't so bad after all.

The ambient light level soared as the restaurant's door was pushed open. Three more Chinese men, all of them in their early twenties, entered the restaurant. Like the other men, they wore black suits and had long hair shot through with streaks of white. The one in the lead stopped dead in his tracks when he saw Oikawa and Willows. His companions bumped into him, and each other. It should have been funny, but wasn't. One of the men yelled something at the two men at the table. Then all three newcomers turned and hurriedly left the restaurant.

Oikawa said, "Kind of hard on business, aren't we?"

"Maybe we're sitting at their favourite table."

Oikawa drained his beer. Willows knew that, if he tried to drink his beer that fast, he'd suffer from terminal brain freeze. Oikawa said, "We aren't going to find out who murdered Colin McDonald, are we?"

"What makes you say that?"

Oikawa said, "Until I was assigned this case, I wouldn't have believed it was statistically possible for anyone to be hated by every single person he ever met in his whole life. Jeez, Jack, it's like he was some kind of deadly virus. Nobody's going to do the right thing and confess that they murdered him, but everybody in the world happily admits they wanted to do it."

The girl who'd served them brought two more bottles of Tsing Tao to the table. She wiped the bottles clean, and uncapped them.

Oikawa said, "Try to be a little quicker next time. Pay attention, 'kay? It's not like you're swamped with customers."

The girl picked up Oikawa's empty. She saw that Willows hadn't finished his beer, gave him a mildly disapproving look, and turned and walked slowly back to the kitchen.

Willows said, "Maybe we'll get lucky."

Oikawa tapped his forehead. He glumly said, "Whoever killed McDonald's going to get away with it. I can feel it in my bones."

Willows tried to think of a snappy rejoinder. His brain failed him. Oikawa stared glumly down at the restaurant's linoleum floor. His eyes were red from lack of sleep, and his skin had an

unhealthy yellowish tinge. Willows, uncharacteristically, wondered how *he* looked. The way he felt, tired and hungry and
borderline cranky, he probably didn't look a whole hell of a lot
better than Oikawa, and might even look a hell of a lot worse.

Oikawa said, "What're you thinking, Jack?"

"That I'm starting to get old." Willows smiled. "I remember
when I first got my gold badge, I could work right around the
clock, no problem. Now, the only thing I do in a hurry is get tired."

Oikawa mimed playing the world's smallest violin.

Willows said, "I'm not asking for sympathy, just stating a fact.
We've interviewed so many suspects, I can't keep track of their
names. That retired guy, had the butcher shop, Walter . . ." Willows
mimed snapping his fingers.

"Krawnkite," said Oikawa. "Walter Krawnkite. Like the famous
TV personality, but spelled wrong. How could you forget a name
like that?"

"It keeps getting easier."

Oikawa said, "You saw the look on Walt's face when he talked
about McDonald. He *hated* the guy. When he told us he wished
he'd had a chance to kill him, *eviscerate* him, he meant every word."

Willows took another sip of his beer.

Oikawa finished his second bottle. He glanced vaguely around.
"By the way, how's Sean coming along?"

"Good, as far as I know."

"What's that mean? When was the last time you saw him?"

"Months ago. Early June." Willows looked over at the two men.
Neither was paying any attention to him. He said, "Sean's keeping
his distance. He wants to make it on his own. Who am I to argue?"

"Nobody," said Oikawa.

"You got that right."

Oikawa said, "I was scared witless, every single minute I worked
undercover. Always watching your ass, piling one lie on top of
another, trying to keep track of it all. Man, I hated it." Oikawa
suddenly rapped his knuckles on the table, startling Willows. The
two gangsters glanced up uninterestedly, then went back to their

meal. A few moments later the young girl hurried towards them with two more bottles of beer. She cleaned and carefully uncapped each bottle, and walked away without a word.

Oikawa drank some beer. Not much, just a little.

Willows' son, Sean, had surprised everyone who knew him by deciding to join the VPD. Like his father before him, he had accepted an undercover assignment as soon as he'd graduated from the Academy. Willows was proud of his son. That didn't stop him from worrying.

Most rookies did some undercover work. If they were good at it, their talents were fully exploited. Oikawa's assignment had lasted two months, and then he'd gone back to patrol division. Willows had worked undercover for eighteen long months. His ambition had been to bust Jake Cappalletti, the city's notorious drugs and prostitution kingpin. He hadn't succeeded, but his evidence had put a serious dent in Jake's chain-of-command, and cost him millions in seized cocaine and heroin shipments.

Willows remembered the undercover work as life on the edge, his glory days. The risk had multiplied as he'd insinuated his way more and more deeply into Jake's distribution system. It was one thing to bust street-level dealers; another thing entirely to gather evidence on the wholesalers, guys who moved large quantities of drugs and even larger amounts of cash. Heavyweight guys who had to cut a deal with the prosecutor's office, or resign themselves to spending the far side of forever in a maximum-security institution. Willows had worked on that level, salting away evidence that would have got him killed, if anybody had even suspected he was a cop. Knowing that his first mistake could be his last had exhilarated him. He'd never felt so full of the sweet juices of life.

Willows believed his early experience as an undercover cop explained his enduring love for the job, and all those countless hours and days and months he'd spent on the street when he should have been with his growing family. Maybe it even explained why his first wife, Sheila, finally packed her bags and walked out on him.

Explained, yes. Excused, no.

Oikawa finished his third beer. Willows was halfway through his second. He felt bloated, and sleepy. Oikawa pointed at Willows' untouched bottle. "You going to drink that?"

"No, I've had enough."

Oikawa stood up. "Might as well get moving, eh?"

"What about the food?"

"You order anything?"

"No, but . . ."

"You don't want to *eat* here," said Oikawa. "I mean, think about it. We're cops, Jack. Who knows what kind of crap they'd put in our food. Rat poison, probably."

Willows reached for his wallet.

Oikawa was a notorious tightwad. He surprised Willows when he said, "Your money's no good here, Jack."

"Well, thanks."

Oikawa took out his own wallet, and shuffled through a thin wad of bills.

Willows said, "Why don't you let me take care of the tip."

"No way."

Willows put his wallet back in his pocket. He turned towards the door, as Oikawa plucked bills from his wallet.

The girl who'd served the beer watched Oikawa from behind the cash register. Her dark eyes were unreadable. She ducked her head when he blew her a sardonic kiss. One of the Red Triangle gangsters said something in a sharp voice. Oikawa had no idea what he'd said but recognized an uncomplimentary tone when he heard it. He turned towards the men and cupped his balls, and sneered.

Willows loitered by the open door. Oikawa walked slowly towards him, as if he were reluctant to leave. He staggered and spread his arms wide for balance. Willows realized that his partner was drunk.

The gangsters shouted something at him, or Oikawa. Both men were on their feet, faces twisted in anger. Willows wondered if they were armed. He let the door swing shut and took a few steps towards them. "What's the problem."

"You no pay! Crooked cops!"

"What're you talking about?"

"You friend never pay! Now you don't pay! Crooked cops!"

Willows detoured towards their table. He saw the bills. A fistful of money. The two men drifted towards him. Where was Oikawa? The cash was bogus – blue and red Canadian Tire "money" in five- and ten-cent denominations. Fifty cents' worth, at most. Willows picked up a menu. The Tsing Tao was three ninety-five a bottle. He dropped a ten and a twenty on the table, and walked out.

star baby

Sandy showed up at two o'clock, just like he'd promised he would. He was the most punctual person Jan had ever known. She and Tyler were waiting for him, Tyler bouncing up and down with excitement, because Sandy had promised he could sit behind the wheel, turn the key and start the truck.

As they walked across the street, Jan said, "I'm not sure we should be doing this."

Sandy said, "Have you ever started a truck before, Tyler?"

"Nope."

"It's easy. You're going to do just fine."

Sandy opened the passenger-side door for Jan, and then he and Tyler walked around to the driver's-side door. Sandy opened the door and Tyler climbed up behind the wheel. Sandy handed him the keys.

Jan said, "Shouldn't he be sitting on your lap? What if . . ."

"Which key is it?" said Tyler.

"That one."

Tyler slid the key into the ignition. He tried to turn the key the wrong way, but figured out his mistake before Sandy or Jan could say anything. The starter motor coughed and then the engine caught. There was a shrill whine.

In a calm voice Sandy said, "You can let go of the key now."

Tyler let go of the key. The whining stopped. He said, "How do I make it go fast?"

"Put it in gear."

"Move this thing?"

"Yeah, but there's a safety feature that stops you from changing gears without pressing your foot down on the brake pedal."

"Which is the brake pedal?"

"That one."

Tyler stretched his legs as far as he could. He said, "I can't reach."

Sandy laughed. He tousled Tyler's hair and said, "That's probably a good thing, because I wouldn't want you to drive off and leave me standing here in a cloud of dust."

"I wouldn't do that."

"Not on purpose, maybe. Shove over."

"You said I could honk the horn."

"That's for later," said Sandy. "After we stop for ice cream."

Tyler moved over. Jan fastened his seatbelt. Sandy got into the truck and put it in gear and off they went.

Sandy's cautious driving was starting to get to her. He was definitely and absolutely the most careful driver Jan had ever known. He never drove a single kilometre over the speed limit, and didn't seem to get the least bit irritated when other drivers cut him off or yelled at him or gave him the finger. A ride with Sandy was like a private driving lesson. He anticipated the traffic lights, signalled well in advance of a turn, and never seemed to get caught by surprise when another driver did something stupid or just plain suicidal. Which happened a lot, in Vancouver. He knew about all sorts of traffic laws Jan had never even heard of, like that the city's speed limit in lanes and alleys was 20 kilometres an hour. Jeez, garbage trucks went faster than that. But not Sandy. It was kind of weird, given the overall careless go-to-hell personality he cultivated.

Funny, how you could have a relationship with a person, go to bed with them and everything, but there were still lots of things you couldn't talk about. Or maybe that was just her . . .

"Jan?"

Sandy turned off the engine. They were parked in the small gravel lot behind the tattoo parlour. Sandy was staring at her, a quizzical look in his eyes. He said, "All set?"

"Yeah, sure." Jan helped Tyler with his safety belt. She pushed open her door, and jumped lightly down from the truck, and fumbled in her jeans pocket for her keys. Sandy lowered the truck's tailgate. Jan unlocked the back door. She took Tyler's hand and the two of them went inside. A previous tenant had painted the windows midnight-blue, then scratched dozens of tiny star shapes into the paint. Jan had never found the time or energy to scrape the paint off the glass, and anyway, it was a neat effect, especially at night. She flicked the light switch. Her studio was exactly as she had left it. Sandy pushed through the door, awkwardly carrying half a dozen cardboard boxes they'd picked up at a nearby liquor store. Jan was suddenly terribly depressed. It hadn't been much of a business, but it had been all hers. It went against the grain to give it up.

She said, "This really sucks."

Sandy nodded. He said, "It'd suck a lot worse if your landlord grabbed all this stuff, and you had to buy it back at auction."

"Like I could afford to do that."

"Well then, there you go."

Sandy and Jan warily eyed each other. Harvey had failed to check in to confirm he'd stolen a getaway vehicle. The robbery was less than twenty-four hours away, and they were both feeling a little tense.

Tyler said, "What am I supposed to do?"

"Help your mom, if she needs help. In the meantime . . ." Sandy reached into one of the cardboard boxes. He handed Tyler a small container of chocolate milk, and a stack of comic books.

"Wow! Thanks a lot!"

"You're welcome."

Jan said, "You can sit over there, on that bench by the window."

Tyler made himself comfortable. He chose a comic, and started reading.

Jan had a padded bench, for customers who needed to stretch out. She also had a dentist's chair that dated from the twenties. The chair was probably the single most valuable item she owned. It weighed about a million pounds, but could easily be disassembled into manageable parts. Sandy went back outside to get his tool kit from the truck. Jan got busy putting jars of dye in the cardboard boxes, wrapping each jar in a protective half-sheet of newspaper. She was hardly aware of Sandy taking the chair apart.

As Jan worked, star-shaped beams of light from the blue-painted windows flowed randomly and silently across her body. Her mood gradually brightened. Life was change. She had hopes and ambitions, but really she had no idea what her future held. All she knew for sure was that she and Tyler were moving on, in their brief flight through space and time. She manipulated her body so a star-shaped beam of light drifted up her arm and across her chest. She turned slightly, so the star settled on her breast like a celestial nipple. Tyler was absorbed in his comic. She softly called Sandy's name.

He smiled when he saw what she was up to, but there was no spark of lust in his eyes, only sadness.

Jan said, "What is it? What's wrong?"

Sandy took her in his arms. He held her close, but didn't say a word.

19

thumb pie

Granville Street was in flux. The street had once been the city's main artery, in the sense that a lot of hot blood had flowed through it. Movies, nightclubs, restaurants. Back in the sixties, Granville had it all. If you were a hip guy from the suburbs, a rite of passage was hanging your naked butt out the window of your buddy's car as he cruised slowly up Granville on a weekend night, mooning a few thousand pedestrians. Traffic had been chaotic, naturally. The city council of the time had decided in its collective wisdom to close the street to all traffic except buses and taxis and cop cars. It was a brilliant solution – assuming they intended to kill the street. An inexplicable ban on neon signs made a bad situation even worse. The construction of the Eaton's building, with its endlessly bland wall of tiny urinal-white tiles, added to the mess. For the past couple of decades, city politicians had toyed with the brilliant idea of reopening Granville to traffic. For reasons not accessible to the general public, they'd always caved in to the Whining Bus Drivers lobby.

Aldo and Jackie waited at the curb for a bus to roar past and then trotted across the street and into the Eaton's building – now reincarnated as Sears. Aldo held his breath as they passed the area of the store devoted to perfumes and toiletries. Jackie inhaled deeply, and winked at an attractive if somewhat over-primped young woman dressed like a dental assistant, who stood in the aisle offering a deluxe boxed set of perfumes. All down the length of the aisle, similarly dressed women mutely offered other products to the passing shoppers.

Jackie said, "It's like Cairo, in that *Lonely Planet* episode . . .

Aldo missed his brother's witticism, because he was already on the escalator, standing bolt upright as he rose majestically into the department store's upper reaches. He made eye contact, tapped the crystal of his watch and loudly hissed at his brother to hurry up. Jackie glanced around. No one had witnessed the insult to his manhood. Lucky for Aldo. Jackie stepped onto the escalator and was carried effortlessly upwards.

Did Heaven have escalators? No, of course not. What would be the point of a system of public conveyance when everyone had wings and could fly about wherever they chose? Aldo retreated down the escalator steps towards him. Jackie took a few steps upwards.

The cavernous self-serve restaurant was busy but not crowded. The brothers, as was their habit, drifted apart as they browsed the dessert selection. Neither risked the calories. They poured cups of coffee, paid separately, and flowed back together like two complicated amoeba.

Jackie said, "Where's Wilbur?" He glared down at his watch. "He's going to be late any minute now!"

Aldo emptied five packets of sugar into his coffee, stirred briskly, and added two containers of cream.

Jackie took his coffee black. He said, "That's a meal all in itself. You've made a kind of soup." He glanced anxiously around. "Cousin Wilbur's a toad. I've only met him twice, but I disliked him both times."

"Me too," said Aldo. He drank some coffee. "But who else do we know who's willing to sell us an unregistered handgun?"

"Nobody."

"You're worried, aren't you?"

"About what?"

"The robbery, what else? We don't know those people. They don't know us, either. Anything could happen." He pointed at Jackie with his spoon. "You know it could."

"What are you talking about?"

Aldo jerked his head sideways. Jackie turned and looked over his shoulder just as Cousin Wilbur slapped him on the back.

"Aldo!"

"No, I'm Jackie."

"You guys look so much alike! You could be brothers!" Seasonally, Wilbur found low-paid employment as a gnome, or Santa's Little Helper. During the rest of the year he sat around plotting and scheming and thieving, and growing his beard. Jackie and Aldo made room as he grabbed a chair and sat down at the head of the small table. Wilbur lived in Surrey, a distant, semi-rural suburb notorious for its high crime rate. Car theft and simple break-and-enter and drug addiction were the municipality's specialties, but the area wasn't above an annual mass murder or two. Wilbur was a small-time thief with a rap sheet as long as his memory. Demographics-wise, he fitted right in. He snapped his stubby fingers. "Where's the money?"

Jackie handed him a sealed envelope. Wilbur ripped it open and counted the thin wad of twenties. He pushed back his chair and stood up and started to walk away.

Jackie said, "Hey, wait a minute. What about the . . ."

Wilbur shook his head and rolled his eyes in mock-exasperation. He said, "It's in your coat pocket, Jackie. Be careful. It's loaded."

Jackie waited until Wilbur had passed from view, then dipped his hand in his pocket. The gun was hard, and warm. He spread his thumb and index finger. "It's this small."

Aldo swung his chair around so he could sit close to his brother. "Show me."

The gun settled into Jackie's hand like an egg into a nest. It was satisfactorily heavy. He pointed the gun at his brother. "Stick 'em up!"

"Give me that, you fool." Aldo snatched the weapon out of Jackie's hand. The gun was chrome-plated. *Made in China* was stamped into the two-inch barrel. It had a relentlessly lethal quality to it, like a small but deadly snake. Aldo's index finger found its own way inside the trigger guard. He pointed the gun at his brother's foot and said, "Bang!"

"Bang! Bang! Bang!" said Jackie.

"*Ka-pow!*" said Aldo. He put the gun in his pocket.

Jackie grabbed him by the lapels. "Give that back, it's mine!"

easy money

When they'd loaded everything into the bed of the pickup truck, and collected Tyler, Sandy said, "There's a guy I know, owes me a favour. I told him what you've got; he said he'd take it all, give you three grand, sight unseen."

"*Three thousand dollars?*" Jan was not much short of astounded. She'd said, "Whoever this guy is, he must owe you a big one."

"Not really. You interested?"

"Three thousand is more than it's worth."

"Better take it, then."

Tyler said, "Can I beep the horn now?"

"Sure."

Tyler leaned on the horn until Jan told him to please cut it out, he was giving her a headache.

Sandy said, "What do you want to do?"

"Sell."

They drove over the hump of the Granville Street Bridge, Fairview's million windows glittering in the light of the sun. Sandy made a right on Broadway. He drove a couple of blocks past Burrard, made a right turn, and then a quick left, down the alley that gave access to the buildings fronting Broadway. He stopped, and then backed up in a wide circle, until the tailgate was inches from a loading dock marked by a faded sign that said Terminal City

Auctions. Tyler had fallen asleep, lulled by the sound of the truck's engine, and the summer heat. Sandy punched buttons on his cellular, put the phone to his ear. He said, "We're here. Open up."

He folded the cellular and started to get out of the truck. Somebody inside the building pushed open a wide door. A tall man wearing black jeans and a black leather vest over a white T-shirt stepped onto the loading dock. He had curly blond hair and a pale complexion, and wore a lot of silver jewellery. Sandy climbed up on the dock. The two men hugged, and then Sandy turned and pointed at Jan, or the stuff in the back of the truck, Jan wasn't sure which. The man said something that made Sandy smile, and then he turned and disappeared into the building. Sandy walked across the dock to the truck. He lowered the tailgate, and then jumped down to the asphalt and got back into the truck.

Jan lit a cigarette. She rolled down her window and flicked the match out of her life.

Sandy said, "He's going to sell it at auction, probably next Wednesday. He gets more than three grand, the usual commission applies."

"What if he gets less?"

"That's his problem."

Jan said, "His, or yours?"

The truck rocked on its springs. Jan turned and looked behind her. Three men were stripping the truck of her possessions. They weren't particularly large or muscular, but they were very fast. When everything was gone, it was somehow as if it had never existed. Sandy handed her a bulky white envelope.

"What's that?"

"Your money. Count it."

The envelope wasn't sealed. Jan opened it. The bills were all twenties. None of them were crisp and new, and as far as she could tell, there were no sequential serial numbers. She counted the money and came up forty dollars short. Frustrated, she scrunched up a fistful of bills.

Sandy said, "Here, let me count it."

Jan pushed him away with her shoulder. She said, "Forget that."

She counted the bills again, laying out stacks of ten on the dashboard and in her lap. She took her time, and when she was finished, she knew the count was right. She gathered the money together and put it back in the envelope and shoved the envelope deep into her purse.

Sandy said, "Okay, you satisfied?"

"Not really."

He leaned against the truck's door, and draped his arm over the steering wheel. "What's the problem?"

"Three thousand dollars in cash, and no receipt."

"It's a cash business, Jan."

Jan rolled down her window and flicked her cigarette butt into the alley. She glanced at Tyler. "Like hell it is."

Sandy sat up straight. He said, "You got three thousand dollars in your pocket. No need to worry about next month's rent or putting food on the table. That's more than most people have got."

"What's your point?"

"You're young, good-looking. You know how to dress, how to behave. You're well-spoken, and healthy. You think for one second that prison made Harvey a better person? He's going to mess you up, Jan. Me too, if he gets the chance. Forget the robbery. There's no such thing as easy money, any more than there's such a thing as an easy death."

Jan stole a quick look at Tyler. Still sleeping.

Sandy said, "Think a nine-to-five job would be hard? Imagine yourself in prison, wearing an orange jumpsuit every single day of your life for the next five years. Think about Tyler in foster care, going to bed every night trying to figure out why his mother abandoned him."

"I'd never do that. Never." Jan lit another cigarette, pulled smoke into her lungs, pinched the match between her fingers, flicked it out the window. "Tyler's the reason I'm doing this, dammit!" She was so angry she could have hit him. She said, "Three thousand dollars is nothing. *Nothing!*"

Sandy said, "I'll drive you home." He'd spoken so quietly she'd hardly been able to hear him. He put the truck in gear, and backed cautiously into the alley.

Neither of them said a word during the ride back to her apartment. When they got there, Sandy shifted into park but didn't turn off the engine.

Jan said, "I guess you wouldn't come up even if you were invited, which you're not. You going to be here, in the morning?"

"Ten o'clock, sharp."

Jan nodded. The way it was set up, she and Harvey and Sandy would meet at her apartment the following morning, and go over the robbery one last time. The heist was set for eleven forty-five that day. If everything went right, the robbery wouldn't take more than fifteen minutes, tops. They'd finish up at noon, just as tens of thousands of downtown office workers hit the street.

Sandy said, "After that, it's over."

"You mean, between us?"

"That's right." Something lurked in Sandy's eyes that Jan had never seen before. A dark, bitter sadness. He said, "You wake up in the middle of the night, decide retail sales might not be so bad after all, call me on my cellphone."

"Yeah, okay."

"I mean it, Jan. Harvey's a loose cannon. And Aldo and Jackie – what does anybody know about them? Less than nothing."

"So what? What does anybody know about anybody? What do I know about you?" Jan jabbed his chest with her finger. "As far as that goes, what do you know about yourself?"

Sandy looked out the windshield at the heat and glare of the world. After a long moment he said, "Doesn't matter what time it is, you have a change of heart, pick up the phone."

Jan said, "Harvey and I don't need you. We can do the job ourselves."

Jan unbuckled Tyler and half-dragged him, moaning and complaining and blindly clutching at his comics, out of the truck. Sandy watched her and Tyler jaywalk across the road, and cut across her building's parched lawn. Jan yanked open the glass door with its faded gilt lettering. She and her son disappeared into the elevator. Sandy told himself he had done what he could, but he didn't quite believe it. Jan appeared at her living-room window. He gave her a tentative wave. She didn't wave back. Maybe she was looking at him and maybe she wasn't. She reached out and pulled the drapes.

butler did it

Willows' pager chirped. He checked the readout, unclipped his cellphone from his belt holster, speed-dialled the coroner's office, and identified himself to the woman who answered the phone.

"One moment, please." There was no canned music. Was that legal? Willows tried to think of a tune. Christy Kirkpatrick, Willows' all-time favourite pathologist, identified himself.

"Jack, that you?"

"Hi, Christy. How's it going?"

"I took a second look at the Colin McDonald photos. Thought you might be interested in the results."

Willows waited.

Kirkpatrick said, "This is just a preliminary, but it's accurate."

"Let's have it, Christy."

"Colin McDonald was attacked with a sharp-edged weapon, either a heavy knife, or a meat cleaver. But not until *after* he'd died."

Willows was stunned. "You're sure?"

"Jack, please."

"How did he die?"

"A shepherd bit him."

Was Kirkpatrick trying to be funny? The pathologist was in his seventies, long overdue for mandatory retirement. Willows had long ago given up trying to figure out who Kirkpatrick knew or how many strings he had to pull to keep his job.

He said, "What did you say, Christy?"

"A shepherd bit him." Christy chuckled. "A dog, Jack. Somebody's puppy used McDonald for a chew toy. Punctured his spinal cord. The cleaver was used to cover up the wound. Any of your suspects own a pooch?"

Willows' mind raced. Most of the interviews he and Oikawa had conducted had taken place in office environments, but they had visited a few of McDonald's business acquaintances at home. He tried to remember if anyone had owned a dog.

"Jack, you there?"

"You sure it was a German shepherd?"

"Arf!" said Kirkpatrick. When he'd stopped chuckling, he said, "We got DNA from saliva in the wound."

"Okay, Christy. Thanks."

"You're welcome. Say hello to Claire, next time you see her."

What was that supposed to mean? Willows didn't ask.

Oikawa waited until Willows had put away his phone, and then said, "What was that all about?"

"Kirkpatrick says what killed McDonald was a single bite to the spinal column. A dog bit him. A German shepherd."

Oikawa said, "I don't remember anybody who owned a dog. I hate dogs. I don't give a damn how small or cuddly or harmless they are, they scare the crap out of me. If we'd interviewed anybody who owned a German shepherd, I'd still be shaking in my boots."

"I didn't know you had a thing about dogs."

"Well, I do."

Willows nodded, only half-listening. If he gave his suspect list to the city, and asked them to run a cross-check to see who had paid for a dog licence . . .

Oikawa continued to ramble on. "I'm allergic. Have been ever since my early teens."

Willows gave Oikawa his full attention. He said, "What are the symptoms?"

"Watery eyes, itchy skin. If it's really bad, shortness of breath . . ."

"Sneezing fits?"

"Big time," said Oikawa. His eyes widened comically. "Jennifer Orchid."

"You couldn't stop sneezing. By the time we left, you were crying like a baby."

"Yeah, but I didn't see any sign of a dog. A place like that, expensive, but a row-house situation, I doubt pets are allowed. Not large dogs, anyway."

"Shouldn't be too hard to find out."

Oikawa said, "We could check with City Hall, see if she bought a licence. Would the application say what kind of dog she owned?"

"Beats me. Probably not. The city doesn't charge by the kilo. Not yet, anyway. As far as I know, all they'd want to know is if the animal was spayed or neutered."

Oikawa's eyes were bright. The possibility of a breakthrough had energized him. He said, "If she owns a German shepherd, that'll be more than enough to get a warrant."

Willows nodded. He said, "Or we could drop by, ask her if she owns a dog."

Oikawa said, "I read in the paper that people don't *own* dogs any more, because ownership implies inequality."

Willows smiled. He said, "Makes sense to me. Everybody knows dogs and cats and humans are all equals. What would *you* like to do?"

"We take the City Hall route, we might bump into the mayor. We could suck up, score a few points. Maybe get promoted. Or better yet, invited to a party."

"True."

Oikawa smiled. He said, "Let's go see Jennifer."

"The direct approach."

"It's never worked before," said Oikawa, "so it stands to reason it might work now."

20

reconciliation, part II

The bedside telephone rang at twenty minutes past one. Jan picked up on the second ring.

Harvey said, "You awake?"

"I can't get to sleep."

"Nervous about tomorrow?"

Jan leaned over and flicked ash into the jam jar on the night table. She said, "A little. What's your excuse?"

"I'm working late."

"Can't find what you're looking for?"

"I'm talking to her," said Harvey.

Jan said, "Oh, please."

Harvey said, "I got a low-mileage PT Cruiser, the Turbo model, 215 ponies. It's black, with tinted windows."

Jan had no idea what he was talking about. She said, "That's great."

"I switched the plates for it, parked it in a safe place. Thing is, I was wondering if I could leave the Firebird at your place. I noticed there's a parking lot at the back of your building . . ."

Jan said, "I don't know, Harve . . ."

"It'd only be until tomorrow afternoon." Harvey hadn't meant to whine. He said, "I don't want to park it on the street, 'cause it's a classic, and I don't want it to get ripped off, or vandalized."

Jan said, "Who do you think you're kidding?" But at the same time, her mind fizzled and sparked at the thought of taking him into her bed. Probably it was true that you couldn't teach an old dog new tricks, but did that matter, when the old dog already knew more than enough tricks to get by?

Harvey said, "I could drop by in a few minutes, if that would be okay."

"You happen to be in the neighbourhood, do you?"

In a comically seductive voice Harvey said, "My heart's never strayed from home, baby. No matter how far from home I've been."

Jan said, "Okay, go ahead. Park the car wherever you want."

"I'll be up in a few minutes."

"No, don't do that."

"I gotta give you the keys."

Jan didn't say anything.

Harvey said, "Be right there."

Outside, a car horn beeped twice. Jan didn't bother to look out. Harvey buzzed her on the intercom five minutes later, as she was brushing her teeth. She spat into the sink, rinsed her mouth, and let him in. He must have taken the stairs, because she didn't hear the rising drone of the elevator. When she opened the apartment door, he thrust a bottle of champagne and a large bunch of bedraggled white flowers at her. The flowers were long-stemmed chrysanthemums. They looked as if they could use a drink. Jan knew how they felt.

She said, "Aren't you sweet."

Harvey walked right past her, bouncing on his heels. He wore an ill-fitting dark blue suit, white dress shirt, and a wide black tie. A large Hudson's Bay shopping bag dangled from his left hand.

Jan said, "What's that?"

"A present." He sniffed the air, grinned at her. "You smoking again?"

Jan led him into the living room. She put the flowers and bottle of champagne down on the coffee table. They sat down on the sofa. Harvey took a big white box out of the bag. He put the box down on her lap. It was surprisingly heavy. Jan opened it up. The box held a two-piece black leather cowgirl suit. The jacket and flaring skirt had a black leather fringe. The jacket was lavishly decorated with sequins and glass beads. Jan looked for a price tag but couldn't find one.

Harvey said, "What d'you think?"

"Where did you get it?"

"From . . ." He gestured vaguely. ". . . the Bay." Without preamble, he wrapped his arms around her and kissed her on the mouth. Jan felt herself responding, despite all her doubts. When Harvey finally came up for air, he had that look in his eyes that she had come to know so well.

He said, "Missed you, honey."

"Well, you didn't have much else to do in there, did you?"

"You've missed me too. I can tell."

Jan reached out and gave his lapel a tug. She said, "Where did you get that suit?"

"It's a Hugo Boss. Don't you like it?"

"It stinks like the grave."

Harvey slyly said, "Well, maybe I better take it off."

"What about the champagne?"

He kissed her again. Leaning back, looking deeply into her eyes, he said, "First things first."

Jan ducked her head. She said, "If we're going to do something stupid, we have to be careful not to wake Tyler."

Harvey touched her here and there, in all his favourite places. He tilted up her head and kissed her on the mouth, and laughed and said, "What're you telling *me* for? You've always been the noisy one."

home sweet home

Willows and Oikawa had loaded up on carbohydrates and coffee from the Parks Board takeout concession stand overlooking the outdoor swimming pool. Arcing out into the pool was a grey-painted, bare-bones plywood stage with a backdrop that hinted at the shape of an old-fashioned paddle-wheeler. The stage was called The Showboat. There was seating for several hundred on the steep slope leading down to the pool. In the summer, people came down to watch amateur dancers and singers and musicians strut their stuff as the sun set over the water and distant mountains. Willows' parents had often taken him down to the pool when he was a child, more than forty years ago. It had been a salt-water pool in those days. He remembered a troupe of local men in old-fashioned bathing suits and handlebar moustaches who'd performed on the pool's outside wall. The men had pretended to run into each other, dived acrobatically into the water, and performed all sorts of skilful and amusing hijinks, never failing to divert the crowd's attention from whatever tame act held the stage. Willows was wondering what had happened to those men, when Oikawa nudged him in the ribs.

"What are you having, Jack?"

Oikawa had ordered the two-piece fish and chips. Willows' family doctor had recently told him his cholesterol level was high. Accordingly, he settled on a burger and fries.

They'd eaten in the car within view of Jennifer Orchid's semi-waterfront home. Between the time they arrived and nine o'clock that night, Oikawa had made five trips to the public bathroom. After nine, he had to use the bushes, because the bathroom was padlocked.

Willows said, "There's a plastic milk jug in the trunk. You keep sneaking into the shrubbery, you're going to get arrested."

At a few minutes past midnight, Oikawa yawned and said, "She's got an all-nighter. What d'you say we get a good night's sleep, nail her when she comes home in the morning?"

Willows was too tired to argue. He dropped Oikawa off on the way home. It was close to three by the time he pulled up to the curb in front of his own house. The porch light was on, but the windows were dark. He let himself in, and sat down on the pine bench in the

hall to take off his shoes. Tripod, their voluble three-legged marmalade cat, rubbed up against his ankles. He went upstairs, checked
on Hadrian, showered, and went to bed. Claire moaned softly when
he slipped between the sheets. He leaned over and kissed her lightly
on the shoulder.

Claire, her voice blurred with sleep, said, "Jack?"

Willows softly said, "Yes, it's me." Claire mumbled something,
sighed deeply, and rolled away from him. Willows lay there, staring
blankly up at the ceiling. The fan was on, but the insect screen
reduced the amount of fresh air being sucked through the open
window, and the room was uncomfortably warm. He tossed and
turned. Why had his wife felt it necessary to ask who'd climbed
into bed with her? He had almost drifted off when he remembered
to set the alarm.

angst

Annie was listening to Nirvana's latest CD on her portable player
when Tripod jumped off her chest and trotted out of her room.
She pulled off the headphones, and heard her father warmly telling
Tripod how glad he was to see him. He was keeping his voice
down, and he sounded sober, but she'd learned that didn't necessarily mean anything. She slipped out of bed and eased shut the
door, and got back into bed. The CD player's laser glowed a weird,
alien-blue. She hid the machine under the sheets, so the light
wouldn't give her away if he looked in on her, even though she
knew he'd never dream of intruding. Anyway, there was no need
to hide the player, because she didn't have to get up in the morning
and could stay up as late as she wanted.

But then, why did she feel guilty? Was it because she couldn't
sleep? Was it because she wanted to be twelve years old again, a
confident little kid in pigtails who didn't have any real responsibilities, and never thought about sex, or worried about what kind
of person she could, or might not, be?

She heard her father going up the stairs. The creak of a floorboard where the stairs turned. His footsteps were slower and more deliberate than they used to be. He was growing older, too.

Annie didn't want to think about that. She didn't want to think about anything, come to think of it. Tripod mewed, and scratched at her door. She got out of bed and let him in, and shut the door, and got back into bed. Tripod curled up on her chest as if he had every right to be there. A sharp claw pricked her breast. She moved his paw away and put the headphones back on.

The music reverberated in her skull. She turned down the volume. Her eyes were wet. A tear rolled down her cheek.

She hadn't known Paige all that long, but they had so much in common that they'd quickly become inseparable, the very best of friends. She missed Paige so much she could hardly bear it, and she didn't know what to do.

arf meow growl hiss

Hadrian rolled over on his belly. He was in the tub, with Claire. Water poured into the tub from the shiny chromed tap. The noise and force of it was exhilarating and terrifying. Claire held him in her arms as he swam against the strong current. She was naked. Her skin felt like rubber. He swam furiously, with all his strength, his arms and legs beating at the water. Claire held him loosely in her hands. What if she let go, or forgot he was there? Sparkly water continued to rush from the tap. He reached out, but couldn't touch the bottom of the tub. The water was frighteningly deep. He shrieked with fear. Claire swooped him up and kissed him. He thought everything was going to be all right, but then she lowered him into the water again. His thrusting legs banged against the side of the crib, hard enough to make the plastic mobile rattle.

Hadrian lay quietly, his chest heaving. The room was hot and stuffy. His eyes gradually adjusted to the light. He was turned sideways in the crib, his legs tangled up in the pastel-striped blanket. He worked hard to free himself and turn so he had more room. It was exhausting work. He squeezed shut his fists and closed his eyes.

The bath was calm and shallow. The yellow duck with the funny red bill swam around Claire's hip. The duck saw him. It stopped, nestled in Claire's hand, and then hurried forward to be with him. He picked it up and squeezed it.

Arf! Meow! Growl! Hiss!

God, but he loved that duck.

roll 'em

Jackie couldn't sleep. He checked his bedside clock and saw that it was almost one a.m. He got up and wriggled into his Calvin Klein robe and went down the hall to his brother's bedroom. A light shone under the door. He knocked.

Aldo said, "Who is it?"

"Me, Jackie."

A buzzer sounded. The lock clicked. Aldo said, "Come in."

Jackie opened the door. Aldo was in bed, reading the latest issue of *Forbes* magazine. His scissors and paste and enormous cartoon scrapbook lay on the night table, next to the sliced-and-diced remains of that week's *New Yorker*.

Jackie said, "Aren't you a busy fellow!"

"I can't sleep. I'm worried about Jan's boyfriend, Sandy."

"What about him?"

"I don't know. I can't put my finger on it. He seemed so . . . *trustworthy.*"

"No, you can't mean that!" Jackie was horrified. He said, "I didn't get that impression at all. He seemed perfectly normal to me."

"You're sure?"

"Absolutely. Listen, I was wondering, since neither of us can sleep, if you'd like to go to a casino. We could gamble the night away. Forget all our cares and woes."

Aldo brightened, as if Jackie had briskly spun his personal dimmer switch to maximum wattage. He clapped his hands together. "What a wonderful idea!" The light faded as swiftly as it had come. "But Jackie, we need every penny of our cash to buy the diamonds."

"We have our credit cards. What we spend tonight will be a drop in the bucket compared to tomorrow's profits."

"You're right!"

Aldo tossed aside his copy of *Forbes* and leapt out of bed. The brothers were on their way to a long night of eating, and drinking, and merrymaking, too.

starry-eyed fool

Dr. Randy Hamilton couldn't stop thinking about Claire. He'd been obsessing about her all night long. The harder he tried to think about something else – like how old he would've been when John Lennon got riddled – the worse it got. At midnight, halfway through his second bottle of Merlot, he phoned Sammy Wong's 24-Hour World of Delicious Chinese Cuisine, and ordered half a dozen of his all-time favourite dishes. Fried Rice with Baby Shrimpettes, Sweet & Sour Boneless Pork, etcetera. The food arrived just as he was uncorking the third bottle. He paid the deliveryman, and carried the food into the dining room. At the table, he poured himself another glass of wine, and levered tin-foil-covered lids off Styrofoam containers. The food was piping-hot and smelled delicious.

Randy's belly didn't growl. His taste buds declined to quiver in anticipation. His nostrils refused to twitch. His gastric juices had never failed him before, but now they lay dormant, and his usually hyperactive saliva glands were playing possum. He stripped the flimsy paper wrapper off his chopsticks and stabbed listlessly at his favourite dish – chicken in black-bean sauce. It was like he needed Viagra for the tummy.

He had no appetite, except for Claire.

To distract himself, he made a list of all the vegetables he could think of, in alphabetical order. He got as far as yam, then put down his pen and imagined himself taking Claire's clothes off. When she was naked, he imagined Claire taking *his* clothes off. She had a delicate, wonderfully sensuous touch. When she knelt down to remove the hand-knitted argyle socks his mother had given him last Christmas, he just about went crazy with desire.

He imagined them in a naked, passionate embrace, flopping romantically about on a white fur rug in front of a blazing fireplace. Hackneyed dialogue, a preposterous orgasm, lots more hackneyed dialogue . . .

By two in the morning Dr. Randy Hamilton had almost finished the third bottle of wine and was falling-down drunk. He stripped off his clothes and, bouncing from wall to wall, made his way into the bathroom, where he stood naked in front of the full-length mirror screwed to the bathroom door, and scrutinized his swaying, slightly out-of-focus image from head to toe. The Chinese takeout was an aberration caused by undue stress. He was usually very careful about what he ate. He spent most of his free time at a local fitness club. He ran for miles on the treadmill, hoisted tons of iron, damn near killed himself fine-tuning his abs. Speaking objectively, he had to say he looked pretty wonderful, for a guy in his late thirties.

He'd hung around Claire's house the past few nights, parked across the street in his Lexus, hoping for a glimpse of Claire, and also wanting a look at her cop husband, because he was curious about what he was up against. The doughnut-eater. Probably had a beer gut, comb-over, flat feet, and breath that would melt a toothbrush. Beady-eyed little sonofabitch who came home stinking of cheap liquor and sudden death.

Randy wondered if Jack smoked. He bet the sonofabitch chain-smoked like a chimney. That didn't mean he wasn't dangerous. Randy knew he could take Willows in a fair fight, but Willows was a cop, and cops didn't fight fair. The bastards had guns, and a licence to kill.

Randy turned off the shower. He towelled himself dry, went into his bedroom, and walked into the walk-in closet. Clothes were his weakness. He chose a pink silk shirt and a lightweight summer suit that had just come back from the dry cleaner, the belt with the mottled silver crocodile's-head buckle. So cool. He got a fresh pair of Jockeys out of the drawer, and a pair of brand new socks, and laid everything out on the kingsize bed. It took him almost twenty minutes to get dressed, but he was not conscious of the passage of time.

When he was dressed, he went back in the closet and stumbled around until he'd found his currently favourite pair of shoes. The shoes were almost new and didn't need polishing. He tossed them on the floor, and then he dove onto the bed, fluffed up his pillow, sighed contentedly, shut his eyes, and was asleep in an instant.

In the morning, he planned to make an unsolicited house call. What a happy surprise that would be. He imagined Claire opening her door. Her eyes widening, a glint of pleasure. Dr. Randy, at your service!

As he slept, Dr. Hamilton's mood was buoyant, and his spirits were high.

21

the end of almost everything

Jack had set the alarm for 6:30, but it was Claire who woke him. She'd made scrambled eggs and toast, and fresh-squeezed orange juice. She handed him the tray, and slipped into bed. He held the tray while she unfolded the legs.

She said, "I've missed you, Jack." She kissed him lightly on the mouth. Her hair was brushed, and she tasted of mint-flavoured toothpaste.

"Me too," said Jack. The words reverberated hollowly among his unbrushed teeth. He ran his fingers through his sleep-tousled hair. "I've missed you too, honey."

Claire took a bite of whole-wheat toast, licked a crumb from her finger. "I thought we could take Hadrian to Science World, run him into the ground, and then maybe go somewhere nice and have lunch."

"You're calling in sick again?"

Parker nodded. She said, "The way I feel now, I may never go back."

Jack put his coffee mug down on the tray. He wiped his mouth with a napkin.

Claire said, "Jessie Waters, that woman down the street who just had the twins? She said that new Italian restaurant on Twelfth

Avenue is really good. Not too pricey, either. If we're lucky, Hadrian will sleep for an hour or so, and we . . ."

Jack said, "Claire, I'm really sorry, but I have to go to work."

"I haven't seen you for three days!"

"Everybody's overworked. It's the Colin McDonald case. Dan and I have a suspect. She isn't much, but she's all we've got. We staked her house out last night. Hopefully, we'll get to talk to her this morning."

Claire was quiet for a moment. She dipped a corner of her toast in her coffee, and chewed meditatively. Jack noticed that her toast was dry, whereas his was buttered and slathered with jam. She knew he had to watch his cholesterol levels. What was she trying to do, kill him with kindness? Finally she said, "All right, fine. If you have to go to work, you have to go to work. I understand that. But I want you to talk to Homer about getting some time off." She gave him a warning look to stop him from trying to interrupt. "You and I need some time together. We have to talk about my career, and our marriage. Especially our marriage, Jack. Do you understand?"

He nodded. They were also going to have a special talk about how in hell they'd manage to pay the bills if she quit working, but he wasn't going to mention it now, because he didn't have the time to argue about it. His stomach turned. He was starving but hadn't touched his toast because he knew that not giving Claire his full and undivided attention would be suicidal. The alarm rasped like a dentist's drill. He reached over and turned it off, but not before Hadrian started crying.

He said, "I have to go."

Claire nodded. She didn't look at him.

He said, "Thanks for making breakfast."

Now she did look at him, and he wished she hadn't. She said, "Shut up, Jack."

Willows showered and dressed, and left the house without a word. Oikawa was parked outside Jennifer Orchid's house when Willows arrived. Willows was driving a Chevy from the motor pool. Oikawa was in a silver-coloured Audi parked halfway up the block. Willows pulled in behind him. He walked up to the Audi and got in.

Oikawa said, "'Morning, Jack." He had a Thermos, a green-and-gold coffee mug from Harrods, and a six-pack of Tim Hortons doughnuts. "Doughnut?"

"No thanks. Nice mug."

"Watching your weight?"

"Cholesterol."

"Want some tea?"

"I wouldn't mind."

Oikawa unscrewed the Thermos's metal lid, which doubled as a cup. He filled it half-full and handed it to Willows.

"Thanks."

Oikawa took a bite of a chocolate-sprinkled doughnut, and said, "Mmmmm."

Willows checked his watch. It was quarter past seven. There were no lights on in Jennifer Orchid's townhouse, and no sign of movement inside.

At seven-thirty, they got out of the car and walked across the street and knocked on the door.

Two minutes later, they walked back to Oikawa's car.

At ten past nine, a dark blue Ford Mustang convertible pulled up to the house. The top was down. The car had a yellow Hertz sticker on the rear bumper. Willows and Oikawa slouched low as Jennifer Orchid got out of the Ford. She hurried across the boulevard and let herself into her condo. She wore a black spaghetti-strap evening dress and black shoes with stiletto heels, and carried a small black purse.

Oikawa said, "I don't think she was wearing anything under that itty-bitty little dress." He added, "I couldn't walk two steps in shoes like that."

"Just as well," murmured Willows.

"Want to grab her?"

"Not yet," said Willows. Their suspect had left the rented Ford's engine running. When he'd knocked on the door, no dog had barked. What was going on? Why had she rented a car? He said, "I want to see where she's going to go next."

"You're thinking a kennel?"

Willows nodded.

Oikawa had two doughnuts left, an Old-Fashioned Plain and a Boston Cream. It was a no-brainer, but he wished he'd brought more napkins . . .

Jennifer Orchid came out of her house wearing a baseball cap, Yale T-shirt, a pair of hot-pink Capri pants, ankle socks, and white sneakers. She put on a pair of sunglasses as she got into the car.

Oikawa started the engine, and cranked up the air conditioner. He said, "I've got Glenn Gould in the CD player. That okay with you?"

"Fine," said Willows.

Oikawa waited until the Ford had disappeared around the corner at the end of the block, then put the car in gear.

Aldo and Jackie played blackjack till dawn. By then, the casino was almost deserted, and they were up a little over three thousand dollars. A somnolent woman offered them another round of free drinks. Jackie turned her down with a grim smile and a fifty-cent tip. He doubled up on a pair of aces and won another four hundred dollars.

When Aldo had finally got his yawn under control he said, "Yee-haw!"

Jackie said, "I'm bored." He mock-punched their pile of chips, scattering them across the table. "This is nothing – it's funny money."

"What d'you mean?"

"It's stupid. It means nothing. Let's have some fun with it."

"I don't understand."

"Three thousand dollars is an insignificant sum. Lady Luck wants to take us for a ride and we are too frightened to jump on board."

"Speak English!"

"Craps," said Jackie. "Roulette. That's where the serious money is to be made. I say let's roll the dice, and see where they take us!"

"Straight to the poorhouse, I bet."

Jackie looked his older but not wiser brother in the eye. He said, "'Life is too short to act as if life is too short.'"

Aldo jerked his head back as if he had been punched in the jaw. "That's *so* profound."

"*People* magazine," said Jackie. "Last week's issue. Goldie Hawn, or maybe it was Brad Pitt, I can't remember."

The brothers went their separate ways. Jackie circled the roulette table like a vulture while Aldo shot craps. They took a pre-scheduled break after one hour. Aldo was up another five thousand, Jackie almost seven. Aldo unstrapped his Timex and pushed tiny little buttons until the watch was in calculator mode. Ten minutes later, he said, "We're up fifteen thousand dollars."

"A good start," said Jackie.

Aldo glanced warily around. He said, "They don't like it. They've encouraged me to bet far above the paltry legal limit, and never stop trying to serve me alcoholic beverages. It drives them mad that I keep winning."

"Me, too," said Jackie.

"Shall we keep playing?"

Jackie clapped his brother on the shoulder. "Why not?"

A little while later, Aldo tired of craps and joined Jackie at the roulette table. Every so often, acting on a whim, he placed a bet. Each time he did this, Jackie lost a sum of money that was insignificant compared to the amount that Aldo acquired by betting against him.

By eight o'clock in the morning, they were up thirty thousand dollars, and the casino's manager was sweating solid silver bullets. He asked Aldo and Jackie if they were interested in a complimentary breakfast, then sent out for orange juice, coffee, and Grand Slam breakfasts from a nearby Denny's.

Aldo and Jackie ate at the table. They placed bets between mouthfuls of food. The Grand Slams were delicious, but, though neither complained, both men thought the orange juice had a slightly bitter aftertaste.

By 8:30, they were up another five grand.

Ten minutes later, both men unceremoniously dropped to the casino's thinly carpeted floor. By 8:45 they were in the trunk of a glossy black Cadillac speeding east on Marine Drive. The Caddy crossed the Fraser River on the Knight Street Bridge. At this point, the driver, Marcus, lost his sense of direction. He drove a couple of blocks and parked in IKEA's massive hundred-acre parking lot, and consulted a magazine-style booklet of maps of the Lower Mainland.

The guy in the shotgun seat was a chubby guy named Kelly Ames. Marcus had never worked with him before. Kelly said, "I hate fucking Richmond. Everything looks exactly like everything else. Santa Claus could get lost out here."

Kelly's hair was thinning. He had the pear-shaped body of a man who had never met a calorie he didn't like. His eyes were the washed-out blue of a country sky, and the way he walked somehow gave the impression his arms were a little too long. He dressed badly. His ill-fitting pants always needed a press. His shirt always needed tucking in. Marcus had taken an intense dislike to him the moment he'd met him. There was something about the guy that made him need to wiggle his toes. His blunt finger stabbed at the map, distorting the lay of the land. He said, "That's where we want to go, Kelly. Right there." His finger moved and stabbed. "This is where we are now."

"Here, in the parking lot?"

Marcus nodded. He said, "I'm gonna pull out of the parking lot and drive down this road right here, back where we turned left at the lights. Then I'm gonna take the overpass over the highway, and head down towards the river. Gimme the lefts and rights as I need 'em, 'kay?"

Kelly nodded doubtfully.

Marcus thrust the map into his hands. "Here, take the map. What d'you think, I'm gonna hold it for you while I drive?"

Kelly studied the map intently for several long seconds, then turned it around so it was right-side up.

River Road was essentially a narrow strip of two-lane asphalt that ran along the top of the dike that kept the Fraser from flooding Richmond. On the Caddy's left, there were big deciduous trees, and log booms tied to the bank. Beyond the trees the mud-coloured river flowed ceaselessly and unhurriedly towards the sea. On the right, there was a twenty-foot-deep ditch, more dark water, the odd jettisoned major appliance, and lots of bright green pond scum. Algae. On the far side of the ditch there were acres of apparently untended fields, a scattering of blocky warehouses with silver- or blue-tinted windows, swampy-looking areas full of dead trees, every once in a while a barbed-wire-surrounded concrete-block office building, a few small houses. The speed limit on the dike was 30 KPH per hour, and Marcus was in no hurry.

After the better part of an hour, they crossed back over the river, into the City of New Westminster. It wasn't anywhere Kelly would want to live. Marcus steered the Caddy into a straggly industrial district that ran parallel to the river.

Kelly said, "You got a particular dumpster in mind?"

"Nope."

"We could chuck 'em in the river . . ."

"Only if they come back to the casino."

"That ain't likely to happen."

"Really? How do you know what they might do?"

"A person wakes up naked in a dumpster way outta town, I'd have thought the message was clear."

Marcus rolled his eyes. He said, "Not if you're an idiot."

"Are they idiots?"

"Well, if they aren't, what in hell were they doing in a casino in the first place?"

"Having a good time?"

Marcus rolled his eyes.

Kelly said, "Yeah, I see what you mean."

The Caddy's suspension worked hard to smooth out a set of railway tracks. The road narrowed to one lane and swung around so the river was on their right. The road fell into a huge, pothole-sprinkled gravel yard. A squat, hangar-sized building made of rusty, corrugated metal loomed above the river. The Caddy splashed through puddles of oily black water. Marcus spun the wheel. They cut around a stack of railroad ties, and drove through a vast doorway, into the empty building. Shafts of light fell through huge mullioned windows, speckling the concrete. Marcus slowly backed the Caddy up against a scabrous, rust-flaked wall. "This outta do it."

"Where's the dumpster?"

"Let's just pretend it's right here, okay?"

Marcus popped the trunk. The high-rollers were still napping. He told Kelly to grab a couple of ankles, and to go easy, concrete was hard.

Kelly said, "So what do we care if the idiot chips a tooth?"

"I never hurt anybody I don't have to."

"Why not? The ones you don't have to hurt are the most fun."

They swung Aldo out of the trunk and lowered him to the cement. A handful of pigeons wheeled high overhead. A pale grey feather came fluttering down. Marcus held out his hand and let the feather drift into his cupped palm. It was shaped like a tiny ark, and it was beautiful. Kelly was watching him, frowning critically. Marcus pursed his lips and blew the feather on its way. They lifted Jackie out of the Caddy's trunk and laid him tenderly down on the ground next to Aldo. The brothers were breathing steadily. They were going to be okay. Marcus said, "Strip 'em naked."

Kelly had been hoping he'd say that. Smiling happily, he got to work. When he'd finished, he manipulated Jackie's body so his head was nestled in the crook of Aldo's arm. He smiled at Marcus and said, "How's that – you satisfied?"

Marcus said, "There are worse things than being a feather."

"What the fuck's that supposed to mean?"

Marcus gave himself a shake to loosen himself up. He had a feeling it was going to be a long ride home.

The night before the robbery, Sandy couldn't sleep. He had pills, but didn't want to take them. In the morning, his head had to be clear. He watched TV for a while, and fell asleep on the sofa in the middle of a truly awful film called *Hercules in New York*, starring a badly dubbed Arnold Schwarzenegger.

The alarm woke him at seven. The diamond-merchant robbery was supposed to go down at quarter to twelve.

Sandy showered and shaved, and dressed in black sneakers, pleated black Dockers, and a loose-fitting black button-down shirt from the Gap. He shoved his holstered Glock inside the waistband of his pants, and let the shirt hang loose. The gun was undetectable – not that it made any difference, since Harvey would assume he was packing. The Dockers were cuffed, and fairly wide at the ankle. Sandy's back-up piece was his blue steel .22-calibre Iver Johnson Pocket Pistol. The gun had a three-inch barrel and a seven-round magazine. It fitted snugly into a black suede thumb-break ankle holster with a Velcro strap. His father had given him the gun. It was fifteen years old, but had never been fired in anger.

Sandy brewed a pot of coffee, and turned on the TV. He usually ate breakfast but he wouldn't eat today, because it was better not to have a full stomach if you got shot in the belly. The weather channel said it was going to be clear and warm, with a mid-afternoon high of 26 Celsius degrees. He turned the TV off and went outside. A robin pecked at his landlord's lawn. Somewhere, not far off, a gas lawnmower roared. He wished the city would ban the damn things. They were noisy as hell and spewed out more pollution than your average dump truck. The mower burped and roared. What kind of inconsiderate fool mowed his lawn at eight o'clock in the morning?

Sandy flung the rest of his second mug of coffee into the lane, darkening an oval of gravel. Startled by the sudden movement, the robin flew away over the rooftops. He reluctantly admitted to himself that it was possible he was a little on edge. Times like this, he almost wished he smoked. He shook the last few drops of coffee from the mug and went back inside his converted apartment.

He phoned Jan, but she didn't answer. Her machine didn't pick up, either. He didn't have a number for Harvey. He waited ten minutes and tried Jan again. The line was busy. He went into the bathroom and emptied his bladder. Man, he was nervous.

He had a few calls to make, and he made them. The first was to the ERT team leader, a sergeant with the unlikely name of Tosh McIntosh. The sergeant asked him if he was going to wear a vest. Sandy said no, he'd decided not to, his thinking being that a vest might encourage Harvey to shoot him in the head, and that a head shot was almost always lethal. They went over the drill. The sergeant sounded so calm, and detached, that he might have been discussing a grocery list. They wrapped, and he told Sandy to take it easy, he'd see him in a couple of hours.

Sandy said, "You mean, it's going down *today*?" Kind of lame, but McIntosh gave him a good laugh.

Sandy hung up, and phoned home. He knew it wasn't a smart thing to do, because as soon as he started dialling, he lost sight of his character, and began to think of himself as Sean. Claire picked up on the seventh ring, just as he'd decided nobody was home.

He identified himself, and told her without being asked that his assignment had almost come to an end.

Claire said, "That's good, Sean. It's been a long time, hasn't it." She sounded a little distracted. More than a little distracted. In the background, the dishwasher hummed. Her flat tone of voice made him feel as if he'd interrupted something important. More important than him, anyway.

He said, "How's Annie?"

"Fine," said Claire.

The roar of the lawnmower was suddenly louder. Sean pressed the phone against his ear, but all he heard was the familiar whir of the dishwasher. After a moment he said, "Did she find a job yet?"

"Not that I know of. I don't know why. We could use some help with her tuition."

Sandy said, "Yeah, I guess so. Dad around?"

Claire told him that Jack had already left, that he and Oikawa were working a stakeout. Hadrian belched loudly into the phone, then started crying. He sounded more mad than upset. Claire told him she'd tell Jack that he'd called. He thanked her and said goodbye and hung up fast, before she could beat him to it. She had no way of knowing that today was the Big Day, but even so, he felt as if she'd let him down. It wasn't rational, but there it was.

He checked the Glock again, and the Titan. Both guns had a full magazine and a round in the chamber.

Jan's line was still busy. He checked the time. It was a little early. He thought he might as well drive over there anyway. He could see how she was doing, find out if she'd decided to take his advice or had chosen, without being aware of what she'd done, to be a criminal and a convict, just like her dim-witted husband.

Harvey and Jan were in the shower the first time the phone rang. By the time Sandy tried again, they'd migrated back into the sack. Tyler was in the living room, watching cartoons on TV. He didn't hear the phone ring, because he'd turned the sound up almost as loud as it would go, to drown out the sound of his mom and the creep who mistakenly believed he was his dad.

Somebody called the cops. Aldo and Jackie had talked things over. They refused to identify themselves or explain why they were stark-naked, or how they'd ended up in an abandoned, half-gutted warehouse on the river. The cops called in the meat-wagon. Aldo and Jackie were involuntarily admitted to Riverview for psychiatric assessment. Their files were lost the day after they arrived, due to a hard-drive failure. Two weeks later, they would still be going crazy waiting for the paperwork to catch up with them.

Sometimes, the wheels of injustice grind exceedingly slow.

Jennifer Orchid drove over the Arthur Laing Bridge towards the airport.

Oikawa said, "Maybe she's planning to leave town."

Willows doubted it. The rental's left-turn signal had just started flashing. The car moved over one lane. Jennifer Orchid made a left turn onto the Dinsmore Bridge, and drove over the middle arm of the Fraser River.

Oikawa said, "Looks like she's headed for beautiful downtown Richmond."

"I don't think so."

"No? Why not?"

Willows said, "She's going to turn right, onto the Westminster Highway."

"No kidding. Where's your crystal ball?"

The line of traffic bumped over the railway tracks that ran parallel to the river. They were on Gilbert Street. There was a dedicated right turn where Gilbert intersected with the Westminster Highway. The blue Mustang swung into the lane, and waited at the red. Oikawa pulled in two cars behind.

Willows said, "I checked the Yellow Pages this morning. There are only a couple of dozen kennels in the Lower Mainland, and most of them are pretty far out of town – in Surrey or Aldergrove. There are two kennels in Richmond. The other one's on Number Three Road."

"How did you know she wasn't going there?"

Willows smiled. "That's where the crystal ball came in, Danny."

Traffic was light, and moving along at a steady 20 KPH over the limit. The drive to Big Dog Kennels took twenty minutes. The kennel was in an area of light industry, farmer's markets, and vast stretches of what appeared to be undeveloped farmland. The road ran flat and unnaturally straight. Oikawa was hanging a quarter-mile back when the Mustang's turn signal lit up. The car's brake lights flashed. Jennifer Orchid turned right, and disappeared.

Oikawa checked his rearview mirror, and tapped the brakes. They crawled past an unmarked driveway surrounded by over-grown brambles. The Mustang was parked in front of a low, flat-roofed stucco building. Oikawa stopped, and backed up a few feet for a better view. He and Willows watched Jennifer Orchid get out of the Mustang and walk into the building. Oikawa backed the Audi up a few more feet, and shifted gears and accelerated down the driveway. On their left there was a mass of brambles. To the right, more parking, and a low, green wooden fence that sepa-rated Big Dog Kennels from the neighbouring property.

Oikawa parked to the left of the Mustang. He and Willows got out. Oikawa said, "You want to go in?"

Willows wasn't sure. How long would it take to retrieve the dog? He didn't like the idea of having to deal with the dog at close quar-ters. He said, "Let's wait outside." He and Oikawa clipped their gold shields to the breast pockets of their sports jackets. Oikawa drew his weapon, the blue steel .38-calibre Colt Police Special he'd carried for more than twenty years. He flipped open the revolver's cylinder, checked the load, and snapped the cylinder shut.

Willows said, "You worried she's going to kiss you to death?"

"I did a little research myself, when I got home last night. If it's a male, it could weigh ninety pounds, or more." Oikawa put on a pair of Decot shooting glasses with rose-coloured lenses. The glasses would help illuminate the target against the lawn's green background. If he had to shoot, they'd protect his eyes from back-flash or metal fragments. He said, "You want to fight the damn thing off with your bare fists, be my guest."

Willows thought Oikawa was being overly cautious but let it go. If Jennifer was involved in Colin McDonald's death, the dog had already killed once. He considered the situation for a moment, and then said, "When Jennifer comes out, the door's going to swing outwards and to the left. The dog should be on her left ..." He was thinking that, if the Mustang wasn't a convertible, they could have waited until Jennifer had put the dog inside the car, then taken her.

Oikawa said, "I'll wait to the left of the door, close up against the building. If you stand by the Mustang, you'll be out of my line of fire. When she comes out, she'll focus on you. If the dog's on my side, I'll deal with it. If it's on her right, and it's aggressive, you shoot it."

Willows nodded. He turned and walked back to Jennifer's car. Oikawa stood to the left of the door. The Colt was in his right hand, close by his side. Both men turned, as a rust-spotted Econoline pulled into the parking lot. Willows held up his badge, and indicated with hand signals that he wanted the driver to turn around and leave. The driver hit the brakes, killed the engine, and climbed hurriedly down out of the van. She strode rapidly towards Willows.

"What the hell's going on here?"

Willows said, "Police business. Get back in your car."

"I'm Milly Feinstadt, and I own Big Dog Kennels." She peered at Willows' badge. "You guys are Vancouver cops. This is Richmond. What ..."

The kennels door swung open, and Jennifer Orchid stepped outside. She had a large male German shepherd on a short leash. She saw Willows, and turned and ran straight into Oikawa.

Claire and Annie were in the kitchen, putting together an Irish stew, when there was a light tap on the back screen door. Hadrian was in his high chair, trying to stuff a plastic spoonful of lime Jell-O into his favourite teddy bear. He pointed at the door and made a cheerful gurgling sound.

Dr. Randy Hamilton opened the screen door. He said, "Hi there, ladies. Mind if I come in?"

Claire said, "Have you been drinking?"

Hamilton rubbed his thumb and little finger together. "Just a little bit, to take the edge off, if you know what I mean." He thought, given the look on Claire's face, that he'd better not mention the cocaine.

Claire said, "Go away, or I'll call the police."

"You mean, call yourself?" Hamilton chuckled. "What are you going to do while you wait for yourself to show up, did you think of that?"

Hadrian held out his arms towards the doctor. He made a pigeon-like cooing sound.

Hamilton said, "Hello, handsome!"

"Stay away from my baby!" yelled Claire.

Hamilton reached out and tried to scoop Hadrian out of his chair. Hadrian's feet got tangled up in the safety strap. He dropped his bear and started screaming. Hamilton yanked even harder.

Annie, standing to the side and slightly behind him, said, "Dr. Hamilton?"

Hamilton turned to look at her. He kept tugging on Hadrian, pulling his arms so hard Annie was afraid they might break.

She swung two-handed, with all her might. The cast-iron frying pan caught Dr. Randy Hamilton flush on the nose. He hit the floor so hard that Hadrian's lime Jell-O was still jiggling when Claire got through to the 911 operator.

Oikawa lost his balance, and fell. His wrist banged against the rough stucco wall. The Colt flew out of his hand. The German shepherd loomed over him, straddling him. Oikawa and the dog looked each other in the eye. Oikawa said, "Good dog." He didn't sound too sure of himself. Milly Feinstadt clutched desperately at Willows' sleeve as he tried to move around her for a better shot. Jennifer Orchid was crying. The shepherd lowered its massive head.

Willows lined up his shot.

Milly Feinstadt yelled, "Don't you dare shoot that animal! Diener, stay!"

Diener licked Oikawa's rose-coloured glasses off his head. He licked Oikawa again, leaving a wide swath of saliva in his close-cropped hair. Oikawa scrambled to his feet. His eyes were red. He sneezed, and sneezed again. The dog gazed up at him as if in sympathy. Oikawa retrieved his gun first, and then the glasses. He wiped saliva from his face and leaned against the wall, sneezing like a runaway steam train.

Willows said, "The dog's name is Diener?"

Milly Feinstadt nodded. She said, "It's German. It means 'Butler.'" She glanced quickly at Jennifer, then looked away. "Diener's a good dog, he wouldn't hurt anyone."

Judging from the expression on Jennifer Orchid's face, Willows wasn't so sure about that. He said, "Have you got a muzzle that we can borrow?"

Milly Feinstadt put her hands on her hips. "That really isn't necessary."

Willows said, "If we muzzle the dog, my partner will put away his gun."

"Well, why didn't you say so in the first place?"

Diener didn't want to be muzzled, but he didn't put up much of a fight. Jennifer Orchid seemed more concerned about leaving the Mustang behind than anything else. Willows assured her someone would take care of the car. He and Jennifer and Diener got into the Audi.

Willows read Jennifer Orchid her rights. He cuffed her, and told her twice that she was entitled to a lawyer and that anything she said could be used against her in a court of law. He asked her if she understood what he had just said.

Jennifer said, "Yes, of course I do. I'm not stupid. Colin liked it rough. I mean, *really* rough. He hurt me, and I cried out. Diener was outside, on the balcony, but he must have heard me. When I left, I was in such a hurry that I forgot all about him. I came back for him a few hours later, at a little past six in the morning, when I knew Colin would be in the shower. I let myself in with my key, and went straight to Diener, and let him in. He brushed past me when I opened the door."

"What do you mean?"

"He went into the bathroom. Diener went into the bathroom. He didn't bark, or make any kind of sound at all. I didn't . . . I was still thinking about what Colin had done to me, and I didn't pay any attention to Diener. I shut the door behind me. Then Colin screamed. I could hear Diener growling low in his throat. I opened the bathroom door. The bathroom was full of steam, from the shower. I called Diener but he wouldn't come. He was growling, and Colin . . . I was frightened. I turned up the music so I wouldn't be able to hear what was happening."

"Why did you . . . the coroner's report said Colin had been attacked post-mortem, with a large knife, or possibly a meat cleaver."

"Cleaver."

Willows stared blandly at her, and quietly waited.

Jennifer said, "I had to cut him. I hated doing it, but I had to."

"Why?"

"To save Diener."

Willows wasn't sure he'd heard her correctly. He said, "What was that again?"

"I had to save Diener. Colin was dead. I didn't want them to kill . . . They *gas* them, can you imagine?" Jennifer started crying again. When she'd collected herself, she said, "Diener's all I've got. He's my only friend in the whole world. I couldn't stand the idea of him being put down."

Willows nodded as if he understood. He wondered how much of her story was true, and how much of it she believed because she needed it to be true, and how much of it was a pack of self-serving lies. Judging by the evidence at the scene, Willows favoured the last option.

Diener stared at him as if he knew what he was thinking. Well, maybe he did.

A commuter jet passed low overhead just as they reached the apex of the Arthur Laing Bridge. Willows saw the plane coming at them when it was still a half mile away. Its lights were very bright, and its landing gear was down. He involuntarily held his breath as it roared past a hundred feet overhead. The thunder of its engines was deafening. The Audi rocked on its springs. For a moment that was as giddy as it was brief, Willows had thought the plane might sweep them all away.

Jennifer Orchid had started crying again. She cried all the way through the city, and was still crying half an hour later, when they walked her through the big glass doors at 312 Main.

Sandy parked his truck in the shade of a plane tree. He kept to the shady side of the street as he walked the two short blocks to Jan's apartment. The temperature was already in the low seventies. He paced himself, not wanting to arrive looking sweaty and worried.

A black PT Cruiser was parked in front of the building. Harvey was slouched low behind the wheel. He wore a black-leather cowboy hat, dark glasses, and a stick-on handlebar moustache that made him look like a refugee from that weird seventies band, The Village People. Jan was in the back. It was hard to see her through the tinted glass. Neither of them seemed to notice Sandy until he'd walked right up to the van. The passenger-side door was locked. Harvey made him wait a fraction too long, then, grinning sardonically, hit the lock.

Sandy opened the door and got in. He turned and said good morning to Jan. She said hello, and leaned forward and pecked him dispassionately on the mouth. Harvey looked on, his face twisted by a benign smile. His apparent total lack of jealousy set off a host of shrieking alarms. Every nerve in Sandy's body, and every brain cell, screamed at him to bail out of the car and run for his life.

Harvey reached out and squeezed Sandy's brown paper grocery bag. "What you got there, buddy?"

"My disguise. Where's yours?"

Harvey frowned, and then, a little too late, got it. He said, "You all set?"

Sandy nodded. Harvey put the car in gear.

The ride downtown took twenty minutes. Harvey parked in a taxi zone around the corner from the Vancouver Block. Sandy put on his Detroit Tigers ball cap, the wire-rim sunglasses with the golden skulls floating in the green-glass lenses. He turned and looked at Jan.

Jan said, "That's you, all right."

"You going to be okay?"

"Don't worry about me."

Harvey and Sandy got out of the car. Harvey wore a big fanny pack that drooped heavily. There was plenty of room in there for a fortune in diamonds, and a gun. Sandy opened the Cruiser's rear door. Jan got out, slid behind the wheel. She handed Harvey a silver-coloured Cobra FRS radio. "Don't forget this."

Harvey shoved the radio into the back pocket of his jeans. He said, "I'll call you when we're done. Drive around the block, and then park right here. You have to move, wait in the lane. Everything goes right, we aren't going to be in a big hurry."

"What if everything doesn't go right?"

"Then we'll probably be in even less of a hurry," said Harvey ominously.

Jan said, "You promised you wouldn't hurt anybody."

"Did I?" He twirled the upswept tips of the handlebar moustache. "You sure that was me?"

Jan turned to Sandy. Traffic zipped past, shards of sunlight flashing on plate-glass windows. The light changed and a tight-packed horde of pedestrians charged across Granville. She said, "Good luck."

Sandy looked like he wanted to say something to her but wasn't sure what it was. He nodded to her in a brisk, businesslike fashion, and stepped away from the car. He and Harvey started towards the sidewalk, and then Sandy turned and hurried back to the Cruiser.

Jan said, "What now?"

"You by any chance remember a skinny black bartender named Billy Zeman?"

Jan stared at him.

Harvey was walking back towards them, frowning.

Sandy said, "I heard Billy used to hang out with your old pal, Matt Singh. Not long before you and I first met, Billy got busted trying to rob a bank over on Main Street. He was looking at quite a stretch. I hear he managed to work something out. Maybe he rolled over on somebody, but who can say?"

Jan said, "How would you know all that?" Her eyes widened as everything fell into place. She wanted to ask him point blank if he was a cop, but Harvey was right on top of them.

Sandy gave her a quick kiss. He said, "For luck."

Harvey said, "We're running late."

Sandy and Harvey headed south on Granville towards the Vancouver Block. It was thirteen minutes to twelve by the clock on top of the building.

Jan didn't see anybody tailing her. That didn't mean they weren't there. She made a U-turn and ran a red, blowing through the crosswalk an instant before it filled with shoppers and tourists. Horns blared. People yelled. Fuck 'em. She drove one short block down Granville, made a hard left on a late yellow, drove another half-block, and ducked down into the cavernous parking lot beneath the old Eaton's building, now Sears. She parked in a handicapped zone, and sprinted towards the escalator. Two minutes later she was in a taxi, punching buttons on her new cellphone, yelling at Tyler that she'd be there in fifteen minutes.

Tyler said, "Is it time for me to go and sit in the red car?"

"Yes, honey."

"Harvey's Firebird?"

"That's right, Tyler."

"Are we going to drive to the Rocky Mountains, and see deer and all kinds of animals?"

Jan said, "You better believe it."

"Is Harvey coming with us?"

Jan said no, and neither was Sandy. Her voice caught as she told Tyler that, from now on, he was going to be the only man in her life.

Sandy followed Harvey into the Vancouver Block's small lobby. A security officer, dressed in the white shirt and dark blue uniform of an Air Canada pilot, lolled behind a desk-on-wheels, reading a newspaper. Harvey studied the building's directory. He obviously hadn't graduated from his speed-reading course.

Sandy couldn't see any of the ERT guys. Hopefully, that meant they were there. Losing patience, he said, "Fifth floor, five-thirteen."

Harvey gave Sandy an evil look. He said, "Thank you for your help."

They joined the gathering crowd waiting at the bank of three elevators. The building was home to several embassies, numerous doctors and dentists, the gold and gems crowd, and various anonymous businesses. Sandy glanced casually around, looking for Friendlies. Nobody paid any attention to him, or to Harvey, despite his stupid moustache and stupid hat. Sandy turned and looked behind him. The security officer ducked his head. Sandy turned away. Harvey studied the three half-clocks with their moving arrows that indicated what floors the elevators were on. A bell pinged. Two elevators arrived at once. The doors slid open. A few people hurried out. Harvey stepped aside, making way for a pregnant woman.

He and Sandy stepped into the nearest elevator. Harvey punched the fifth-floor button. He adjusted the set of his fanny pack, caught Sandy watching him, and gave him a conspiratorial wink. The elevator stopped at the third floor. A shabbily dressed woman carrying a large white florist's box got on board. The elevator door slid shut. They ascended to the fifth floor. Harvey and Sandy and the woman with the flowers stepped out. The woman turned left and walked down the hall. Harvey and Sandy went in the opposite direction. The building had been around forever, and renovations had been kept to a minimum. The office doors were varnished oak. Some had frosted-glass panes, but most were solid wood. The door to suite 513 had a peephole at eye level. Harvey pressed the wall buzzer. He held an oval-shaped silver badge up against the peephole.

Sandy said, "Where'd you get that?"

"Tooth fairy."

A muffled voice asked who was there. Harvey said, "Police." His voice was loud and authoritative. He pounded on the door with his fist, and then he reached down and unzipped his fanny pack and pulled out what appeared to be a solid-gold pistol, the biggest damn handgun Sandy had ever seen.

The door opened on a safety chain. Harvey stepped back and kicked hard. The chain snapped and the door flew open. Harvey followed his gun into the office. Five hard-eyed men dressed head to toe in black ballistic nylon pointed their weapons at him. Somebody yelled, "Police! Drop your weapon! Hands above your head!"

Harvey retreated backwards. Sandy stopped him with the palm of his hand. He pressed the Glock's muzzle into the small of Harvey's back.

Sandy said, "Give it up, Harvey."

Harvey turned his head so he could glare at him. He said, "Think it's gonna be that easy, do you?" He raised the gold-coloured Desert Eagle and fired. The roar of the gunshot was deafening. The recoil jerked the muzzle upwards. The .50-calibre round hit an ERT cop named Hannigan an inch below his widow's peak. Hannigan's cheeks and pale blue eyes bulged. His head exploded into bloody shrapnel.

Harvey drew a bead on another officer.

Sean tilted his Glock's barrel so it was tilted downwards at an acute angle. He pulled the trigger three times in quick succession. The bullets shattered Harvey's spine, paralyzing him. Two rounds exited through his belly, below his belt. The third lodged in his right thigh, midway between hip and knee. Harvey crumpled. He doubled over and then he threw his head back, straightened, and fell backwards onto the bare wooden floor.

Sandy kicked the Desert Eagle under a desk. The overhead fluorescents were reflected in Harvey's unblinking eyes – vertical bars of white light that gave him a feral, unworldly look. Blood poured suddenly out of his mouth and nose, the gaping holes in his stomach. Sandy stared down at him. He was still trying to think of something to say when an anvil-jawed ERT cop roughly shoved him out of the way. The cop leaned over Harvey. His tears fell into Harvey's eyes, blurring the white bars of reflected light.

Harvey licked his lips with his bloody tongue. His mouth opened and closed, as if he were a fish on a carpet. The cop lifted his leg like a dog at a fire hydrant. He rested his black boot on Harvey's gaping mouth, silencing him, and then the cop shot him straight through the heart.

Harvey had been front-page bad news since he was old enough to take his first step. Now, far too late, he was gone.

22

family reunion

Harvey was cremated ten days after his sudden but entirely predictable death. There was no service. If there had been a service, it is unlikely anyone would have attended, because Harvey had no friends and his few surviving relatives loathed him. His wife and son were thousands of miles away, their backs to the West Coast. Jan didn't want to know how the diamond robbery had gone down, if Harvey was a rich man or dead, or a reincarnated felon. In the days following her flight from Vancouver, she'd deliberately avoided watching television or scanning newspaper headlines or listening to the news on the car radio. If she had somehow learned about her husband's death despite all these precautions, she would have grieved, and been relieved.

Jack took some of the vacation time he was owed. Claire arranged an unpaid leave of absence of indeterminate length. Jack knew a retired VPD cop who owned a romantic beachfront summer cottage in Seaside, Oregon. The cottage was rented for most of the summer but happened to be empty due to a cancellation. Jack rented it for a week at a rate that wasn't exactly cheap, but was borderline affordable. He and Parker and Hadrian were going to leave early Monday to avoid the lengthy weekend lineups at the border, and hoped to arrive at the cottage sometime the following day.

Claire suggested they host a family barbecue. She phoned Sean and, after a lengthy conversation, managed to talk him into dropping by for dinner on the Sunday evening before they left for Oregon. Claire told Annie she was welcome to invite a friend. Annie declined without explanation.

Sunday morning, Claire went to the local Safeway and bought a couple of thick T-bone steaks, two chicken breasts, a packet of wooden skewers, new potatoes, and onions and green peppers and cherry tomatoes. When she got home, Jack used the car to drive to a nearby wine and beer store, where he picked up a bottle of Chenin Blanc, and two six-packs of Sean's favourite imported beer.

The gas barbecue, stored under the back porch, hadn't been used all summer. Jack took a broom, swept away the cobwebs, and rolled the barbecue out onto the patio. The grill was filthy. Worse, large pieces of the glossy white paint on the propane tank had flaked away, and the bare metal was bubbled with rust. Jack gave the tank an experimental shake. It was empty. He unscrewed the tank from the brass coupling and carried it around to the front of the house. The car was gone. He went inside, and found Claire in the dining room, feeding Hadrian tiny slices of fresh peach.

"Where's the car?"

She looked up. "Annie's got it."

Jack felt as if he was about to explode. He told himself to calm down, it wasn't all that important, they could always order takeout Chinese. He said, "Where'd she go?"

"I don't know. Why, what's the problem?"

"There's no propane – the tank's empty."

"Can't we use briquettes?"

"We don't have any briquettes, either."

"Yes, we do. There's a bag in the garage. Some friends of Annie's brought it over last summer. I'm sure it's still there, on the shelf by the window."

Jack went into the kitchen and splashed cold water on his face and the back of his neck, and then he went out the back door and walked down the brick sidewalk to the garage. The door was locked, and he didn't have his keys. He went back into the house, found his key ring after a brief but irritating search, and returned to the garage. The five-kilo bag of briquettes was right where Claire had said it would be. He ripped it open. The shiny, black, weirdly shaped lumps of fuel seemed to have aged well. He used a small axe to chop some scraps of wood into kindling, and carried the kindling and briquettes back across the lawn to the barbecue. Now he was all set, except he needed a beer.

Annie came home half an hour later, with a brand-new tank of propane. Jack thanked her for her help, and carried the kindling and briquettes back into the garage. He and Claire were skewering vegetables and chunks of meat when the back screen door slammed shut, and Sean called out a cheery hello from the porch.

Jack told his son there was a cold beer in the fridge. Sean disappeared back inside the house, and came out again a few minutes later, with his arm slung across his sister's shoulder, and a beer in each hand. Claire hugged Sean, and Jack slapped him on the back, and told him he was looking well. There was an awkward silence. Sean's eyes were bloodshot, and he was a little unsteady on his feet. Jack put him and Annie to work setting the picnic table. He tended the grill while Claire went inside for glasses and cutlery. Sean sat heavily down in one of the chairs.

Tripod came into the yard through the open gate that led to the lane. The cat stopped dead in its tracks, lifted its head and stared at them, and then raced diagonally across the lawn, and jumped up onto the wooden fence that ran along the length of the property. It trotted along the fence for a few feet, and then, with a prodigious effort, leapt up onto the garage roof, and stretched out on the peak in the sun, where it had a clear view of the backyard.

Sean said, "That cat's just amazing." He finished his beer and put the bottle down on the table and started in on his second bottle.

Jack said, "You'd better slow down, or you're going to have to walk home."

Sean laughed harshly. "Who you think you're kidding. I'm a cop. I can drink and drive if I want to. Who's gonna arrest me?"

Annie brought out a bowl of taco chips, and salsa, and the worn leather football Jack had been given on his sixteenth birthday. The ball was deflated.

Jack said, "The pump's in the basement. I'll get it."

Sean pushed himself out of his chair. "I'll help you look for it."

Jack was mildly surprised, but didn't say anything. Father and son walked side by side across the yard. As they entered the basement through the ground-level door, Willows paused to give his eyes a moment to adjust to the light. The pump was in its customary place, hanging from a hook over the work bench. Jack was reaching for it when Sean rested his hand on his arm.

Jack glanced over his shoulder at his son. What he saw in Sean's eyes broke the rhythm of his heart.

He said, "What is it – the shooting?" What else would it be? Jack felt stupid for asking. He said, "Sean, you did what you had to do. The guy was a killer. It was you or him. You're getting trauma counselling, aren't you?"

Sean told him how Harvey had died. His tone was flat and unemotional. He chose his words carefully, for their ability to describe the unimaginable as an everyday event. He would not meet his father's eyes. Halfway through his story his shoulders began to shake, and he fell apart, dissolving in tears.

Jack eased shut the basement door, and locked it. He took his son in his arms and held him tightly, as he hadn't held him in half a lifetime.

When Sean had finally regained control of his emotions, he said, "What in hell should I do?"

"What do you think you should do?"

"Turn the sonofabitch in."

"Is that what you want to do?"

"Sometimes." Sean wiped his eyes with the back of his hand. He said, "I'm not saying anybody ever deserves to die, but if anybody ever did, Harvey would've been pretty close to the top of the list. You could even say he committed suicide when he shot Hannigan, instead of choosing to give it up. I mean, he was up against five ERT cops. He must've known he wasn't going to take all of us out."

Jack said, "You got that right."

"He would've died anyway, if that ERT cop hadn't shot him. Hell, if the ERT guy hadn't put a bullet in him, the three rounds I gave him would have killed him. So you could even say I owe the ERT guy a favour." Sean's mouth twisted. For a split second that Jack knew was burned into his memory and would stay with him until the day he died, his son was transformed into something mean, and ugly.

Sean said, "If I rat on the guy, it isn't going to bounce off you, is it?"

"Of course not. Don't worry about it."

"I feel so goddamn naive. I thought we were supposed to be the good guys."

Jack said, "Most of the time, we are." He could hear Annie calling to them that dinner was ready. He said, "Are you okay to go back out there?"

"Yeah, sure."

"We'll talk about this after dinner, okay?"

"That'd be good."

Jack put his arms around him and held him close for a long moment. He said, "We'll figure something out, son."

Sean nodded. He laughed and said, "Or if we don't, at least we can knock back a couple more beers."

Jack unlocked and opened the basement door, and he and Sean went back outside, into the brittle sunlight, and lengthening shadows.